John

The Journal don't figure very strongly in the story, but there is a clipping from it (p. 88). I hope you might find some bits of interest in it.

Best Wishes

Bill Cave

This is a true story. It begins with the birth of my father in August 1914 and ends with my own birth in March 1952. Of course, real stories don't have beginnings and ends, but those are convenient markers for this one. The events in it all actually happened and almost all of the characters are real – they can be distinguished from the small number of fictitious ones by their inclusion in the index. All of them are now dead, apart from myself, although of course I'm not really in this story. However, there are certainly a number of people still alive who knew characters in the story, and maybe also were involved in some of the events in it. I hope that at least a few of them may read it.

True stories are evidently different from fiction. They are simultaneously much easier and much harder to write. There is no need to conjure up a plot, although inevitably there is a requirement to do some background research - this is much easier now than it used to be, and I should emphasize that I have no pretensions to being an historian of any kind. It's also possible to provide documentary evidence concerning people and events, which can help readers to place them in context and to note relationships to other historical activities. I've tried to do this throughout the book. I've also provided a "Timelines" Appendix, to help clarify the historical context and sequence of events. While I've made every effort to ensure accuracy, and I have included a fair amount of documentation, it's inevitable that there will be some errors - hopefully only small ones.

Concerning this issue of true versus fictional stories, it's obviously not possible in the former to mould characters or events so as to convey messages or to stimulate responses in a reader. Any significant distortion of a true story will quickly become apparent. There are no particular messages in this story. There are also no heroes or villains. In general, they only really exist in fiction. There is adversity - indeed it's common in real life - and there are sometimes ways in which adversity is tackled that are of interest to us all. If there is some sort of theme, then perhaps it is the remarkable tenacity in the threads of individual lives that together form the tapestry of our continued existence. All of the threads break eventually, but extensive cross-links hold the fabric together.

A final point that is perhaps worth addressing in a preamble such as this is my motivation for writing the book. In a way, I write for a living, but I mainly write scientific papers, plus the odd textbook. The objective there, at least in principle, is to search for knowledge and understanding (even if it concerns rather specialized areas, of interest only to a distressingly small number of people). This is different, and I suppose that I've done it partly because, since my formal retirement from the University about 3 years ago, my teaching activities have virtually stopped. As it happens, my involvement with a start-up company in Cambridge has meant that I have continued with some research and development work, but I have had a combination during this period of some spare time and at least some background in writing.

However, that doesn't really explain my motivation. Perhaps it's to put on some kind of record my appreciation of the threads that ensured I had an ideal springboard in life - largely those of my parents, although many others have in effect contributed to this. I've learned a lot about my family history during preparation of the book, which was mainly done between early 2021 and mid-2022. Perhaps surprisingly, I knew rather little beforehand and I've been unable during this period to talk to anyone with personal knowledge of the events concerned. In general, my parents' generation tried to avoid burdening their children with history that was often traumatic and, to my shame, I didn't really show very much interest while they were alive. Perhaps the book is an attempt to redress this. We should all aim to understand history – both global and personal. I'd like to dedicate the book to my wife, Gail, and to our two children and four grandchildren. They currently know little or nothing of this story. If they were all to read it eventually, then I'd consider it to have been worthwhile. Put more simply, it's just been a labour of love.

Bill Clyne
Cambridge, 2022

Chapter 1: Setting the Scene (August 1914)

1.1 New Life

The morning of Wednesday 26th August, in 1914, dawns bright and clear in North Kent. Alice Clyne has a feeling that her 11th child will be born today, and that it will be a boy. Of course, she's had plenty of experience. Her first, William, was born 18 years ago and since then she's had 6 more boys and 3 girls. They've all been born in this area (although they've moved house six times during the period) and they've all been trouble-free home births. The first took a while, but subsequent ones have been quick and easy. For the previous two births she's had the same midwife, who lives nearby, and they both know the ropes. This one has certainly been kicking a lot and, while her girls had also been very active, she feels that it is going to be a strong boy.

Alice is still in good shape, and still an attractive woman. This is, however, a bit of a mixed blessing in some ways. They really should call a halt soon, and her husband (also William) has agreed that this must be the last one – although he'd also said that after Douglas, who is now two years old. Still, William is a good man and Alice feels happy with her life. The children have mostly been very healthy, although she has lost two. Poor little Alice Minnie died from typhoid just before her third birthday. She had struggled with the horrible illness for over a month, but she had succumbed in the end. That was 11 years ago now. Also, Alec died just three years ago, also from typhoid, and he'd been just over a year old. She still thinks about them quite often, but she's come to terms with the sadness and pain – after all, she knows women who have lost whole strings of their children, and never recovered. She's really quite lucky. She tries to focus on today, and to get a feel for when her waters will break, and what will need to be done. William is still snoring away next to her and he'll be no help – well, men never are with these things.

Of course, she's not entirely carefree. War with Germany was declared earlier in the month, which is hardly conducive to peace of mind. However, many people don't seem to be at all worried about the outcome – life has gone on through what has been a glorious summer and the beaches in East Kent are still very busy. In fact, many people seem to actively welcome the war. Unemployment is quite high in the area and war often helps to provide economic activity and jobs. Britain hasn't been involved in one for quite a while – there was something in South Africa, but the Dutch were put in their place in the end without too much trouble. She'd heard about an unpleasant episode with the Russians half a century before, but she didn't really know what that was all about – it was, of course, before she was born. That brings her back to her age – she'll be 40 next year and it really is time to call a halt.

Anyway, while most people seem to think that we will easily see off the Boche, and sort out any other foreigners who get in the way, she isn't thinking in those terms. Firearms have improved so much recently - she knows a bit about this, since William's job in the Metropolitan Police brings him into contact with guns and he often talks about how people can be killed much more efficiently these days. Surely this also applies to wars and it's not just a question of who wins a war – she's much more concerned about lots of people getting killed - particularly her elder sons, and especially William. He seems determined to join up and they now have arguments about this almost every day. He's a bright boy, but he left school several years ago and is drifting between jobs. There aren't a lot of jobs in the area for young men like him. His father keeps pressurizing him to join the Met – he's sure that he'd be able to swing this, despite the strong competition, but the lad is quite headstrong and he doesn't want to just follow in his father's footsteps.

Her husband has certainly done well in the Met. He was promoted to Detective a couple of years ago and, with the older boys making a contribution to the family finances, they're now able to pay the rent fairly comfortably, with enough left over for clothes and food, and even the odd trip to the seaside. They stopped having a lodger when they moved from Erith to St. Paul's Cray about 5 years ago, so there's a little more room now – although it's certainly still quite crowded - these are solid houses, but not big enough for a family of 10 (shortly to be 11!) to stretch out much. There's also the annual hop-picking expedition, which is like a holiday, but doesn't cost anything. Yes, they've done well. William was brought up in Caithness, which is literally the back of beyond, and had shown the initiative to move down to Glasgow (to work in a Singer factory) and then down to London to join the Met.

That wasn't such an easy thing to do and she reflects that it was really the development of the railways that allowed people like her husband to escape from restricted backgrounds – the railway had reached the Far North of Scotland just a decade or so before he left his home near Wick. Of course, it's still far away – about 700 miles – and he's largely lost touch with his roots up there. She's only been up for one short visit, but she knows that the Clyne Clan is still very strong in the area. Actually, as he's explained in some depth, it doesn't have its own Clan or tartan: it's a "Sept" of the Sinclair Clan – a sort of sub-Clan. The name is very common in the far north of Scotland and there's even a Parish called Clyne. He'd told her that there's a church in the Parish of Clyne that can seat a thousand people. (He didn't say whether it had ever been full – that's probably the complete population within a radius of several miles!)

In fact, it all seems to her to be a bit strange up there, but he has settled in down here and he's turned out to be a successful policemen. The Met takes on many thousands of people – it's one of the biggest employers in the country – and many of them inevitably don't get promoted much, so he's done very well. She rather doubts that he's quite in the Sherlock Holmes mould; those stories are incredibly popular these days, although the few that she has read seem very contrived. Still, he's certainly a good and popular policeman. Nevertheless, her eldest son has dismissed this option. On the other hand, he seems to regard the war as a great opportunity. A lot of his friends, and many of the neighbours, seem to think similarly and she has a sinking feeling that she won't be able to stop him from joining up. He's a man now, but he's always held the most special place in her heart and she can't bear the thought of losing him.

She shakes off these negative thoughts, gets quietly out of bed and gives her husband a nudge:

"I think it might be today, dearest, so I'll just pop down the road and check that Jessie Craddock will be able to come over soon."

She quickly gets dressed and sets off down the road to make the arrangements with her. The Clyne family lives in Hearns Road, in St. Paul's Cray. It's a pleasant and respectable neighbourhood, although certainly not prosperous or pretentious. Most people work somewhere in the metropolis, with many thousands employed in the docks, shipyards, railways, manufacturing industries etc. Most of them commute via the dense network of railway lines in the area – there certainly aren't many people here with cars. It only takes William about an hour or so to get to work at the Victoria Embankment – the "New" Scotland Yard as it's now called. Nevertheless, it would be nice to live somewhere a little different. Perhaps eventually, if William continues to do well, they'll be able to move right out into the Kent countryside, or maybe to somewhere west of the city. He's shortly due to complete 25 years in the force, at which point he will become eligible for a pension. This is one of the attractions of working for the Met, since the pension scheme is a generous one. It's actually very common for policemen in the Met to retire in their late 40's or early 50's, once they've earned this entitlement. Possibly he could then find another job for a decade or so. Maybe, one day, they'll even be able to think about buying their own house, although that seems to her to be a distant dream.

She calls on the midwife, who also lives in Hearns Road. She examines Alice and agrees that it will be soon. They walk together back to number 20, which only takes a few minutes, and get things ready in the main bedroom. The contractions are coming quickly now and the waters break soon afterwards. William had asked her whether he should stay, but she indicated that this wasn't necessary and he has already gone to work. Most of the children are now at school, but William Jnr. (ie William Thomas, although he continues to make every effort to drop his middle name) is currently between jobs and he has made it clear that he will stay at home until the birth, so there's help available. He's a very capable young man, and deeply attached to his mother.

Still, these events really are routine in the Clyne household and this one goes as smoothly as everyone expected. A healthy boy is duly delivered in the early afternoon and, by the time that the rest of the family return, he's sleeping happily, having already had a couple of good feeds. Mina (10) and (Alice) Lena (7) are enchanted and soon start to take turns to look after the new arrival. The other boys, Herbert (17), Frank (15), Stan (12), Harry (8) and Douglas (2), are a bit more blasé, but they also at least take a passing interest. It looks as if the Clyne family is now complete and about to start making its way in the world.

Registration District BROMLEY.

1914. BIRTHS in the Sub-District of CHISLEHURST in the County of KENT.

Columns:— 1		2	3	4	5	6	7	8	9	10
No.	When and Where Born.	Name, if any.	Sex.	Name and Surname of Father.	Name and Maiden Surname of Mother.	Rank or Profession of Father.	Signature, Description, and Residence of Informant.	When Registered.	Signature of Registrar.	Baptismal Name if added after Registration of Birth.
436.	Twenty sixth August 1914 20 Hearns Road St Pauls Cray R.D.	Leonard James	Boy	William Clyne	Alice Clyne formerly Pollard.	a Detective Metropolitan Police	William Clyne Father 20 Hearns Road St Pauls Cray.	Sixth October 1914.	R. Hamlyn Deputy Registrar.	

Fig.1.1: Birth certificate of Len Clyne.

Of course, the latest arrival has some way to go before entering the wider world and the first issue is to give him a name. Alice and William have had quite a few animated discussions about names over the years. William was keen to retain a strong Scottish flavor. Despite the fact that they had seen little or nothing of their "homeland", he wanted the family to be aware of their (paternal) heritage. That the first one should have his father's name went without saying, and William is certainly a name with strong Scottish links (some traceable to the "French connection" going back to the time of the Conqueror). The Sinclairs, with strong links to the Clynes, came from France (St. Clair, in Normandy). The connections between Scotland and (the northern parts of) France have always been strong. Actually, Franco-Scottish alliances have mainly stemmed from a mutual loathing of the English, although in the case of the Scots the attitude to those south of the border has always been something of a love-hate relationship.

William's middle name of Thomas is in fact that of Alice's father, who was an Organ Builder in Worcestershire, although William himself dropped it soon after being the butt of some crude jokes from his friends along the "John Thomas" lines. Herbert was given the middle name of William's own father, George, who was a seaman – one of the few lines of work readily available in Caithness. It started to get a bit random after this, with Alice having an increasing say. Herbert was named after Alice's brother, and it's certainly popular – for example, it's the name of Lord Kitchener and of the Prime Minister, Asquith. Frank (Francis) was named for a cousin of William's, who's now in the Navy. Stanley was effectively named after the street where he was born (Stanhope Road). It wasn't very clear how they'd come up with Alec, but the next one, christened Walter Douglas, was always just called Douglas by most of the family, presumably because they favoured the Scottish theme.

The first girl was naturally given the name of Alice, with a middle name of Minnie – another strongly Scottish name. Sadly, she died before it became clear which she would have chosen. The next girl was named Williamina, after William's mother, which is clearly a Scottish name. She has always been called Mina. Alice made one final effort with the last girl, who was named Alice Lena. Actually, the name of Lena is found in many languages and cultures, usually with a meaning along the lines of "shining light". It's not clear how Alice came to choose it, but the girl herself clearly liked it, and the "Alice" was dropped from an early age.

Anyway, William is keen for this latest (and last!) addition to the family to have a name with Scottish links (since, to be fair, several of the other names do not). In the end, they settle on Leonard James. The name of James has strong links to biblical times (Jacob) and to Scotland, where there has been a string of Kings, not to mention the Jacobite revolution. The name of Leonard is chosen by Alice, who likes the aura of lions and bravery. They register the birth, and the name, about 6 weeks later. He will always be known as Len.

1.2 Reflections

William Clyne (Snr.) is a busy man. He would have been prepared to see his wife through the birth, but he's somewhat relieved when she insists that there is no need. After all, he knows that he would be of no possible use if anything were to go wrong – in fact, he'd be both petrified and useless. They've always been very close and the thought of her suffering in any way is unbearable. In fact, the chances of this are small. Not that childbirth is without its hazards – far from it – but she's a strong and healthy woman and clearly well-suited physically for childbirth. The pregnancy was trouble-free and the midwife is very competent. Going to work – perhaps coming home a little early – seems the obvious option.

Part of the motivation is that he does enjoy his work these days. Also, this is a very busy time. The Met is taking on various extra duties and responsibilities with the advent of war. These include having a presence at the Royal Dockyards and at major railway stations. There is now a strong security issue associated with such locations, with a state of high alert having been raised concerning spies – apparently the country is full of them. Army personnel can't be spared for such duties, but the Metropolitan Police, with a strong central organization and high quality personnel, is deemed to be ideal for such purposes.

Of course, the detection and prevention of ordinary crime still has a high priority and they're making strenuous efforts to use the latest technology. Fingerprinting has been in use to help solve crimes since around the turn of the century, although the Met is sometimes accused of being slow to use it effectively. In fact, this is very unfair. The first case in which a conviction was achieved by Scotland Yard via fingerprint evidence was a dozen years ago and it's almost 10 years since the Stratton Brothers were hanged for murder (during a burglary), based mainly on matching of the prints on a cash box that was left at the scene (which was nearby, in Deptford). The Fingerprint Bureau, which was established in Scotland Yard at around that time, now has hundreds of thousands of prints on file and they continue to develop improved methods for searching them. Furthermore, they have many excellent people working with the Forensics Department. These include Bernard Spilsbury: still only 37, he has already used autopsy evidence to secure several convictions for murder – including that of Hawley Crippen, four years ago. Spilsbury was able to show that the body buried in his cellar was that of his missing wife, from some scar tissue found on the body.

Nevertheless, they're often asked why Sherlock Holmes seems to do so much better than them – not helped by Sherlock's apparent disdain for the efforts of the Met. Actually, William does admit that Conan Doyle seems to be generally on the ball - Sherlock did start to use fingerprint evidence some years ago, although it hasn't figured very prominently in his work. His disparagement of the Met is in any event very unfair and they've had to put up with over 20 years of this - Holmes had supposedly met his end almost 10 years ago, but had been resurrected by popular demand and is still going strong. They're all expected to read all of his stories. Whenever William has actually tried to apply the apparently foolproof methods of Holmes to real cases, the outcome has usually been laughable.

"Having eliminated the impossible, I've decided that Mrs. Smith was pushed into the river by her horse. Her husband has assured us that he has a morbid fear of going near rivers and the horse hasn't denied it, so logic has led me to that conclusion." William does sometimes use humour to make a point, although the general public still seems to feel that Holmes (ie Conan Doyle) can't possibly be making it all up.

William has mixed feelings about the war. He recognizes the economic benefits, but he's far from sure that it will be either easy or quick. Britain is still a dominant nation in many ways, but he knows that German industry is highly efficient and that they have a very strong military tradition. He also has mixed feelings about his sons. He sympathizes with William (and also with Herbert and Frank) being keen to do their duty, while perhaps also getting to see a bit of the world, learn new skills, make new friends etc. In any event, the pressure on young men to join up is becoming very difficult to resist. Groups of young women are already handing out white feathers in the streets to young men not in uniform. To a proud young man like his eldest son, who is already attracting quite a lot of attention from young women for other reasons, this creates almost unbearable pressure.

While sitting in the train, William thinks back to his own youth a quarter of a century before. He'd had different pressures. Caithness in the late 19th Century was a very long way from London in the early 20th, both physically and culturally. Wick is a small town, although it has a history going back over 500 years. That part of Scotland had long been very independent, with Gaelic the predominant language until the start of the 19th Century. One of the key industries started around then, as the herring shoals moved north and Wick quickly became an important fishing centre – in fact, the largest herring port in Europe. The great Thomas Telford built a substantial harbour there in 1810. By the time of William's birth in 1869, there were around 500 boats in the Wick fishing fleet, with several thousand fishermen and a similar number of associated workers.

Fig.1.2: Photo of William's parents, George and Williamina Clyne, taken at the famous Johnston photographic studio in Wick in 1880.

His father was a fisherman and he did well, managing to bring up a large family in relative prosperity. His parents are both dead now, but the larger Clyne family is well known, both in Wick and more widely in the Far North of Scotland – particularly down the East Coast of Caithness and Sutherland, and this has been the case for centuries. William had been born in a croft (small cottage), in a tiny village called Latheron, about 15 miles south of Wick. Of course, everything is relative. Being from an established family in a remote and parochial region is not necessarily so attractive. Also, William didn't want to be a fisherman. It's a hard life and also a limited one. The pungent smell of fish hung perpetually over the town.

There is still a strong folk memory in the area of the events of Friday 18th August 1848, when dozens of fishermen from the region were drowned. Much of the fishing was done overnight, during the summer months. A huge fleet of small herring boats, mostly from Wick, set off that evening in excellent weather, but a terrible storm arose very quickly soon after night fell. Some boats managed to get back into the harbour, but many were caught outside. The sea conditions were atrocious and visibility very poor. Many boats were smashed against harbour walls or nearby rocks. Most of the town's population – largely the wives and children of the fishermen - were on the quayside throughout the night, but there was little they could do to help. William's father had been in the fleet that day as a young lad and had come close to death. Such dangers were accepted, since the fishing had brought great prosperity to the town. Also, a national weather forecasting system started in the 1860's, which helped to avert such tragedies.

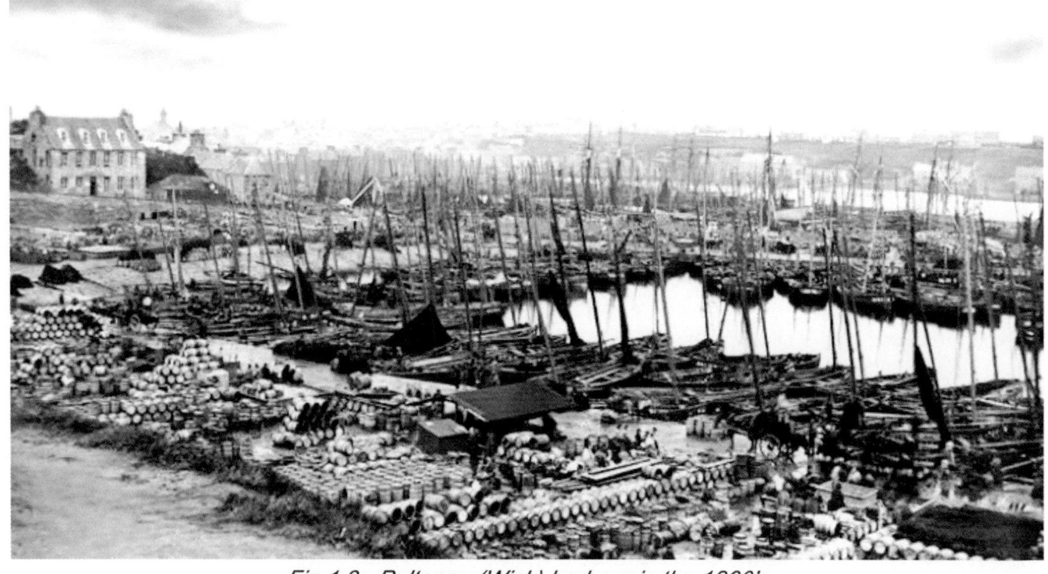

Fig.1.3: Pulteney (Wick) harbour in the 1860's.

However, problems were starting to arise. For example, the dangers of over-fishing were becoming clear to the fishermen of Wick. In particular, by the 1880's large, steam-powered trawlers were using the port – mostly having owners from outside of the area. Unlike the "drifters" used by local men, this type of fishing involves dragging of nets along the seabed, which was thought (correctly) to damage herring spawning grounds. By 1885, unrest among local fishermen was leading to minor rioting and attacks on steam trawlers bringing their catches into Wick. Such attacks were, of course, illegal and no steps were taken to control the type, or extent, of fishing in the area. Whatever the causes, the industry has declined quite significantly over the last couple of decades, with the herring stocks having certainly become depleted. William's decision not to follow in his father's footsteps has thus proved to be a good one. The Wick fishing fleet is now a fraction of its former size and his brothers who entered the industry have often found times to be hard. Many fishermen have joined the Royal Navy over recent years – a period during which the "Grand Fleet" has expanded considerably.

Pulteney Harbour in 188 .

Wednesday 4 Mar 188

Blowing a strong gale of wind

The Trawlers all left today being accompanied to the Quay head by crowds of fishermen.

Some five or six of the ringleaders of the rioters were taken before the Sheriff today & were remanded for a week, the Provost bailed them out

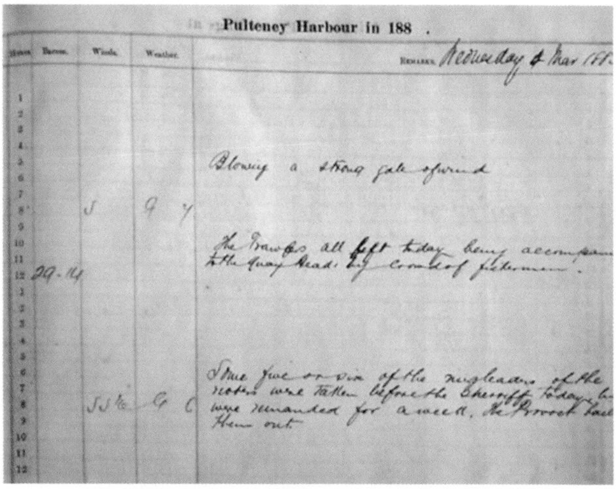

Fig.1.4: Entry in the Pulteney (Wick) harbour-master's log for 4th March 1885, referring to attacks on steam trawlers and the "ring-leaders" of rioters being brought before the Sheriff.

Other types of employment are not so widespread in the area and indeed many people still live mainly by subsistence farming in a harsh climate. Another option for young men is to join the army: for the past several decades the Seaforth Highlanders regiment, which recruits mainly from Caithness and Sutherland, has had a strong and proud tradition. That is certainly a hard and precarious life: many who join up never come back. The traditional weight that the Scots give to education is strong throughout the country and William did attend school. At that time, the educational system was still developing, and was more advanced in Scotland than in England, at least for poor children. However, fees were not abolished until 1890 and the family was far from rich. He therefore left at the age of 13, despite having done well.

Fig.1.5: Locations of the fishing villages in East Caithness in the mid-19th Century.

He was determined to seek his fortune in the South and the coming of the railways at least meant that this was physically now a viable option. The Highland Railway had arrived in Wick in 1870 - the year after he was born. While his parents were very sorry to see him go, knowing that they might see little of him in the future, they understood and supported his aspirations. Aged 16, he saw an advertisement for workers in the huge Singer sewing machine factory that had just been opened in the western suburbs of Glasgow – shortly to become the largest factory in the world, employing 3,500 people.

He applied for a job at the Singer factory and was invited to attend for an interview. His parents paid his fare and within a few weeks he had moved down. He recalls those days with a complex mixture of emotions. The area was developing rapidly. Shipyards on the Clyde, close to the centre of Glasgow, had grown quickly over the previous decade or two. The Singer factory, however, was set up several miles downriver, on the northern bank, in the area now known as Clydebank. There was little else there at the time, although it has since become highly developed. He therefore had to take digs in Glasgow – in a tenement block in Simpson Street. The Glasgow City and District Railway had just been created and there was a line out from the centre to the west. Like most of the Singer workers, he commuted out by train, together with thousands of others – there were a dozen special trains every morning between 6am and 7am. The overcrowding was terrible and conditions in the tenement blocks were dreadful. The notorious Duke Street Prison was just a stone's throw away from where he lived. On the other hand, Glasgow offered things that Wick could not. He lived only a mile away from the beautiful Botanical Gardens, and a similar distance from the famous Mitchell Library. His commute involved a

Fig.1.6: Photo taken at Wick in 1888 of William (second left), on a visit home from his job in Glasgow, with his three brothers.

walk of about a mile to the station at Charing Cross – he smiles as he reflects that a different Charing Cross is now his daily destination.

His work in the factory was hard – he was employed as a labourer in the foundry - and the pay was less than ten shillings a week. People looking for work were flocking to Glasgow, with both the shipyards and the Singer factory expanding rapidly. Some of this influx was from Ireland and friction between communities was starting to develop along religious lines. This copious supply of workers kept wages low and he had little prospect of promotion. It was an exciting and demanding time, but also very stressful. It all came as a severe cultural shock to a young lad who had rarely travelled more than a few miles from his small and isolated hometown – Wick has its boisterous aspects, but this was something else. Still, determined to stick with it, he survived and learned quickly. However, he recognized that this wasn't really what he wanted, so he started to look around. He didn't have any particular skills, but he was bright, able-bodied and literate, putting him a notch or two above many in the job market.

Fig.1.7: Photo of the workforce outside the Singer factory in Clydebank, taken in the early 1890's.

1.3 Taking the Plunge

It's well known that the streets of London are paved with gold. William rather suspected that the reality down there would be a little different, although he doubted that general city conditions could be any worse than those in Glasgow. Anyway, he felt that London would be the place to really offer him some opportunities, so he kept his eyes open. After a few years in Glasgow, getting back to see his family once or twice a year, he spotted an advert for the Metropolitan Police, which was rapidly expanding the size of the force and recruiting a lot of constables. He applied, was interviewed, got accepted and started work there towards the end of 1889. Of course, this really was a long way away - although the train journey to London took no longer than the one back home. Nevertheless, he would now be 700 miles away from his family. Still, he felt that this was what he needed to do.

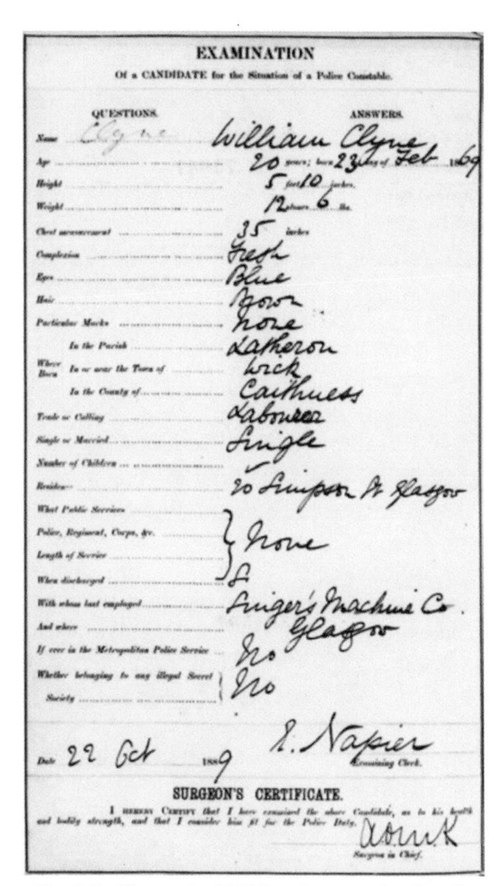

EXAMINATION

Of a CANDIDATE for the Situation of a Police Constable.

QUESTIONS.	ANSWERS.
Name	William Clyne
Age	20 years; born 23 day of Feb 1869
Height	5 feet 10 inches.
Weight	12 stone 6 lbs.
Chest measurement	35 inches
Complexion	Fresh
Eyes	Blue
Hair	Brown
Particular Marks	None
Where Born — In the Parish	Latheron
Where Born — In or near the Town of	Wick
Where Born — In the County of	Caithness
Trade or Calling	Labourer
Single or Married	Single
Number of Children	—
Residence	20 Simpson St Glasgow
What Public Services, Police, Regiment, Corps, &c., Length of Service, When discharged	None
With whom last employed	Singer's Machine Co.
And where	Glasgow
If ever in the Metropolitan Police Service	No
Whether belonging to any illegal Secret Society	No

Date 22 Oct 1889 — I. Napier, Examining Clerk.

SURGEON'S CERTIFICATE.

I hereby Certify that I have examined the above Candidate, as to his health and bodily strength, and that I consider him fit for the Police Duty. [illegible signature], Surgeon in Chief.

Fig.1.8: Record of William's examination for entry to the Metropolitan Police on 22nd Oct. 1889.

He thinks back to those early days with the force. His warrant number is 74941, so almost 75,000 people (all men) had been recruited since it all started in 1829. The actual number employed when he arrived was about 13,000 – so even more than at Singer, although of course they never all congregated at the same time, as the workers did in Glasgow every day. One of the reasons that the Met was often criticized was their failure to catch "Jack the Ripper". A string of similar murders in Whitechapel, involving mutilation of the bodies of the victims (all prostitutes), occurred during the year before he arrived and they received a lot of publicity. There were also further murders of women in the area after he arrived. He and his colleagues were frequently sent into Whitechapel to make enquiries.

Even by the standards of the East End, in which there was a lot of deprivation, conditions in Whitechapel were terrible. There were many prostitutes in the area, but he sympathized with them – just surviving each day was a challenge and without money it was hopeless. The housing was unbelievably bad and over-crowded, but a bed in even the most horrible doss-house cost 4d per night and without a bed nobody would survive many nights. The area contained many desperate people, including large Jewish and Irish contingents. Within these communities, some support might be offered, but outside of them it was very difficult. Many survived only via criminality. Drunkenness was rife, offering the only (temporary) escape from the horrors of life. It was hardly surprising that there were murders. In fact, in this area at least, conditions were worse than in Glasgow. It actually seemed likely that only the murders that were committed in 1888 were down to one particular individual. Who knows what happened to him? Anyway, the only long-term way to stop crimes like this is to improve the conditions under which people are living. To be fair, this has happened over the past 25 years or so, although there are still parts of the city that are very bad.

Of course, even in those days, other parts of the city were much better, the Met was, and still is, a very supportive community and there has always been this feeling that London is an exciting place to be. Getting around the city was relatively cheap and easy by this time. Soon after he arrived, the main headquarters of the Metropolitan Police was moved from Whitehall to a large building on the Embankment – "New" Scotland Yard. He now spends most of his time there, particularly since his promotion to Detective a few years ago. All in all, a lot has happened since he arrived in the city and he has absolutely no regrets about his move down.

Fig.1.9: Photo taken at the Elephant and Castle in 1890.

Part of the reason for this is that he met Alice in London. She was a bright and beautiful girl – still is, as far as he's concerned. He had met her in the course of his professional duties. She was from a small village in Worcestershire and, like him, she'd been attracted to London by the employment available – she was working as a maid in a large house in the area. That was hard and poorly-paid work, but she was provided with accommodation and she was able to save a few shillings. For such girls, no matter how bright and able, marriage is often the only way out of a life of drudgery – certainly at that time. Current trends, including a lot of activity by the Suffragettes, and a widening of the range of work open to women, are slowly changing the situation, but in the Victorian era the lives of most young girls and women were terribly constrained. Alice did in fact have several suitors at the time, but William had plucked up the courage to ask her out and they started going to local music halls and some of the more respectable pubs. William being a policeman certainly helped in terms of the attitude of landlords and customers.

Those were happy times. After a courtship of a couple of years, they decided to get married, although the fact that William Jnr. was on the way did slightly accelerate things. It was a small wedding, but a very enjoyable occasion. His parents and brothers did come down for it, although it was a long (and expensive) journey for them and there were certainly some difficulties in fitting everyone into the small house in Woolwich that they were renting at the time - particularly since Alice's parents were also there. He rather suspected that his parents had been relieved to get back to their simple life in Wick – London was really rather overwhelming for them.

CERTIFIED COPY OF AN ENTRY OF MARRIAGE

GIVEN AT THE GENERAL REGISTER OFFICE

Application Number COL872026

1896. Marriage solemnized at the Parish Church in the Parish of Woolwich in the County of London

No.	When Married.	Name and Surname.	Age.	Condition.	Rank or Profession.	Residence at the time of Marriage.	Father's Name and Surname.	Rank or Profession of Father
173	Eighth February 1896	William Clyne	26	Bachelor	Police Constable	Police Station William Street	George Clyne	Seaman
		Alice Pollard	21	Spinster	———	52 William Street	Thomas Pollard	Organ Builder

Married in the Parish Church according to the Rites and Ceremonies of the Established Church by ——— or after Banns by me,

This Marriage was solemnized between us, William Clyne, Alice Pollard

in the Presence of us, William John Vine, Ester Vine

H G Veazey

Fig.1.10: Certificate of marriage between William and Alice.

So many things happen here that make it seem like another world. For example, the first electric power station in the world opened next door in Deptford, just before he arrived in London. It was a while before any ordinary houses started get electrical power and even now it's mostly only for affluent households. There are certainly none in the immediate neighbourhood, although perhaps they will get such facilities one day fairly soon. During the year after their marriage, there were major celebrations in the city, marking Victoria's 60 years on the throne and generally highlighting the power of the British Empire - the envy of the world. There are now trams and cars on the streets, trains everywhere, produce of every kind in the shops etc. There's even a cinema in Dartford, which opened last year – not that they have much time for that kind of thing these days. He shakes his head in disbelief just thinking about the contrast with his childhood, and how his parents had lived – although he does sometimes yearn for the peace and simplicity of that life – the overcrowding, dirt, crime and general pressure of life here can be overwhelming.

Fig.1.11: Photo taken at Southwark in 1897, with the area prepared for the Diamond Jubilee celebrations.

Still, there is unquestionably rapid progress in many areas, with London always being at the forefront. Sewage treatment is a good example. The huge pumping station at Crossness, next to Erith marshes, was a key part of the revolutionary system setup by Joseph Bazalgette in the 1860's. The pumping station - the first in the world - was opened in April 1865. When William first arrived in London, raw sewage was simply pumped into the Thames at Erith and, while the rest of the city certainly benefitted, it created a dreadful stink in the local area – particularly in the summer. The system was, however, improved during the subsequent decades, with large holding tanks being created and solid matter being collected by sedimentation, for removal by barge out into the estuary. Pumping of liquid sewage was also limited to periods of outgoing tide. Nevertheless, the Erith area still tends to be a bit smelly and the family was pleased when they managed to move a bit further out.

1.4 A Hectic Time

Coming out of this reverie about his youth, William looks out of the train window, noting the evidence of increased activity that has already been stimulated by the war. For example, the Vickers factory in Crayford, which is quite close to the line, is already gearing up for massive production of their machine gun, which can fire 500 rounds per minute. Special buses are already bringing in large numbers of workers – he'd heard that there were already about 10,000 people working there (including a number of women!). Unfortunately, the Germans are already producing large numbers of the same gun themselves under licence and it seems very unlikely that this can be stopped. A few miles to the East, in the Chatham area, building of warships is now being stepped up – mostly of light cruisers, destroyers and submarines, now that the production and servicing of the huge Dreadnoughts has largely been moved to the new Dockyard at Rosyth, in Scotland.

Fig.1.12: Photo of the Vickers FB5 (Gunbus), taken in 1914.

The Vickers aircraft factory is also nearby. They started a few months earlier to produce the FB5 ("Gunbus"), which is more or less the first viable plane with serious armament. Production is now being stepped up enormously. There is no doubt that, from being a rather depressed region economically, with a lot of unemployment, this part of Kent has been rapidly transformed into a hive of activity. He thinks back to his early days in London, when the Met helped him to find suitable digs, quite close to the centre. The Met is certainly a good employer. His starting pay was 25 shillings a week – not a fortune, but a lot more than he was getting in Glasgow. They also provided supplements for various purposes, including rent. It was only a couple of shillings a week, whereas most rents were much higher than this, but every little helped and he was able to start looking around for houses suitable for his growing family. Housing conditions close to the centre were very poor in this district and working people tried to move out to less crowded areas, with some countryside nearby. This had been helped by

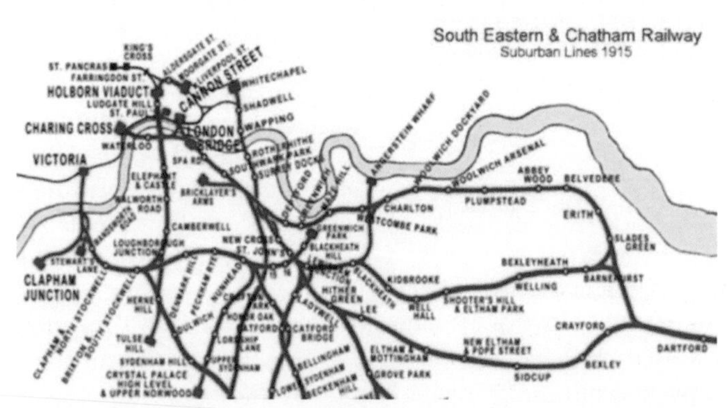

Fig.1.13: A SECR map showing their suburban lines close to London.

the "Cheap Trains Act" of 1883, which removed the tax on trains costing less than a penny a mile and obliged the railway companies to operate more cheap trains – making it viable for working men to live further out.

As William thinks about the house moves they have made, he reflects that they have really just progressively migrated along the suburban lines of the South Eastern and Chatham Railway, with "his" station changing from the original of Woolwich Arsenal to Plumstead, then Erith and now Crayford (close to St. Paul's Cray). The commuting time has remained much the same, at about an hour into Charing Cross, from where New Scotland Yard (on the Victoria Embankment) is just a few minutes walk. In fact, there has been a Police Station in St. Mary Cray since 1896, and he sometimes has stints there, but mostly he still goes into the city - which is fairly inexpensive and not too bad a journey.

Still, looking out of the window as they go through the rabbit warrens of New Cross and Southwark, the poverty, overcrowding and deprivation are only too apparent. It's no surprise that such areas still incubate unrest, strikes and periodic rioting. He sometimes has to deal with such problems and he often feels much sympathy for the people involved. Policing is an important and valuable activity, but it can't cure underlying issues of deprivation and exploitation. That is down to the politicians and it's clear that they're often not to be trusted – blundering into this war is a good illustration of that.

Fig.1.14: Photo taken at Sidney Street on 3rd January 1911, with Churchill (front of main group) directing police (and army) operations.

Reflecting on the role of politicians, he thinks back to the time in January 1911 when Winston Churchill – only 36 years old at the time, but already rapidly moving up through the system – had taken personal charge, as Home Secretary, of how the Met was handling the infamous "Siege of Sidney Street". The East End was, and still is, a dangerous and unruly place, but a gang of Latvian refugees was causing particular problems around 1909-1910, partly because they frequently used guns – which was, and still is, quite rare among criminals. They were heavily engaged in extortion, robbery and murder. Several Met policemen had been killed by this time and there was national outrage. Something certainly needed to be done, but the idea of having a politician out on the streets personally directing operations was rather ludicrous. Still, Churchill is no ordinary politician. The gang was finally eliminated, although only after a 6-hour gunfight, with Churchill calling in a company of Scots Guards. In fact, Churchill did have "previous" in resorting to use of the army to deal with civic matters, having done so to disperse striking miners in Wales (Tonypandy) the year before. Anyway, there were certainly mixed feelings in the Met about all this.

Eventually, the train pulls into Charing Cross. William recalls the day, almost ten years ago, when part of the roof collapsed, shortly before he arrived to go home. The station was then shut for several months, although the repair was a simple and rather unattractive structure. They really should do a proper rebuild soon – after all, this is an important and busy station. Still, the war is likely to result in many such projects being put on hold. He walks out of the main entrance, with a wave to a couple of constables stationed there, and it's then just a very short stroll to the elegant headquarters building overlooking the Thames. As he goes in, and is greeted by the receptionist, he gets his usual kick from having such a place of work. As he enters the main office on the first floor, he's greeted by several of his colleagues:

"Morning, Bill. How's the family – I thought that Alice was due to be adding to it about now?!" This is from his immediate boss, Harry Collis, who joined the force at the same time as William, and is now an Inspector.

"Aye, it could be soon." William's Scottish brogue has become diluted over the years, although it's still clearly detectable. "We need more Scots in this part of the world."

"Away with ye. Your kids are cockneys through and through! They take their lead from Alice, and just as well – she's a lovely girl. Anyway, we need to go over the latest duty rosters – these railway people don't seem to understand that we're supposed to be chasing criminals, instead of standing around in draughty stations trying to work out what a spy might look like!"

Chapter 2: The Gathering Storm (September 1914 – March 1915)

2.1 The Next Generation Steps Up

Fig.2.1: Recruitment poster of 1914.

William (Jnr) has made his decision. It hasn't been a difficult one. It seems that every young man of his age (18) is joining up. Posters of Lord Herbert Kitchener, pointing his finger and highlighting the need of the country, are absolutely everywhere. He's already been handed several white feathers by groups of young women prowling the streets. It isn't as if he has an important job. He'd actually liked school, but he'd had to leave four years before and since then he's had a series of rather unsatisfactory jobs. He does want to help his country, but also he yearns for adventure and new experiences. He's never been abroad, unless one counts a single visit to the North of Scotland, when he'd been quite young, and had in any event found the place desolate and primitive. It seems clear that this war is to be short and easy, so he feels that it's important not to miss the boat, literally and figuratively. His only hesitation arises from the knowledge that his mother will be devastated. Still, he's sure that she'll come round as she sees that it is turning out to be an exciting adventure for him. After all, his brothers Herbert and Frank, who are one and two years younger than him, are already showing definite interest in joining. It's his clear duty, as head of the next generation, to step up first.

He therefore turns up at the recruiting station in Dartford at 9am sharp on Monday 1st September. There's already a long queue. He's in good health – indeed one might call him a strapping young man – and he quickly sails through the medical inspection and interview. Several of his friends are in the same batch and virtually everyone seems to be getting accepted. He signs the forms and is told to report to the Army Centre in Tonbridge on the following Monday. Most new recruits are joining the army. He isn't offered a choice, so the navy is apparently not an option – they seem to need far fewer new people and in any event he has no experience of the sea. He's told that he'll be joining the Queens Own Royal West Kent Regiment, and that it has a long and proud tradition. They're already forming several new battalions, which are expected to see action abroad very soon. This is music to his ears – the last thing he wants is to find himself kicking his heels for years in some barracks in an army town in England.

Photo by] [Elliott and Fry, Ltd., Baker Street, W.

Colonel C. N. Watney, C.I.E., T.D.
Commanded 1/4 Battalion until April, 1919

Fig.2.2: Photo of Lieutenant-Colonel Watney.

Fig.2.3: Cap badge of the Royal West Kents.

He has to break the news to his mother, leading to a difficult few days, but the rest of the family are supportive and he heads off to Tonbridge in high spirits. He's issued with kit and starts to learn how the system works. A few days later, he and a batch of new recruits are moved to a barracks in Sandwich. He starts to get to know his new comrades and the traditions of the regiment. He's allocated to the 1/4th Battalion. The nomenclature is a bit confusing. The original 4th Battalion had been formed from volunteers about 15 years earlier, but it was now being split up, as thousands of new volunteer recruits arrive. There are four Battalions of this type in the West Kents – termed 1/4th, 2/4th, 3/4th and 4/4th, but something similar is also happening to other Battalions in the regiment. He learns that a Battalion is usually composed of about 500-1,000 men, with a Lieutenant-Colonel in charge. The man in charge of the 1/4th Battalion is Charles Watney. He doesn't get to meet him in person, but he gives a stirring speech to an assembly of the new recruits.

Regiments are composed of several Battalions, but these don't usually fight alongside each other. Larger (multi-Regiment) units are Brigades (several Battalions) and Divisions (several Brigades). A Division typically comprises about 15,000 men. Sometimes a few Divisions are assembled into a Corps, which may also be termed an Army. Battalions are also broken down into smaller units, including Companies (~100-150 men) and Platoons (~25 men), the latter usually commanded by a Lieutenant or Second Lieutenant. William finds it all a bit overwhelming, particularly since he's also trying to absorb the various traditions and conventions that are associated with the West Kents. There is fierce rivalry with the East Kents, often called the "Buffs". In any event, he is now in the 1/4th Battalion of the QORWK (or just RWK) Regiment, which will always be his affiliation or "home". He learns about the "Invicta Horse" symbol of the Regiment, their nicknames (such as the "Celestials" – from the original sky-blue facings on their uniforms) and previous battle honours etc. He quickly makes new friends and starts to take part in some intensive training. It's an exciting time.

2.2 Rapid Developments

The new recruits, with no experience of soldiering, are initially told that they will receive at least about 6 months of training in the UK before there is any possibility of seeing active service. However, it soon becomes apparent that this guideline is likely to be relaxed in some cases, in view of the way that the war is rapidly developing. A few weeks after his arrival, volunteers are invited for overseas service in the near future. Most of the new recruits in 1/4th Battalion eagerly accept this invitation and William joins them. They're expecting to be sent to France or Belgium, where many thousands of soldiers have already arrived (in the "British Expeditionary Force") and a couple of battles have already been fought. Indeed, the 1st Battalion of the Regiment had arrived in France in the middle of August and had already taken part in a one-day battle at Mons, in Belgium, although apparently the overall outcome on that day had not been so good. Still, the lads had fought back hard, together with Battalions from several other Regiments, and they had since won a great victory near the River Marne. Clearly, things are already starting to go our way and enthusiasm is sky-high.

William and his new friends and comrades are looking forward to joining them soon. However, in mid-October, they get a bit of a shock, as a rumour starts to circulate that the 1/4th Battalion is going to India! This seems to be confirmed when they are issued with tropical kit, and also get vaccinated against typhoid. This isn't quite what they had in mind, but they're assured that they will soon see action and that India, and British Indian troops, will be an important aspect of this war – the Germans have been eyeing up parts of the British Empire, particularly around the Suez Canal, the Persian Gulf and India, for some time. The immediate intention is that they will be relieving seasoned troops currently in India of their duties there, so that they can be released to go immediately to areas where fighting is taking place. Also, it appears that 1/4th will be the first of the volunteer Battalions of the RWK to see some sort of action – the others are already starting to get distributed around the country for extended training. In any event, they will be going on an interesting voyage, seeing an exotic part of the world and starting to do a useful job. Everyone seems to be very positive about this development.

A week or so later, he hears that they will be embarking on 29th October – that's this Thursday! They've been given less than a week's notice, but he appreciates that things are happening very quickly, and he's also starting to understand that the lower ranks usually get told very little about what's going on. They've still not been informed by anyone in authority about their destination, although everyone seems to know. He's allowed a quick visit home, but reports back on the Wednesday. Everyone is very excited. The next day, they march through the streets of Sandwich to the railway station, where a special train is waiting for the Battalion – about 700 men. The streets are lined with cheering crowds. Most members of his family have made the journey to Sandwich to see him off. It's a bit emotional, especially for his mother, but the general feeling among both troops and relatives is that they're off on an adventure.

The journey to Southampton is a bit slow, and the train is very crowded, but they get there in the early afternoon, arriving at the docks to scenes of great activity and confusion. It's clear that several troopships will be leaving today, with many special trains arriving and departing. There are several non-commissioned officers (NCOs) controlling the movements of the Battalion into various holding areas, and a lot of waiting around. Security is high, with everyone frequently being asked to show ID cards. He also has an ID disk around his neck, with his regimental number, which is 1356.

Fig.2.4: Photo of RMT Grantully Castle in 1914.

The identity of "their" ship eventually becomes clear. It's the "Grantully Castle", which is now prefixed by "RMT" (standing for Requisitioned Military Transport). The government has taken over huge numbers of the vessels being run by various shipping lines, together with their crews. One of his new comrades, Ernie Mortby, comes from a family with a maritime background and, as they assemble in front of the gangplank, he starts to give William some background about the ship.

"These are very solid ships, Billy boy. This one was built on the Clyde about 5 years ago. About 7,000 tons displacement and it would normally carry about 400 passengers. Of course, that's fare-paying passengers and you can be fairly sure that they're going to cram us in a bit more densely than that! It's probably been used on the run to Bombay – the Union Castle Line would be my guess. They'll probably have the same crew – or at least have offered them the chance to stay on. She can probably manage 20 knots and so will easily be able to outrun any U-boats. We'll have a Royal Navy escort and no German surface ships will come near us – we'll be safe as houses, mate!"

The prediction about passenger density turns out to be quite accurate. The more luxurious fittings have been largely stripped out. In fact, they're going to be sharing the ship with two other Battalions – he'd heard that one of them was the 1/6th East Surrey. There are apparently going to be about 1,800 soldiers on board. It soon starts to become clear that there will be a lot of hammocks, and perhaps also some primitive beds on the open decks. He manages to grab a hammock in a fairly spacious corner, close to several of his new friends.

William is starting to feel that this is not going to be a luxury cruise, but nevertheless he has the impression that everything is being well organized. It's also clear that a number of similar-looking ships are being readied to sail in the same timescale. He's told that all of them are carrying Territorial troops (ie recently-formed volunteer Battalions). When, shortly before midnight, the Grantully Castle slips her moorings and moves down Southampton Water and out into the Solent, several other ships have already left, and several more are close to departure. They move out into the Channel, to the South-East of the Isle of Wight, but remain in the area until it becomes light. He comes up on deck after an early breakfast to see that there are actually ten troopships being assembled, with several Royal Navy warships around them – Ernie was right about this. He can see now that they're going to be sailing in a sizeable convoy. He had heard that U-boats might be a threat - his mother had been particularly concerned about this – but in view of Ernie's information, and the impressive array of destroyers and cruisers in sight, he feels sure that they're going to be very safe on this trip. He can't help reflecting that Britannia really does rule the waves – this is an impressive display of maritime power. Huge resources are clearly being deployed very quickly and efficiently.

The voyage itself turns out to be rather long. Ernie had told him that it's about 7,000 miles to Bombay, so, averaging about 10-15 knots, it should take something like 3 weeks. In fact, it takes quite a bit longer than that. However, it's still a fairly relaxed and pleasant voyage, despite the overcrowding. There's plenty to see along the way. The weather is a bit rough on the second and third day, while crossing the Bay of Biscay, and William does find then that keeping his breakfast down is not so easy. However, he soon gets his "sea legs" and he's not one of those having a lot of trouble. In any event, the sea is quite calm for virtually all of the rest of the voyage. They pass through the straits of Gibraltar on the fifth day and William is amazed to see the towering cliffs and the huge number of British and Allied warships in the naval base there.

They carry on through the Mediterranean, with balmy weather and no alarms of any kind. He had heard rumours of German, and possibly Austrian, warships in the area, but they see nothing to cause any concern. He and his regimental mates are subject to some strict discipline, with mealtimes being carefully regulated, but they do have spare time and they devise various games and other activities on the deck. There are few actual duties, but they do learn various skills, such as how to disassemble and clean a rifle – although they don't actually have their own rifles yet – such has been the speed at which events have evolved. Their first port of call is Malta – another huge naval base. A night is spent there, although they're not allowed ashore. The British naval escort is swapped next morning for a French one, with various complimentary and uncomplimentary messages being shouted across to the crews of these Allied ships. They then move on to Port Said, at the northern end of the Suez Canal, reaching it about two weeks into the voyage.

Clearly, no escort is needed through the canal and it makes logistical sense for a separate set of escorting warships to pick up the convoy at the other end, at Port Suez – which is about 100 miles to the south. William and his mates marvel at the various sights seen during the two days of transit – including ships coming north, which are passed in a number of bays and lakes. They also see camel trains and local boats, as well as preparations being made to defend the canal – there are rumours that the Ottomans (Turks), against whom war had been declared just a few days after they'd left Southampton, may attack it soon.

It is starting to get hot and there is less of a breeze in the canal than in the open sea. Most of the soldiers are not really used to very hot weather and, with the mercury climbing into the 90's around mid-day, there is a certain amount of fretting.

"Strewth, Sarge, you didn't tell us about this when we signed up. Is this normal round here?"

"I'm afraid that you ain't seen nuthin' yet, me old cock-sparra! It's actually winter at the moment. Also, it's nice an' dry. Keep yer hat on in the sun an' ye shud be OK. Ye're headed for India, ye know. Ye should have popped down the Turkish Baths before ye came on this little trip."

One or two rather anxious glances start to get exchanged, although they're not really sure whether he's joking. Anyway, they're seeing a lot of interesting sights and the general perception is that this is a lot better than a freezing winter's day in Rotherhithe.

Unfortunately, when they arrive at Port Suez they hear that their escort has been delayed and in fact a very tedious 6 days is spent there waiting for it to arrive. It's not possible to keep all of these soldiers cooped up in their ships for the whole of this period, particularly since it's now very hot. They are therefore allowed to do some local sightseeing, including some visits during the evenings. They're given very detailed and graphic information about the dangers of fraternizing with local women, although this is naturally ignored by a number of them (although not by William).

Finally, a new escort arrives to take them the 1,500 miles down the Red Sea to Aden – another strong British naval base – and another delay of 4 days. They're again allowed ashore for a couple of brief visits, during which they start to hear some details about what caused the previous delay. Apparently, there has already been action against the Ottomans near Aden, with the escorting warships getting involved and an attack beaten off. William starts to feel that the war is getting closer! Then their escort for the last stretch to Bombay arrives, in the form of some powerful Japanese battleships and cruisers. They've been escorting a large convoy - dozens of ships - full of troops from Australia, New Zealand and India, bound for Gallipoli or France. William starts to get some sort of feel for the scale and complexity of the operation that is under way

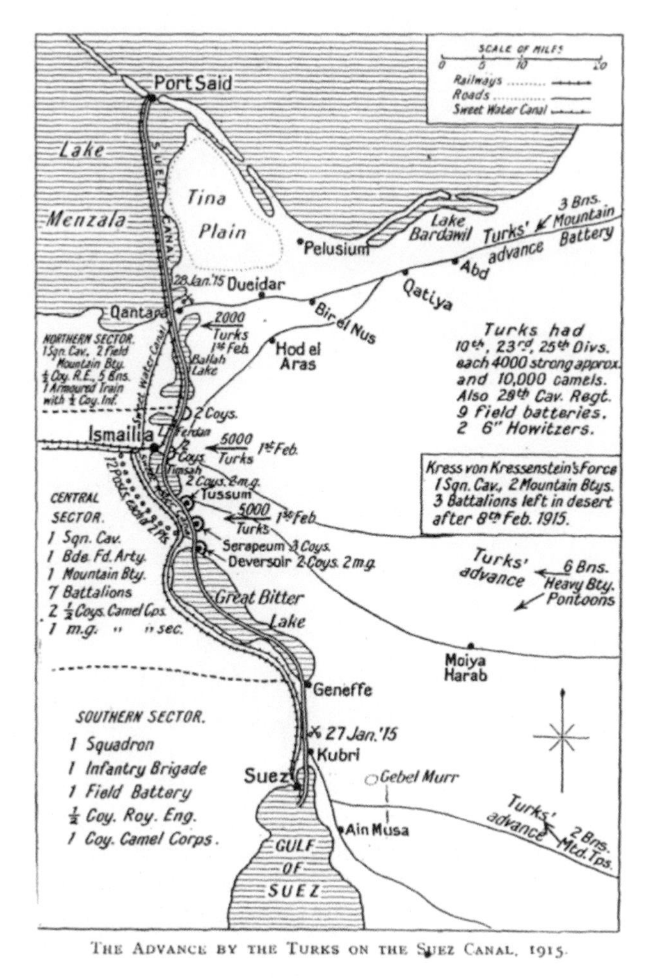

THE ADVANCE BY THE TURKS ON THE SUEZ CANAL, 1915.

Fig.2.5: Map showing the Suez canal area, with lines of attack by Turkish troops in 1915.

The Japanese escort quickly hands these ships over to the warships that have brought William and his shipmates through the Red Sea and it accompanies the convoy on their final leg of the 1,700 miles to Bombay. It's certainly hot, with virtually everyone having to sleep on deck, and they've been on the Grantully Castle for what seems like a very long time. However, spirits are still high and they enjoy the seaboard routine for the remaining five days of the voyage, arriving at Bombay on Wednesday 2nd December – 5 weeks after their departure from Southampton. William looks forward to the final stage of the journey, having heard a host of views about where in India it's likely to end.

It's clear that this part of the trip will be by train and William wonders just what the Indian railway system is going to be like. Nobody is expecting luxury or speed, but their

Fig.2.6: The Punjab Mail waiting to leave Ballard Pier Mole station in 1914.

confidence that the army system will manage something workable is quite high, and it could be that their new home will be somewhere nearby. In fact, it turns out to be a long way from being nearby. One of the more likeable NCOs, Sergeant-Major Willoughby, tells them what he's heard as they assemble on the dockside.

"We're off to Jubbulpore, you lucky lads! Right in the middle of India, a little trip of 700 miles, and a temperature of 100 degrees in the shade (if you can find any)! You'll love it!"

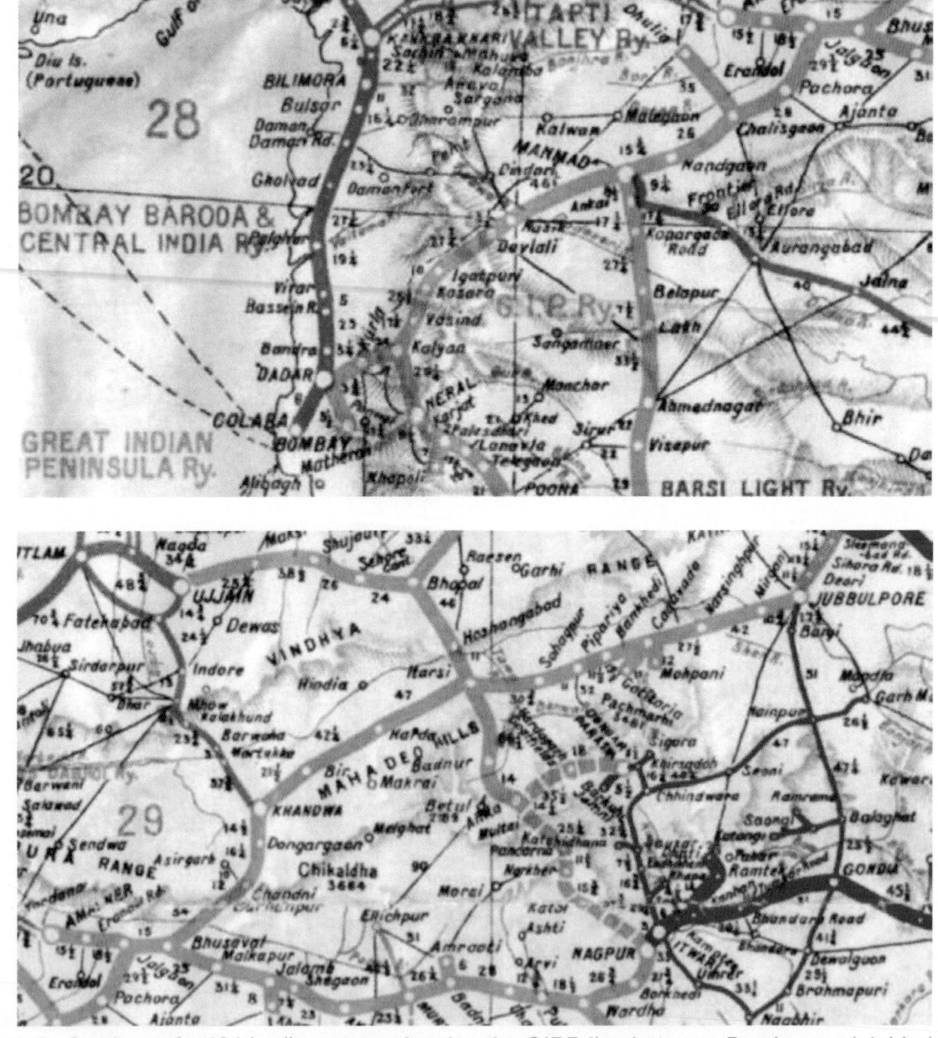

Fig.2.7: Sections of a 1914 railway map showing the GIPR line between Bombay and Jubbulpore.

Actually, the temperature here isn't too bad, with some onshore sea breezes. It's often difficult in the army to tell who is or isn't making jokes, or even who actually knows about things. Anyway, William and his mates are preoccupied with absorbing the sights and sounds of Bombay docks. It's certainly a captivating scene. There are dozens of ships of all possible sizes, shapes and types. Thousands of Indian seamen and soldiers mingle with arriving British troops, local workers, beggars and purveyors of various services. The assaults on the nose, ears and eyes are almost overwhelming. William and his mates are approached by all sorts of people, but the NCOs quickly shepherd the Battalion to the dockside station – the famous Ballard Pier Mole station - where their train is waiting. They see signs proudly proclaiming that this is the headquarters of the "Great Indian Peninsula Railway".

It's clear that they're not very high in the pecking order and they wait patiently in a large holding area while some important people – evidently high-ranking British Army officers and their families – sweep down from their majestic P&O liner and onto a gleaming train proudly proclaimed as the Punjab Mail, which will take them to the great colonial centres of Delhi, Lahore and Peshawar. Nevertheless, the system does work for 1/4th RWK and they're eventually met by a British Indian Army Sergeant based in Jubbulpore, who happens to be in Bombay and will be accompanying them to their new home. William is within earshot as he greets Sergeant-Major Willoughby:

"So this mob only joined up 3 or 4 months ago, eh? Well, they may find that this isn't quite what they had in mind! Still, it could be worse – for one thing, this train isn't too bad and hopefully it will be leaving fairly soon. The tracks and signaling aren't up to the standards in Blighty, so we'll be lucky to average about 30 miles per hour when moving. There'll also be plenty of stops to water the engine – water supplies are always a problem round here. We'll also stop at quite a few stations – with this heat, and no facilities of any sort on the train, that's essential. It'll be at least a 2-day journey. Of course, it's much worse in the summer!"

"How's the accommodation on the train going to work out?" asked S-M Willoughby.

"Well, these are mostly 2nd Class carriages, but there is a first class one for the officers and a few hangers-on. I'm afraid that the NCOs are going to have to travel with the other ranks – at least one per carriage – to keep some sort of order. As you can see, there's no provision for moving between the carriages, or even between compartments in a carriage for many of them. There should be enough seats for everyone, but it's going to be a tight squeeze."

Just then, an employee of the GIPR, resplendent in a garish uniform, comes bustling up: "Sahib, please to get your men on the train quickly now – we're due to leave in 30 minutes."

William and a few friends quickly grab seats in a nearby carriage and throw their packs onto the luggage racks. The NCOs run up and down the platform, herding everyone on board and discouraging them from buying anything from the throng of locals that are busy trying to hawk various drinks, fruits, samosas etc carried on trays above their heads. "Come on, you horrible crew, you'll get fed en route and we don't want these carriages stinking of curry all the way to Jubbulpore. Anyway, most of this stuff will make you ill. In particular, don't drink any of the water that this bunch might try to sell you."

Actually, acquiring a few melons would have been a good idea, since it is hot in the train, which doesn't in fact leave Bombay for over two hours and the first stop, at the railway junction of Kalyan, is only reached after a further couple of hours of jolting through crowded tracks in the region around Bombay, with bullocks, dogs and people providing obstacles throughout. Everyone is very happy to tumble out onto the platform for a break. The stationmaster comes out of his office to check that everything is in order. "The toilets are round the back and these merchants are all approved purveyors of food and drink of the very highest quality", he assures the bemused-looking soldiers, pointing to a motley collection of impoverished locals who have set up various stalls on the platform. He's also extremely proud of the steel bridge over which the train has just passed, pointing it out to anyone who will listen. "Just completed earlier this year, double track, built by the Indian Army – a most brilliant engineering achievement!"

William isn't terribly interested in this, but notes that they've been sitting in this train now for 4 hours, but are still only about 30 miles from Bombay. However, things are not so bad – it's getting cooler as the sun goes down and they're soon on their way again, having bought some food and drink for the next stage of the journey. He and his friends soon realize that most things in India are incredibly cheap. The basic unit of currency is the rupee, divided into 16 annas. One anna, which is worth about thru'pence, buys a lot of melons! William is getting paid about a shilling a day, but most of his basic needs are being provided free, so he has already been able to accumulate a few pounds. He and his mates are starting to feel that they're effectively quite rich in this country! In fact, he's already been able to send some cash back to his mother – a little more than he contributed when he was living at home!

They settle down for the rest of the journey, managing to get some sleep during the night and entertaining themselves playing cards, telling various yarns and circulating a few books and newspapers. It's a bit claustrophobic to spend a couple of days cooped up like this, but they get to know each other well and they also absorb the sights that are slowly unfolding outside of the windows. It's clearly a poor country, with many people working on the land, but there are also a lot of beggars – often with some physical disability – and they congregate around the railway stations, which are effectively community centres. They move slowly into the interior of the country, with extended stops at the big junction stations of Manmad, Bhusaval, Khandwa and Itarsi.

Fig.2.8: Photo of Jubbulpore station in 1914.

Eventually, on the morning of Saturday 5th December, they roll slowly into Jubbulpore station. It is a little hotter here in the middle if India, compared with Bombay, although still not too bad. It's just a short march to the huge "Hugh Rose" Barracks, with everyone welcoming the chance to stretch their legs. They spend the rest of the day settling into their new home, although they also get a chance to chat to some of the British Indian Army soldiers that are now leaving to take part in the fighting in France and Mesopotamia. William and his friends start to get an idea of the duties and activities that will be expected of them here.

Fig.2.9: Photo of 1/4th RWK personnel, soon after arrival in Jubbulpore at the end of 1914.

The following days are busy as they start to settle into their new accommodation and roles.

There are several battalions here, from various parts of Britain, and new ones continue to arrive. William starts to understand the relationship between the British Army units in India and the British Indian army, which has mainly British officers, but other ranks drawn from various parts of India – "Sepoy" troops, as they're usually known. It slowly dawns on William and his friends that a large part of their function in the country concerns the suppression of internal dissent of various types. The Indian Mutiny was almost 60 years ago, and is starting to recede into history, but the underlying causes have certainly not all disappeared. British officialdom has since made serious attempts to respect the various religious and caste-related sensitivities of local people, but they're still very much second class citizens in their own country. The overt racism and arrogance of many of the "ruling classes" here comes as something of a shock to William, although he and his friends naturally feel that they should just accept the situation in their new environment.

In any event, there doesn't seem to be very much trouble in this part of India with the locals, who mostly appear to be reverential, or at least respectful, towards William and his mates. They have contact with some of them, mainly the servants employed to help them in various ways. While there are occasional signs of resentment, it doesn't seem to be too serious. It also becomes clear that the Army in India does have a role in protection of external borders. This relates particularly to the "North-West Frontier" and the border with Afghanistan. The Russians have been threatening to encroach from this direction for many years, which was part of the causes of the Crimean War about 50 years ago. The Russians are now Allies against Germany and the Ottoman Empire, with which they have had conflicting interests for centuries. There are still, however, regular skirmishes on the NW Frontier, where the complex tribal system is very difficult to understand, and the British Indian Army often gets embroiled in attempts to keep the peace.

Fig.2.10: Photo of the 1/4th RWK cookhouse crew in Jubbulpore ("Hugh Rose") barracks, taken early in 1915.

Still, there seems to be little likelihood of the 1/4th RWKs getting involved in anything like that. In fact, as the New Year starts and a regular routine gets established, the main problem is that of boredom – plus the heat, which starts to get worse as they move into spring and peak temperatures creep up into the 80's and 90's. Also, it's very dry. William is told that there's not much rain at all until around June, when it will start to get heavy as the monsoon season begins. He's starting to feel that some rain would be welcome, although none of the tales he's heard really prepare him for the reality.

March 1915 sees many of those in the Battalion accepting their lot as having its drawbacks, but not being too bad. However, disturbing news about how the war is developing in Europe keeps coming through. There are various reports of major battles at Arras, Messines, Ypres and Neuve Chapelle. While many of these stories are confused and limited, it seems clear that the anticipated easy victory is not materializing at all. These battles have evidently been very hard fought, with many casualties on both sides. The term "trench warfare" is starting to be bandied about, although talk of impending breakthroughs is widespread. In any event, William himself feels that he is far from the action and unable to contribute as he should. He can't stand the idea of being marooned here while momentous events are taking place elsewhere. His thinking starts to move towards whether there might be an opportunity to get more involved in some way.

2.3 Leadership and Strategy

It has been a long, tiring meeting and the atmosphere is tense and fretful. Every member of the newly-created War Council recognizes that things are not going according to plan. The date is Wednesday 25th November 1914. The key people involved in decisions related to the war are all present. Lord Kitchener, at the height of his powers at the age of 64, is the Secretary of State for War. He has a high public standing, partly due to his perceived success in running the Boer Wars. His recruitment campaign for raising a large army is already very successful. His word is virtually law in the Council. However, other strong characters are also present. These include Winston Churchill, a highly ambitious, well-connected young (39) politician who has been appointed First Lord of the Admiralty. He has a close relationship with Lord John Fisher, whom he recently brought out of retirement, aged 73, to take up the post of First Sea Lord. Fisher, like Kitchener, has a high public reputation, having been responsible for massive strengthening of the Royal Navy between the turn of the century and his retirement 4 years earlier. This was largely in response to the growth of the German Navy, the pride of Kaiser Wilhelm, and it involved the development of the Dreadnought type of battleship, with greatly improved speed and armament capabilities. As a result of this, Britannia still rules the waves, although the German Navy is certainly a threat.

Others present include the Prime Minister, Lord Herbert Asquith (62), who tends to act as a neutral chairman, and David Lloyd George (51), a Welsh firebrand with little time for most admirals and generals. He is currently Chancellor of the Exchequer, although taking an increasing interest in military aspects of the war. Also present is Richard Haldane (58), currently Lord Chancellor, although he'd been Minister of War until two years earlier, and had instigated a lot of useful Army reforms. He has German links that are already being used publicly to vilify him.

Reviewing the situation, it's very clear that the quick and easy victory anticipated just a few months earlier was a complete delusion. The Royal Navy has triumphed in a couple of minor skirmishes, and the German Navy is now staying in port, but on land it's a very different story. The German Army is evidently strong and well-organized. Huge armies now confront each other in muddy trenches running from the Channel to Switzerland. Moreover, when either side attempts to advance, wholesale slaughter from machine gun fire results. Unbelievably, Britain and France have between them already lost a million men. Attempts are being made to suppress this information, but a lot of bad news is certainly becoming public. There is a consensus on the Council that "something must be done".

It's Churchill, with his active brain and strong powers of persuasion, who proposes opening up a new theatre of operation – preferably one where British sea-power can be exploited. This concept commands wide support, although Kitchener feels that the war has to be won by persevering in France and Belgium, and he supports the Commander-in-Chief of the British Expeditionary Force, Sir John French, who insists that throwing waves of men into machine-gun fire is the only way forward.

"Surely we all recognize that we must stop sending men to chew barbed wire in Flanders?!" Churchill implores. "We must open up a new front – one where the strength of the Royal Navy can be used, instead of our powerful ships endlessly cruising around the North Sea!"

"Moreover, there is a place where it could play a key role in turning the course of this war. I'm talking about the Dardanelles."

Churchill is referring to Turkey and the shipping connection between the Black Sea and the Aegean Sea (and from there to the Mediterranean and the oceans of the world – either via the Straits of Gibraltar or the Suez Canal). At the Eastern end of this link lies the relatively large Sea of Marmara, connected to the Black Sea by the short Bosphorus channel, where the ancient city of Constantinople is located. However, at the Western end, there is a narrow, 40-mile long waterway called the Dardanelles. On one side of this channel is the Turkish mainland and on the other is the Gallipoli peninsula. There is a continual flow of water, typically at several knots, westwards through this channel, caused by the discharge of several large rivers into the Black Sea. The Dardanelles is a heavily-used and important waterway - particularly for Russia, which has no warm water port for exports and imports other than those on the Black Sea.

Russia is now an ally of Britain and France, and is engaging the Germans strongly in Europe on the Eastern Front. Russia is also a long-term antagonist of Turkey – ie of the Ottoman Empire, which is somewhat teetering these days, but is still a significant force. Britain has tended to keep on reasonably good terms with it in the past, and in fact was allied with them in the Crimean War against Russia, some 50 years earlier. However, they're certainly not allies now.

"As you know, we've been at war with the Turks for almost a month now" says Churchill. "They've closed the Dardanelles. It's clear that the Germans are sending men and arms to Turkey."

"Also, I need hardly repeat the story of the Goeben. Three months ago, we had it trapped in the Mediterranean. Unfortunately, it escaped into the Aegean and thence into the Sea of Marmara, with Turkish connivance. We decided not to attempt to enter the Dardanelles, which has gun emplacements on both sides. The presence of this single German warship was a major cause of the Turks going into alliance with them. Closure of this channel is now bleeding the Russians white. Needless to say, if they're forced out of the war, then millions of German troops will be released from the Eastern Front."

"We must do something about this!" urges Churchill. "What's more, the Royal Navy could play a crucial role. They could pound the forts protecting it and support troops to be landed there. A strong naval force entering the Sea of Marmara could sink the Goeben and threaten to bombard Constantinople. This might well persuade them to withdraw from the war – we all know that the Ottoman Empire is on the point of collapse."

Two different types objection are raised to the plan. One, promoted by

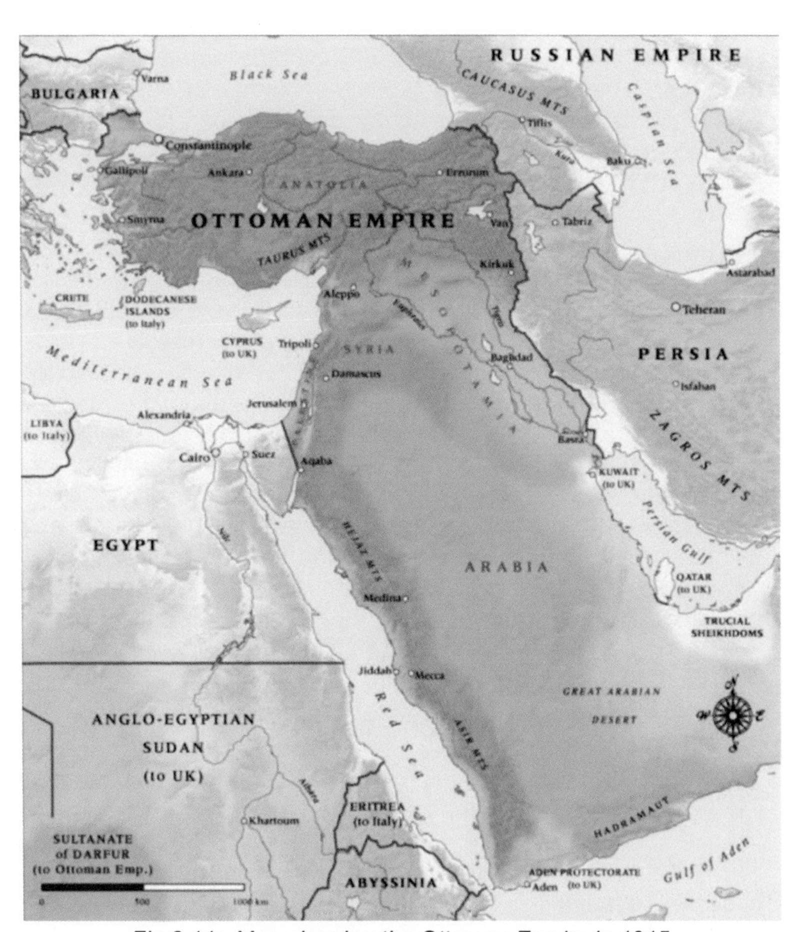

Fig.2.11: Map showing the Ottoman Empire in 1915.

Fisher, is that retaining control over the North Sea, blockading Germany, is of paramount importance and the ships to be used for this venture must not detract at all from the dominance of the Grand Fleet in home waters. This isn't really a valid objection, since Britain has many warships that are effectively "spare" and even older ships that are slower and less powerful should be suitable for this venture, in the absence of strong enemy sea power in the area. Nevertheless, Fisher is to put it forward in increasingly strong terms over the coming months.

The other objection, repeatedly voiced by Kitchener, is that no troops can be spared from the French/Belgian theatre of operations. This also does not seem to be a show-stopper, particularly as the naval-only plan starts to take centre stage. In fact, Kitchener is prepared to consider usage of troops from other nations, with those from both France and Greece being mentioned. In the event, that does not happen, but he is to withdraw his objection to use of British troops (coming from the UK, rather than being transferred from the Western Front) and also agrees to use of British Empire troops, particularly those from Australia and New Zealand. In any event, a definite decision is deferred at the meeting on 25th November, but a consensus is starting to emerge in favour of the venture. It can certainly be argued that, carried out quickly and well, it could and should have been pivotal in swinging the outcome of the war towards the Allies within a relatively short period. Of course, that is not how it turns out.

Churchill's hand is strengthened early in January by a desperate plea from the Russian Tsar, Nicholas II, for help against the Turks. The King, George V, who is a cousin and close friend of the Tsar, makes it clear that assistance should if possible be given. The War Council therefore decides on 28th January to go ahead with some action. Churchill pushes this through on the basis of it being a purely naval action. This has the support of Kitchener, although Fisher is becoming increasingly antagonistic. A strong force of (mostly old) warships is sent to the Aegean and they start to bombard the forts at the entrance to the Dardanelles on 19th February. The range of the naval guns is greater than those of the forts and this exercise is initially quite successful, with the forts being severely damaged and no naval losses suffered.

However, instead of pushing on with attempts to enter the Dardanelles, the action is halted for further consultations. This delay is partly due to the timid approach of the admiral in charge, Sackville Carden, who is stressed and unwell, although a lack of clarity in the instructions from the War Office contributes to this. He is relieved of his duties in early March by Admiral John de Robeck, with an emissary of Kitchener, General Ian Hamilton, being sent out at the same time to assess the situation. Attempts to enter the Dardanelles are started on 5th March and continue until 18th March. These are disastrous, with the combination of floating mines in the channel and mobile howitzers on the banks proving very difficult to overcome. Part of the problem is that the Turks and a number of German advisors have had a period of several weeks to prepare their defences and this has been done very well. One of the arguments in favour of a purely naval attack was that, if things went badly, the venture could be abandoned without heavy losses, but, predictably, this is not done.

It's possible that, even in the face of this strong defence system, a purely naval "forcing" of the channel could, with better planning and coordination, have been achieved, but at this point a decision is made (effectively by Kitchener) to move to a combined naval and land attack. This is to be under the overall control of General Hamilton, with Admiral de Robeck in charge of naval operations. The idea is to rapidly move in a large army that will overcome what is expected to be feeble resistance (to be subjected beforehand to intense naval bombardment), occupy the peninsula and remove the howitzers and mines, allowing the fleet to move into the Sea of Marmara. The difficulty of this task is grossly underestimated.

In parallel with these preparations, another British initiative is already underway against the Ottoman / German axis. This has attracted less public attention, but it is based on a genuine strategic concern. The British-controlled oilfields in Persia (run by the Anglo-Persian Oil Company – APOC, later to become British Petroleum, BP) are increasingly important, particularly for the Royal Navy - which is rapidly shifting towards oil, rather than coal, to power its warships. This oil is transferred via a pipeline to Basra and thence to the oil terminal on Abadan Island. This is a key resource that is increasingly needed in the war. This region is towards the southern limits of Ottoman influence, but the local Arab population is sympathetic towards them – or at least is not well-disposed to the Allied powers (Britain and France).

Churchill actually knows all about this issue and he was involved in the decision early in the war to move troops to Basra. These are largely to be Anglo-Indian troops, transferred from India, which is much closer to the Persian Gulf than is Britain. There are concerns about whether Indian troops will be happy to fight against soldiers who might be quite close to them in cultural and religious terms. However, there are hundreds of thousands of soldiers there under arms, while none can at present be spared from the growing conflict in Europe. It seems the logical thing to do. Some Indian troops are also to be moved to France and Belgium.

The first contingent from the British Indian army starts to arrive at Basra in September 1914 and this largely ensures the security of the oil pipeline. However, as so often happens, there is "mission creep" and it is decided to push on and drive the Ottomans out of Baghdad, so as to control the whole of lower Mesopotamia. This starts to take place during the early months of 1915.

2.4 A Family at Home

Meanwhile, the war starts to have an effect on the Clyne family in Kent, as it does on almost everyone in the country. Herbert finally joins up in March 1915, aged 17 years and 9 months. He follows his brother into the Royal West Kents, and into the same Battalion (1/4th). This only happens in the face of bitter opposition from his mother, but he manages to overcome this, partly by using the argument that no harm of any sort has come to William, who is now seeing the world and appears from his letters to be enjoying his new life. Herbert had hoped to be able to join up with his brother quite soon, but sending soldiers abroad soon after they join up is now much less common and he has had to resign himself to at least 6 months of training in Britain.

Frank, now aged sixteen and a half, is also pressing hard, although he's expressing a wish to join the Seaforth Highlanders – partly to promote the support of his father. Alice keeps threatening to report both of them to the authorities for lying about their age and joining before they are 18. She knows that hundreds of thousands of young men are doing this, largely with the connivance of the Army, and she might even run the risk of being branded as insufficiently patriotic. Alice is an intelligent woman and, while not normally interested in politics or wars, she can sense from various reports that young men are already being killed in large numbers and that this is likely to continue for some considerable time. It's a terrible dilemma for mothers such as her.

Still, for the moment, life is going on much as before. She gets regular letters from William, which are very reassuring. Her husband is busy with his work and, while he seems a bit stressed with the new pressures, he appears to be in good spirits. The other children are all doing well at school in St. Mary Cray, with Douglas keen to start soon at the Infants. Len is still at home, although running around now and chattering away.

They continue to take part in various local events, including weddings and other celebrations. There are also activities associated with the war, such as looking after refugees from Belgium – there are now substantial numbers of these housed in the Dartford area. Talking to these people starts to bring home just how serious and destructive this war is becoming. While putting on a brave face, Alice, and many people like her, are starting to have terrible misgivings. It's becoming clear that the German war machine is formidable, and can even deliver death and destruction to the homes of British people. Concern about the "Zeppelin raids", which were initiated in January 1915, is becoming widespread. In practice, there are many difficulties in guiding these cumbersome airships over the Channel (at night) and dropping bombs in targetted areas. Nevertheless, the fact that it's a possibility, with little or nothing that can be done to defend people against such attacks, creates widespread panic and horror.

Fig.2.12: Photo of the Clyne family in March 1915, with (left to right) Frank (16), Lena (7), William (46), Len (18 months), Alice (41), Douglas (3), Stan (13), Mina (10) and Harry (9). Herbert and William are away in the army.

The technical challenges involved in building an airship of this type are formidable. The rigid, 500 feet long framework is made of a strong, lightweight aluminium alloy ("Duralumin") specially-developed for this purpose – the formulation being kept secret for several years. The internal bags that hold the hydrogen must be light, flexible, have a low gas permeability and be easy to mould and bond: the material used is derived from the intestines of cows, with those from a quarter of a million animals needed for each airship. The procedure is derived from expertise in the country concerning the production of skins for frankfurters. The resourcefulness of the Germans in ventures such as these is impressive indeed.

By May of 1915, airships have successfully dropped both explosive and incendiary bombs on London. On the night of 7th September Alice and William watch one pass overhead and hear the bombs exploding just a mile or so away. People are being killed and property is being damaged. Such raids never become extensive, but their psychological effects are substantial. By that time, there are also many other ways in which the war has started to impinge on the lives of ordinary people – in fact, virtually everyone in the country is being hit in various ways. The main feeling is that we must all redouble our efforts, so as to finish things off as quickly as possible. However, it is becoming increasingly clear that this may turn out to be very much harder than was originally thought.

Chapter 3: Into The Maelstrom (April 1915 – February 1916)

3.1 A World at War

The war is now expanding out of all control and expectation. All of the conditions are in place for a "perfect storm". Most of the populations involved were supportive of war originally, having been led to believe that their side would win and that, in any event, it wouldn't have much direct impact on civilian populations. Memories of the Napoleonic Wars a century earlier – the last major European conflicts to impinge strongly on ordinary people – have faded. Furthermore, most people simply didn't understand the significance of recent rapid increases in the level and destructive power of military technology, the efficiency of transportation etc. Indeed, most military leaders and politicians didn't really understand this properly either. In fact, there was distinct enthusiasm for the war in many countries, or at least patriotic fervour, causing millions of young men to enlist voluntarily during the early days. Their actual experiences, of course, are very different from their expectations and by April 1915 the reality of this war is starting to hit everyone – particularly the troops in the field.

Also poorly understood originally was how the colonies of the major powers would be dragged into the conflict, with a host of geopolitical and cultural complications. Britain in particular is very keen to retain control over India – the "Jewel in the Crown" – and over other important assets, such as the Suez Canal and the oilfields in Arabia. Now that the Ottomans (Turks) are involved, they are perceived as a distinct threat to these interests, particularly since they have strong German infrastructural support – they have already started on a joint project to build a railway from Berlin to Baghdad, and on to Basra.

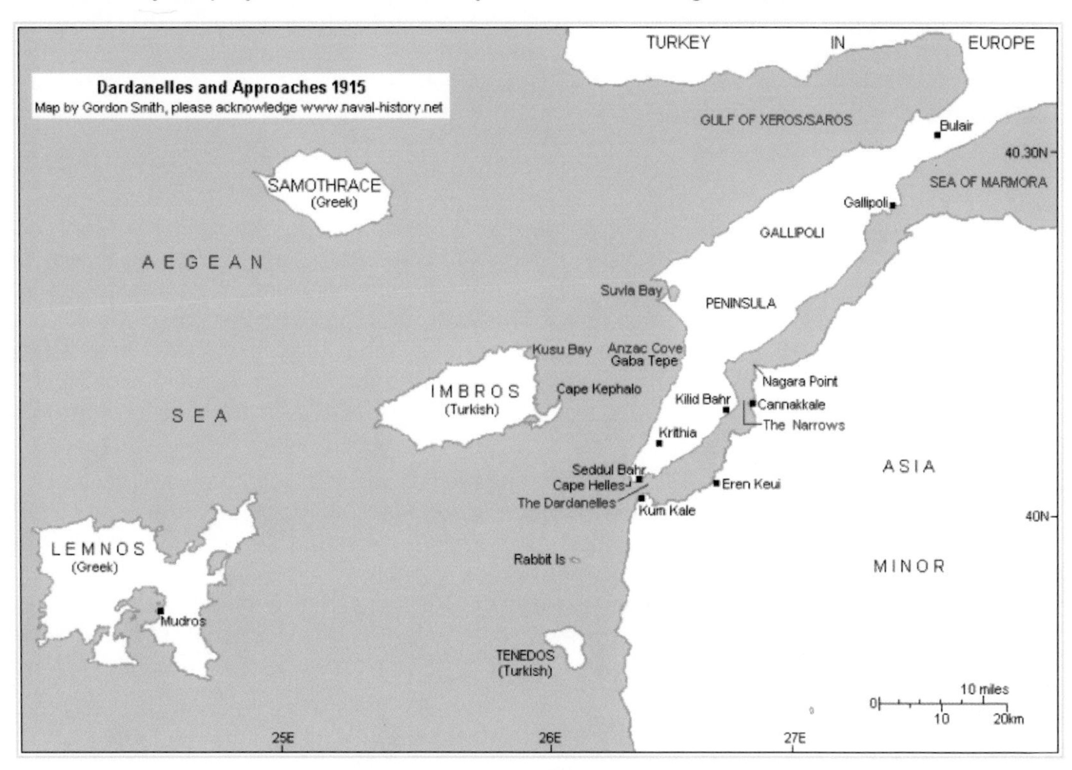

Fig.3.1: Map showing the Dardanelles area in 1915.

Preparation for the Gallipoli landings is haphazard and relatively slow, particularly in view of the fact that the Turks and their German advisors are using this time to bolster their defences. The initial onslaught takes place on Sunday 25th April 1915 (subsequently to be known as Anzac Day). It is a complete and utter disaster. The landing of large numbers of

British troops on the tip of the Gallipoli peninsula (at Cape Helles), mainly of the 29th Division, is met by coordinated fire from well-prepared Ottoman positions, such that many are killed as soon as they emerge from their landing craft. Even on beaches that are not so well-defended, the landings are poorly-coordinated and penetration inland is far less extensive than had been planned. Some of the fire from the British warships falls on troops who have established precarious footholds.

Simultaneously, a landing is undertaken further north, at Gaba Tepe (subsequently to be known as Anzac Cove), using troops from Australia and New Zealand. Casualties are enormous on the first day, with well over 10% of the 16,000 Anzac soldiers being killed, others wounded and only tenuous beachheads established. The story is similar at Cape Helles, with about 6,000 casualties among the 30,000 or so troops attempting to land. After a few days, there are several established beachheads in both areas, but penetration inland is minimal and a stalemate position is reached. The high level of courage and organization shown by the Ottoman troops comes as a shock. This is not at all what the British and Allied troops had been led to expect.

William is in touch with a school-friend from Dartford, who joined up at the same time, but ended up in the 2/4th Battalion of the RWK. In the 9 months since then, they had been moved to various bases in England for training, so he'd been rather jealous of William's quick and adventurous start. However, at the end of June they hear that they are to be part of the "Mediterranean Expeditionary Force" and sent to Gallipoli. In fact, the response of the authorities to the disastrous initial outcome of the Gallipoli landings has been to send massive reinforcements, strengthening the beachheads so that the planned penetration and takeover of the peninsula can be effected. Of course, ordinary soldiers such as William and his friend know little or nothing of what is actually happening in Gallipoli, where many have already died and the survivors are faced with a desperate struggle to maintain footholds on the beaches. The RWK 2/4th Battalion sails in mid-July, reaching Alexandria at the end of the month. They then take part in a set of landings at a new site in Gallipoli over the following week or two.

3.2 The War Arrives in Scotland

The history of participation of Scottish people in the defence of the realm is a long and illustrious one. While cross-border raiding and skirmishes date back to Roman times, the Scots have contributed strongly to the military strength of Great Britain ever since the Act of Union at the start of the 18th Century. This has most prominently taken the form of Scottish regiments with proud independent traditions, many dating back to that period. There have been many famous battles, including Waterloo, at which their contributions have been pivotal. Many young lads from Scotland had lost their lives in foreign fields during the preceding 200 years.

However, until 6.45am on 22nd May 1915, leaving aside the odd case of illness or the effects of wounds, no serving Scottish soldier in the British Army has died on Scottish soil. On this date, that changes when a troop train carrying soldiers of the 1/7th Battalion of the Royal Scots, bound for Gallipoli, crashes into a stationary local passenger train near Quintinshill, which is just north of the border at Gretna. Within a minute, a northbound sleeping car express ploughs into the wreckage. About 95% of those who die are soldiers, with over 200 of them losing their lives – almost half of those on the troop train. Many others are badly injured.

This is, and will remain, by far the worst rail disaster in Britain. It's also a huge casualty rate to be suffered by a Battalion in a single action, although even higher levels have been reached at Gallipoli a month earlier, with some Battalions being virtually wiped out completely. The Royal Scots is the oldest regiment in the British Army – its formation actually predates the Act of Union, since it was first raised in 1642 by the 1st Marquess of Argyll. Many of the deaths at Quintinshill are due to the carriages being engulfed by fire, with persistent rumours to the effect that a substantial number of soldiers are shot by others in order to spare them further agony. Many of them are burned beyond any possibility of identification or even clear recognition as bodies.

3.3 The Hell where Youth and Laughter Go

Siegfried Sassoon has had plenty of personal experience of life in the trenches on the Western Front by the time that he writes lines such as the one above. It's certainly beyond dispute that life is hellish for millions of young men, pinned down for months at a time in horrible muddy trenches, with continuous severe discomfort and death never far away – particularly when ordered to attack against resourceful and well-organized enemies.

However, there can also be no doubt that, while there is much in common between the situations of Allied troops on the Western Front and those in Gallipoli, the conditions faced by the latter are much worse. There are several reasons for this. One is that the Turks hold the high ground. Another is that, while the Turks have copious fresh water bubbling out of many springs along the heights, the Allied soldiers have none – it has to be brought by ship from Alexandria, 700 miles away. A third is that there is no possibility of respite – nowhere to retreat to for rest or recreation: they have their backs to the sea. A fourth is that the weather is often hellishly hot and there is a continuous plague of flies, particularly at the lower levels where the Allied troops are pinned down. Furthermore, the Turks build their trenches very close to those of the allies, to make it difficult for the British warships to fire shells at them. Movement out of the trenches is highly dangerous, particularly since there are many Turkish snipers in the bushes on the surrounding hills. The situation is such that many corpses are left to rot, causing a terrible stench. Disease, particularly dysentery, is absolutely rife.

Conditions are also bad for the Turks, but they turn out to be a resolute, stalwart and courageous foe, despite also losing many thousands of men. None of this has been foreseen and both the planning and the leadership have been abysmal on the Allied side. The venture should have been abandoned at an early stage, but in practice many young men suffer and die in a hopeless cause over a period of 8 months, before the decision is finally made to evacuate.

The story of the 2/4th Battalion of the RWK Regiment typifies the experiences of soldiers on the Gallipoli beaches. They land at Suvla Bay, a few miles to the north of Anzac cove, during the evening of 10th August. Landings had actually started there four days earlier, when two Battalions had managed to storm the Anafarta Hills above the beach. However, amid widespread confusion, two days later they withdraw back to the Suvla Plain. The Turks, who had originally been weak in the Suvla Bay area, quickly establish strongholds in these hills and the surrounding heights. During the Suvla Bay landings of 6th – 12th August, there are 20,000 casualties in total, of which only a few tens are from the 2/4th RWK: they therefore suffer less than many other Battalions during this period, but their situation is now perilous.

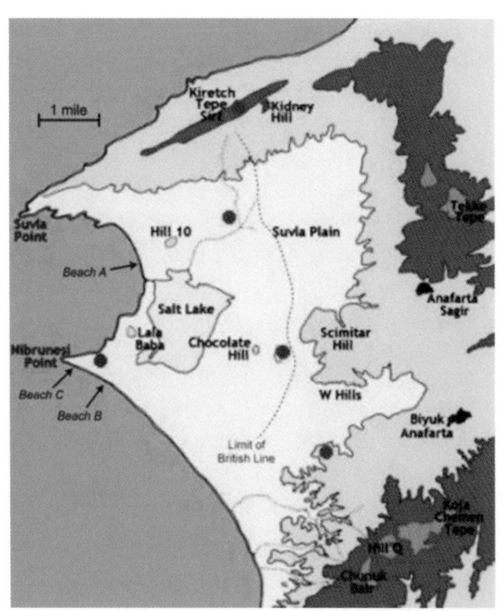

Fig.3.2: Map of Suvla Bay, for illustration of operations of the 2/4th Battalion of the RWK during August-December 1915.

It isn't until the 13th August that the 2/4th reach the firing line, having spent three days digging in and unloading stores. When they do reach the front line, at a 700 yard long stretch of it that has been allocated to the Battalion, they face an horrendous situation, with shallow trenches and the flat area in front of them dotted with bushes and trees that conceal many Turkish snipers. It's difficult to imagine a worse "baptism of fire" for raw troops who volunteered less than a year before and have not previously seen action of any sort. The Battalion commander, Colonel Alfred Simpson, is wounded and evacuated on the 15th. Nevertheless, they do manage to dig in and, after plans to penetrate further are abandoned, they make their trenches deeper and better equipped, while a more substantial and integrated overall line is established.

The following weeks and months, however, are a time of monotonous hardship for the Battalion. Stints in the front line trenches alternate with periods in reserve in the beach area, although facilities there are minimal and they're still within range of enemy shell-fire. They do suffer losses from this and from snipers, but even worse is the effects of disease, which is rampant due to the heat, widely scattered corpses, flies and generally insanitary conditions. As the autumn wears on, the weather becomes more variable and in the middle of November there is a terrible blizzard, which is so severe that many men suffer from frost-bite. There is no real prospect of any advances being made towards the centre of the peninsula, much less occupying the whole of it.

By the time that the decision is finally made to abandon the whole venture, with the 2/4th Battalion being evacuated on 13th December, it is down to about 200 men, despite the fact that some replacements have arrived since August. About 700 have been killed or evacuated due to wounds or disease. William's school-friend does survive, although he is badly wounded and it's quite a while before William hears from him again. The evacuation (of all of the beach-heads) during December is successful, being well-planned and involving virtually no casualties. This is in sharp contrast to the planning of the landings, which was appalling. The total number of Allied casualties is around 250,000. While the corresponding figure for the Turks is less well-established, it's probably similar. However, there is no doubt whatsoever that this is a crushing and humiliating defeat for the Allies.

As the full story starts to become widely known, heads inevitably roll. Several of the commanders in the field are sacked, but the repercussions also extend back to London. Lord Fisher, furious at how his precious warships are being used, resigns in May 1915 and Churchill is sacked as First Lord of the Admiralty shortly afterwards – a victim of political maneuverings and a perception that the Dardanelles fiasco is primarily his fault. He is kept in the government, and of course his star is destined to rise again later, but he no longer has much say in the management of this war. Needless to say, prolonging the venture for a further 6 months is also a terrible mistake, for which Kitchener is effectively responsible. His standing also plummets, although he stays in post for the present.

Overall, the war becomes a bitter and nightmarish struggle as 1915 unfolds. Attempts to break through the lines of trenches in France and Belgium continue to result in huge casualties, as advancing soldiers are mown down by machine gun fire. The Royal Navy still dominates the North Sea, but the Germans are increasingly using their submarines (U-boats) as their main naval weapon and moving their operations out into the Atlantic. They're sinking large numbers of Allied ships, particularly those bringing in much needed food and other resources. They also repeatedly warn that civilians travelling on British passenger ships are putting themselves at risk. On 7th May, a German submarine sinks the "Lusitania" off the Irish coast, towards the end of a voyage from New York, causing over a thousand deaths (including over a hundred American citizens). In fact, the ship was carrying munitions, but the sinking does cause revulsion in the USA and increases the pressure for it to enter the war on the side of the Allies.

3.4 William's Journey Continues

The (regular) 2nd Battalion of the RWK was based in several garrisons in India at the outbreak of war, including Jubbulpore. They expected to be moved quickly to Mesopotamia, but in fact much of it did not move until mid-January – mainly because the relieving troops from Britain did not arrive until around then. However, the 6th Indian

(Poona) Division had been moved to Mesopotamia in August 1914, as the Indian Expeditionary Force, and they quickly started to push the Turks north from the Basra area, and to secure the vital oil pipeline. By December 1914 they had occupied Basra and Qurna, but it quickly became clear that it would need to be reinforced in order to ensure security against Turkish counter-attacks, and to inhibit potential attacks by local Arab tribes. The move of the 2nd Battalion of the RWK is part of this reinforcement operation. They arrived at Basra in late January, from where they moved up-river by small steamers to Qurna, where the Tigris and Euphrates rivers meet. The whole Basra/Qurna area is a "wetlands", with the locations of various swamps and small lakes in a state of perpetual flux, depending on the season and weather conditions. Establishing stable garrison bases, and carrying out various troop movements, is thus difficult, particularly since both Arabs and Turks in the area frequently destroy riverbank supports and carry out other operations designed to flood out the 6th Indian Division troops. Their knowledge of the local geography and aquatic conditions is helpful in this.

The 2nd Battalion RWK eventually establish their headquarters in Basra, from where several companies of the Battalion take part in movements up the two rivers into the interior of Mesopotamia. Despite the extensive harassment and resistance from the enemy, the Division manages to penetrate along both rivers during the first half of 1915, establishing secure bases at places such as Nasiriyah on the Euphrates and Kut-al-Amara on the Tigris. The 2nd Battalion RWK plays a full part in these operations. The idea starts to emerge of pushing deeper into Mesopotamia, and perhaps taking Baghdad, which is further along the Tigris from Kut-al-Amara. This would effectively drive the Turks out of the whole Mesopotamian area, but it's recognized that further reinforcements will be needed to achieve this.

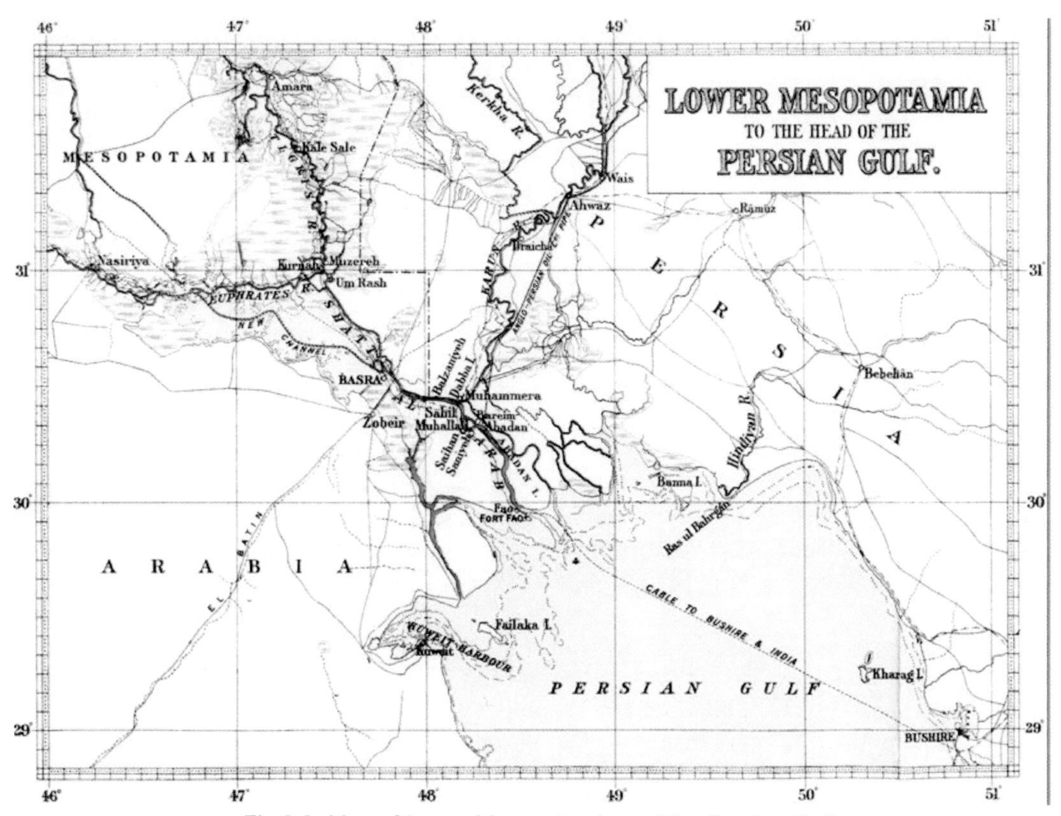

Fig.3.3: Map of Lower Mesopotamia and the Persian Gulf.

Meanwhile, things have been very quiet during this period in Jubbelpore. However, in view of the need for further reinforcements in Mesopotamia, volunteers for transfer are invited from territorial troops in India, including all of those based in Jubbulpore. William has not been very happy over the past few months. From March to May it became progressively hotter, with temperatures reaching the 90's or above every day. He realizes that he really doesn't like the heat. When the rains come in June it's initially a relief, but the temperatures remain high and it's now terribly sultry and oppressive. They also start to suffer more from the attacks of insects, which are thriving in these conditions. Malaria is a constant danger, but just getting some sleep at night is a major challenge.

"How on earth do people survive in this country?" he asks his friend Ernie, for the umpteenth time.

"Well, Billy," says Ernie, also for the umpteenth time, "the natives are just used to it. They don't seem to get upset by the heat and they appear to be immune to these blasted mossies. Of course, most colonials don't like it, but I've worked out what the rich do in this country – they move further north, where it's not quite so hot, and they also build little hill stations wherever there's higher ground – also mostly in the north. I've heard that the weather is marvelous in places like Shimla, Darjeeling, Pachmarhi etc. In fact, there are dozens of places like this – most of the well-to-do never leave them in the summer. There's no option like that for the poor bloody infantry and nobody explains all this to us beforehand!"

"We've been taken for mugs, and what makes it worse is that there's absolutely nothing to do here. It's too hot to even march around and anyway we'd just get soaking wet. This is going to drive me nuts in the end!"

"Calm down, Billy boy. Most Tommies are just pleased to be out of the firing line." William reflects that this is simply not how he feels. If he can't have an enjoyable time, he at least feels that he should be doing something useful. Actually, Ernie feels the same and they often discuss how they might get relocated in some way.

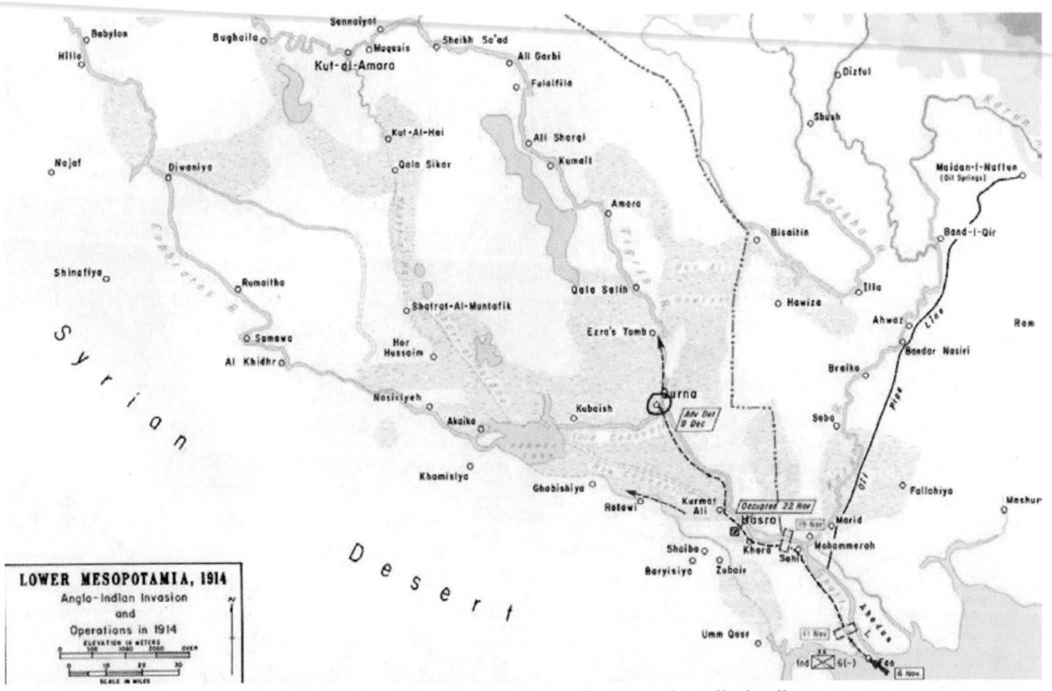

Fig.3.4: Map of the Basra area, showing the oil pipeline.

Therefore, when the offer comes for a transfer, they both jump at it. Not everyone feels this way, but about 40 members of the 1/4th Battalion volunteer. This small group thus finds itself, under Lieutenant Wilf Haslam, on board RMT Elephanta (requisitioned from the British India Line), arriving at Basra in early August of 1915. This is a slightly smaller ship than the Grantully Castle, with a displacement of about 5,000 tons, but there are again about 2,000 troops on board, drawn from a range of bases and regiments in India. This voyage, however, is much shorter than the outward one, with the distance being only about 1,800 miles. It's another uncomfortable journey by train and boat, but at least they're seeing somewhere new, and it's not nearly as hot or stifling when they arrive at Basra.

William and his group are now incorporated into the 2nd RWK Battalion. There is a valuable influx of about 200 men who are volunteers from RWK Territorial Battalions in India. William welcomes this change, not only in terms of seeing new people and places, and the weather becoming cooler, particularly as autumn advances, but also in terms of the prospect of taking part in some useful activities. He is now integrated into a Battalion of regular soldiers (still in the RWK Regiment) and he feels sure that he'll learn from their higher levels of professionalism and experience. He also knows that there is an improved chance of getting involved in some serious actions. He feels that this has been absolutely the right thing to do when he hears that the 2/4th Battalion, to which he might easily have been allocated on joining up, is now heavily engaged on the beaches of Gallipoli.

He now starts to get familiar with the terrain, climate and geography of lower Mesopotamia, which is very different from that of central India. Many operations are water-borne and it's a challenge to keep kit dry and serviceable. Nevertheless, the rain is not incessant and he finds this environment preferable to that of Jubbulpore. There are certainly more challenges and interesting activities. He becomes based at Basra as part of the "HQ group", although it does go on various "outings" to the north.

3.5 Comrades on the Tigris

Two companies (about 300 men) of the 2nd Battalion of the RWK leave Basra in November 1915 (as part of the 6th Indian Division) to travel up the Tigris. William has got to know several of them quite well in the 3 months or so since he arrived. He himself stays in the Battalion HQ in Basra. Although the oil terminal and pipeline have been secured, it's increasingly being thought that there is an opportunity here to drive the Turks completely out of lower Mesopotamia, while also subduing the local Arab tribesmen. This move up the Tigris, in native sailing boats, is part of a push towards Baghdad.

The overall situation regarding the Turks, Arabs, British and French is highly complex. The Arabs, themselves composed of various factions and tribes, with a lot of rivalries and feuds, have long been part of the Ottoman

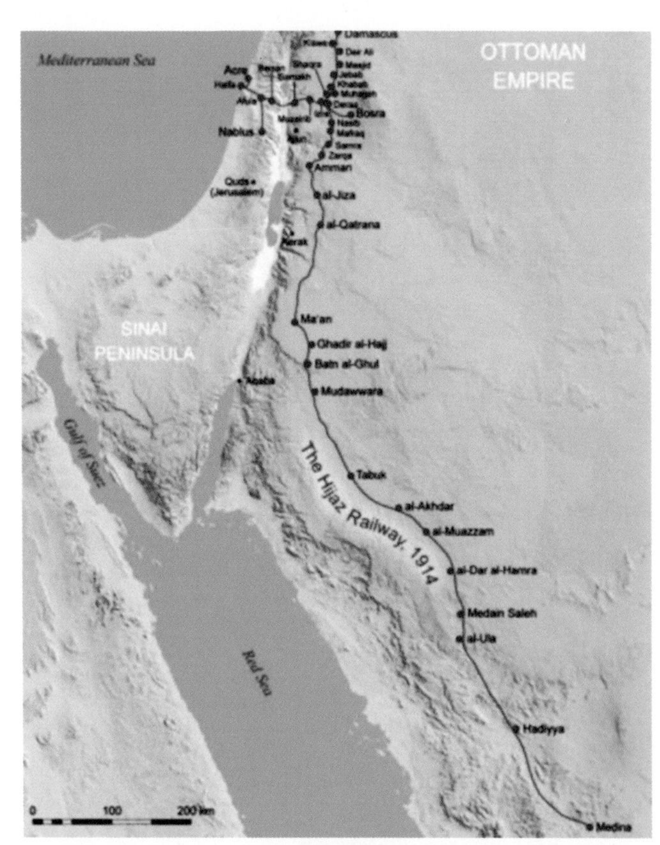

Fig.3.5: Map of 1914, showing the Damascus-Medina (Hejaz) Railway.

Empire. However, they're not happy with this at present, particularly since the "Young Turks" movement of about ten years earlier seems to presage a strong nationalist (Turkish) trend in which they're likely to end up sidelined. The British are very keen to foster some kind of Arab rebellion against the Turks, since this will help considerably in safeguarding the Suez Canal and other assets in the area. They're aiming to do this by promising the Arabs that they will become an independent nation after the war.

Fig.3.6: Photo of the interior of a carriage on the Hejaz Railway, taken in 1915.

The British therefore enter into prolonged negotiations with the Arabs – particularly Hussein bin Ali, the Sharif and Emir of Mecca, who claims that he'll be able to stage an Arab uprising against the Turks. Among the complications is that the Turks completed (at great expense) the Hejaz Railway from Damascus to Medina in 1908 – a distance of around a thousand miles. The main justification was that it would facilitate pilgrimages of the Islamic faithful down to Mecca, although the railway never actually reached that far – Mecca is a further 300 miles to the south. Still, Medina itself is a holy city that is visited by many pilgrims and the railway certainly makes the trip to Mecca much easier.

The real motivation of the Turks for building the railway, however, was to speed up the movement of troops and military equipment to the southern parts of the Ottoman Empire. Moreover, although it is in extensive use for pilgrimages, many of the Arabs (Bedouin tribesman) in the region object strongly to it, since it deprives them of the lucrative business of helping these pilgrims through the desert. They've been attacking trains and damaging track for a while.

Thomas Lawrence ("of Arabia"), whose original interests in the region were archeological, is working for the British Army during the war. He develops strong links with the Arabs, who come to trust and respect him, and he helps to foment this rebellion against the Turks. Part of this

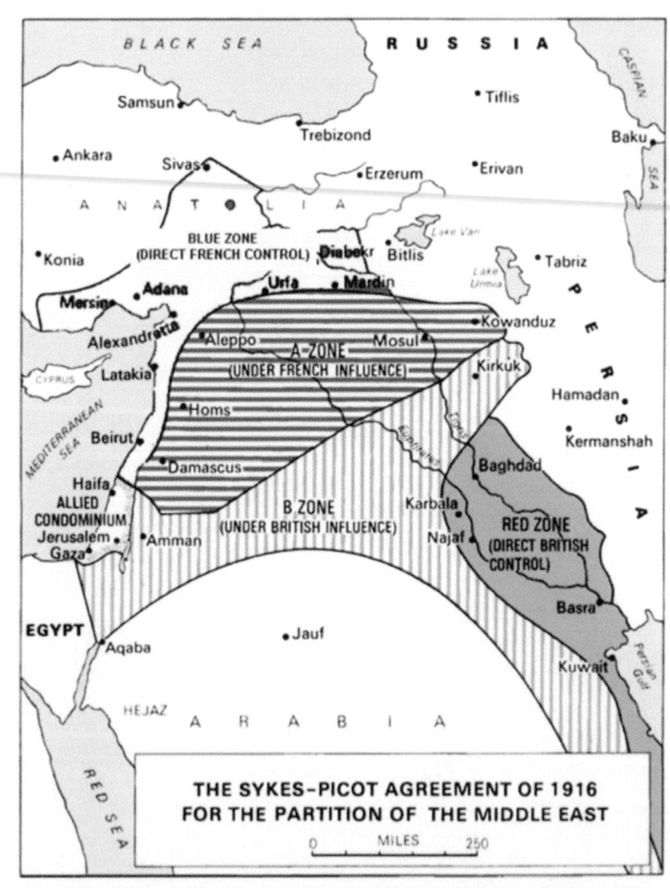

Fig.3.7: Map of 1916, showing the (Anglo-French) Sykes-Picot plan for a post-war division of control in the Middle East.

takes the form of repeated sabotage of the Hejaz Railway, with Lawrence heavily involved in many movements and attacks during the period from 1916 until the end of the war. He also supplies, via the British government, arms and finances for these activities. It is all done on the clear understanding that the Arabs would achieve independence afterwards, with Hussein, and subsequently his son Faisal, as Head of State and Damascus as the capital.

However, the French have long been in control of Syria, which is almost entirely inhabited by Arabs, and they are determined that it should continue as a French protectorate after the war. The British have their own interests further south and they need to keep on good terms with their ally. Their promises to the Arabs are not kept. A secret Anglo-French (Sykes-Picot) plan is drawn up in 1916, carving up the whole Arabian area between them. Lawrence is aware of this arrangement, but his commitment to the Arab cause is real. He tries hard to make the Arab state materialize, but in the end he fails. He is plagued with guilt and regret afterwards, even after he becomes a national hero in the West - largely as a result of the promotional activities of the American writer and broadcaster Lowell Thomas. The deception and bad faith shown by the Western governments will, of course, lead to many problems in the future. In any event, during 1915 and the early part of 1916, most Arabs are still on the side of the Turks, or at least they are certainly not well disposed towards the British.

William, like most ordinary soldiers, naturally knows nothing of such politics or machinations. They just know that the Arab inhabitants of the region may cause trouble, and also that some of their own Indian troops may be sympathetic towards them (partly on religious grounds – something like 30% of the British Indian Army are Muslim). The 6th Indian Division as a whole comprises mainly Indian soldiers. They're not entirely happy in Mesopotamia. The organization is not perfect – well below that in Europe – and the liaison with the commanding (British) officers is often poor, with a number of linguistic and cultural barriers. The weather is sometimes cold and wet, and the provision of suitable clothing and rations is often inadequate. Their feelings are often reflected in their performance during battles. There are some desertions, and deliberate self-mutilations.

Troops of the 2nd Battalion of RWK reach Kut-al-Amara, located in a loop of the Tigris, in mid-November. From there they move closer to Baghdad, partly by marching on land and partly by river steamer, meeting up at the end of the month with the bulk of the 6th Indian Division at Aziziya. The Division has just had a major engagement with the Turks at Ctesiphon, close to Baghdad. This was a victory of sorts, but with heavy losses. Furthermore, strong Turkish reinforcements have since arrived and the Division is now retreating back down the Tigris.

The situation starts to get difficult, with word arriving that Turks and Arabs are massing on the Tigris below Kut. The complete group now retreats back down the river, mostly by forced march, with a large force of Turks hard on their heels. They arrive back at Kut on 3rd December and the decision is made by the commanding officer, General Charles Townshend, to establish a strong base there and await reinforcements from Basra. This is duly done over the following few days, with an encampment being established that is about 2 miles by 1 mile in size, surrounded on three sides by the Tigris. The Arab town of Kut, with a population of several thousand, is within this area. Trenches are dug on the fourth side and a strong defensive position is established by the time that the Turks arrive in force and begin preparations to attack. This starts on 9th December. The Turks attack repeatedly over the following weeks, hoping to achieve a crushing victory before the relieving force, already being assembled lower down the river, can arrive. However, the defensive position that has been established is strong and, despite a number of intense skirmishes, the British and Indian force holds out. In January, however, the Turks change their strategy and start to simply lay siege to the town, while also sending more troops downriver to prevent any relieving force from reaching it.

The soldiers in this embattled group, comprising about 10,000 men, are slowly starving. They make one or two attempts to break out, but they have no river transport and the Turks have them encircled with a large and well-organized force. Several attempts are made to relieve the siege via attack by reinforcements from the direction of Basra, but they are poorly organized and they fail to break through. Disease takes a terrible toll and eventually, towards the end of April, General Townshend decides to surrender. There are about 8,000 British and Indian troops, including about 300 from the RWK. Some of the wounded are exchanged with Turkish prisoners, but most of these soldiers are taken into captivity and harshly treated, being forced to march long distances and given little food. Most of them die during this ordeal. Well over 200 of the 2nd Battalion of RWK become prisoners, but only about 70 survive. The whole episode illustrates the depths of depravity that can be reached during war, with great courage often displayed, but the real outcome just being terrible suffering and waste.

3.6 The End of a Long Road

William has been based at Basra Battalion HQ for about 3 months when he moves towards an area where some kind of action is more likely. There is a base for British and Indian troops at Nasiriyah, a town of several thousand inhabitants on the Euphrates, about 150 miles upriver from Basra. Nasiriyah had been taken from the Turks in a battle the previous July and a garrison left there, partly to keep the local Arabs under control. The Turks have been trying to persuade the Arabs to join in fully on their side, using various cultural and religious arguments, including the suggestion that this should be treated as a Jihad (holy war). There's concern that they might start to make concerted attacks. In addition, with the Allies withdrawing from Gallipoli, large numbers of Turkish troops are being released to move to the south. The 34th Indian Brigade is therefore moved up the Euphrates to reinforce the garrison at Nasiriyah and a "HQ group" of the 2nd Battalion of the RWK goes with it. On 7th January 1916 this force joins an encampment just north of the village of Butaniyeh, about 10 miles from Nasiriyah. Shortly after this, on 14th January, a reconnaissance party is attacked by a large group of Arabs. The RWK Battalion, including William, is called out to help cover their retreat. This is the "baptism of fire" for William and the rest of the small contingent from the 1/4th Battalion. They perform well and lose just one man killed and three wounded. A large number of Arabs are killed. The atmosphere in the group afterwards is mixed, but they at least feel that they're finally getting properly involved in the war and making a contribution. Fighting Arab tribesmen who don't really belong to a well-defined country, against whom there has been no formal declaration of war, is not what they had in mind when they signed up, but they just feel that they're doing their duty, whatever that turns out to be.

The encampment at Butaniyeh is maintained for just one month, with the main activity being to provide escorts for convoys to and from the garrison at Nasiriyah. After that period, it is decided to close down the encampment. The local tribesmen appear to be doing little or nothing of an aggressive nature and there are no indications of any Turks in the vicinity, or of any intentions on their part to move down the Euphrates or across from Kut (on the Tigris) via the Shatt al Hai network of lakes. Part of the column decamps to Nasiriyah on 5th February, with the rest, including the RWK Battalion, to follow two days later.

The final withdrawal over the 10 miles or so from the camp at Butaniyeh back to Nasiriyah is carried out on Monday 7th February, with the 2nd Battalion of the RWK acting as rear-guard. Although the Arabs in the vicinity have given no trouble recently, it becomes clear as the withdrawal gets under way that those from nearby villages intend to harass the column as it withdraws. As Butaniyeh village itself is passed, at about 10.30 am, these people bring out concealed weapons and start to subject the soldiers to intense fire. The number of Arabs who become involved is much larger than might have been expected and it quickly becomes evident that this is a major, pre-planned attack.

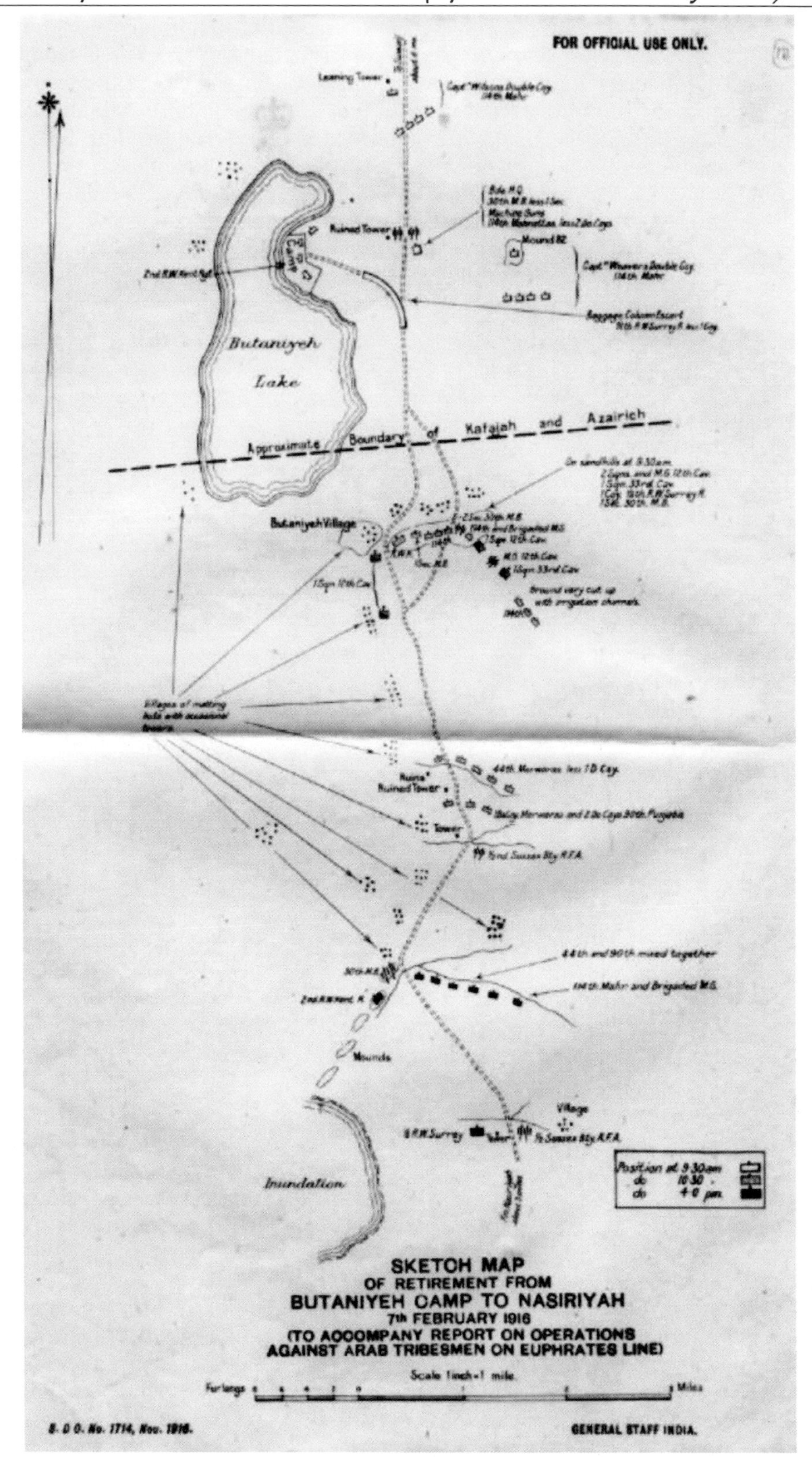

Fig.3.8: Map showing the withdrawal of the Column from the Butaniyeh camp towards Nasiriyah on 7th February 1916.

A couple of Indian Battalions fall back in some disorder, apparently reluctant to fire at people with whom they have certain cultural and religious ties, and the situation starts to become chaotic. The RWK Battalion, however, covers the retreat in a disciplined way, standing their ground and returning intense fire. However, the Arab attackers show considerable courage and skill, using their knowledge of the terrain and being prepared to get involved in desperate hand-to-hand skirmishing. What becomes a relatively major battle rages on for several hours. The total number of British and Indian troops in the column is about 2,000, but the 250 or so of the RWK Battalion are in the thick of the most intense fighting. The attackers finally withdraw at about 4 pm, with the steadiness of the RWK troops being a major factor in their reluctance to continue. Nevertheless, the column suffers about 400 casualties. While this episode might be considered relatively minor in the overall context of the war, partly in view of the low profile of the struggles in Mesopotamia compared with those in Flanders and Gallipoli, it is in fact a major engagement, and one in which considerable bravery is shown on both sides.

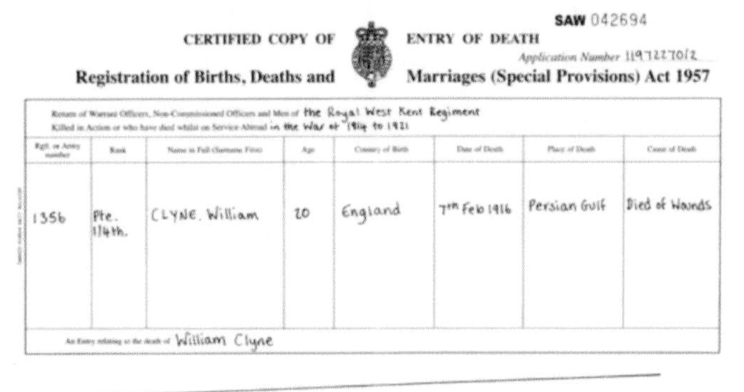

SAW 042694

CERTIFIED COPY OF ENTRY OF DEATH

Application Number 1197227012

Registration of Births, Deaths and Marriages (Special Provisions) Act 1957

Returns of Warrant Officers, Non-Commissioned Officers and Men of the Royal West Kent Regiment
Killed in Action or who have died whilst on Service Abroad in the War of 1914 to 1921

Regtl. or Army number	Rank	Name in Full (Surname First)	Age	Country of Birth	Date of Death	Place of Death	Cause of Death
1356	Pte. 1/4th.	CLYNE, William	20	England	7th Feb 1916	Persian Gulf	Died of Wounds

An Entry relating to the death of William Clyne

CERTIFIED to be a true copy of the certified copy of* an entry in a Service Departments Register.
Given at the General Register office, under the seal of the said Office, the 28th day of July 2021

CAUTION: THERE ARE OFFENCES RELATING TO FALSIFYING OR ALTERING A CERTIFICATE AND USING OR POSSESSING A FALSE CERTIFICATE.

WARNING: A CERTIFICATE IS NOT EVIDENCE OF IDENTITY

Fig.3.9: Certified copy relating to the death of William Clyne.

Despite their prominent role, casualties in the RWK are relatively light at about 30, with only 8 killed. Sadly, one of these is William and another is Ernie Mortby, who stays with his machine gun emplacement until overwhelmed by the enemy. William is just a few yards away and he dies at the same time. Neither photos of William, nor any of his letters etc, are destined to survive into posterity. Lieutenant Wilf Haslam, who has been a kind and considerate commanding officer to William ever since he joined up, is also among those killed on this day. The bodies are carried back to Nasiriyah, and eventually down the Euphrates to Basra.

Clout, A.	G/18292	Pte.	Colebrooke, W.	L/8047	Sgt.
Clout, G.	L/8423	Pte.	Coleman, A.	G/2220	Cpl.
Clover, B. J.	G/29503	Pte.	Coleman, A. G.	S/8466	Pte.
Clutterbuck, A.	G/7607	Pte.	Coleman, F.	G/19015	Sgt.
Clyne, W.	TF/1356	Pte.	Coleman, G.	G/71	Pte.
Coachworth, E. S.	205679	Pte.	Coleman, G. B.	G/10895	Pte.
Coates, J. C.		2nd Lieut.	Coleman, H.	205583	Pte.
Cobb, J. C.		Lieut.	Coleman, J.	G/2212	Pte.

Fig.3.10: Small section in the list of ~7,000 names of men who lost their lives while serving with the QORWK Regiment in 1914-18.

Two days later, the Battalion returns (as part of a large force) to the villages from which the attackers were apparently drawn. They are abandoned by their inhabitants, then laid waste by the British and Indian troops. What this achieves is difficult to say. This desperate war is not about winning hearts and minds.

Fig.3.11: Photo of Lieutenant WHW Haslam.

This is pure speculation, but if William and Ernie had survived the battle of Butaniyeh, then they would have returned to Basra and, in all probability, been quickly shipped up the Tigris, in February or March, as part of the force trying to relieve the siege at Kut-al-Amara. Most of his Territorial RWK colleagues were integrated into this group. This was a rushed, desperate and poorly-organized operation. There were several battles in which British and British-Indian forces advanced long distances in the open towards well-defended enemy locations, often across completely waterlogged, boggy ground – the Tigris often floods its banks in this area at this time of year. The casualty rates were horrendous – amongst the highest of the whole war. Very few of his erstwhile comrades survive. Even some British units refused to obey orders to undertake what were effectively pointless suicide missions. It is, of course, possible that William could have survived this, but it may be that his death at Butaniyeh spared him an even more harrowing one a month or two later.

For many soldiers, life or death is now the outcome of a mad game of Russian Roulette, largely determined by the timing and location of military postings imposed by a mindless system. There is no escape, even for volunteers. Full conscription is now in place (from March 1916 in the UK), so there is no longer any meaningful distinction between professionals and volunteers. Deserters face the firing squad.

Chapter 4: Home Fires (February 1916 – February 1918)

4.1 A Terrible Blow

"I'm so sorry, Missus – I'm so very sorry."

Alice becomes hysterical as soon as she opens the door and sees the messenger. These days, telegrams arrive for one reason only. She tears it from his hand and rips it open, but she already knows its import. It has to be William. Herbert arrived in India a few months ago, to join the rest of the 1/4th Battalion, and the dangers there appear to be minimal, while Frank is still under training in Britain. Stan is still only 14 and she's certainly not going to stand by if he tries to join up.

There is the faint hope that William could be just reported missing, but this is unlikely. She'd had a letter from him just a week ago and she knows that "reported missing" telegrams are only sent after every possibility has been checked: in the vast majority of cases, the final outcome is the same. Anyway, it's there in black and white – "..killed in action". There is little further information – just an indication that he died in the "Persian Gulf". Alice has only a vague idea where that is and she never hears anything further about his death. She screams in horror.

"I'm afraid that I need you to sign this, Missus". He feels that his job, so innocuous before the war, has become one of the worst in the world. He's not in physical danger, but he's exposed every day to such raw mental pain and anguish in others that he wonders whether physical pain would be preferable. He has several more telegrams to deliver this morning just in this neighbourhood and he knows that the scene will be much the same each time. He feels that requiring a signature makes it even worse, but he knows that, without this, the temptation to just put it through the letterbox and run would be irresistible. Having at least someone there when it's opened must be better, even if it's only him. There's nothing he can offer – words are meaningless in this situation.

This blow falls in mid-February and of course the whole family is bereft. This war is no longer any sort of adventure, but an ongoing nightmare. Britain has now lost several hundred thousand men, with many more disabled and/or traumatized. Some parts of the country, including London, have contributed strongly to the increased size of the army and a sizeable proportion of the families in the metropolis has already suffered bereavement. Despite all the efforts of the British government to conceal bad news, everyone now knows that there is widespread carnage and that conditions for the fighting men are often terrible. People are becoming desperate, but the only solution being offered is redoubled effort and sacrifice.

There are similar feelings in many other parts of the world – in Germany, the Austro-Hungarian Empire and the Ottoman Empire, as well as in France, Russia, India, Australia, New Zealand, Canada, Egypt and Italy on the Allied side. There is widespread destruction even in regions that were not originally in either camp – Greece, Albania, Rumania, Bulgaria and several parts of Africa. The Germans in particular are proving extraordinarily resourceful and organized, managing to remain strong on both Western and Eastern Fronts, despite being blockaded by sea. Normal commercial activities, and life in general, have been totally disrupted throughout the world. Hunger is becoming widespread.

4.2 William Moves On and the War Drags On

The news of William's death is a terrible blow for his father, as well as for Alice. He's in a state of turmoil. He's been thinking of resigning from the Met for a little while, mainly in order to augment his net income by taking another job: hopefully this income, plus his pension from the Met, will come to a little more than his current salary on its own. There is, however, a further motivation, which is that he feels that he should be making a slightly more direct contribution to the war effort. His elder boys have all stepped up – William at terrible cost – and he feels that he should try to do a little more himself. At 46 years old, the army would not take him, but there is the option of working for Vickers, which has several places nearby, all of which are devoted to production of materiel for the war effort. The death of his son pushes him in this direction and he resigns with effect from 21st February. He immediately takes up a post as Warden at Vickers. It's a step down from being a Detective, but he feels that it's the right thing to do. His farewells at the Met are difficult all round, but of course the whole country is in a state of turmoil.

Life in the Clyne household carries on, albeit with overtones of sadness and trepidation. Herbert and Frank write regularly. Herbert joined the RWK in March 2015 and Frank enlisted in the Seaforth Highlanders Regiment in June 2015. He felt that he wanted to strengthen ties with his northern roots and he's now in contact with several relatives from there. These include his namesake Frank William Clyne, who's now a 40-year old seaman in the Royal Navy, based at Rosyth – part of the enormous fleet that is so vital for the security of the country. "Uncle" Frank has told him about some of his exploits as a member of the crew of HMS "Invincible", a powerful Battlecruiser – the first of its type in the world when launched in 1907. With eight 12-inch guns and a top speed of 25 knots, it's a formidable ship. For example, he hears about the dramatic dash to the South Atlantic, where Invincible was a key ship in the chasing and sinking of the powerful German Cruisers Scharnhorst and Gneisenau near the Falkland Islands at the end of 1914. Frank feels that his uncle really is making an important contribution to the war effort and he feels that he must try to do the same. While Herbert seems to be safe in Jubbulpore, and Frank is still under training in Britain, Alice still lives in daily dread of them getting some perilous posting abroad. She keeps telling Herbert that he is not to accept any invitations to move out of India to anywhere more dangerous, which probably means almost anywhere else.

Fig.4.1: Photo of the interior of part of the Vickers factory in Crayford, showing machine guns being made.

Meanwhile, news of the war continues to be a series of horror stories, despite all of the censorship. It soon becomes clear that there is a titanic struggle going on in the vicinity of Verdun, about 140 miles east of Paris. The Germans launch a massive attack against French strongholds in late February. Although British troops are not directly involved, it's clear that they may need to go to the aid of their French allies if the situation becomes desperate. Also, it leads to the British having to take a major part in a joint offensive planned for later in the year, at the River Somme, rather than the minor role that was envisaged. In fact, the struggle around Verdun goes on for many months, with huge casualties on both sides. Although the French are not in the end overwhelmed, they eventually suffer 400,000 casualties, of which 160,000 are killed. It significantly weakens the ability of the French to continue fighting.

4.3 Jellicoe Meets the Challenge

The one area in which the British have maintained a clear upper hand, and it's a vital one, is command of the seas – particularly the North Sea, in which the British Grand Fleet confronts the German High Seas Fleet. The British fleet has been blockading German ports since the start of the war and this is starting to have a major impact on the ability of Germany to continue to fight – particularly in terms of imported food reaching the German civilian population. They cannot survive on home-grown food alone and even that is partly dependent on imported fertilizer. The German navy is strong, although not quite as strong as the Royal Navy. They hope, however, that careful tactics – ie choosing their battles carefully - will allow them to whittle away the difference and eventually break the stranglehold of the blockade.

The man charged with stopping this is John ("Jack" to his friends) Jellicoe. He's the epitome of the great British Naval tradition. Excelling throughout his career, he was earmarked for overall command from an early stage and was given the top job, slightly ahead of schedule, at the start of the war – propelled there by John Fisher and Winston Churchill. Fisher was the man who, recognizing the danger posed by Kaiser Wilhelm's determination to make the German Navy the equal of Britain's, ensured that the Royal Navy maintained superiority. He was involved in development of the revolutionary Dreadnought type of battleship – combining high speed with massive armament – and managed to persuade the British government to spend enough through the early 1900's to maintain numerical superiority, and also to keep up with the development of submarines. Throughout this period, he had Jellicoe in mind to be in charge when the inevitable confrontation took place. Jellicoe is technically outstanding, being fully aware of all the relevant issues, but he's also a superb leader of men. He takes a keen personal interest in all of those under him – down to large numbers of ordinary seamen – and he's also modest and approachable. He works like a Trojan. He has the respect and affection of the whole navy – a worthy successor to Nelson. He has a heavy burden – in Churchill's words, he's "...the only man on either side who could lose the war in an afternoon..." – but he carries it lightly.

Fig.4.2: Photo of John Jellicoe, aboard his flagship, HMS Iron Duke.

By the early months of 1916, those in charge of the German Navy are becoming frustrated and are increasingly looking for opportunities to break out of their base in Wilhelmshaven and inflict serious damage on the Royal Navy. There have been various minor skirmishes in the North Sea over the preceding two years, mostly with the British coming out on top, but nothing at all decisive. Both sides are continuing to build further warships, but if anything the numerical superiority of the British is creeping up as a consequence of this. There have been other calls on the resources of the Royal Navy – including the fiasco of Gallipoli and the much more successful episode in the Falkland Islands in December 1914, when a large task force tracked down and destroyed a powerful German Cruiser Squadron that had escaped across the Pacific from their base in China, sinking several British warships at the battle of Coronel, off the coast of Chile, on the way. Nevertheless, the Royal Navy

Fig.4.3: Map of the main anchorage for the British fleet, in Scapa Flow.

has maintained its control over the North Sea. The Grand Fleet is now securely based at Scapa Flow – a huge natural harbor in the Orkneys enclosed by several small islands. It was potentially vulnerable to submarine attack in the early part of the war, but, under Jellicoe's urgings, it's now been made virtually impregnable. It's also such a huge area that various fleet manoeuvres, target shooting practice etc can be carried out within it.

There are several other major Royal Navy bases around the North Sea. While the Grand Fleet itself, comprising dozens of warships of various sizes, is based at Scapa, the famous Battlecruiser fleet has its home at Rosyth in the Firth of Forth (upstream of the famous rail bridge). This group of about a dozen fast, powerful ships is under the command of the swashbuckling David Beatty. He is very well-connected – including Ethel, his wealthy, and rather pushy, American wife – and he has a high public profile, although his seamanship (and reliability) is far inferior to that of Jellicoe. Rosyth is 300 miles south of Scapa Flow, and hence that much closer to the German base at Wilhelmshaven. Between the two Scottish bases is another important one at Invergordon, on the Cromarty Firth. It's the home of the 2nd Cruiser squadron, under Hugh Evan-Thomas, and also the location of many large storage tanks for fuel oil – increasingly being used to power these ships – and a lot of accommodation for naval and army personnel, a major naval hospital etc. Finally, a large number of small, fast ships (light cruisers and destroyers), commanded by Roger Tyrwhit t, are based much further south at Harwich. This is also the main base for submarines, under Roger Keyes.

Fig.4.4: Photo of David Beatty.

The German naval command structure has recently been overhauled. In January, the cautious Hugo von Pohl was replaced as Commander of the High Seas Fleet by Reinhard Scheer. This was partly due to Pohl's failing health, although in fact he had been ineffective and Scheer was very critical of previous tactics and strategy. He's determined to go on the offensive and comes up with a plan to provoke British ships to come out of their bases into a trap composed largely of waiting submarines and torpedo boats. The provocation is to be a sortie by a group of powerful Battlecruisers under the command of Franz von Hipper. In fact, the trap turns out in the end to be an encounter with the main body of the High Seas fleet, rather than by hidden submarines. The attack takes place on Wednesday 31st May 1916. It evolves into the greatest ever sea battle (at least in terms of the number of ships), eventually involving about 150 British ships and about 100 German ones in a confused and complex encounter over a large area of sea, covering a period of about 12 hours. The numerical advantage of the British fleet is even greater (a factor of 3) when expressed in terms of weight of broadside. Nevertheless, the outcome is far from being a foregone conclusion. The accuracy of German gunnery is known to be outstanding, assisted by superior ranging and viewing equipment. Also, their ships have thicker armour, reducing their speed, but making them more durable. Finally, they are better trained in night fighting, which turns out to be relevant.

The encounter is to become known as the Battle of Jutland, named after the large peninsula near the area of the North Sea where it takes place. It's often perceived as having had no clear outcome, and is sometimes even regarded as a German victory. In fact, its clear effect is to reaffirm British domination over the North Sea and to strengthen the blockade of Germany, albeit at a heavy cost in terms of loss of British lives, and also at a (very unfair) cost to Jellicoe's reputation at the time – fortunately reversed by historical perspective and analysis. It is in any event a battle of pivotal importance in the war as a whole.

Frank (William) Clyne has been part of the crew of HMS Invincible now for almost a couple of years, having joined up at the outbreak of war. His wife, Jessie, has never been keen on this, but she is realistic. Frank has always been a seaman and, put bluntly, he's probably at lower risk on a ship than in the army – particularly in this war. Also, it means that he stays in the area, since most of the Royal Navy is now based in Scotland, so it's easy for him to come home to Wick during leave. This is certainly not true for everyone in the Navy.

Frank has various duties, but during actions he is part of the team of about 50 men operating one of the large gun turrets. There are 4 of these, each carrying a pair of 12 inch (bore) guns. There is one at the front (A turret) and one at the back (X turret), plus two (P & Q) located amidships between the second and third funnels. Frank is in the P turret. There is keen rivalry between the turret teams, particularly with turret X, which is operated by Royal Marines. The tasks involved in loading and firing these huge guns at high speed are demanding. Shells and propellant are put into a hoist in the magazine below the turret, lifted up to the breech of the gun, pushed in, the breech door shut and the gun fired, ready for a repeat sequence. A good gun crew can do this 2 or 3 times per minute.

Frank is based in the turret itself, where shells and propellant are transferred to the breech. The shells weigh about 800 pounds (a third of a ton) and the propellant about 250 pounds. Any mishandling can be disastrous: the propellant is highly unstable and large amounts are stored in the magazine. Part of Frank's job is to make small adjustments to the gun elevation and direction – following instructions from the gunnery officer, who monitors the fall of shells from a suitably elevated position. In Invincible, this is Lieutenant Commander Hubert Dannreuther (who happens to be the godson of the German composer Richard Wagner). There are also 12 smaller (4 inch) guns (reduced from the original 16) and 5 torpedo tubes. However, it's the large guns that are usually critical during encounters with other capital ships. Those on Invincible have a range of up to about 18,000 yards (10 miles). Depending on weather conditions, it may be difficult to see enemy ships at that distance.

Fig.4.5: Photo of HMS Invincible.

Since the start of the war, Invincible has been part of Beatty's Battlecruiser force, based at Rosyth. She and her two sister ships, Indomitable and Inflexible, constitute the 3rd Battlecruiser squadron, under Admiral Horace Hood. At this point, however, they're temporarily attached to the Grand Fleet under Jellicoe. This was done to allow some target practice in Scapa Flow, following a recent refit. That has gone very well and spirits in the ship are high. Hence, today (31st May) she's at the head of her group of

Fig.4.6: Photo of P and Q turrets, trained in-board, on HMS Indomitable.

three, sailing south-east as part of the Grand Fleet. It's carrying out a sweep of the northern part of the North Sea, as it has done many times before. It all looks routine, although there has been a report that the German High Seas Fleet, under Admiral Scheer, may venture out today. However, such reports are common, and not always accurate. As Frank and his shipmates scan the horizon, on a typical summer's day, all looks calm and normal. The Germans just don't seem at all keen on any kind of pitched battle and they certainly don't want to tangle with the Grand Fleet. Looking around him, Frank can understand this - the dozens of ships, of all shapes and sizes, constitute a truly formidable force. The formation includes about 25 huge Battleships, which carry powerful guns up to 15 inch in size, and massive armour. Battlecruisers, such as Invincible, are slightly different, also having large guns, but with thinner armour – giving them higher speed. Invincible and her sisters can race along at 25 knots, while some of the more recent Battlecruisers in Beatty's group can go even faster. The Grand Fleet as a whole can't steam at much more than 20 knots. Today they're cruising at 15 knots.

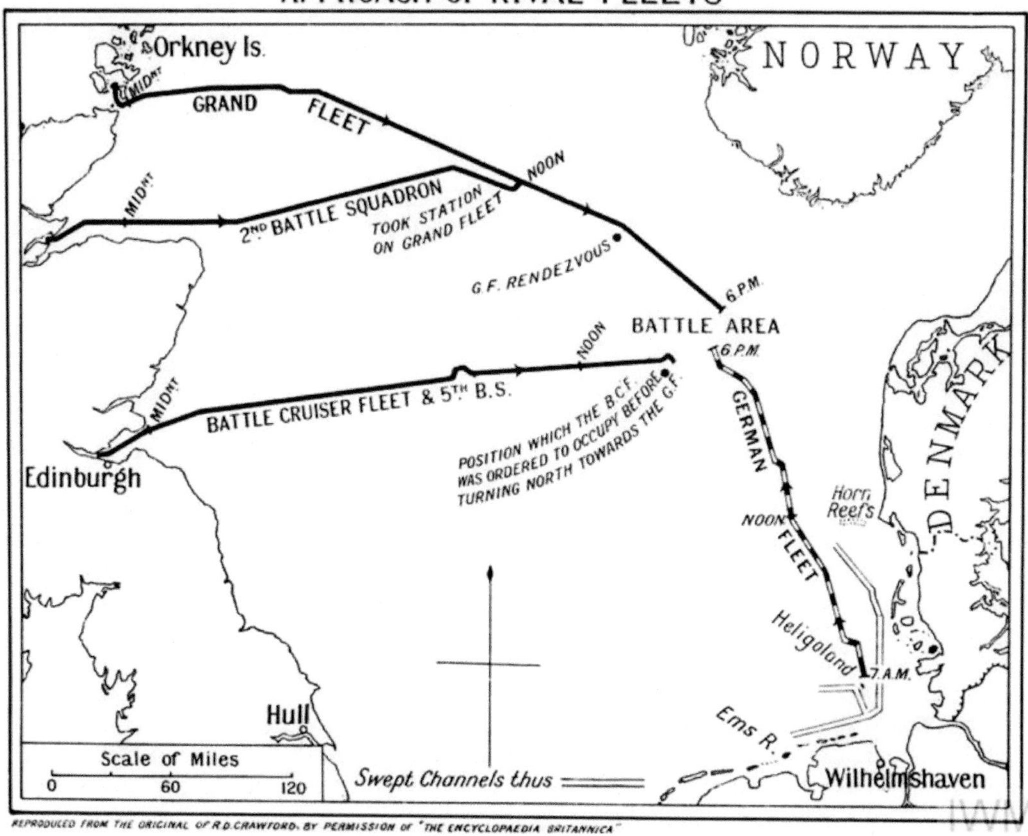

Fig.4.7: Map showing approaches of opposing fleets.

Beatty is also at sea today. His Battlecruiser group (1st & 2nd Squadrons) has been temporarily reinforced by the 5th Battle Squadron of Evan-Thomas, who is now under his command. In fact, three groups left port late the previous night: his from Rosyth, that of Vice Admiral Martyn Jerram, with the 2nd Battle Squadron (of the Grand Fleet), from Cromarty Firth and the Grand Fleet itself from Scapa. The last two are due to meet up at midday and then rendezvous with Beatty a little later. Rather typically, Beatty has not given clear instructions to Evan-Thomas about tactics in the event of meeting enemy ships. Beatty tends to just charge ahead regardless and he generally takes the line, understandably, that his famous "Cats" – the first two ships in his group are Lion and Tiger – are more than a match for any force of similar size.

Meanwhile, Franz von Hipper has been leading his Scouting Group northwards, in hopes of encountering a weaker British force, or possibly one that he could entice southward towards the complete High Seas fleet of Scheer, which is following him about 50 miles behind. Hipper's group is a small but powerful squadron of Battlecruisers – on a par with that of Beatty, except that he has 5 ships against the 6 of Beatty, who today also has the 4 Battleships led by Evan-Thomas. The visibility is variable – a lot of haze and mist patches, but occasionally good. Hipper has more or less given up hope of finding suitable prey, and has turned round to head towards Scheer, when, at about 3.30 pm, he sights Beatty's fleet. After verifying their identity, he opens fire at a range of about 16,000 yards (9 miles).

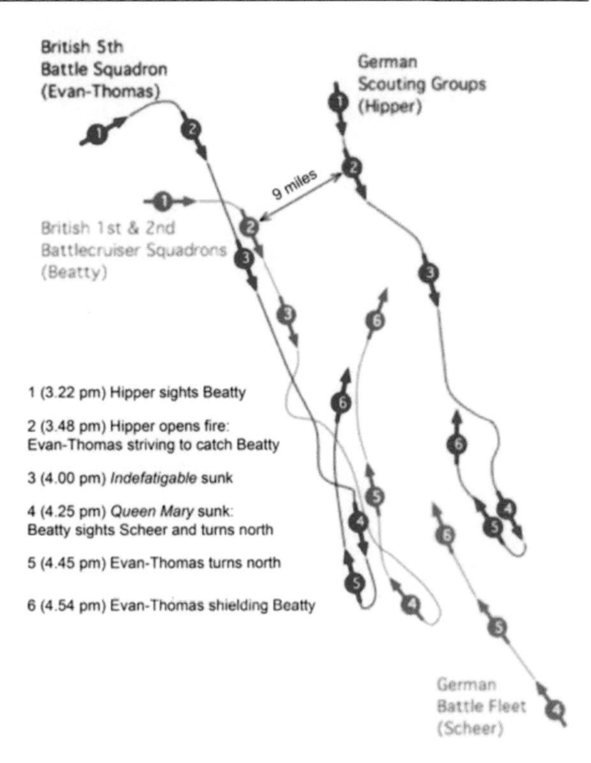

Fig.4.8: Timeline map for the Battlecruisers.

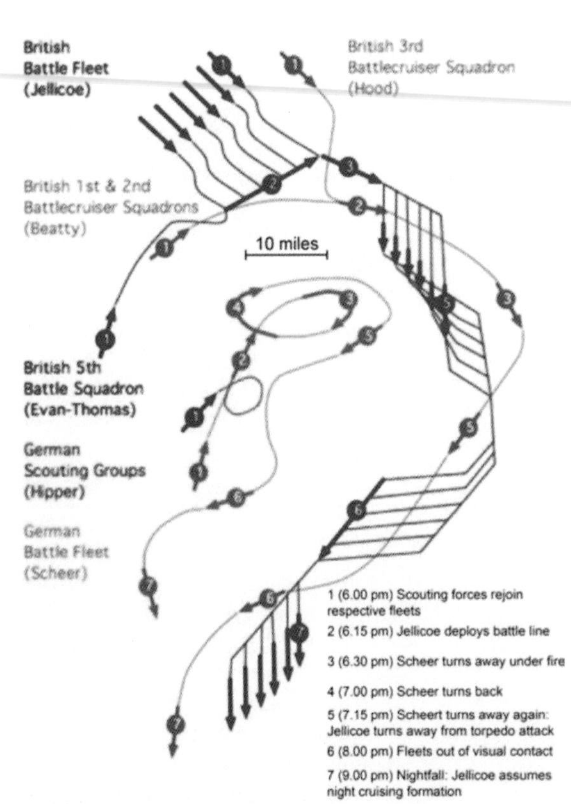

Fig.4.9: Timeline map for encounter of the main fleets.

Beatty takes up the challenge, swinging onto a parallel course so as to bring all his guns to bear and tearing along towards the South-East at high speed. Rather typically of Beatty, he doesn't make sure that Evan-Thomas, already several miles behind, knows where he is going and why – although this is partly due to signaling problems. Evan-Thomas belatedly realizes what has happened and swings his squadron around to follow the Battlecruisers. A running battle develops between the Beatty and Hipper groups, with Beatty's ships reaching speeds of up to about 28 or 29 knots. Hipper knows that Beatty's group has a slight advantage, but his plan is to lead it to complete destruction at the hands of Scheer's Battleships. Nevertheless, Hipper gets the better of the running battle, as a consequence of accurate German gunnery and some vulnerabilities concerning the handling of shells and propellant in British ships. One of Beatty's ships, Indefatigable, blows up when a German shell penetrates a turret and ignites the magazine underneath. Just two of the crew of over 1,000 survive. Less than half an hour later, an almost identical catastrophe befalls another of Beatty's ships, HMS Queen Mary. Of her crew of almost 1,300, only a handful survive. While Beatty can't be blamed directly for these losses, his leadership and tactics have been very poor – particularly in terms of keeping Evan-Thomas and Jellicoe informed about the situation. Both of them eventually realize what is happening and both follow him at high speed, but valuable time is lost.

Most of the other ships in Beatty's Squadron have also been taking heavy punishment. Complete obliteration looms for him, particularly when he spots Scheer's huge fleet approaching from the south, soon after losing his second ship. He turns back towards the North-West, apparently in dire straits. However, the situation is evolving rapidly. Firstly, Evan-Thomas has finally caught up and he uses his powerful Battleships to provide a shield for Beatty. Even they can't fight the combined German fleet, but they're able to take the brunt of the firestorm away from Beatty's battered force. Furthermore, they both know something that the Germans do not – that the Grand Fleet, now only about 60 miles to the North-west, is steaming towards them at full speed, with the net rate of approach being almost 50 knots. In about an hour (ie at around 6 pm - still some time before nightfall on this summer's day), a real shock awaits the Germans – who currently believe that a famous victory is in their grasp.

The first indication for Frank Clyne and his shipmates on Invincible that this might not be just another routine trip comes at about 4.30 pm. Nothing much can be seen in the vicinity, but Jellicoe has heard from Beatty that his running battle with Hipper has led to contact with the High Seas fleet of Scheer and he orders Hood's 3rd Battlecruiser Squadron (ie Invincible and her two sister ships, together with some light cruisers and destroyers) to steam at full speed to the south-east. This is aimed at providing Beatty and Evan-Thomas with some substantial support as soon as possible. It's also logical in the sense that Hood is normally under Beatty. The call to action stations is made and it's soon clear that this is not an exercise. Rumours run through the ship like lightning. Frank and his team set up P turret for firing. Speed is rapidly raised to 25 knots, with the stokers and others in the engine-room working flat out. The whole ship vibrates as it flies through the water, gradually drawing ahead of the rest of the Grand Fleet.

At about 6 pm, Scheer catches up with Hipper's rather battered group, which has now been in a running battle with Beatty and Evan-Thomas for about 2 hours. Hipper has come out on top, particularly relative to Beatty, but his ships have been hit a number of times, suffering considerable damage. However, Scheer's powerful Battleships are virtually untouched and they move in for the kill against Beatty and Evan-Thomas. Suddenly, however, out of the murk to the north, they see a dreadful sight – dozens of powerful ships, starting to deploy in a line in front of them, bringing all of their guns to bear. This is their first indication that the Grand Fleet is at sea. Jellicoe's deployment is masterly – the classic "crossing of the T" in front of an oncoming column of enemy ships.

Meanwhile, other things are happening. Some of Hood's small screening ships, positioned ahead of him, meet a similar force ahead of Hipper's group. In the ensuing confusion, another group that was steaming ahead of the Grand Fleet, under Robert Arbuthnot, charges in, unaware of the nearby presence of the capital ships of Hipper and Scheer. His flagship, the large armoured cruiser Defence, is hit by a storm of 12 inch shells and becomes the third large British ship to explode and sink within a matter of seconds, again taking an entire crew of almost 1,000 men to their deaths. Hood, on a westerly course, is now aware of the Grand Fleet starting to deploy off his starboard bow and he also sees Beatty coming towards him. His normal place would be behind Beatty, but it's logical in this situation to turn through 180° and take up a position at the front of Beatty's squadron. Beatty and Hipper are still on parallel courses, and still exchanging fire, so Hood starts to do the same, finding himself in conflict with the two leading German ships, Lützow (Hipper's flagship) and Derfflinger. Fresh from gunnery practice, and in pristine condition, Invincible, Indomitable and Inflexible immediately start to make an impact.

It's about 6.20 pm when Frank and his team in turret P are given the green light. Their recent target practice pays off as they operate their two guns like clockwork every thirty seconds. Invincible initially targets Lützow and fires 50 shells at her in 8 minutes, with 8 direct hits. This is gunnery at its very best. The hits cause extensive damage, including large holes in the hull below the waterline, which will cause her to sink later tonight. They then switch to Derfflinger and start to inflict heavy damage on her. Hood shouts encouragement up to Dannreuther – "Keep it up – every shot is telling". Frank and his team, aware that their ship is performing heroics, are euphoric, with adrenaline fuelling their frantic efforts. Of course, nothing is certain in war, and nothing can be taken for granted. Seconds after Hood's shouted encouragement, transmitted to the gunners by Dannreuther, Invincible is consumed in a huge explosion.

Viewing conditions are often critical in long-range ship actions. Both Jellicoe and Beatty have now managed to get the German ships framed against the setting sun, while their own ships are less visible towards the murky north-east. However, the conditions on this day are variable and quirky. As the gunnery officer on Derfflinger, Commander Georg von Hase, reports later: "The veil of mist in front of us suddenly split like a curtain at a theatre: sharply silhouetted against the horizon we saw a powerful ship on a parallel course. A salvo from it straddled us completely." Hase quickly fires 3 salvos at Invincible, the last of which leads to a shell penetrating turret Q, igniting the magazine below it and also the magazine below turret P. It is 6.30 pm.

NAME, (Surname first).	Decorations (if any).	Rating.	Official No. and Port Division.	Branch of Service.	Ship or Unit.	Date and Place of Birth.	Date of Death.	Cause of Death.	Address of Cemetery.	Location of Grave. Plot, Row, Grave No.	Relatives notified and their address.	Remarks.
CLYNE, Francis William	—	Smn.	2161.D. (Po)	R.N.R.	H.M.S. "INVINCIBLE".	18.3.76. Wick.	31.5.16.	1.	ø	— — —	Wife, Jessie L. 40, Louisburgh Street, Wick, Scotland.	

Fig.4.10: Scottish Naval Deaths entry for Francis William Clyne.

At least the end comes quickly and painlessly for Frank and his team, with no warning. In fact, most of the crew die quickly, as the ship is immediately blown into two halves by the massive explosion. Bizarrely, both halves come to rest vertically on the sea bottom: since the ship is almost 600 feet long and the sea is less than 200 feet deep here, 100 foot lengths of both halves can be seen above the waves for quite a long time. One of the 6 survivors of the crew of over 1,000 is Hubert Dannreuther. Only those high up in the superstructure of the ship stood any chance. Horace Hood is among the dead. The Hood family has a long and illustrious history of service in the Royal Navy. Ellen Hood writes to the next of kin of every sailor who died with her husband, emphasizing the major role played by the ship, and that the end was very quick for all of them. It does provide some comfort for Jessie Clyne, and for many other widows in Louisburgh Street and other parts of Wick.

Fig.4.11: View of British ships in the Firth of Forth, near Rosyth, taken in 1916 from Airship R9.

It's evident from these events

that there is a difference between the likelihood of a catastrophic magazine explosion in the British and German ships. The main cause of this illustrates the technical complexity of war. One of the most important developments towards the end of the 19th Century has concerned explosives – particularly as a propellant for bullets and shells. Gunpowder – a mixture of potassium nitrate (saltpetre), sulphur and carbon – has been around for many hundreds of years. However, it's not ideal – its explosive power is limited and it creates a lot of smoke. The development of nitro-glycerine in the 1880's represented a major step forward. However, it's highly unstable, and hence very dangerous to handle. Intense effort went into finding ways of mixing it with other constituents, giving a product that is safe and convenient to handle – while still delivering a powerful and progressive release of energy when ignited. Most of the mixtures involved constituents such as guncotton (nitrocellulose), petroleum jelly and acetone. Alfred Nobel was heavily involved in this area (and made huge amounts of money – much of which was ploughed back into the provision of prestigious prizes). Such work was often kept secret and several countries came up with slightly different formulations. In Britain, chemists such as James Dewar and Frederick Abel, working at Waltham Abbey, came up with Cordite – named because it was in the form of cords or rods. In various forms, it became the standard for British military use in the early decades of the 20th Century. It performs well, but it can still be dangerously unstable under certain circumstances. Arguably the best Chemists in the world during the late 19th and early 20th Centuries are German. People such as Fritz Haber and Carl Bosch were pioneers in many areas, particularly related to nitrogen chemistry. Haber is to achieve notoriety for his promotion of the use of poison gas, but arguably the more important type of "chemical warfare" concerns explosives. In any event, while the differences are very subtle, the bottom line is that the propellants used by the Germans during this battle are as effective as those used by the British, but less prone to explode prematurely. The price paid for this by Frank Clyne and several thousand other British seamen at Jutland is a heavy one. Such are the vagaries of war.

There is more of the battle yet to unfold, although perhaps not quite as much as would be hoped on the British side. At 6.30 pm, the complete German fleet appears to be at the mercy of the Grand Fleet, which is spread out in a huge arc to the north-east, now steaming on a south-easterly course. The visibility to the north-east is very poor and all that the Germans can see as the bombardment starts is a "ring of fire", with just the flashes from the muzzles of the guns clearly visible. Furthermore, most of Hipper's ships are now in poor condition, having been subjected to prolonged combat, including some severe recent punishment from Hood's squadron. Now, as the intensity of firing from the Grand Fleet builds up, Scheer's Battleships rapidly start to suffer significant damage. His position looks desperate, but he quickly issues a command for all of his ships to reverse direction immediately – a difficult manoeuvre that his fleet has practiced repeatedly. In the fading and variable light, the German fleet appears to simply vanish. This is a bit mystifying, but Jellicoe realizes that they must now be steaming towards the south-west and simply alters his course towards the south, knowing that they must lie to the west of him and cutting them off from escape towards their base.

Scheer is in a panic at this point. His position is starting to look hopeless. He realizes that he must somehow buy some time: if he can survive until darkness falls, then perhaps he might yet escape. At 7 pm, he again reverses the course of his fleet. It's not really clear what he has in mind, but 10 minutes later the two fleets are in sight of each other again, with the distance between them closer now, and Jellicoe still having all of his ships broadside-on to the approaching columns of the German fleet. The Grand Fleet again subjects it to a firestorm, with the Battlecruisers at the front of the German columns suffering further serious damage. Destruction of the complete High Seas Fleet looms, but Scheer then plays his last card, ordering several flotillas of his destroyers to move ahead towards the British fleet and launch their torpedoes. This is potentially dangerous, since a single torpedo can sink a capital ship and the British Battleships, lined up at right angles to this stream of torpedoes, are vulnerable to this type of attack. About 15 German destroyers, carrying about 60 torpedoes, are able to respond to this call and they hurl themselves towards the Grand Fleet.

They're met with a hail of fire, but they are too small and fast to be easy targets and Jellicoe quickly orders the stock response to this situation, which is to turn the ships away, so that they are running in the same direction as the torpedoes. While a ship can't quite outrun a torpedo, it can certainly reduce the relative velocity substantially, raising the time to impact and introducing the possibility that it will run out of fuel before that happens. Also, the target area for a torpedo is sharply reduced and it may even be deflected by the wash of the ship's propellors. The manoeuvre is successful: of about 30 torpedoes launched, 10 run out of fuel and the other 20 are avoided in some way. However, it has at least postponed the destruction of the main German fleet, which reverses direction for a third time as soon as the attack by the destroyers begins. They're again well out of sight. Jellicoe, however, still has the upper hand. His escape from the torpedo attack is in a south-easterly direction, so afterwards he is still positioned to the south (and east) of the German fleet, and hence still cutting it off from its base. He has handled the whole of this encounter in a masterly fashion.

However, it is now getting dark. Jellicoe knows the location of the enemy fleet approximately, but not exactly. He also can't be sure by what route they will attempt to get home. What he does know is that he should not risk a night battle with them. The German fleet is much better trained for night fighting, and has better equipment for it – things like very high intensity searchlights. Even having a strong numerical superiority would not guarantee a favourable outcome to a night action. The Germans, on the other hand, don't want a battle of any sort. Their ships are mostly in a very bad way by now, many of them holed, having reduced power and/or reduced functioning armament. Also, they have lost several major ships – not as many as the British, but overall they are in a much worse state - their only objective now is to somehow get home without too much further loss. As darkness falls, Jellicoe organizes the fleet into several columns and heads south at 17 knots. It will be light within about 5 or 6 hours – a period during which Jellicoe grabs some well-earned rest. He expects to be still between the Germans and their base at daybreak, ready for the final confrontation. This is based on the idea that Scheer also must head approximately south. He can't possibly overtake the British fleet, and he's certainly to the north-west of it at present. There is the possibility of him cutting eastwards, to reach the safety of Horns Reef, from where there is a protected waterway along the west coast of Denmark. However, that would involve cutting across the British fleet and it seems unlikely that Scheer would try that.

Fig.4.12: Photo of Jellicoe's flagship, Iron Duke.

In the event, however, it is exactly what he does, driving his battered ships through the rear of the extended columns of British ships during the night. There are a number of confused contacts and fights during this period. Jellicoe actually expected something of this type at the rear of his columns, in the form of attacks by German destroyers, so hearing some gunfire from the north is not unexpected. However, it is actually the complete German fleet that is cutting eastwards, desperately driving through the fairly scattered rearguard of the British columns. Of course, this does become apparent to at least some of the British ship captains involved, but, inexplicably, the news is not conveyed to Jellicoe. This is the latest of several incidents in which he is badly let down by certain subordinates during the Jutland battle. Scheer manages to make it to Horns Reef without any major confrontations and eventually his battle-scarred ships reach Wilhelmshaven without any further losses.

The final reckoning of the outcome does not look so good for Jellicoe – about 6,000 British lives lost, compared with 2,500 Germans, and 14 ships sunk, against 11 German ones. Once they realize that these are the numbers, the Germans start to trumpet this as a great victory. Moreover, at least for a while, this is also the story in the British press. Jellicoe is criticized as having been too cautious and hence losing the chance of obliterating the German fleet. Particular emphasis is laid on his "retreat" in the face of the torpedo attack, since it is suggested that it would have been possible to simply ignore it and push on to destroy the German fleet, even if a few ships might be lost to torpedoes. In fact, it would have been foolish to do this, risking the loss of perhaps half a dozen or more of his powerful Dreadnought Battleships – in the event, none of these were lost in the whole battle. Jellicoe well understood that preserving the status quo was all that was needed in this battle, and risking major losses would be foolhardy. Nevertheless, this view of him as over-cautious is promoted by supporters of Beatty, and even, surreptitiously, by the man himself. They spread the idea that he effectively delivered the enemy on a plate to Jellicoe, who proceeded to squander the opportunity.

The truth is very different. Not only does Jellicoe do virtually everything right, whereas Beatty is cavalier and ill-disciplined, but the actual outcome of the battle is far from a German victory. Damage to German ships is so extensive that the fleet is not able to emerge from port again as a fighting unit for several months. Jellicoe, on the other hand, is immediately able to resume normal activities in the North Sea, carrying out the usual sweeps and patrols as before. The numerical advantage of the British fleet in ships and firepower is undiminished. Perhaps even more importantly, the battle has damaged the morale and attitude of the Germans. They had briefly faced the full might of the Grand Fleet and they're now very reluctant to risk any sort of repetition of this.

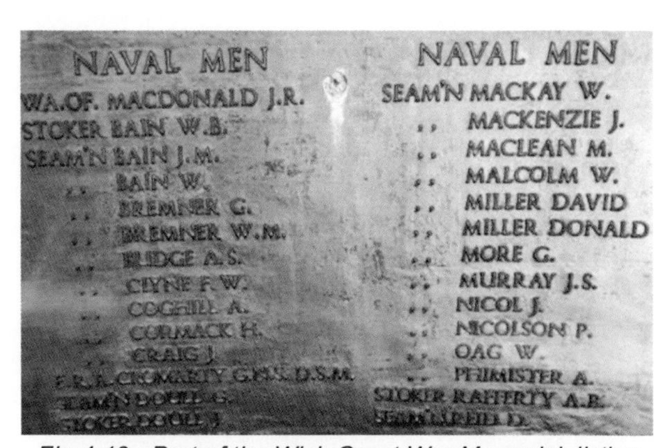

Fig.4.13: Part of the Wick Great War Memorial, listing some of the 53 men from the town who died at Jutland.

They never really try anything similar again and their ships spend the rest of the war rusting in port, their crews becoming increasingly disaffected. The blockade of German ports continues unabated. From this time, the German high command switches the marine focus from surface ships to submarines, encouraging them to attack shipping indiscriminately. This does have an effect on the supplies reaching Britain, but it also alienates neutrals, particularly the United States – leading to them joining the Allies the following year. In fact, the real outcome of the Battle of Jutland is to swing the whole course of the war decisively towards the Allies, although that is not how it is generally perceived at the time. Moreover, Jellicoe's reputation does suffer, with a lot of lobbying against him. He is replaced by Beatty as Admiral of the Fleet in November 1916, being "kicked upstairs" to become First Sea Lord. The various awards and titles he eventually receives from the country tend to be slightly inferior to those showered on Beatty.

Nevertheless, he was the one who fully understood what was needed at the critical time, and delivered it. It takes a long time, but eventually this comes to be widely recognized.

4.4 The Family Hangs Together

News of the death of his namesake hits Frank Clyne quite hard. He'd been too young to remember any details of the family's single visit to Scotland, but he had been in correspondence with his "uncle" more recently and they'd met up a couple of times in the year or so since he joined the Seaforth Highlanders Regiment. The events at Jutland have hit the whole Scottish community, particularly Wick. Over 50 seamen from the town die in the battle, so it has literally been decimated – it has lost about a tenth of its menfolk in a single day. Virtually every street is hit. While it's true that Jellicoe performed well in the battle, and the outcome is in effect an important victory, it's also true that the cost in British lives is high. This is partly due to certain deficiencies in the technical details of their equipment and procedures – leading to greater vulnerability to magazine explosions – rather than to any tactical mistakes, but nevertheless the price paid by the naval crews and their families is high.

Overall, this is a very difficult time for the country and for the Allies. Just a few days after Jutland, Lord Kitchener drowns when a cruiser on which he's a passenger, headed for a meeting in Russia, sinks after hitting a mine near to Scapa Flow. He is no longer seen as a man who can do no wrong, having received a lot of criticism over Gallipoli, but he's still something of a national icon and the country reels from the blow. Furthermore, a month after the battle, and the associated criticism and frustration, the British and French armies launch a long-planned offensive from the region where their trenches meet, about 150 miles to the north-east of Paris.

The attack starts on 1st July 1916, along a line between the Somme and Ancre rivers, near Albert. From the British point of view, the day becomes etched in memory as the worst ever disaster, with over 50,000 casualties – of which 20,000 are killed. The French do much better, advancing appreciably and losing far fewer men. There are several reasons for this, but one of them is that the British troops are mostly quite inexperienced. In fact, they're largely composed of "Kitchener's army" – the throngs of volunteers who heeded the call of their country almost 2 years before. So many of the British officers and regular army soldiers in France have died or been wounded that many young, raw recruits have been drafted into the front line for this battle, sometimes as rapidly-promoted officers. It's the first major battle of the war in France and Belgium in which the British have played the major role, rather than the French. This is largely because of the huge demands being placed on French resources by the ongoing battles at Verdun, further south. The British troops are among the best of the new recruits, but nothing could have prepared them for this.

The several days of bombardment prior to the battle does little damage to the German lines, although it does convert much of the "no-man's land" that the British troops have to cross into a sea of mud. Tanks are used (for the first time), but they're still experimental and give various problems. Furthermore, the Germans have obtained details of the planned offensive, and make extensive preparations. The battle drags on for several months, with the Allied troops advancing a few miles along a broad front, but the cost is enormous (on both sides) – casualty levels over the period up to a cessation of conflict in this area, about 5 months later, are over half a million men for both the Allies and the Germans. It's just another part of an enormous, tragic stalemate across the heart of Europe.

The attack at the Somme was a plan by the French, Italian, Russian and British, hatched in December 1915 (at the Second Chantilly Conference). The idea was to launch major attacks simultaneously on three fronts. In fact, the Russians do launch a major attack (the Brusilov Offensive, named after one of their generals) in June 1916, in Galicia (present day Western Ukraine), against both German and Austro-Hungarian armies. It achieves its objectives, with the Russians breaking through en masse and forcing the Germans to send reinforcements from Verdun, so that the conflict there grinds to a halt. The losses sustained by the Austro-Hungarians are so heavy that their subsequent contributions to the war become small. However, the Russians also suffer huge losses, with this becoming a major factor in its own withdrawal from the war the following year, as the Bolshevik Revolution takes place. The casualties dwarf even those at the Somme and at Verdun, with both sides losing well over a million men.

SCALA THEATRE,
CHARLOTTE STREET, FITZROY SQUARE, W.
THE BRITISH TOPICAL COMMITTEE FOR WAR FILMS
THURSDAY NEXT, AUGUST 10th, at 11.30 a.m. prompt,
OFFICIAL PICTURES
"BATTLE of the SOMME,"
WAR OFFICE

Fig.4.14: Ticket for entry to a theatre to view the film "Battle of the Somme" in August 1916.

In any event, while the Russians certainly make every possible effort, the Brusilov Offensive doesn't significantly weaken the German defences at the Somme. The original hopes on the Allied side are nevertheless high. In fact, the British expect it to be a famous victory. They even commission a small company to create footage during the battle, so that a film can be shown to the general public. Geoffrey Malins is attached to the 29th Division and John McDowell to the 7th Division. They start filming a week or so before the start of the attack and return to London, with 8,000 feet of film, a week afterwards. The film, called "The Battle of the Somme", is a silent black-and-white production running for 77 minutes. It is released on 7th August. It is, of course, vetted by the War Office and it has to be regarded as largely a propaganda exercise. Nevertheless, although some of the scenes are staged, it does include some harrowing and genuine action. However, when it goes on general release – being shown in 34 London cinemas from 21st August, it is for the most part received enthusiastically. In fact, it's a great commercial success, being seen by an estimated 20 million people in the first 6 weeks of its release. The cost in human lives of the battle, which is to continue for another couple of months, is not made clear to the public – although it inevitably becomes known eventually. The film can still be easily viewed in the 21st Century.

Fig.4.15: Still from the film "Battle of the Somme", showing a wounded man being brought back to the trenches: this was a genuine action and in fact the man died 30 minutes later.

Along with most of their friends and neighbours, William and Alice Clyne attend the showing of the film, in Dartford cinema, in September. This is an area that has already lost many young men and the reception is more mixed than in some places. There is certainly some response to the strong appeals to patriotism in the film, but some of the horror of life at the front can still be seen and it appalls people like Alice. She lives in constant fear of losing more of her sons. Herbert is now in Jubbulpore, where there seems to be relatively little danger. Frank is still under training in Britain. She lives, however, in constant dread of hearing that they are to be posted – there are clearly very few postings where they won't be in considerable danger.

The Clyne family has just moved house again, this time to 24 Green Walk. It's still in Crayford, so the children don't need to change school. As Alice and William come out of the cinema, Alice notices a new neighbour, who has also just moved to Green Walk.

"Edith, it's nice to see you again – your baby was very good in there", says Alice.

"Eddie is fine – he's just a couple of months old now and he sleeps a lot" replies Edith. "I don't think you've met my husband, William – he's just started working at Vickers. He's a skilled carpenter and they've brought him here to help build these new aircraft."

"It's very nice to meet you," says Alice. "This is my husband, also William – he's been a Detective in the Metropolitan Police for a long time, but he moved to Vickers about 6 months ago, so that he can contribute more to the war effort."

The two men have a quick chat. It turns out that William Heath was briefly in the West Kents. William explains that he has a son with the RWK in India, and also that his eldest lad was with them until he was killed earlier in the year. William Heath is a bit sniffy when he realizes that the older man just has a security job at Vickers, but of course he's sympathetic about him losing his son.

"I can't say that I like the area round here much" he says. "We're from Broadstairs and we'll move back to the coast once this war is over. I plan to make sure that young Edward has a good education and is brought up in a nice area. I've got great hopes for him. Hopefully he won't get caught up in any of this soldiering stuff. I was very pleased to get out before I was sent to get slaughtered in some muddy trench."

Fig.4.16: Dartford Cinema in 1916.

William understands the feelings of young men like this, particularly if they have children. He doesn't say that nevertheless some people have to be prepared to make sacrifices, although it certainly crosses his mind.

4.5 More Hammer Blows

This is not something that was planned or welcomed, but by the late spring of 1917 it becomes clear that Alice is pregnant again. Condoms are in quite widespread use, but the technology is still a little unreliable. Furthermore, abortion is illegal and also very much against the teachings of most churches. William and Alice decide that they don't really have any alternative to proceeding with the pregnancy. After all, Alice is still only 43 and she has had little or no trouble with any of her previous births. There's no doubt that the stresses of the past 3 years have taken their toll on both of them, but hopefully she'll be able to manage this last one OK. Maybe, by the time that this one is born, the war will be coming to an end and things will be starting to look brighter.

This pregnancy feels a little different to Alice and, by the late summer she's starting to think that perhaps it's twins. There's no routine way of being sure about these things, but she occasionally feels that the movements inside her are rather uncoordinated and perhaps these could be due to two babies moving at the same time. In any event, she feels that perhaps she's a little bigger than previously at corresponding stages. In some ways, it's an exciting prospect, but she's not at all sure whether, given the various other pressures and difficulties, this is a good time to be having to cope with two babies. Also, as the year wears on, it certainly doesn't look as if the war is going to finish any time soon. In fact, the deprivations are, if anything, getting worse. Since Germany's decision at the start of the year to carry out unrestricted submarine warfare, supplies of food are being progressively cut. There are now long queues at virtually all shops selling food and there is much talk about rationing being introduced soon. It's already illegal to feed wild animals like pigeons or ducks. There are also rumours that Russia may be about to withdraw from the war and everyone knows that this would be a disaster for the Allies.

Another concern for Alice relates to medical services. There are now huge numbers of casualties in the country – mostly soldiers who have suffered various wounds and trauma. Life-saving interventions carried out at the Front, such as blood transfusions, have been developed and improved over the past 3 years, but this has actually led to an increase in the demands being placed on medical services within the UK. Convalescence periods for war-wounded are often quite long. A lot of hospitals, and also the services of many nurses and doctors, are now dedicated to coping with wounded veterans. Inevitably, provision for routine medical needs has been reduced. Also, the supply of experienced midwives has been decimated, as any women with medically-related skills are increasingly been called on to help in nursing the injured. Alice has been able to find a young women in the area who has agreed to help her, but it's clear that she has very little previous experience.

Alice goes into labour on Thursday 22nd November. Things go wrong from the start. The first baby becomes a breech presentation. Alice has no experience of this, and nor does the midwife. The effect is that the labour is exhausting and painful, with a lot of bleeding, but with no progress being made. Alice should be moved to a hospital, for a probable Cesarean section. It is becoming a more widely-accepted procedure these days, although still not entirely routine. However, the limited availability of resources is such that even getting her to a hospital is a challenge. William is present, but he has no idea what to do. Eventually, he and the midwife manage to persuade the cottage hospital at Bexley to arrange an ambulance for her. She doesn't actually arrive there until early the next day. She is in a state of utter exhaustion. Even then, there is nobody available at the hospital with sufficient experience to recognize that a Cesarean represents the only chance, or to be able to carry one out. Alice passes away, dying from exhaustion and loss of blood. The two babies also die. William is in a state of shock.

Registration District DARTFORD.

1917. DEATHS in the Sub-District of BEXLEY in the County of KENT.

Columns:—	1.	2.	3.	4.	5.	6.	7.	8.	9.
No.	When and Where Died.	Name and Surname.	Sex.	Age.	Rank or Profession.	Cause of Death.	Signature, Description, and Residence of Informant.	When Registered.	Signature of Registrar.
145	Twenty third November 1917. Bexley Cottage Hospital Bexley Heath Bexley U.D.	Alice Clyne	Female	44 years	of 24 Green Walk Crayford Wife of William Clyne Pensioner Metropolitan Police	(1) Parturition (2) Septicaemia Exhaustion Certified by Thomas W. Hinds M.D.	William Clyne Widower of deceased In attendance 24 Green Walk Crayford	Twenty third November 1917.	W. J. Weaving Registrar.

Fig.4.17: Death certificate of Alice Clyne.

This is not a blow from which the family can easily recover. Alice has always been the bedrock of the family, organizing everything and dearly loved by all of them. The grief and pain are overwhelming. It affects them all, but Len, now 3 years old, is completely inconsolable. Of course, many families have lost their menfolk recently, but the death of a relatively young woman, who is still the mainstay of a growing family, is much less common than it had been in Victorian times. Even in the midst of the ongoing trauma of the war, there is much sympathy from neighbours and friends – Alice was a very popular woman. Those closely affected include Alice's younger brother, Herbert Pollard, who lives nearby. He's present in the hospital when she dies, but he's as helpless as everyone else.

William tries to pick up the pieces, for the sake of the children, but it's very difficult. Alice did so much in the home and now he also has to spend hours every day in queues, just to get enough to eat. Except for Stan, all of the children are at school (or away in the Army). William is overwhelmed with grief and worry. Christmas and New Year, far from being a holiday or festival, is a time of chaotic trauma and desolation in the house in Green Walk. William considers resigning from Vickers, but money is tight and it would be even tighter if he only had his pension.

Registration District DARTFORD.

1918. DEATHS in the Sub-District of BEXLEY in the County of KENT.

Columns :—	1.	2.	3.	4.	5.	6.	7.	8.	9.
No.	When and Where Died.	Name and Surname.	Sex.	Age.	Rank or Profession.	Cause of Death.	Signature, Description, and Residence of Informant.	When Registered.	Signature of Registrar.
197	Second February 1918 24 Green Walk Crayford U.D.	William Clyne	Male	48 years	Pensioner Metropolitan Police — Warden at Messrs Vickers	(1) Cerebral Haemorrhage (2) Heart failure No P.M. Certified by R. Davis Stacy M.R.C.S.	H. E. Pollard Brother in law Present at the death 20 Royal Oak Road Bexleyheath	Fourth February 1918	W. J. Deaving Registrar.

Fig.4.18: Death certificate of William Clyne (Snr.).

His health had previously been good, but the stress of the last few years has taken its toll and this latest blow has left him completely prostrated. He's not eating properly and he starts to suffer palpitations and headaches. He should visit a doctor, but there is little time for such things these days. His blood pressure is extremely high. The end comes in early February. He suffers a cerebral hemorrhage and a heart attack at home. It's very quick and there is no time to get medical help or move him to hospital. His brother-in-law, Hebert Pollard, who has been helping over the past couple of months, is with him at the end. For the children, who were at school when he died, it's another body blow. Their world has collapsed in a few short weeks.

Chapter 5: On the Jellicoe Express (March 1918)

5.1 A Family on the Brink

"It's good of you to spare a few minutes, Sir Edward." Inspector Harry Collis does actually know Sir Edward Henry quite well, but the Head of the Metropolitan Police is naturally a busy man. However, he's known to take a personal interest in his officers, even those who've retired. Harry is quite happy about asking him to help.

"Not at all, Harry. I understand that you wanted a quiet word about an officer who's died recently?"

"Yes, it's Detective William Clyne. His wife died in childbirth a couple of months ago, leaving him with a string of young kids on his hands. Well, he's just had a heart attack and died. He was still in his 40's, but his wife's death hit him very hard. He retired a couple of years ago, but I've kept in touch – we actually joined up at the same time, almost 30 years ago, and he's been a good friend." Harry had actually been promoted a little more quickly than William, but it's true that they had remained friends. He came from a similarly humble background, but they had both thrived in the force.

"Actually, I did hear and I was very sorry about it. I do remember him well – a Scotsman, I seem to recall, a very good cop and a nice bloke as well. I used to have a chat with him occasionally. What's the situation with his family?"

"The key question is what on earth is going to happen to those kids – he had a lot of them, but his family are still up in the far north of Scotland and Alice didn't have many relatives round here either. I had a chat yesterday with Alice's brother, Herbert, who registered William's death and in fact was with him when he died. As you'd expect, it's complete chaos. Their eldest lad was killed in Persia two years ago and the next two are both away with the army. The oldest one still at home is Stan, who's just turned 16 and apparently plans to stay in the area with the family of a friend. There are then a couple of girls, aged 13 and 10, and three boys, aged 12, 5 and 3. Of course, they can't stay in the house – apart from anything else, there's no income to pay the rent and I don't think that they had much in the way of savings. I've just checked on the rules – it seems clear that William's pension will now stop. If his wife were still alive then she'd get something, but there's no provision for dependent children on their own to receive anything."

"Yes, I'm well aware that there are some deficiencies like that. We should look into the possibility of modifying certain rules", says Sir Edward. "In fact, the whole pay and pension structure of the Met should be overhauled – for one thing, pay has slipped badly behind inflation over the past few years. Still, I'm afraid that we can't do anything that would help this family. Were you hoping that we could make some sort of payment to them?"

"No, that's not what I had in mind – I'm well aware that there are procedures to be followed and we can't make exceptions just because we feel some sympathy in particular cases. No, it just concerns exactly what will now happen to the kids. Herbert was clear that his family can't help. He himself lives in Bexleyheath, but he's still in his thirties and not married. There's just nobody who could take them on. They're currently with neighbours, but something has to be done quickly. There is a plan to move the younger ones up to Scotland. There are lots of family connections in the area, although it's going to be a big change from London and the kids don't actually know anybody up there. Anyway, what are the alternatives – the Workhouse?! They're a lovely bunch of kids and they've got to somehow retain some family links. In many ways, their real roots are in Scotland."

"There's something in that. They need to know who they are. They certainly can't be left to somehow fend for themselves down here. Are there particular families up there who can take them?"

"It's a bit unclear", replies Harry. "There's apparently a couple of cousins who could take some, although they're not themselves very much older than the kids. Still, at least there are plenty of others in the area with connections to the Clyne Clan, so they'd be sure to get some general support. Communications are far from easy. There are virtually no phones up there and letters are slow. It's already clear, however, that nobody will be able to come down to pick them up. There's just no money around and of course travel is so difficult anyway these days. What I actually wanted to ask you is whether they could go on a Jellicoe Express. Otherwise that journey would be a complete nightmare and they'd probably never get there, even if the cash could be found. I can't see any other way that this could work."

"Absolutely. As you know, normally only military personnel are allowed on those trains, but we're in charge of the security arrangements and we can certainly issue them with special passes. If the elder girl is able to go with them, then she should be able to make sure that they get there OK. In fact, I'll tell you what I'll do – I'll also have a word with a friend of mine in the Navy and make sure that a good man is in the same compartment, to keep an eye on them and make sure that they come to no harm."

"That's extremely kind, Sir Edward. My understanding is that Mina would be able to go up with them. She's a very sensible girl and she'll make sure that they get there in one piece: Still, having someone involved who knows the ropes on these trains is a brilliant idea. If it's OK with you, I'll confirm with Herbert Pollard and hopefully we can get them onto a train sometime next month?"

"That's fine – it's the least that we can do. I just pray that those kids are going to be OK in the end. God knows there are many casualties in this war, but not many families have suffered quite as much as that one."

Fig.5.1: Photo taken just before their departure in March 1918, showing (left to right) the newly-orphaned Mina (13), Harry (12), Lena (10), Douglas (5) and Len (3).

5.2 The Journey Starts

The arrangements have been made. The journey is to start on Monday 18th March. There have been meetings at which things have been explained to the five children who will be on the train, with Stan and Herbert Pollard also present, plus some of the neighbours who have been helping. There have also been discussions with their schoolteachers. Of course, the children are distraught and confused, having lost both of their parents so recently. Some of them, such as Mina, understand the implications only too well. The younger ones, particularly Len and Douglas, don't really know what is happening – only that there is sadness and pain, that their stable and loving environment has been torn apart and that the future is very uncertain.

They have, however, been reassured – that they will soon have a new home, where they will be looked after very well, and that they will be all be going on a long and exciting journey. They try to be brave and positive, although they can sense in the older people that all is not well – children are often very sensitive to feelings of insecurity in adults around them. They're told to pack the things they want to take with them, although they won't be able to have very much.

William's old colleagues in the Met are very helpful, and even provide a car to take the children to Euston. They're dropped in front of the huge Doric Arch at the entrance.

They've never been to Euston and they look around in awe. As with all of the Jellicoe Expresses, it will leave at 6 pm. They run every day, and they're usually full. They're nominally restricted to military personnel – predominantly naval – but of course there are occasionally others, such as administrators, contractors who service the ships and other facilities etc. Security is strict, but having a pass is all that's required in order to be allowed to board and the children do have these, provided by the Met.

Jellicoe is no longer Admiral of the Fleet, so he travels on these trains himself much less frequently. Nevertheless, they're strongly associated with his name – he effectively moved the fleet to Scapa Flow and he was the one who organized much of the associated infrastructure etc. He's a great organizer. Most people in the Navy still regard him as their leader – and indeed in a way he still is, as First Sea Lord. Nevertheless, they miss his physical presence. In any event, these trains still carry his name.

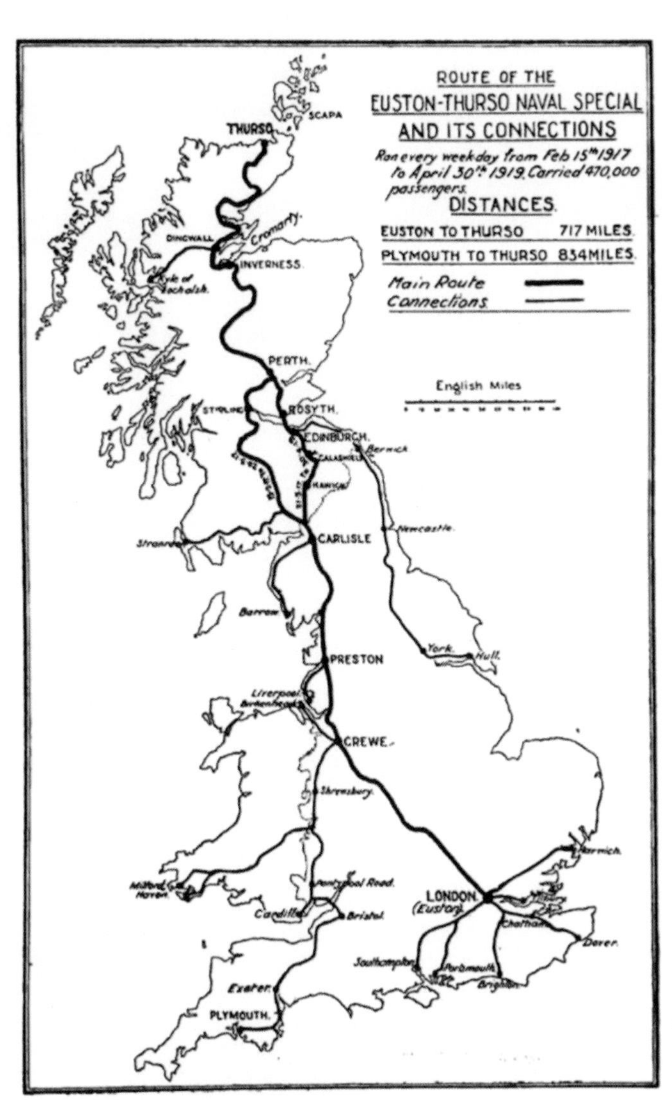

Fig.5.2: Routes of the "Jellicoe Express" trains.

They're actually run by three companies – the London and North Western Railway as far as Carlisle, the North British Railway from there to Perth and the Highland Railway beyond to Thurso. In principle, the government now controls the entire railway system (for the duration of the war), but in practice it's still the employees of these companies, and also their locomotives and rolling stock, that run the trains over their territories. The counter-productive rivalries, blocking of trains from competing companies etc, have been stopped, but the pride in their own operations remains.

The children arrive in good time, but there is already a lot of activity around Platform 15, on the far left, where the long train is waiting. They gaze at the bustle of hundreds of passengers – mostly sailors in uniform – milling around, laughing and shouting. They have a compartment reserved in the first coach. They walk the length of the train – well over 300 yards of it – find their way to the first coach and sit down, in a state of shock. A couple of sailors are already there.

"Well, lads and lasses, are ye sure that ye're on the right train – this one's nae going to the seaside – at least not what ye might think of as the seaside!" Mina assumes the role of spokesperson for the little group.

"We're the Clyne family and we're going to stay with our relatives in Scotland."

Fig.5.3: Photo of the entrance arch at Euston station in 1914.

"Are ye now. Well I'm Jock Sinclair and I'm a stoker on the Iron Duke, the flagship of the Grand Fleet. We'll be together for a wee while – we're also headed for the far north. Clyne – ye ken tha's a brae Scottish name, but ye dinna sound as if ye're from those parts?"

"No, we're from Kent, but our family is from Scotland. I think we're going to Caithness, to somewhere near Wick."

"Are ye now, well it's gud old haul. Look, lassie, we'll nae be off for a wee while yet – would ye all like to come along wi me and hae a look at the front of the train – do ye like trains?"

"I don't know - we've not been on very many, at least not trains like this – I didn't know that trains could be this long."

"Well, there's nae many as long as this one", says Jock, as they all climb down onto the platform and walk a few yards forward, the two younger boys jumping up and down with excitement.

They soon reach the first of the two gleaming engines, steam gently issuing from chimneys and pistons. They're right at the end of the platform, but there's a low bridge over this part of the station and the area is quite dark. The glows from the fires in the cabs of the huge engines are clearly visible. Harry, who is interested in trains, reads off the number, 2408, and name, Admiral Jellicoe, of the first engine.

Fig.5.4: A LNWR 1st class corridor brake coach, dating from 1906.

"Who's Admiral Jellicoe?" he asks.

"Ye've a fair wee bit to learn, m'lad! He's nae but the finest seaman in the Royal Navy. Also a bonnie wee man – we all love him, nae more than the crew of the Duke. He's moved on, but the Duke is still his ship. Did'ya ken that these trains are called the Jellicoe Expresses?"

"No", says Harry, "Does this engine always pull these trains?"

"Well, it cannae do that, but I've been on these trains several times and it's been up front on a couple of them - I guess that they like to use it. They often use the same drivers, too, and they're also the best. Hey, Archie", he calls up to the driver, "Can these three lads jump up and hae a look around up there?"

"If you're quick", Archie calls down, "We're away in 15 minutes". The three lads clamber up into the crowded cab, gawping at the roaring fire as the fireman throws in a few more shovelfuls. Archie shows them a few dials and gauges, including that for the steam pressure, nudging at the 175 psi limit. "She'll blow soon if we're not careful, which would be a waste of steam - we'll need it all shortly." "You'll have all you need!" grunts the fireman, as he takes a short break. The boys are entranced.

They soon jump back down to the platform and walk on a few yards with Jock, to look at the pilot engine at the front – a sister engine, No. 233, named Suvla Bay.

"These are magnificent engines, lads", says Jock, "They're Prince of Wales 4-6-0s, if ye're interested in details. The London & North Western's finest. Can ye see the three sets o' coupled driving wheels, each taller than a man? These locos were built at Crewe a couple of years ago. They'll make short work o' the run up to Carlisle, including the climb to Shap."

Just then a rather fussy man in uniform bustles up, a little out of breath. He's the "Despatcher", responsible for making sure that the train leaves in good order. He approaches Archie as the senior driver.

"You do realize that you've got 16 on today?" he says.

"Well, I could see that it's a bit longer than usual – what's going on?"

"Between you and me, it's Lady Muck again. She's always causing trouble, but we just have to swallow it. Sir David gets annoyed as well, but he'll do anything to keep her happy. Anyway, they're both on board today. She's demanded an extra couple of coaches at the back, both sleepers, since she has a lot of friends coming along. Sir David's in a different coach, so heaven knows what's going on there – we don't ask. They're only going to Rosyth, so 5 will come off there."

"I'm not interested in his domestic problems, or in what happens after Carlisle, but that's a long train. Are we full?"

"We certainly are – there's probably about 900 on board tonight and I've estimated around 550 tons."

"That's a lot", says Archie. "We might have trouble getting it out of here – this bank is a bugger with wet rails like today."

"Don't worry – I've given you a banker. It'll drop off once you're over the hump. Will you be OK on Shap?"

"We'll sail over Shap, as long as we've got a clear road."

"You'll always get that – you know that these trains have absolute priority. Anyway, it's just 3 minutes now – you need to be off – best of luck!"

Jock and the children had been quietly listening to this exchange, shouted above the noises of escaping steam and much yelling and general bustle, but they realize that they need to get on board quickly now, as whistles start to blow along the length of the train. Mina herds them in, aware that she has to take responsibility for them all.

Both engines give a blast on their whistles and they slowly start to move. There are a few moments of dramatic wheel-spin from Suvla Bay, before the massive banking engine digs its heels in and starts to push the huge train forward. They slowly gather speed up the steep incline out of the station and soon the front of the train is over the hump that crosses the Regent Canal and it starts to move forward in earnest. The banker eases away from the train and slowly goes off onto another track, heading for a break at Willesden shed until its next call of duty.

As they accelerate away, the children settle down, excited, but also apprehensive about the whole situation. A little later, when the others are chattering away, Jock has a quiet word with Mina.

"What's the story here, lassie – visits to relatives are pretty rare these days?"

"We're orphans", she says sadly, "Both of our parents have died within the last 3 months. The only relatives who can take us are in Scotland. We've never met them, or even been to Scotland. In fact, we're not even very sure who will be looking after us."

"My God, lassie, there are so many tragedies these days. Tae tell the truth, my captain had a wee word with me, and asked me tae keep an eye on ye all during the trip, but he did'nae know much about ye or why ye're on this train. Anyways, we just need to win this damn war and move on, although it's a tough fight. We all thought that the Boche would be a pushover, and also Johnny Turk, but we were very wrong. Still, we'll win through in the end. I'll look after ye all on this trip, and Scotland's a bonnie place to live – it's nae a soft place, but it's a bonnie place, and the Scots always look after each other. Ye'll find out all about the Clans – and I'll let ye intae a secret – the best Clan in the far north of Scotland is the Sinclair Clan, and the Clynes are an important part of the Sinclair Clan!"

Mina is heartened by his words, and by the thought that he'll be travelling with them. Jock, on the other hand, has serious concerns about what might await these bairns at the end of the line.

5.3 On the West Coast Main Line

The Express quickly gets up to 60-70 mph, with a clear road all the way – every signal is "off", in railway parlance. They hurtle through the northern suburbs of the capital, with the smoke from thousands of coal fires rising into the cool evening air, and they're soon flashing through Harrow. Suddenly, water starts cascading through the open part of the window, near the top. Jock quickly jumps up to close it.

"What's happening?" asks Mina.

"We're at Bushey Troughs" Jock replies. "Archie, or more likely his sidekick, has left the scoop down a bit too long. They're always keen tae fill up the tank completely and they're nae too bothered about a few passengers at the front getting a wee bit wet!"

Fig.5.5: A Prince of Wales class 4-6-0 heading up the 10 am "Scotch Express", shown picking up water from Bushey Troughs in 1918.

There is plenty to see as the train ploughs on towards the north-west, passing through the huge cutting at Tring and the long (mile and a half) tunnel at Kilsby, roaring through some stations, but going slowly through others – such as Rugby, with its long platforms, each capable of holding two full-length trains.

Fig.5.6: Photo of Rugby station, taken in 1917.

After an hour and a half of high speed running, it starts to get dark, and also to rain. There's less to see out of the windows and the children start to doze. The normal bedtime for Len passes, but of course there's little normal about life these days, particularly on this journey. They're also starting to get hungry. Jock tells them that the train will stop at Crewe, where they'll be able to get some food and drink. There is a restaurant car on the train, but it's a long walk and in any event it's probably not a good idea – there's more drink dispensed there than food, and some of the sailors in the vicinity may already be a bit rowdy.

At about 9.30 pm, they slow down as Crewe is approached, passing the huge engine shed and railway works by the side of the line. They pull into the station and stop, with hordes of sailors then flooding out to stretch their legs. Both engines are to refill their water tanks here and they're to stop for about 30 minutes. The children manage to buy some food – Mina has been entrusted with some funds – and settle back into their compartment. Before long, they're off again, heading ever towards the north. The rain falls more heavily and the temperature drops: that this might in some way be associated with their northwards migration is not a possibility that occurs to the children.

In the cab of the Admiral Jellicoe, all is fairly routine. Archie and his mate are somewhat exposed to the elements, but there's a lot of heat coming from the fire and they're used to this environment. As they cruise through Preston and Lancaster, their focus is on the signals and on the performance of the loco. One effect of the war is that these engines are not being maintained as well as they would be normally, with the intervals between servicing being stretched, so they need to be on the lookout for defects that might become serious. The engines are certainly being worked hard on a train as heavy as this one, with a demanding schedule and few stops. As they pass through the Lune Gorge, the beauty of the surroundings is rather lost on them on a night like tonight and their focus is more on the upcoming climb to Shap summit – 4 miles at a steady gradient of 1 in 75 is a challenge for any heavy train, and this one is very heavy. Still, as Archie had predicted, they take it in their stride, the two locos working in close partnership, building up speed to 75 mph at the foot of the climb and eventually breasting the summit without dropping much below 40 mph. These enginemen are masters of their trade.

They ease up on the gentle run down to Carlisle, coasting into the magnificent Citadel station just after 1 am. The station is a hive of activity, with various trains, passenger and goods, still running at this time of night. The children wake up and take in these new sights. The crews of the two locos, having had over 6 hours of continuous hard labour – at least for the firemen, although the strain of concentration is equally demanding for the drivers – have certainly earned a rest. The locos are also in need of relief, with their coal-bunkers almost empty. They're uncoupled from the train and taken off to Kingmoor shed, just a couple of miles away. The replacement engines, and their crews, are ready and waiting. The train is now passing from the stewardship of the LNWR to that of the North British Railway. The handover will take a while and the train is scheduled to spend almost an hour in Carlisle.

The children again come down onto the platform with Jock, having recovered some energy after a few hours of sleep. Jock again takes on the role of instructor about the train. Harry listens carefully, but Douglas and Len are mostly running around causing minor mayhem, with Lena and Mina trying hard to minimize this. By now, the children have attained the status of mascots in the first coach, with a number of sailors taking an interest in them and keeping them entertained.

"Harry, these locos are Atlantics – that's tae say, they have a 4-4-2 wheel arrangement", says Jock. Harry reads off the numbers 902 and 903, and the names of Highland Chief and Cock of the North. "They can pull about as hard as the twa' that hae just come off, but they weigh a wee bit more. That does add tae the total weight of the train, but it helps with adhesion tae the rails. On the other hand, there are just the twa' pairs o' powered wheels, while there are three on the 4-6-0s, which can make slipping more likely."

Harry isn't following all of this, but he's still fascinated by these enormous engines, which seem to live and breathe. Just then, the stationmaster arrives, accompanied by a signalman from the main box in the station.

The signalman calls up to the driver of the train engine – Highland Chief, who has just climbed into the cab. "Jimmy, you're on the Waverley today – there's two sleeper expresses heading north shortly and a couple of heavy goods up from Settle - I just can't fit you in over Beattock. Also, did you know that you've 16 on today?"

"Ye dinna' say", calls down Jimmy. "Tha's a heavy load over the Waverley. We're 20 minutes doon already and we cannae make up any time on that route. Also, I dinna' like the weather much – there's a storm an' a haf' brewing here."

"Ally", he calls to his fireman, "Ye ken tha' we're on the Waverley tonight, with 16 on – we need tae hit the road soon."

"Aye, we do that. I dinna mind the Waverley. It keeps us awa' from those awfu' wee spirits at Quintinshill."

"Awa' with ye, man. Ye've nivver seen a ghost in yer life."

"Ye're right, but ma' mate Tommy says he's heard them there – screams, followed by gunshots. It's always at first light", so he says.

"We dinna' have time for this – we're awa' in 5 minutes."

Whistles start to blow and the senior guard, who's based in the last coach, comes up for a last minute check. He's been on the train since Euston and he'll be staying with it all the way. He has a quick chat with Jimmy and the driver of the pilot engine about the extra two coaches and the fact that they'll be on the Waverley route. The latter is not at all unusual, although they can't recall taking 16 over it before. Still, they're all confident that this can be managed. Meanwhile, the children clamber back into the train, along with hundreds of sailors. It shortly starts to ease its way out of the station, switching quickly onto the Waverley line. The next stage of their epic journey has begun.

5.4 On the Waverley

They settle down again. The rain is now pouring down, and it's pitch black outside. It's about 2 am. They're going a little slower than on the West Coast main line, with this route having more curves and gradients, although the initial stretch of about 15 miles is across flat country. Speed builds up to around 60 mph and most people on the train drift quickly off to sleep. The train then starts to climb a little, as they move towards the Pentland Hills. As they pass Newcastleton, the gradient quickly rises to 1 in 70. It will stay at this for the 10 miles to Whitrope summit. This is always a challenge, particularly for heavy trains. The rain is making the rails slippery and the battle often concerns traction as much as power.

On Highland Chief, however, the atmosphere is calm. This is a very heavy train, but these two engines are working hard and well, with the initial speed of 60 mph dropping only slowly as the gradient starts to bite. Ten minutes later, just two or three miles short of the summit, it's still about 35-40 mph. All should be well. Suddenly, however, they're in a real crisis.

"My God, it's on!", shouts Jimmy. They're just coming round the curve into Riccarton Junction station. The signal at the end of the platform is showing starkly red. He heaves on the whistle cord, just as the driver of Cock of the North in front does the same. The night is rent with piercing noise. "It's not coming off - the bugger must be asleep! I'll kill him!"

"We cannae stop here – ignore it", yells Ally.

"That I cannae do!" says Jimmy grimly, repeatedly blowing the whistle, but also easing the regulator and starting to apply the brakes. The driver of the pilot engine reaches the same conclusion and the train grinds to a halt a few yards from the signal-box. The signalman jumps down and runs over to them. At least he wasn't asleep.

THE WAVERLEY ROUTE
WITH BRANCHES AND OTHER LINES

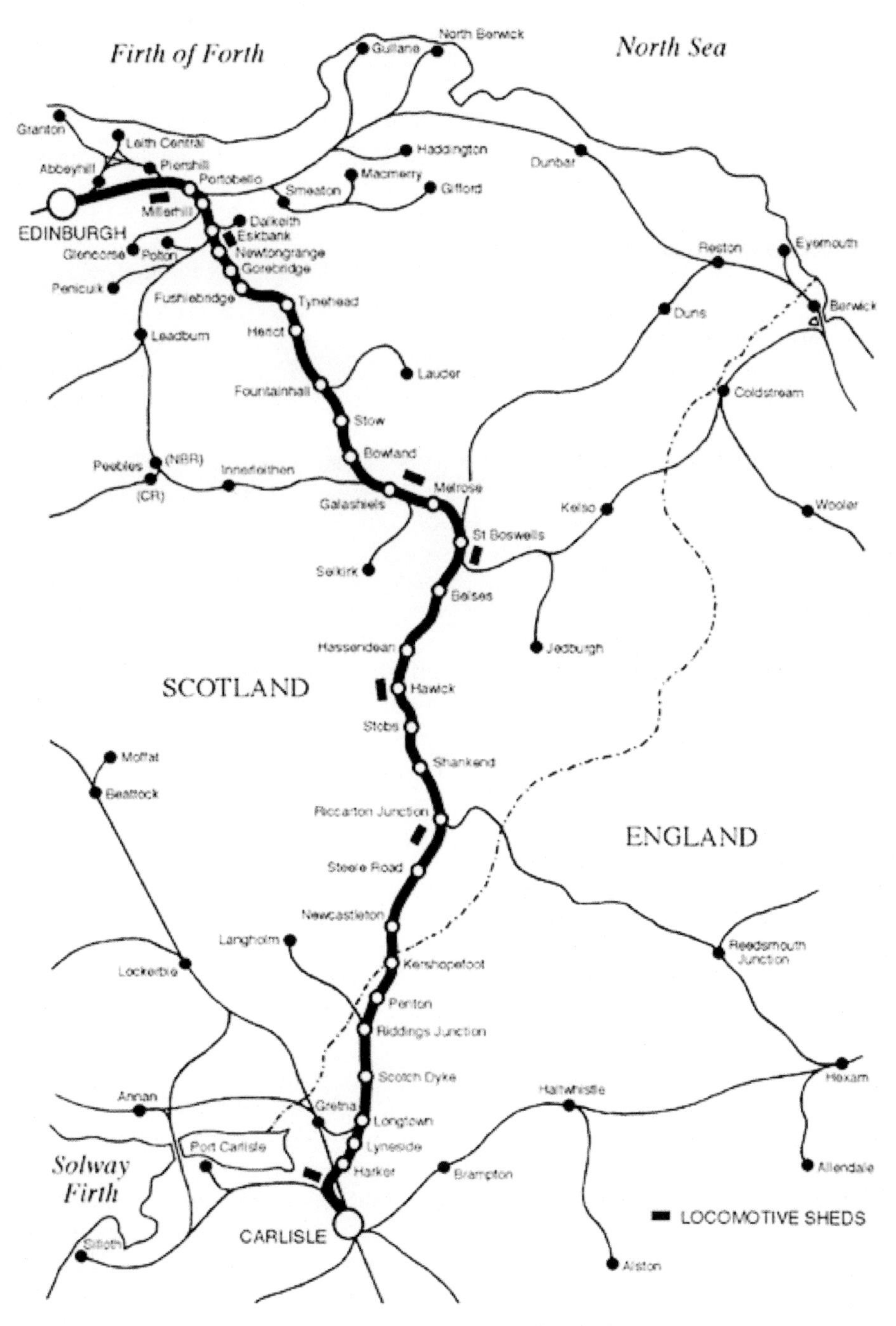

Fig.5.7: The Waverley Route in 1918.

"Ye're mad – do ye ken what ye've done", shouts Jimmy. "This is a Jellicoe Express and we've 16 on. We'll nivver get over Whitrope now."

"I did'na ken that ye had 16 on, but this is an emergency – there's a man doon there who's gonna die if he does'na get tae the hospital at Hawick soon." says the signalman. "There's nae another train fer 4 hours, ye ken. He's a logger an' he was hit by a falling tree this afternoon. It's taken 10 hours tae get him here on a stretcher, thro' 4 miles o' forest in the dark. Ye ken that there's nae roads tae this place – there's only the rails!"

"I ken that well", says Jimmy. "Get him on board, while we hae a good think about what the hell we're tae do." The senior guard arrives at that moment. The other guard is supervising the operation of bringing the injured man into the train and making him as comfortable as possible. It's clear to all that he's in a bad way. Most of the passengers are now awake and heads are appearing out of windows along most of the length of the train.

"Fortunately, I don't think that Sir David and Lady Beatty have stirred – they're quite a long way from your manic whistling", says the guard. "Still, we've got a problem here – the one place we needed a clear road was here! What should we do?" The ultimate responsibility actually lies with the guard, but he's always going to involve the drivers. "I think we need a banker to be sure of getting over the top. Do you have any engines at the shed here?" he asks the signalman.

Fig.5.8: Riccarton Junction station in 1907.

"Nay, there's nothing here tonight."

"Please call Kingmoor, Canal and Hawick at once and see what they've got." The signalman quickly runs up the stairs to his box.

"What are the other options?" he asks Jimmy. "What about splitting the train?"

"I was thinking aba' that", says Jimmy, "But it's nae a quick or easy option. We'd have tae stop the other half from slipping back – there's a bit of a gradient even along this platform. We'd have to break the vacuum. Also, ye ken that they'd lose the steam heating – it could get awfu' cold in those coaches."

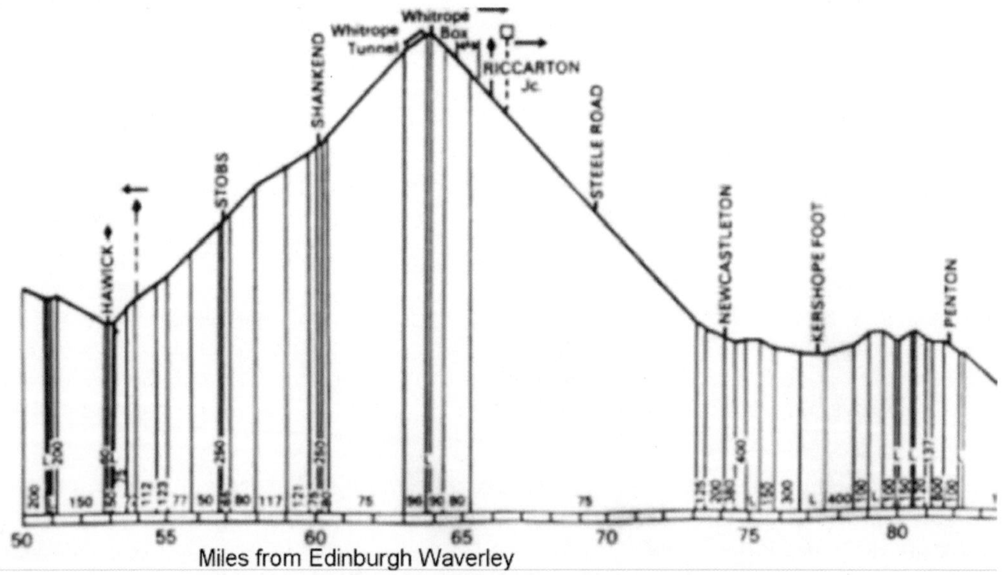

Fig.5.9: Gradient profile in the vicinity of Whitrope summit.

They continue to discuss the technical challenges, but this is cut short as the signalman runs up to them.

"I've tried them all", he says. "None hae a suitable engine in steam at present. It'd be 4 or 5 hours before anything could be here. Surely we canna' wait that long?"

"Ye're right, man, we canna. That injured lad must be moved soon.'", says Jimmy. "We could mebbe' split the train."

"I dinna' think that's a guid idea", says the signalman. "Ye cud run round the train a' Hawick, but ye'd need an awfu' lot o' shuntin' tae get it back t'gether agin. Ye'd be sure tae lose a guid few hours, an' ye ken there'd be nae heat fer awl tha' time."

"We can't do that", says the guard. "Sir David would be livid. Anyway, if anything bad is going to happen to this train, I must at least be with it. We can't split it. You'll just have to get it over the top somehow – can you do it?"

Jimmy looks long and hard at the other driver.

"Aye, I think we can. It's a wee bit flatter just here and we should be able tae get it moving. The crunch will come after we're aroun' that curve an' the grade starts tae bite again. Andy – is yer sandbox full?"

"Well, I've used it a wee bit over the past few miles, but there should be plenty there – I filled it myself at Kingmoor."

"OK, well ye're going to need it. We must'nae let the wheels go. If we both spin at the same time when the grade's high, then she'll start tae go backwards fur sure an then we really are in trouble."

"Aye. Well, we'll gi' it our best shot."

With everyone back on board, after a couple of quick blasts on the whistles, both drivers cautiously open their regulators, fighting all the time against wheel-spin. The precious sand grains are now running in a continuous stream to all of the driving wheels. To run out before the summit would be disastrous, but the risk has to be taken. Both sets of valves are lifting, with the pressure at the 180 psi limit – the firemen have sweated blood to provide this, but now it all comes down to the experience and skill of the drivers. They both push the cut-off to the 85% limit, using almost the full stroke of the pistons to maximize the torque, but they throttle back the steam pressure, to reduce the danger of wheel-spin. As they start to move, an evolving balancing act is needed that would test the best of drivers. The deep staccato bark of the two exhausts echoes for miles over the desolate countryside. They literally feel through the soles of their feet how their charges are responding and how they can somehow be coaxed to perform this Herculean task. Slowly, they gain precious speed and height. There are a couple of sharp curves before the summit, with a 30 mph limit, but this is not relevant tonight, as they struggle to get above walking pace on the steep gradient. The banshee screeching of wheel on rail through the curves can be heard by everyone, but this precious friction actually helps to keep the train moving.

Some of those on board, familiar with trains and with the Waverley route, silently urge on the crews in their struggle, while the guards in the two brake coaches are rigid with tension. On this grade, the strain on the first few couplings in this heavy train is enormous and a breakage would cause the automatic train brake system to fail. Getting those in the brake coaches on manually as soon as possible could be critical. These people know the perils here, with not just Quintinshill in everyone's thoughts, but also the Armagh Disaster – it was a quarter of a century ago, but the terror of a heavy train slipping back down a steep gradient has been burned into the psyche of all railway-men. In fact, they've heard rumours recently of a terrible crash in the French Alps, at a place called St. Michel de Maurienne, just 3 months ago, when an over-filled troop train ran away down a steep slope, killing many hundreds of men – witnessed by some Scottish troops in the vicinity – although it's all being hushed up.

There would in any event be the certainty of a long and stressful wait if they were to grind to a halt here. If this were to happen, and the Grand Fleet had to sail without its Admiral, heads would roll, and those might well be the heads of blameless men given impossible tasks. Meanwhile, most of the passengers go back to sleep, or perhaps start to think about the discomfort and dangers that await them at the end of the line. The older children, sensing the tension in those around them, look at each other, totally lost in a situation, not just beyond their experience, but beyond their imagination. Len and Douglas quickly go back to sleep.

After two relentless miles of working at the endurance limits of men and machines, the gradient starts to ease as the summit is approached. The situation quickly changes and the train starts to speed up - 20, 30 and 40 mph are reached as they move past the summit.

"Ye ken, ye're nae a bad driver – fer a Campbell", say Ally.

"Aye, and ye're nae a bad fireman – fer a MacDonald" says Jimmy, "but we're doon below 140 now, so ye need tae get back tae yer work, instead o' leaning on yer shovel." Ally grins as he opens up the firebox door and starts to build the fire up again.

They now enter Whitrope Tunnel – at 1,200 yards long, and 1,000 feet above sea level, this is the most daunting railway tunnel in Scotland. Notoriously wet and dank, it's a challenge for trains toiling up the gradient when heading south, but there's no problem now – unless one counts the horrendous conditions for the crews in their exposed cabs. Still, at least it's passed in just a minute or so, followed by easy running down the gradient to Hawick, 12 miles to the north, where the injured man is taken off to the hospital there. The signalman had warned them in advance and an ambulance is waiting at the station.

They quickly set off again, across flat and open country, followed by another climb up to the summit at Falahill. This one is not so bad and there are no holdups over this stretch, with the engines working hard and speed being maintained. After Falahill, there is a long descent down to Waverley station in Edinburgh. They drift smoothly into one of the premier cathedrals of the railway age – the largest station in Britain. In the twinkling pre-dawn light, the magnificent North British Hotel can be seen dominating the night skyline high above. It's now about 5 am and, as usual for the Jellicoe trains, the canteen here puts on a huge free breakfast for everyone, with plenty of porridge, tea, jam, scones, bacon etc, and even a haggis option – a real Scottish welcome. The passengers from most of the carriages, including the children, are delighted to take part, although there is not so much stirring by the officers and other notables in the handful of sleeper coaches. By 6 am, the whole circus is ready to roll again. The journey, at least for those going to the end of the line, is still not much more than half over.

5.5 Over the Forth Bridge

In fact, a sizeable proportion of the people on the train are now very close to their destination. The Forth Bridge, and the large naval base located in its shadow at Rosyth, are only about 10 miles away. The train slows down slightly as it approaches the magnificent structure, illuminated by the sun as it rises over the horizon on the North Sea. The weather has improved and it's now a sparkling spring day. As they start to cross the bridge, dozens of warships, large and small, can be seen at anchor below them in the estuary to the west.

Five coaches are to be detached here, including the sleepers containing David Beatty and his wife. He tends to spend a lot of his time here, despite the fact that the Grand Fleet is still based at Scapa. His wife would certainly never go that far north and in fact she regards even Edinburgh as being rather parochial and boring. Beatty also is much more at home here, where for several years he commanded his famous "Cats" - the buccaneering squadrons of high speed Battlecruisers. There're still here, now commanded by Rear-Admiral Richard Phillimore.

Meanwhile, the necessary train movements now need some attention. The train pulls into a siding just past the bridge and the set of coaches to be detached is uncoupled from the rest of the train. The senior guard now moves to the other brake coach and the guard who was there switches to the detached section. He'll stay with this set of coaches in Edinburgh, taking a break until it forms part of a sleeper heading south this evening. A tank engine is coupled up at what was the back and guides this detached set down the steep gradient towards the naval base and onto the private Admiralty siding next to the Naval Dockyard. The officers and other dignitaries finally stir from their slumber and walk across to their offices or nearby homes. The other ranks are herded across to their barracks, or in some cases straight onto their ship – the passengers have included a contingent on leave from HMS Repulse – the fastest large warship in the world, although with a reputation of tending to need quite a lot of dockyard attention. The whole area is already a hive of activity. It's the start of another day in the Royal Navy.

Fig.5.10: Map of the rail lines near the Forth Bridge in 1918.

5.6 Through the Highlands

The train moves on, now down to 11 coaches – still a heavy load, but less likely to be a real problem on steep grades, at least with two engines up front. There's still a long way for the train to go, so Jimmy and Ally push the speed up again as they navigate the tangle of tracks around Dunfermline and get onto the line heading for Perth, about 30 miles to the north. In fact, Jimmy and Ally will stop there, with control handed over to the Highland Railway. Engine crews still tend to stick with the locomotives and routes that they know, despite the fact that the whole railway system is now being run centrally. This makes sense, since there are many important points of detail that take years to learn. Only rarely have Jimmy and Ally ventured north of Perth, or driven engines other than those of the North British Railway.

As they pass through Kinross, Mina asks Jock about life in the Navy.

"What's it like being on a warship – it must be terrifying when other ships are firing at you?"

"Well, ye ken we hae little tae do most o' the time, but we stokers hae tae shift a lot of coal when the cap'n wants tae move fast, an' that happens a lot – mainly just tae keep the ship up tae scratch. Our own guns are fired a lot, just fer practice – we ken fer sure doon below when we fire a broadside – the whole ship heels over and th' noise is fit to wake th' dead. As fer being under fire, we hav'na had much o' that on the Duke. Just at Jutland, tae tell the truth, and we were nae hit then. Many other ships, ye ken, were hit many times. Anyway, ye need tae understand that most o' the crew, an' fur sure the stokers, cannae see or hear much in a fight. Ye dinna ken if a shell is on its way tae blow ye tae kingdom come. It happened tae thousands o' men at Jutland."

"Yes, one of our relatives, Frank Clyne, was on the Invincible."

"Ye dinna say. A lot of bonnie lads were lost on that ship – I didna' know many of them – she was based in Rosyth – but she was a brave wee ship fur sure. She blew up right in front of us – I cud'nae see anything, but the lads on deck saw her go, an' thought she was a Boche, so there were cheers as we went past. It was a sad day for the north of Scotland – many o' those who died were Highland lads. Still, we've nae seen much o' the Germans since then, an' they canna' get any cargo ships through – this will win the war fur us in the end. "

They soon drift slowly into Perth General station. It's still only about 7.30am. The children have been dozing, but they wake up as the train stops and a further change of engines gets under way. Jock and Harry again have a look at the operation.

"Harry – these are 4-6-0's again", Jock explains as the two new engines slowly back up against the train. "They're the famous 'Castle' class", he says, as they read off the numbers - 27 and 28 – and names – Thurso Castle and Cluny Castle. "They're the pride o' the Highland Railway." Harry writes all of this down in a little book, in which he's chronicling the journey.

"Doug – it's gud tae see ye again", Jock calls up – he seems to know all of these drivers.

"Jock – have ye had a gud break?" Doug calls down. "Back tae a bit o' sailing on the pond?"

"Aye, back tae freezin' our bollocks off in a Force 10, keepin' the likes o' ye an' yer sidekicks safe an' warm!"

"It's true, Jock, I wouldna' fancy bein' tossed around oot there – but I'll tell ye this – a couple o' months ago, we ran intae weather like I've nivver seen up in Caithness – drifts o' 15 foot. We got stuck at Altnabreac an' we were running very short o' coal. We were in real trouble, I can tell ye. It's lucky it was a Jellicoe, so a few hundred sailor lads could dig us out, but even then we could only go back – we had tae reverse all the way tae Helmsdale. We couldnae get through after that fer 10 days!"

"Aye, I mind that time well. When the storm sprang up, two destroyers were wrecked on the rocks trying tae get back into the Flow – just a single man survived out of 200. As it happens, I know him – Bill Sissons. He spent 36 hours in a cave on South Ronaldsay – as tough as they come. It was bad even inside the Flow. You couldnae see yer hand in front of yer face in that blizzard, which lasted fer a week. "

Doug notices that Harry is looking a little worried.

"Dinna fret, laddie – the weather is fine up there today!" Of course, he doesn't know that Harry is about to start living in that part of the world.

After the usual bustle of changing engines, legs being stretched, and a cacophony of whistling, the train sets

Fig.5.11: Map of the Highland Railway line between Perth and Inverness.

off to the north again. There are still a couple of sleeping cars in the train – one in the last three coaches, which will be detached at Invergordon and one in the remaining set of eight that will go all the way. However, virtually everyone is now up and about, and the restaurant car is again operational, having been restocked at Perth. Some of the officers gather there for breakfast. The scenery gets a little more spectacular as they start to enter the Highlands, skirting the flanks of the Cairngorm Mountains.

As they pass through Dunkeld and Birnam, on a bright spring morning, spirits rise throughout the train. Just after Pitlochry, they start to follow the River Garry, entering the beautiful gorge of Killiecrankie.

"Mina, how's yer knowledge o' history", asks Jock, "d'yer ken the name o' Killiecrankie?"

"I'm sorry, Jock, but I'm afraid that I've never heard of it. We didn't get taught very much history at school – and certainly very little about Scotland. Papa used to tell us a few things about his life up there, but not much about the past. Is this place famous?"

"Well, I would'na quite say that, but there was a time when things were in the balance an' there was a brave fight here a long while ago."

Jock goes on to give a very brief summary of the Jacobite Rebellion, when for several decades there was a lot of uncertainty about the inheritance of the English and Scottish crowns. It's a very complex story, but Jock does know a bit about it – Scots are often well-educated and they do take an interest in their own history. It was partly about religion and in 1688 James II (of England) and VII (of Scotland) had been King of England, Scotland and Ireland for 3 years. He was the latest of the Stuart Dynasty. He was also a staunch Catholic. Five countries were involved – England (largely Protestant, although with areas that remained loyally Catholic), Scotland (almost entirely "Church of Scotland" – ie Presbyterian), Ireland (strongly Catholic), France (Catholic, and always keen to create trouble for England) and Holland (largely Protestant).

The majority in England and Scotland simply wanted no trouble from their monarchs, and a reasonable level of religious tolerance. They were prepared to put up with James (aged 55), hoping that the succession would lead to someone who was less keen on Catholicism (and on the divine right of Kings). His daughter, Mary, a Protestant who had married William of Orange in Holland, was next in line. However, in 1688 a son was born to James – also called James, changing the line of succession to one who would be brought up as a Catholic. At the same time, James started to pass pro-Catholic decrees and was coming into serious conflict with the English and Scottish Parliaments. They decided to act and depose him, inviting William and Mary to take over the throne. This was enacted at the end of 1688 – the so-called "Glorious Revolution".

Fig.5.12: Photo of the railway viaduct at Killiecrankie.

James, who was based in Scotland, naturally reacted against this and made various attempts to raise armies against the Scottish Parliament. He had strong moral, and to some extent physical, support from France, and also from Ireland. He also had some support from Clansmen based in the Northern part of Scotland – Gaelic-speaking and often in conflict with Lowland Scots. A relatively small, but bitter, battle took place in the Killiecrankie Pass in the evening of 27th July 1689, when 2,500 Clansmen trapped about 4,000 Scottish government troops in the narrow (2 mile long) gorge of the fast-flowing River Garry. A traditional Highland charge with claymores led to about half of the government troops being killed or wounded, while only about 800 of the Highlanders were lost. Still, the Jacobites could ill afford to lose even that number of men, and it included their charismatic leader, John Graham. The Clansmen largely dispersed afterwards, taking some booty back to their homes. It wasn't a decisive event, but the bravery of the Highlanders was clear: Scottish folklore tends to revel in heroic, but doomed, causes. James was strongly supported by the French and was in exile there when he died in 1701, but his son, also James, continued to claim the throne – he became known as the Old Pretender. In fact, Jacobite resistance stuttered on for another half century or so, with various highs and lows. A son of James, called Charles (the Young Pretender), also claimed the right be king. These claims were wiped out with brutal finality after Culloden.

Passing through Killiecrankie Gorge doesn't attract any attention from most of the passengers – there are in fact relatively few Scotsmen on the train, and Jock is slightly unusual in spending his leave time in England. Up front, the engine crews knuckle down in preparation for the most testing part of their stint. They now face the rigours of the 15 mile run up to Druimuachdar (pronounced Drum-ACH-ter) summit, climbing by over 1,000 feet – an average gradient of about 1 in 75, with a long stretch steeper than 1 in 70. At 1,484 feet, Druimuachdar is the highest point in the entire British railway network. This is also the most demanding climb – there are a few short sections elsewhere that are steeper than this, although they're often routinely tackled with a powerful banker engine, but there's nothing with quite this combination of length and gradient – the climb to Whitrope is similar, but a bit shorter.

The train now has fewer coaches, and the weather is better, but this still presents a challenge, and a need for a "clear road". This is provided, and these engines have been designed for this task, so they are able to climb steadily with the speed dropping only slowly. As they pass through Blair Atholl, and the gradient starts to bite, the scenery changes sharply, becoming much bleaker and more desolate. There are no trees in this region. Snow-covered peaks start to appear on both sides and soon the whole area around the train is covered in snow. Both engines are working hard as they finally breast the summit, with speed having dropped to about 25 mph. Doug and his footplate colleagues can now start to relax. The children have seen snow before, but these mountains, and this bleak pass between them, is a new sight for them.

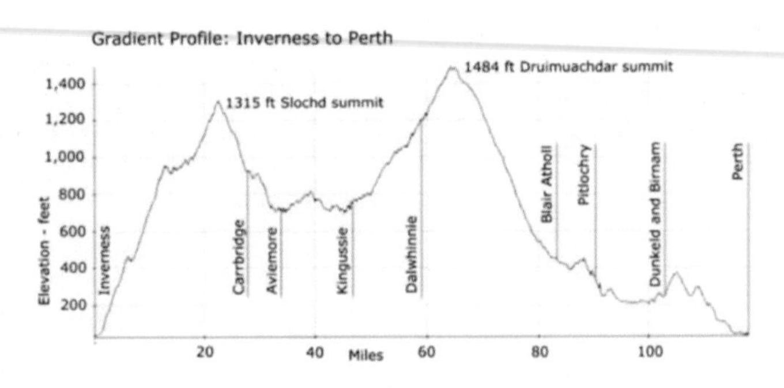

Fig.5.13: Gradient profile between Perth and Inverness.

As they reach the summit, they come to the end (or rather the beginning) of the River Garry, which they've been following for 20 miles. This is a watershed and they now start to follow the River Truim as they descend. This whole stretch is desolate and, as they pass below the snowline again, the peat and scrubland show no trace of colour at this time of year. They enter the valley of the River Spey a little further down, around Kingussie. These streams, which pick up a hint of peat, are well-suited for whisky production and there are several distilleries in these valleys, starting with the one at Dalwhinnie - built 20 years ago. These establishments do attract the attention of some on the train, since many of the passengers are whisky drinkers, if not connoisseurs. Soon they're passing through Aviemore, where the Highland Railway has recently built the Aviemore Hotel. The area is starting to acquire a reputation within Scotland's embryonic tourism industry.

After Aviemore, the train takes the line towards Inverness, and a further climb. This is up to the Slochd summit - another challenge for the engine crews. While not quite as high as Druimuachdar, and involving less of a change in height, there is an ascent of 400 feet over a distance of 5 miles, giving an average gradient of about 1 in 65. This also has to be taken very seriously – it's tougher than the Shap and Beattock banks, or even the "long drag" from Settle to Blea Moor (15 miles at 1 in 100). Nevertheless, these two powerful engines take it in their stride. After that, steam can almost be shut off completely during the descent to Inverness, although parts of that section are a challenge for trains heading south.

A few miles before Inverness, they pass the rather bleak station at Culloden Moor. The historical battle there is better known than the skirmish at Killiecrankie. On 16th April 1746, the Jacobite army of Charles Stuart, the grandson of James II & VII, was slaughtered by a stronger and better-equipped British government force – Scotland and England having been joined by the Act of Union in 1707 – under the Duke of Cumberland. The battle only lasted an hour, but around 2,000 Jacobites were killed or wounded in that time, while there were only 300 casualties on the British side. Both French and Irish troops were in the Jacobite army and the French also provided weaponry. Although about 5,000 Jacobites were left after the battle, they quickly dispersed, effectively ending the rising. A brutal operation ensued over the following weeks and months, with Highlanders being ruthlessly pursued and the whole Clan system being undermined.

Charles himself ("Bonnie Prince Charlie" of the story-telling) got away and hid in the Western Isles for several months, managing to evade pursuing government troops - partly via a boat trip to Skye with Flora MacDonald. He eventually escaped to France and never returned to Scotland. The French were still keen to see a Catholic on the British throne, although, failing that, they were also interested in generally causing problems for the English. The much-vaunted plan for them to land an army in the south, while the Jacobite army moved down from the north, never quite materialized. Their support, while considered important by the Jacobites, was always going to be a very negative factor for the vast majority of British people.

The whole saga is rather tragic, since the only real division between the sides was that they had decided to support different claimants to the throne. Religion was relevant, but it wasn't really a clash between supporters of different religions – very few of the Highlanders were Catholics. For these Scots, it was more a way of expressing their independence, and their personal loyalty within their Clans. In any event, the Highlands were subsequently brought properly under the rule of law of Britain, albeit slowly and reluctantly – their independent, but unsustainable, family-based system had to be modified if they were to move into modern times. Jock explains a bit of this to Mina, although the attitude of Highland Scots like him to their history has always been a mixed and complex one. As the train steams into Inverness, Mina wonders about the nature of this proud, but slightly strange, society into which they are apparently to be integrated.

Fig.5.14: Southbound train, headed by a Highland Railway Castle class 4-6-0, about to leave Inverness station in 1906.

"By the way, Mina", says Jock, "we Sinclairs are a canny bunch! We've always been the staunchest o' Scots. The Bruce would nivver have won at Bannockburn without us. We were also right behind the Jacobites for most o' the time. Still, just before Culloden, we switched sides, an' we fought there with the English. We cud' see which way the wind were blowin' an' it meant that we did well in the aftermath. Ye ken that our current Head, Archie Sinclair, owns a quarter o' Caithness – an' the best quarter at that! We ken well how tae survive in this part o' the world!"

5.7 To the End of the Line

At Inverness, which is a terminus station, a rather complicated set of movements is needed, using a triangle of lines, to get the engines at the front, facing the right way, and with the coaches in the same order – this will facilitate dropping off the last three shortly. The water tanks also need to be refilled here. The operation therefore takes a while. This is built into the schedule and in fact they'll be here for almost an hour. This is partly because Inverness is another station that takes pride in looking after the people on this train. A lunch is provided free for all of them, as for every Jellicoe Express. It's again a traditional hearty Scottish meal, with haggis now figuring quite strongly, but plenty of alternatives – the canteen managers do appreciate that most of the passengers are not actually Scottish. It's another new experience for the children, by now established as celebrities in the midst of these hundreds of sailors. By the time that they're ready to leave again, it's about 11.15am.

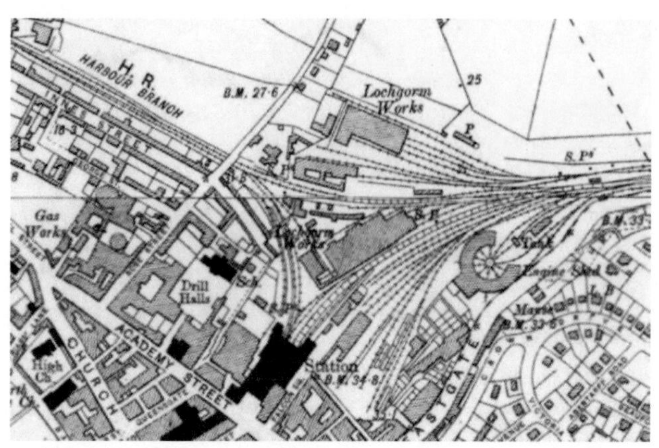

Fig.5.15: Rail layout of Inverness station around 1918.

There is a large naval base about 30 miles beyond Inverness, which is journey's end for another contingent on the train. This is Invergordon, located in an outstanding natural harbour. They set off again, passing through junction stations such as Beanly, Muir of Ord and Dingwall (for the Kyle of Lochalsh, on the West Coast). They're now skirting the beautiful Cromarty Firth, with views across the water to The Black Isle. They're soon pulling into Invergordon station, which is very close to the naval port facilities. This area has grown enormously since the start of the war and it now includes accommodation for many thousands of military personnel,

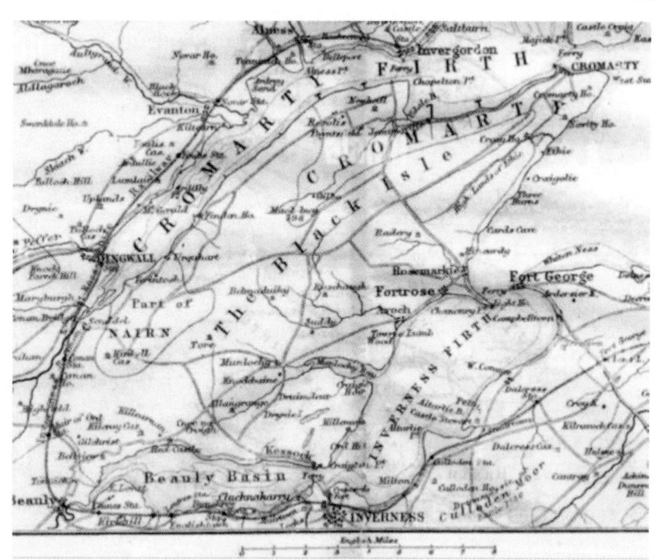

Fig.5.16: Map of 1887, showing the rail route from Inverness to Invergordon.

huge storage tanks for fuel oil, extensive docking facilities and anchorage for dozens of warships.

The last three coaches of the train are detached here, along with about 200 men. A few of them walk up to the front of the train to say goodbye to the children and wish them well. There is some concern here about the recent outbreak of influenza ("Spanish 'Flu"), with there reputedly being over 25,000 men in the base who have come down with it and are being quarantined. In any event, those from the train are able to walk quickly to their quarters. The train, now down to 8 coaches, leaves at around midday. There's still another 120 miles to go for the 500 or so rather weary sailors still aboard, plus 5 very tired children.

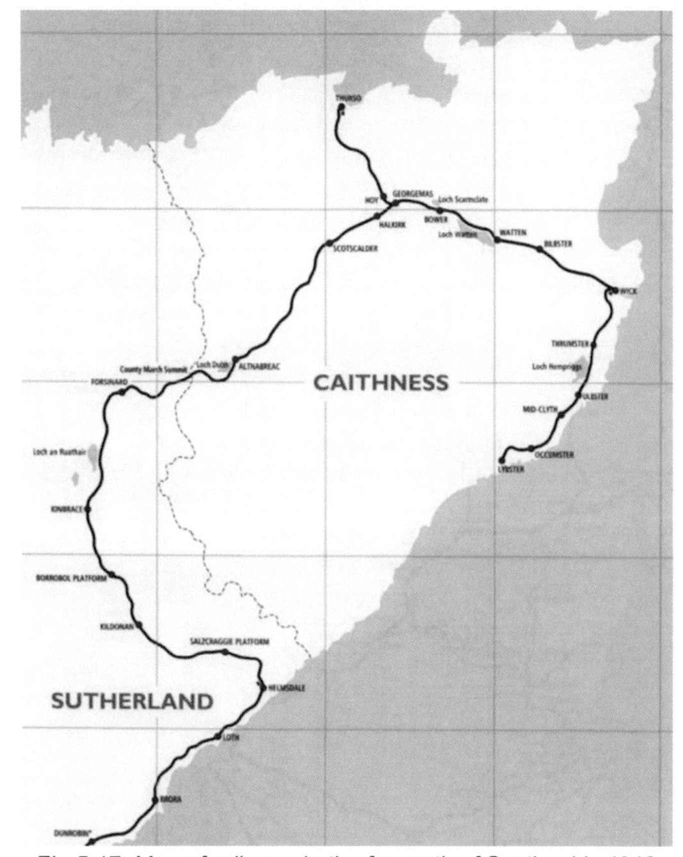

Fig.5.17: Map of railways in the far north of Scotland in 1918.

The next stretch is very circuitous, as the line makes a big detour inland around Dornoch Firth and the Kyle of Sutherland. They make rapid progress, racing along through flat open farmland, with yellow gorse lining the track along much of its length. They pass the golf course at Tain, pleased to see some sort of normality in the form of people playing on the links, although there are no young men amongst them. They eventually cross the Kyle on the beautiful viaduct at Invershin. The countryside around here is very attractive and memories of the desolate Highlands between Killiecrankie and Inverness start to fade. They reach the coast again at Golspie, from where the line runs alongside stretches of beautiful (completely deserted) sandy beaches.

They soon move slightly inland and pass through the station at Dunrobin, where there's a short (private) drive down to the famous castle on the seafront. This is the ancestral seat of the Sutherland Clan and the Dukes of Sutherland (and, previously, the Earls of Sutherland). They were closely involved with the building of the railways through this region, and also with attempting to promote industrial developments in the area. Prominent among these is the coal-mine at Brora - just a few

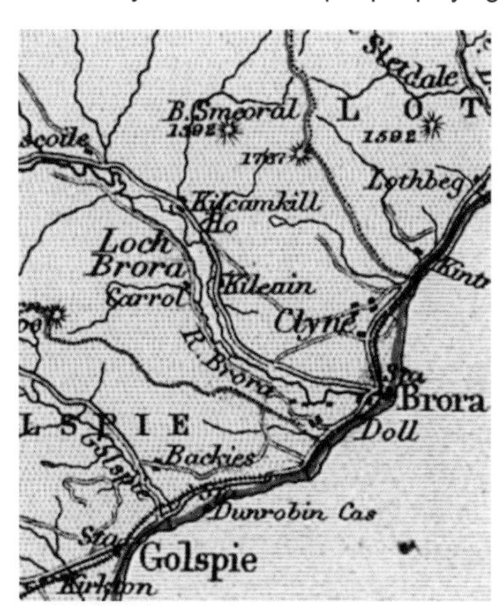

Fig.5.18: Map showing the region around Brora.

miles further on, with the track now hugging the coast again. As they pass through Brora station, the winding-house of the mine is visible, a few hundred yards away, from where a short branch runs up to a junction with the main line. This is one of the few examples in the far north of Scotland of the kind of industrial development that has become so important in much of the rest of Britain, including the lowland areas of Scotland.

In fact, attempts to mine the (small) coalfield here date back hundreds of years, because a seam reaches the surface close to the beach and has thus long been visible to the locals. Unfortunately, the coal is not of very good quality, being contaminated with high levels of sulphur and iron pyrites. It doesn't burn so well, but it's also prone to ignite spontaneously. Nevertheless, after a half-century of closure, the 2nd Duke of Sutherland, who had inherited vast wealth via other family connections in England, provided the funds for it to be reopened, almost 50 years ago (in 1872). While never profitable, it has been operating ever since, providing many economic benefits for the area.

The proximity of clay deposits, and also of the sea, has led to the creation of a large brickworks nearby, and to the setting up of salt-pans next to the seashore - both activities being dependent on the supply of coal from the mine. Bricks from here have been important in improving the quality of buildings in the Far North, while the salt is extensively used for the preservation of herring caught around the coast of Caithness. There have also been other spin-off benefits. Brora was the first place north of Inverness to have electricity, which was first generated about 5 years ago - using steam generators powered by coal from the mine. Electricity has been used for street lighting, and for some other purposes, ever since. Brora is known, at least locally, as "The Electric City".

Fig.5.19: Photo of Brora mine, taken in the 1960's.

Immediately after passing through Brora, Mina is excited to see a sign on the left pointing to the village of East Clyne, which is apparently a cluster of house on a gorse-covered hillside, with spectacular views of the sea a mile or so away.

"Jock", says Mina, "Papa told us that there was somewhere round here with our name. This must be it."

"Aye, and ye ken that it's nae just a couple of wee villages – the whole Parish round here is called Clyne. Yer kinfolk are well known in these parts, an' have been for a long while. There's a big pit a couple of miles away called the Clynelish Quarry, and there's even a unique kind of stone found there, called Clynestone. Also, I'll let ye into another wee secret, which might interest a few more people. The building ye can see just up that road is the Clynelish Whisky Distillery – started a hundred years ago and it's one o' the oldest (and best) in Scotland. Mostly they blend with other brands, but real connoisseurs know that the Clynelish 14-year single malt is the best."

Mina takes all this in and is starting to feel more positive about the whole venture – the countryside around here is beautiful and it doesn't seem to be such a primitive place. They continue to follow the coast, reaching another sizeable settlement at Helmsdale. The line turns sharply to the left here, away from the coast, hugging the west bank of the River Helmsdale. It immediately becomes clear that there are very few people living along this beautiful valley, although there is evidently a lot of fertile land alongside the river – most of it being grazed by sheep. There are a few houses, but most of them are derelict and deserted. This region provides a good illustration of the effect of the Clearances, which took place between the late 18th Century and the mid 19th Century. While they were particularly dramatic and cruel in the Western Isles, and in Ross and Cromarty, they also happened extensively in Sutherland – mostly controlled by the Earls and Dukes of Sutherland, who have long owned much of the county. In fact, this valley (Strath Kildonan) was for centuries a thriving and well-populated place, but most of the people here were compelled to move to the Helmsdale area on the coast, to survive as best they could. The few stations along this stretch of line are completely deserted, apparently in the middle of nowhere.

Fig.5.20: The west bank of the River Helmsdale in 2022, showing an area dedicated to sheep farming and the ruins of an abandoned house dating from the early 19th Century.

Areas such as Strath Kildonan originally supported a reasonably large population, farming the land in small strips under the “run rig” system, with shared grazing for their Highland Cattle. However, as the old patriarchal Clan system began to break down after Culloden, the position of the Chieftains started to change. They had more contact with well-to-do Lowland Scots and English, who were becoming rich as the Industrial Revolution gathered pace towards the end of the 18th Century. The pressures on them to get better returns from their landholdings began to build up and they started to act more like conventional landlords, rather than paternal heads of large families. It also became clear that they could get much better returns by letting their lands to people who would use them to graze large flocks of sheep. The markets for wool, and also for mutton and lamb, were becoming substantial. Of course, this was incompatible with having large numbers of subsistence farmers living on the land.

Furthermore, the previous value of the members of a Clan to the Chieftain, in the form of periodically providing military force, more or less disappeared. These changes led inexorably to many people in the Scottish Highlands and Islands being forcibly evicted from the land. The details of what happened differed between different parts, and it’s true that some landlords tried to reduce the hardships faced by their tenants. In fact, the Dukes of Sutherland, and also the Duchess, who was very influential in the early decades of the 19th Century, did try to help provide employment and resources for the people being displaced – as evidenced by their injection of huge amounts of money into the mine at Brora, initially around the beginning of the 19th Century and again later. Nevertheless, in common with many other landlords, they did forcibly evict many people. The whole saga of the Clearances can be expressed in just a few stark sentences.

The tenants were forced off their small-holdings, to which they had no legal right under British law. They were moved to “crofts” (small cottages) created for them, mostly on the coast. Surviving on what they could grow in much smaller plots than previously was often impossible. They were mostly expected to make ends meet by also collecting kelp (seaweed – used in making glass and soap) or by fishing. Kelp was a good cash crop for a while, particularly in the Western Isles, but the price collapsed after the end of the Napoleonic Wars in 1815 and never recovered. Potato blight reached Scotland in the late

1840's, hitting the main source of homegrown food for "crofters". The famine wasn't quite a bad as that in Ireland, mainly because most were able to obtain at least some fish and shellfish, but it was similarly devastating. Many crofters became destitute and a lot of them were left with the sole option of emigration – often to the United States or Canada. Landlords often assisted with the cost of this. The overall population fell sharply, particularly in the interior. Survival was precarious for many crofters, with them often needing, not only to grow what they could on their tiny plots, but also to spend part of the year elsewhere – fishing off the coast of Caithness in the summer, where herring catches were good for many years, or perhaps working as domestics in large houses further south. Much of the 19th Century was a terrible time for these people. While the Clans survived as a concept, and family members certainly continued to help each other, the previous hierarchy, and the strict allegiance owed to the head of a Clan, largely disappeared.

In fact, things have improved somewhat over the past quarter of a century. By the 1880's, the crofters finally began to rebel against the unbelievably cruel and unfair treatment to which they had been subjected during the previous hundred years. They also started to receive political support in the South, as communications improved, and also as the Land League set up in Ireland led to at least slight alleviation of the (rather similar) mistreatments to which many Irish "share-croppers" had been subjected. There have been reforms to the law concerning ownership of land and other issues relevant to the life of crofters, although there has still been no large-scale repopulation of interior regions. Extreme hunger is no longer so common, and nor are people forced to emigrate against their wishes (although it's still true that many young people still decide to move South, or possibly to leave the country).

"Jock", asks Mina, who of course knows nothing of any of this, "Why is this place so quiet? Does nobody live around here?"

"As ye can see, there's mostly just sheep here – they dinnae need much care", replies Jock. "The people that used tae live here moved tae the coast a long while ago."

"Why does the line come this way?", asks Mina. "Were there people still here when it was built?"

"Tae tell the truth, they'd mostly moved before the trains came, but there was hope that building the line intae these parts would help tae open up the interior to people agin'. Sadly, it has'nae happened so far."

The train moves on, climbing into an area that again starts to look rather bleak and windswept. This is the Flow Country – mostly composed of peat bog, with rolling hills and a few high peaks. There are dozens of small lakes (lochs) and the whole area is very poorly drained. There are no trees. As they reach the higher levels, there is again a lot of snow on the ground. In fact, there are snow barriers along the sides of the track, clearly designed to stop deep drifts from impeding the passage of trains. There are a few stations, but they're all in the middle of nowhere – they're really just passing places, where the track is doubled for a short distance. Shortly after passing through Forsinard ("Frozen 'Ard" to railway men, referring mainly to problems with the points), they reach the summit of this stretch of line and pass from Sutherland to Caithness. This part of Caithness is different from the rest of the Highlands. There weren't any "Clearances" here. Much of it is peat bog and nobody has ever lived here. However, in the North-Eastern part of the county there has long been a small, but close-knit and thriving, population – the land is more fertile, there are some substantial stone quarries and fishing has been an important industry in the area for well over a hundred years. Nevertheless, as the train starts to go through Caithness, even recognizing that there is a stark beauty in the wide skies and distant hills, it's undeniably desolate. There aren't even any deserted stations. There's simply nothing here and the train seems lost as the track meanders through the wilderness.

"Are we going to the end of the earth, Jock?" asks Mina eventually, almost wondering if there really is such a place.

"Dinna fret, lassie – there's some brave villages and towns near the end of the line, and some good people waiting there who'll do a famous job o' looking after ye all", says Jock, offering up a silent prayer that this will in fact be what happens.

Eventually, they pass through a station called Halkirk. There's also nothing here, although they can see a few scattered houses about a mile to the north. They don't stop, but a few minutes later they steam slowly into a station called Georgemas and come to a halt. There's also nothing here – the hamlet of Georgemas is some distance away. However, this is where the lines to Wick and Thurso divide. It's now about 3pm and they're nearing the end of this long journey. In fact, the line that they're currently on continues to Wick, with a reversing operation being needed to go in the direction of Thurso. The engines therefore need to run around the train here, since the destination for the sailors is the harbour of Scrabster, which is a couple of miles from Thurso station. There'll be lorries waiting there when they arrive, and a small warship in the harbour at Scrabster, ready to take them to Scapa Flow.

Fig.5.21: Georgemas station in 1912. The train on the left is leaving for the south. On the right, the engine at the end of the platform is taking on water, before its short trip along the branch line to Thurso.

The plan is for the children to be picked up from Georgemas station. It's not, however, a very well-defined plan, since communications have been far from easy. Mina's understanding is that a couple of fairly distant cousins will pick them up – a brother and a sister who are not so very much older than she is – about 18-20, although they are living on their own and they apparently have some room in their house. The children aren't really sure where they live. It also turns out that there is some uncertainty on their side and they're not entirely clear about how many children are involved – they certainly don't think that it's as many as five, although it's always been understood that Mina herself would probably return to London quite promptly. The children therefore don't know quite what to expect and, as they look around them on the platform in the gathering gloom, there doesn't seem to be anyone here. Jock reassures them that he'll stay with them until someone arrives, or at least make sure that someone like the stationmaster has taken them in hand. However, after a few anxious minutes, while the engines are still moving to the other end of the train, two figures do loom out of the mist. Jock stays to check that these are indeed their new guardians – John Don Dunnet and Lizzie Dunnet. The Dunnet family is well-known, and extensive, in these parts. Jock has a quick chat with them before taking his leave of them all and climbing back into the train.

Chapter 6: Into the Roaring Twenties (March 1918 – August 1932)

6.1 Culture Shock

John Don Dunnet and his sister are a little shocked to see that there are 5 children waiting on the platform – they thought that there would be just two or three. John assumed that the older ones had just accompanied the younger ones on the journey, and indeed this is effectively what Mina turns out to have done, but the initial impression is that all five need somewhere to stay. He has been in touch with Frank, who'd joined the Seaforth Highlanders almost 3 years ago. John is in the same regiment, in the Transport Corps, although he only joined recently and they've not actually met – in any event, Frank is based further south. They'd only communicated by letter and it had all been a bit confused. Still, he'd been keen to help, and his sister had also felt that they should do this – there are long-standing links between the Dunnet and Clyne families, although the former tend to be based in the North of Caithness, while the latter have their ancestral base along the South-eastern coastline of both Caithness and Sutherland.

Fig.6.1: Map of the region around the Parish of Bower.

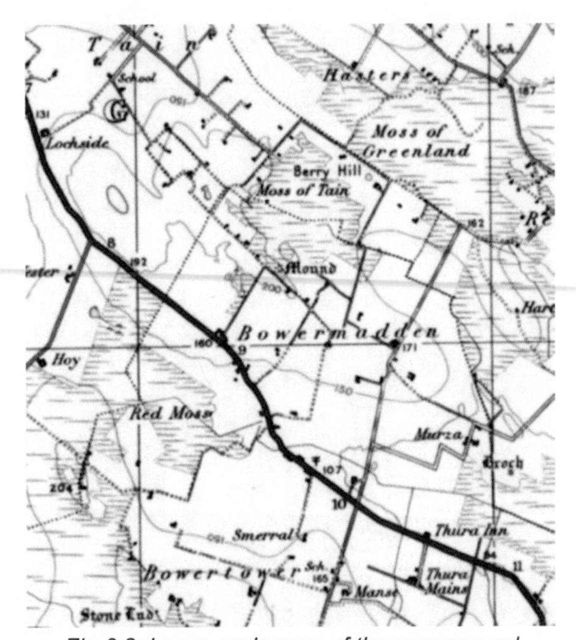

Fig.6.2: Large scale map of the area around Bowermadden in the 1920s.

The Dunnets have brought a small horse and cart, borrowed from a neighbouring farmer, and they manage to get everyone on board, plus their luggage – fortunately, they just have a small suitcase each, with Len and Douglas sharing one. The Dunnets' house is in Bowermadden, which is about 8 miles away. The journey takes an hour and it's starting to get dark by the time they arrive. Bowermadden is a tiny hamlet with just two very short streets – Auchorn Square and Thura Place, although there are also a few scattered houses and farms nearby. The population of the immediate area is just a couple of hundred souls. There are no shops or other businesses. There is, however, a church, which is just a stone's throw away – Bower Holy Rood Church. This serves the whole Parish of Bower, which covers quite a large area, but has a population of only about 1,200. (It was 1,500 thirty years ago.) It's also the location of Bower Parish Primary School. Unlikely as it sounds, Bowermadden is the largest collection of houses in the Parish.

John and his sister have inherited the tenancy of a house, although he is working on improving it: he's already a skilled carpenter and bricklayer. They have a traditional broth waiting to be heated up on the stove – a recent acquisition - and they sit around the small table and make a hearty meal of this, together with some home-made bread, by the light of a paraffin lamp. There's plenty to discuss, but the children are very tired and a sleeping arrangement is sorted out for everyone, deferring everything to the next morning.

Fig.6.3: John and Lizzie Dunnet with their mother in 1905.

This is a very remote and quiet place. Having been used to life in London, it creates a profound culture shock for the children. There is a barrel to collect rainwater, but water for drinking has to be collected from a small stream about 100 yards away. Heating is from burning of peat. Still, at least they have a secure place to sleep and eat. Mina rapidly decides, however, that she can't possibly stay here. She only has a further year or so of schooling left and the idea of spending it here seems outlandish. Stan has said that she's welcome to come back down to stay with him, and return to the school in St. Paul's Cray, and this seems the sensible thing to do. They'll certainly be able to find somewhere to live down there, one way or another. She's perfectly capable of travelling back down on her own. She might even be able to sort out another trip on a Jellicoe Express. She sets about organizing this and John Don doesn't try to discourage her – he's wondering how he's going to feed and clothe 4 children, never mind 5.

Fig.6.4: John Don Dunnet in 1918, as a member of the Transport Division, 5th Battalion of the Seaforth Highlanders.

One of the first things to sort out is schooling for the other children. There are actually four (very small) schools in the Parish of Bower – the Scots set great store by education and the Parish Council are very supportive. The children will attend Bower Parish Primary School, which is in a hall that is part of the Parish Church, and hence just a stone's throw away. This is very helpful, since walking any distance in the winter in this part of the world would be very challenging for young children. Len is keen not to be left at home for too long and it's agreed that he'll start in the autumn, when he'll be 4.

Life in Bowermadden settles into a stable pattern. For John Don and Lizzie, it's a big change to suddenly be responsible for four children. They're well-behaved, but recent events have been very traumatic for them. Lena has always taken a very maternal attitude to the two young boys, so Douglas and Len still feel a measure of security. It's not so easy for Harry to adjust, since, as a 12-year old, he has become more accustomed to life in London. The minimum school leaving age in Scotland is 14. The 1918 Education (Scotland) Act introduces the principle of universal free secondary education, allowing pupils to stay on until an age when they could progress to University, although in fact this isn't to be properly implemented for a couple of decades. What the Act does do is bring the various religiously-oriented schools into a uniform state-funded system. The schools in Bower Parish only take children up to the age of 14. There are schools in places like Wick and Thurso that take children beyond that age. The nearest such school is actually in Castletown, which is about 5 miles to the North-West of Bowermadden, and it turns out that Len will switch to there when he reaches that age.

Fig.6.5: Photo of the Dunnets' house in Bowermadden, taken in 1914. The people in front of the house have not been identified.

Fig.6.6: Bower Parish Primary School photo, taken in 1912, with the Parish Church in the background.

Fig.6.7: Bower Parish Church in 2022. Bowermadden is about 100 yards along the road to the left.

In fact, Castletown is important for the people in Bowermadden, since it's the nearest settlement of any size, having about 1,000 inhabitants. It's relatively prosperous. In addition to the school, there's a post office, a bank, a hotel, a library, a reading room and three churches. Its main commercial activities centre around the large quarry located between the town and the coast, which produces high quality Caithness flagstone that is exported all over Britain, and indeed also to Europe and America. Easy access downhill to the small harbour at Castlehill facilitates this. Several hundred people are employed in this business. However, the industry is now somewhat in decline, as the production of concrete paving slabs starts to ramp up in many places around the world. The beautiful 2-mile long sandy beach of Dunnet Bay, adjacent to Castletown, starts just beyond the harbor, next to the large Castletown Mill (powered by the Stanergill Burn), which is still being used for grinding of corn. The houses are largely built from local stone. Castletown Football Club is one of the strongest in the area, with a good pitch and facilities.

Fig.6.8: A large piece of local layered flagstone on the beach at Castletown in 2022, with the sweep of the initial part of Dunnet Bay visible in the background.

Travel to Castletown from Bowermadden, at least for most of its inhabitants, is either by bike or on foot – a good hour and a half's walk. This is along a road that is little more than a grassy track. It's fairly straight and level, with a slight rise about half way along. On reaching this point, on a clear day, a fantastic view is revealed of Castletown to the left and the beautiful curve of Dunnet Bay to the right, ending in the dramatic cliffs of Dunnet Head. It's an uplifting landmark during the trip, although of course the weather isn't always good.

The children start to adapt to their new way of life. The house is not large, and there's some sharing of beds, but it's more comfortable and solid than many of the crofts and other dwellings that are common in some parts of the Highlands. They have a small plot of land, on which vegetables are cultivated. Potatoes are the main crop, but several other vegetables are also grown, such as leeks. As they move into summer, daylight hours get longer, and the weather is often pleasant, but they all understand that the winters are going to be hard. Every house needs a supply of peat for heating in the winter. This is tackled on a communal basis, with groups of families doing the cutting together in the summer and then stocks being left to dry out before being stored. The children are expected to contribute to tasks like this, of which there are several, but they're happy to do so.

Fig.6.9: Peat cutting in Caithness around 1920.

There is a railway station that is nominally called Bower, but it's a long way from any habitation and it's about 8 miles from Bowermadden. (Most railway companies have a long-standing tradition of choosing routes dictated by the lie of the land and then putting stations at points as close as possible to small towns and villages, although in many cases they're not close at all: the Highland Railway has been particularly bad in this respect, especially in remote areas.) Thurso is about the same distance away. The train therefore isn't so useful to people in Bowermadden for local travel, although, once Thurso has been reached, it's easy to get to Wick, or indeed to travel to the south – perhaps even as far as the metropolis of Inverness, about 150 miles away by train – this is just about feasible as a day trip, although it's not a cheap one.

There are a few buses (and taxis) in the area, but they're rare - and not to become common for another decade or so. There are, however, a relatively large number of bicycles in the area, with establishments that sell and maintain them starting to appear in several of the towns in Caithness. There are currently two bikes in the Dunnet household and in due course the children will all get their own. Most of the roads, however, are rather rough and ready – mainly designed for horse and cart, and potentially hazardous after dark even for those. Walking or cycling the 5 miles to the beach at Dunnet Bay is an attractive prospect for a sunny summer weekend, although sea temperatures are such that actual bathing is only for the hardy.

There are thus options for occasional visits to the attractions of a sizeable town, but it's not something to be done easily or frequently. Day-to-day living has to be very self-contained, and focused on the most basic requirements. They also appreciate that, while it will be possible for them to receive visitors from the south, and in particular to see Mina and their elder brothers occasionally, this also is likely to be relatively rare. Of course, while the war goes on, even that kind of thing is not going to be possible. Although the war now seems a long way away, they all appreciate the importance of it coming to an end.

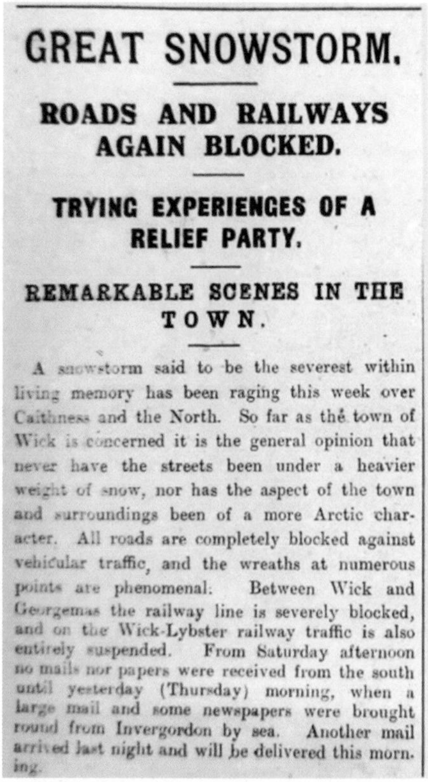

GREAT SNOWSTORM.

ROADS AND RAILWAYS AGAIN BLOCKED.

TRYING EXPERIENCES OF A RELIEF PARTY.

REMARKABLE SCENES IN THE TOWN.

A snowstorm said to be the severest within living memory has been raging this week over Caithness and the North. So far as the town of Wick is concerned it is the general opinion that never have the streets been under a heavier weight of snow, nor has the aspect of the town and surroundings been of a more Arctic character. All roads are completely blocked against vehicular traffic, and the wreaths at numerous points are phenomenal. Between Wick and Georgemas the railway line is severely blocked, and on the Wick-Lybster railway traffic is also entirely suspended. From Saturday afternoon no mails nor papers were received from the south until yesterday (Thursday) morning, when a large mail and some newspapers were brought round from Invergordon by sea. Another mail arrived last night and will be delivered this morning.

Fig.6.10: Article in the John O'Groats Journal of 18th January 1918.

6.2 The Spring Offensive and the End of the War

As far as the course of the war is concerned, two pivotal events took place during the previous year. One was the entry of the Americans on the side of the Allies, in April 1917. The American President, Thomas Woodrow Wilson, had long been reluctant, but the pressure of public opinion, particularly after the sinking of the Lusitania and other loss of civilian lives from the German campaign of submarine attacks, had become very strong. By now, substantial numbers of American troops are starting to arrive in Europe. The other development relates to Russia. The Russians have lost huge numbers of men and their economy is in a state of collapse. This, and a lot of previous episodes that created widespread dissatisfaction with Tsar Nicholas II, led to the Russian Revolution and to him being deposed, in March 1917 (and to his murder, and that of his wife and children, the following year). Initially, the Provisional Government that took over the country made no changes in policy regarding the war. However, factions in the revolutionary movement (often termed the Bolsheviks, meaning "of the majority") seized control in October 1917, with the promise to secure peace (and also "land and bread"). Central to this movement was Vladimir Lenin (and also Leon Trotsky). Initially, Lenin was in exile in Switzerland, but the Germans were understandably keen on his policy and they arranged for him to be taken secretly to Russia in a sealed train. Once in power, Lenin made good on his promise to pull Russia out of the war, with the details being formalized by the Treaty of Brest-Litovsk, signed on 3rd March 1918. It ceded huge areas to the Germans and also involved large payments in gold being made to them. Moreover, the Germans knew that this was coming and they made preparations for a huge switch of resources from the Eastern to the Western front. This, then, is the German background to their Spring Offensive – millions of men, and huge amounts of materiel, being freed up and the knowledge that, if they don't move quickly, then the arrival of massive American reinforcements in the near future is likely to swing the course of the war away from them.

What follows is a desperate time for the British and French. A ferocious attack starts on 21st March, preceded by the largest artillery barrage of the war – over a million shells are fired. Elite German troops are in the forefront and they penetrate rapidly into British and

French lines, aided by a heavy mist on the first morning. Casualties are high on all sides. The 7th and 8th Battalions of the Royal West Kents are among those that are completely overwhelmed and virtually wiped out over the following few days. Casualty rates exceed even those incurred during previous ill-conceived ventures. However, the resistance that they and other Battalions put up takes a heavy toll on the attacking forces. As the German infantry advances, supply lines become stretched and their tactic of penetrating deeply at weak points in the British and French lines leaves them vulnerable to flank attacks. Their momentum, apparently irresistible initially, slowly falls off and the attack peters out over the next 3 months. Their territorial gains are small and their casualty level of about 700,000, while slightly lower than that of the Allies, leaves them greatly weakened. In contrast, while the Allies also lose many men, the growing flood of American troops and equipment more than compensates for this.

A massive counter-attack by the Allies now follows – the so-called "Hundred Days Offensive", which starts in early August. This turns out to be different from virtually all of the previous battles in Europe, with the Germans quickly being forced into virtually continuous retreat. Combined forces of French, British, Australian and Canadian troops, together with over 500 tanks – now a fully-developed weapon, pour forward near Amiens on 8th August, against an exhausted and demoralized enemy. The long sea blockade has taken a terrible toll, with not only the civilian population of Germany being on the brink of starvation, but the soldiers also going hungry.

Fig.6.11: British tank and troops near Amiens in August 1918.

Over the next two days, there are 75,000 German casualties, including 50,000 taken prisoner. Their allies of the Austro-Hungarian and Ottoman Empires have already capitulated, or are about to do so. Their military leaders, Erich Ludendorff and Paul von Hindenburg, are on the verge of mental breakdown and many in the army and navy are close to rebellion, with the attractions of communism being widely promoted. The Spring Offensive has been their last, desperate throw of the dice. While the Central Powers might have been able to achieve a negotiated peace earlier in the year, it's now clear to the Allies that they need settle for nothing less than unconditional surrender. Kaiser Wilhelm resists to the last, but on November 9th the German Chancellor, Prince Max von Baden, announces the abdication of the Kaiser anyway, effectively surrendering on behalf of the country. The Armistice is signed in a railway carriage in France just two days later. It is pure coincidence that the guns fall silent at 11am on the 11th day of the 11th month.

Fig.6.12: German prisoners near Amiens on 9th Aug.1918.

There are many issues to be resolved and arrangements to be

made. There is widespread agreement that major changes are needed, such that no war like this can ever happen again. There are strong feelings, particularly from the French, that the Germans must be totally emasculated – made to pay huge reparations and deprived of land and resources. The French leader, Georges Clemenceau, is particularly outspoken on this. Others, particularly Woodrow Wilson, take a more measured stance, insisting that the Germans must not be driven into desperate straits. The British Prime Minister, David Lloyd George, sympathizes with the French, but wants to remain on good terms with the Americans. Initial anti-German feelings are strong in Britain, but tend to fall off a little with time, as people focus more on the future, with some recognizing that the economies of Europe, particularly the markets in Germany, Austria etc, need to recover if prosperity is to return.

Looming large in the minds of many Western leaders are the dangers of communism. In fact, in parts of Germany, communist movements are already strong and there are inclinations in this direction in France and Britain. It is decided that a major Peace Conference is needed, at which most of the many nations involved in the war, at least on the side of the Allies, will be represented, although it is the "big three" of France, Britain and America that will be calling most of the shots. In principle, it's actually a "big four", with Italy also playing a strong role, although in practice the Italians are something of a junior partner. There is an argument for the Japanese also being at the top table, although they certainly are not to have much of a say. However, the total number of participating nations, or in some cases groups with aspiration to nationhood, is very large. The whole map of Europe and the Middle East, and the redrawing of many boundaries, is to be in the hands of this momentous gathering. The conference is to be held in Paris, and the final treaty signed at Versailles. It starts on 18th January and the treaty is signed on 28th June 1919. Many of the hopes and plans that emerge, including the "League of Nations" (much beloved of Woodrow Wilson), will crumble into dust, but that is still in the future at this stage.

Among the issues to be resolved is the fate of the German Navy. While their morale is now very low, they still have many powerful ships and submarines. There are two concerns here. One is that leaving Germany with such a resource is potentially dangerous – there are still those in the German military who might be tempted to use it in the future. The other is that there are many Navies around the world casting envious eyes on these ships. Unlike most other military hardware, these could be easily transferred. The British are not in favour of this. They already have far more warships than they need and they're not particularly keen on seeing other Navies getting strengthened.

The immediate solution is for the entire German Fleet to be impounded in Scapa Flow, with skeleton German crews. The fate of these ships is to be decided later. Over 70 warships are escorted to Scapa Flow towards the end of November, where they are kept under surveillance. Over the following months, the German crews, who are not allowed to leave their ships, become very disaffected, even with their own officers. The normal command structure breaks down. In the end, however, the Germans manage to scuttle their own ships. This happens on 21st June 1919. Everyone has been awaiting a decision from the Paris Conference about the fate of the ships. There is confusion about the expected outcome, but there is a fear on the part of the Germans that they are likely to be given to their enemies, or possibly that the German delegation in Paris might reject the Treaty, in which case it is conceivable that the ships could be taken over by rebellious sailors and used against Germany. Admiral Ludwig von Reuter, in command of the fleet, gives the order to scuttle. This order, unlike most others, is obeyed by the sailors – it's seen by all of them as a reassertion of the pride of the German Navy. The British forces that are overseeing the fleet attempt to stop the operation, but it is well planned and they're largely unsuccessful. They manage to beach some of the ships, but 52 of the 74 vessels sink. While the attempt made to save them was genuine, the authorities in Britain are not unhappy with this outcome.

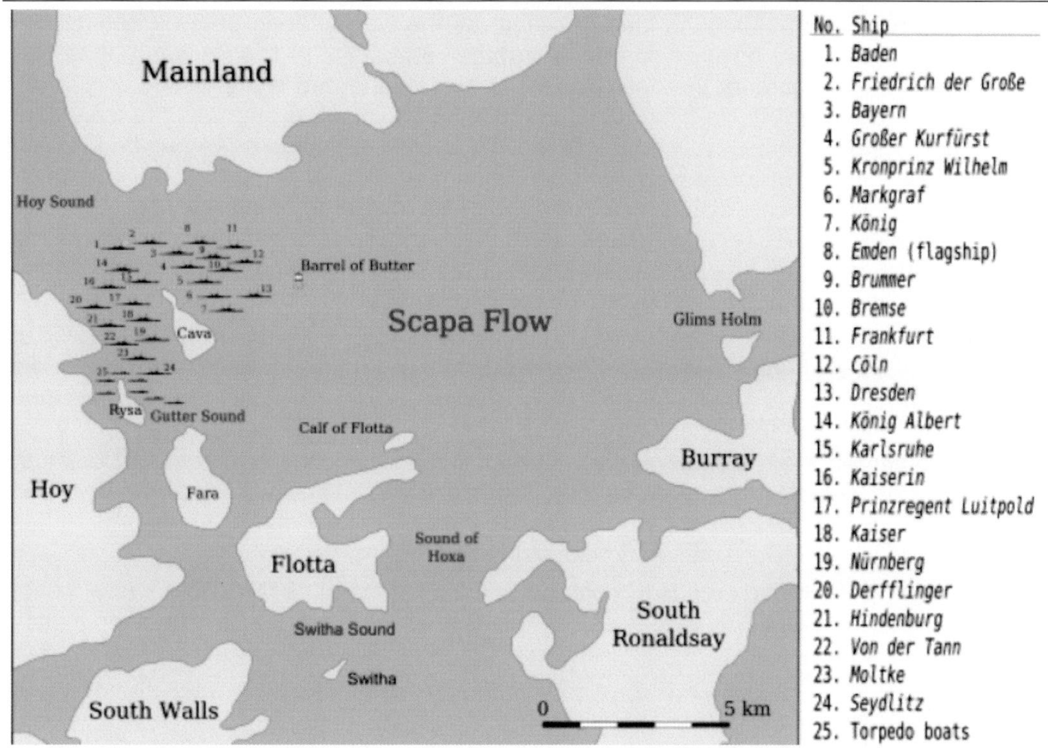

Fig.6.13: Map showing the locations of the scuttled German warships in Scapa Flow.

As far as the children in Bowermadden are concerned, none of this has much impact. Of course, the end of the war is welcome, although its effects are much diluted in this part of the country, and are partly in the form of increased unemployment as the size of the Navy is reduced. The Jellicoe Expresses are stopped in April 1919. This is naturally associated with a reduction in the activities of the British Fleet at Scapa Flow, which in any event has been partially transferred down to the ports in the mainland. The Orkneys largely revert to being something of a backwater, albeit one that is periodically visited by the sailors who were based there, and later by many tourists – partly to view the spectacle of the remnants of the scuttled German Fleet.

6.3 Herbert finally sees some Action

Herbert Clyne has not had a happy time over the last few years. Having joined up less than a year after William, and in the same Regiment and Battalion, he's had a very different experience. While William was posted abroad soon after he joined, Herbert had to wait almost a year before he was able to join the Battalion in Jubbulpore. This almost coincided with the sad news of William's death. This was a particular blow to Herbert, who was very much looking forward to meeting up with his brother again, although he knew about his transfer to Persia. N o more opportunities were offered for volunteers to leave Jubbulpore for places where more was happening. He spent the next two years doing very little, apart from the rather low-key garrison duties expected of the Battalion. Towards the end of this period, he heard the even sadder news of the death of both of his parents. He did consider asking for compassionate leave, but getting back to England would have been a slow and difficult process and, by the time he arrived, there would have been little he could do regarding the arrangements for the younger children. He knew that Stan and Mina would be able to sort out something.

Everyone in the Battalion knew that, if they had been given a more hazardous posting, then their chances of being killed or wounded would have risen enormously. By this time everyone is aware of the level of carnage throughout Europe, and even in places like

Mesopotamia. Nevertheless, the idea of sitting out the war, hearing of the accolades and suffering being heaped on their comrades in other Battalions of the Regiment, has been hard to take. The argument that the "Raj" must be safeguarded is impressed on them by their officers, although it's clear that even they are becoming frustrated with the tedium, not to mention the heat and dust, of this posting. Of course, shipping huge numbers of men around the world does require resources, so it's understandably being limited these days - although there is probably also a feeling among those in charge of the war effort that there must be less exposure of untried volunteers to the rigours of front line action, even if they had been recruited 2 or 3 years earlier. Experiences of battles such as that of the Somme are now starting to be etched deep into the national psyche.

In fact, the Battalion does not stay in Jubbulpore during 1918. The main concern of the British in India has long been with the North-West Frontier, where the border with Afghanistan has always been ill-defined and subject to various incursions and uprisings. Early in 1918, the Battalion is moved up to Quetta – a city at high altitude (over 5,000 feet) near to the border. It's in a strategically important location, and also has a much cooler and more pleasant climate than most of India, so the British Army has established a base there, with a large Staff College – formed about a decade or so earlier. In fact, the College was converted to a Cadet Training School at the start of the war.

The news of the move comes through around Christmas of 1917 (before Herbert hears of his mother's death). He, and most of the Battalion, greet the prospect of a move enthusiastically.

"You know, if we'd stayed here for another summer, I'm sure that we'd all have gone crazy" he says to one of his friends.

"Well, maybe we would, but at least there's nobody shooting at us here."

"I really don't care about a few towelheads with some pea-shooters. At least we'll be able to fire back. You can't do that with mossies – I've tried. They literally drive me mad every summer, particularly at night."

Their Company Sergeant-Major passes by at this point.

"Are you having a moan, Herbie Clyne? You've got your mossie net, haven't you?"

"Yes, Sarge, but, as you know, most of these nets are full o' holes. Once a mossie gets in, an' you hear that infernal buzzing, that's it for the night. The only thing that keeps them away is cigarette smoke, but you can't spend the night smoking fags – anyway, I can't afford it. The only net without holes in it round here is yon Bertie's," nodding towards a slim lad reading in the corner. "He's good with a needle and thread, and, to be fair, he's always inviting other lads in to share his bed during the night if they're having mossie trouble, although nobody does that more than once!"

"Yes, well I certainly didn't hear that. An' another thing, you shouldn't call these lads up in the mountains towelheads – they're not Arabs. What they actually are is mad bandits, but you'll soon realize that they need to be taken seriously. Anyway,

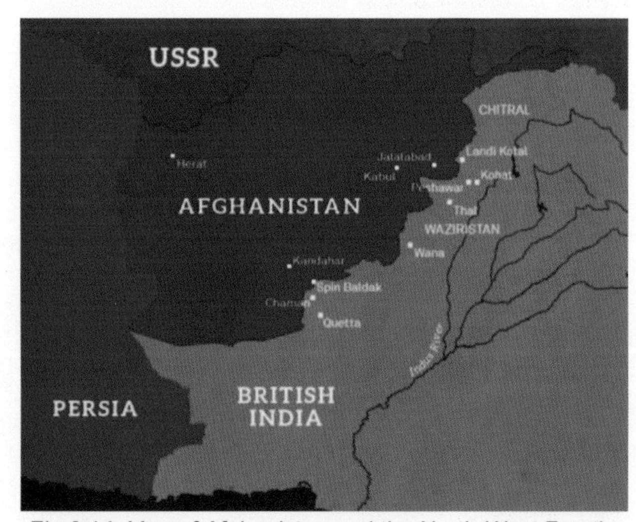

Fig.6.14: Map of Afghanistan and the North-West Frontier region in 1919.

you're right that it'll be a lot cooler up there. We'll also have a bit more to do"

Actually, while it is a lot cooler, and everyone is happy with the move, there's not that much to do, since the Afghans are quiet (and, at least in principle, not involved in the war). The Battalion has another soporific year, very relieved when they hear in the summer about the war in Europe finally going well. As the end comes, they naturally expect to return quickly back to Britain, to pick up the threads of their lives. There has been much trumpeting of the concept of rebuilding Britain as a "land fit for heroes", and indeed there is real optimism around the idea of creating a fairer and better-balanced society. The Bolshevik Revolution, while universally denigrated in the West, has made those in power much more receptive to the idea of improving the lot of ordinary working people, or at least trying to ensure that nothing truly revolutionary takes place. Herbert and his comrades are naturally keen to get back and start thinking about jobs, families, housing etc. In the event, however, the Battalion is one of the very last to get home.

As the war ends, there is naturally a requirement to move troops around, with many going back to Britain, but also large contingents returning to the colonies. The pressure on marine transport is therefore high, particularly since many ships have been sunk during the war. Moreover, there is no intention to strip places like India of British troops. The 1/4th Battalion of the Royal West Kents is thus one of those left in place for some time after the Armistice. They're therefore still in Quetta at the start of the 3rd Anglo-Afghan War in May 1919, when the Emirate of Afghanistan invades British India. The background to this is complex. Afghanistan has remained neutral during the Great War, despite pressure from the Ottoman Empire, with calls for a Jihad ("Holy War"). The Afghans expect some sort of reward for this, which is turned down by the British. They're also annoyed that their request for a place at the Paris Peace Conference, which started at the beginning of 1919, is rejected. In addition to these resentments, and a hope that they might be able to capture the land West of the Indus River, which had been lost many years before to the Sikhs, they sense that there is a growing feeling of resentment against the British in India. This has been particularly stoked by the so-called Massacre of Amritsar on 13th April 1919, when almost 400 innocent civilians in an enclosed square are shot dead by a detachment of 50 British Indian troops under Brigadier-General Reginald Dyer – a disgraceful episode that will have long term repercussions. The Afghans also hope that the British will be war-weary after the long struggle of the Great War. Moreover, they are being encouraged by the new (Bolshevik) regime in Russia, with Russian links extending back a long way. Finally, there is a power struggle within the Afghan royal family.

In fact, the British have a substantial advantage in this war in terms of numbers of troops, and also in terms of equipment – which includes significant air power. It should, however, be noted that the majority of these British troops are, like those in the 1/4th RWK, Territorials with little or no battle experience, and also with strong feelings that they just want to go home now. In this sense, the calculations of the Afghans are correct. In any event, this war doesn't last very long. It's terminated by an Armistice after a couple of months. During the conflict, about 1,000 Afghans are killed, compared with 250 British troops (plus 650 wounded). The outcome in political terms is not very significant – just a slight redrawing of the border and some promises that Afghanistan will have more independence in the future, although it's certainly destined to be a region of turbulence and periodic

Fig.6.15: Photo of the fort at Spin Baldak, after its capture from the Afghans in May 1919.

disturbance for many decades to come.

In fact, the 1/4th do play a role in the conflict. One example is the capture on 27th May of the Afghan stronghold at Spin Baldak, which is stormed after an action lasting 8 hours, in very hot weather. This is important, since the fort commands the strategically vital road from Kandahar to Quetta. There are also several skirmishes along the Khyber Pass. At least these battles give the Battalion a feeling of having done something real. Herbert is centrally involved in the Spin Baldak battle and he feels that perhaps he has in the end done something vaguely similar to the exploits of William, and is, of course, thankful that he has come through it unscathed.

After this conflict is resolved, they really do want to just come home. The Battalion returns to Quetta in September and eventually leaves Karachi on October 30th. They arrive at Plymouth on 21st November, and Tonbridge on 24th November. Demobilization follows, so that Herbert is finally able to go "home". Of course, home as he knew it no longer exists – there isn't a house where they can congregate and his siblings are dispersed between Kent and Scotland. The country as a whole is also almost unrecognizable. There are many unemployed and also many struggling with long term injuries and other types of trauma. The influenza epidemic is also rampant, with many ex-soldiers, already in a poor state of health, being vulnerable to it. Herbert receives a sum of money, calculated in a rather complex way (depending on length of service and a few other factors), which adds up to about £10. He also has some modest savings. Overall, he has enough to survive for a while, but it's not a huge sum. He needs to take stock and start to rebuild his life, as do millions of others.

Fig.6.16: Detachment of Indian Army troops overlooking the Khyber Pass in 1919.

6.4 Life in the Early 1920's

Life moves on, both in Caithness and in North Kent. Harry finishes school in Scotland and moves back to the South, staying initially with Stan. The new decade starts. Lena is now 12, Douglas is 7 and Len is 5. There is an initial "mini-boom" in Britain as the Government tries to stimulate the economy. However, it's difficult to create enough jobs for the millions of demobilized soldiers and sailors coming onto the market, and there is a large national debt – mainly incurred during the war. The boom doesn't last long and by 1921 there is high u nemployment and little investment. Things are, of course, much worse in Germany, which is forced to pay large reparations and is given little or no economic help. It also has to give up territory, including Alsace-Lorraine, which had been taken from the French after the Franco-German War of 1870. This has been an outcome of the Paris Peace Conference, with the French largely getting their way. Economic

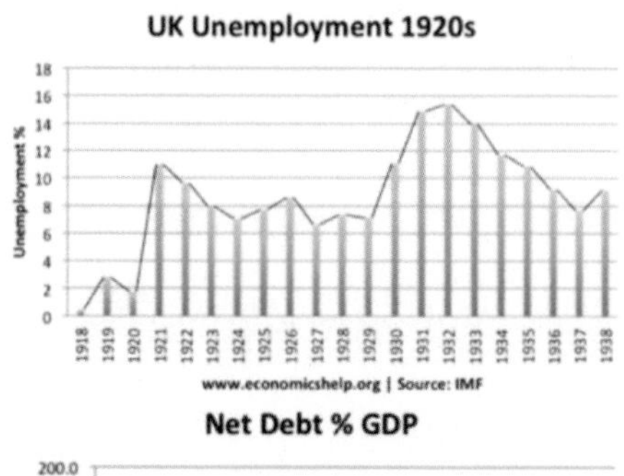

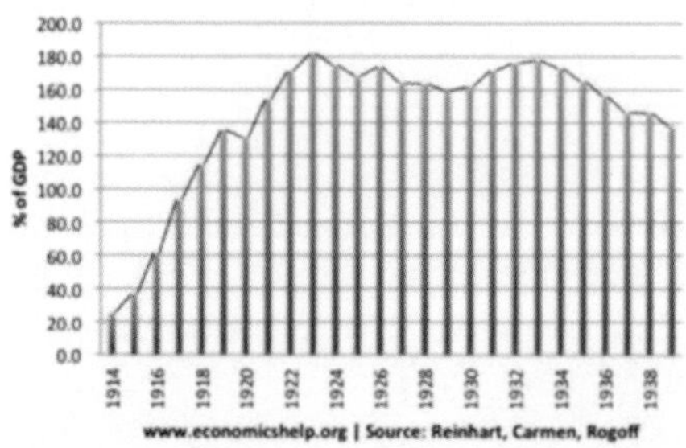

Fig.6.17: Unemployment and National Debt data for the UK in the 1920's.

productivity in Europe is low, but the American economy is surging – such that industry in Britain starts to lose many of its markets. The anticipated social changes are very slow to develop, leading to resentment, a string of strikes and a lot of general unrest. The Labour Party is on the rise, starting to supplant the Liberals.

To some extent, Caithness is insulated from these fluctuations. Life has always been something of a struggle, but the people are hardy and self-sufficient. It's true that, certainly in many parts of the Highlands and Islands, the Clearances, and other ill-treatment by landlords, in parallel with limited interest from those further south controlling the levers of power, have created terrible hardships. That is slowly being remedied, following (long overdue) direct action by crofters during recent decades, although they're still largely at the mercy of the weather and economic forces. In Caithness, there are certain local problems. For example, the stone quarry at Castletown closes. There are other quarries in Caithness, but this hits the immediate area hard – there had been several hundred people employed there just a couple of decades ago. There has also been a decline in the herring industry, largely due to over-fishing. Wick still has a reputation for being a relatively lively place, particularly in terms of the activities of people brought in on a temporary basis by the fishing. In fact, it often becomes rather over-boisterous and 1922 sees the introduction of "prohibition" in the town, with all of the pubs forced to close and even off-license sales of alcohol banned. As in the USA, this is largely circumvented, particularly since it applies only to Wick. Much of the hard drinking is simply moved to Thurso, creating a lot of late night traffic on the railway between the two towns. It is still destined to persist for 25 years, so that it will outlast the ban in America by about a dozen years. In fact, this is largely due to pressure from temperance societies, and also from the ultra-conservative Church of Scotland (and the even more conservative Free Church of Scotland). Nevertheless, it is true that the fishing industry is in sharp decline. Unemployment is getting very high. While this is no longer the only way to avoid starvation, as it often was during the Clearances, high unemployment has driven periodic waves of emigration, particularly to Canada, and another of these starts to get under way in the early 1920's.

Economic viability for people like the Dunnets, on the other hand - while marginal in many ways - is reasonably stable overall. Their annual rent is £10. This is small when considered in national terms – the average annual wage of a (male) factory worker is about £250 (but only £100 for women!). However, it's a lot lower for people working on the land – well under £100 for farm labourers, although sometimes accommodation and/or meals might be provided. Moreover, rates in the Highlands are lower than in the rest of Britain. For the Dunnets, £10 is significant. Also, people in their particular situation often have no job as such. They might do some casual work – there are opportunities for this in the fishing industry, although not in Bowermadden, which is not in "commuting distance" of the ports. They might also be able to sell home-grown produce – for example, John Don keeps bees and sells honey at local markets and to large houses in the area. He's also a skilled carpenter and occasionally sells small pieces of furniture or farm implements. The Dunnets pay very little for "services" – the peat for heating is effectively free, as is the water, although they do need to buy paraffin for the lamps.

Nevertheless, it's a precarious living, with very limited cash-flow. There is nothing to spare for anything superfluous – the essentials of food and clothing take up all of the available resources, with the children representing an additional burden. It has been a kind and generous act for the Dunnets to take them. It is true that the broader Dunnet family is extensive and prominent in the area, with some branches being more affluent than others. While "cross-subsidies" are rare, with Scots in general being extremely proud about their independence, families in dire straits would not be allowed to starve. However, the gross inequalities that are still so common in the rest of Britain certainly extend to these parts. In a large house, such as that at Stanstill - just a couple of miles along the road to Wick from Bowermadden, and one of several mansions in the area owned by the Sinclair-Wemyss family - there are now privately-owned cars, and a chauffer, whereas it will be several more years before even public bus services are common in the area.

VALUATION ROLL FOR THE COUNTY OF CAITHNESS FOR THE YEAR 1923-1924—PARISH OF BOWER. 87

No.	Description and Situation of Subject	Proprietor	Tenant	Occupancy	Inhabitant Occupier not Rated	Annual Value	Feu Duty or Ground Annual	Yearly Rent or Value	No.
						£ s.	£ s. d.	£ s. d.	
140	aLand and House (Granton Mains), Bowermadden	John Keith, Granton Mains		Proprietor	Margt. Matheson, spinster, farm servant Malcolm Munro, farm servant Robert McGregor, farm servt.	4 0 4 0 4 0		157 0 0	~~140~~ 140
141	Shootings do.	do.		Proprietor				5 0 0	141
142	aLand and House, do.	Wm. Mackenzie, cattle dealer, Castletown	Wm. Donn Dunnet	same				~~20 0 0~~	142 25.0.0
143	a do. do.		John D. Dunnet	same				10 0 0	143
144	a do. do.	Peter Mowat		Proprietor				2 12 0	144
145	a do. do.	James Dunnet and Mrs Christina Black or Dunnet, 27 Viewforth, Edinburgh	Mrs Jessie Murray	same				11 3 0	145
146	a do. do.	Alexander Auld and Christina O. Auld	Alexander Auld	same				5 0 0	146
147	a do. do.	Robert Baillie, Rangoon, Burma, per Miss Christina Magrae, Bowermadden, Bower		Proprietor				3 0 0	147
148	aFarm and House (part), Murza	Peter and John Bain		Proprietors	David Nicolson, farm servant John Nicolson, farm servant David Henderson, farm servt.	4 0 4 10 4 10		165 0 0	148
149	Shootings, do.	do.		Proprietors				2 10 0	149
150	aFarm and House, Upper Thura	Trustees of Miss H. L. E. Dunbar Sinclair Wemyss, per Mackay & Macdonald, factors, solicitors, Thurso	William Sinclair	same	James Gunn, farm servant Jeannie Gunn, farm servant	4 0 4 0		181 17 1	150
151	aLand and House, Seater		William Morrison	same				50 8 6	151
152	a do. do.		Hector Sinclair	same				6 0 0	152
153	a do. Lower Thura	do.	William Waugh	same				68 15 0	153
154	aFarm and House, Stanstill	do.	Alex. David Campbell, Stanstill	same	John Mowat, grieve Alex. MacLeod, farm servant Charles Leith, cattleman John Lockie, shepherd Donald MacLeod, farm servt. David Bremner, farm servant Donald Bain, ploughman John Malcolm, chauffeur John Mowat, jun., farm servt.	4 0 4 0 3 0 4 0 4 0 4 0 4 0 5 0 3 0		363 7 10	154

Fig.6.18: Part of the Valuation Roll for the Parish of Bower, for 1923-24.

For the children, the transition has been shocking. From being in a relatively prosperous situation, with no real problems about food, clothing, warmth etc - even having some pocket-money to spend at local shops, and being able to travel around freely, life is now mainly just a question of survival. The winters are long and hard, and simply keeping warm is a challenge. There's not much entertainment, at home or outside. There is a public house – the Thura Inn – just up the road, but the Dunnets are teetotal, like most of the locals, and it doesn't do much business. On the other hand, there is much less danger of infectious disease – the water supply is clean, unlike that in London, which certainly carried typhoid in earlier decades, and still isn't completely safe. They do in general manage to get enough nutritious food, with plenty of porridge. A certain level of hunger is common, but there's no real danger of starvation. There's also plenty of fresh air and exercise, and certainly no danger of obesity. They are, in fact, robust and healthy. Still, the two young lads do nip regularly into fields on the way back from school, to pick up the odd turnip and eat some of it raw before they get home – since such "theft" would not be tolerated by the Dunnets. This kind of thing is not common in Kent.

The change has naturally been more traumatic for the older children. Harry returns to the south after just a year or so, grateful to be able to get away. Lena, who is now entering her teens, finds it hard. She had become accustomed to life in Kent and, like all young girls, was looking forward to the freedom and excitement of becoming a young adult. She's a vivacious and attractive girl: to be spending these years in such a restrictive environment is very frustrating. This isn't just a question of physical limitations. The social climate in this part of Scotland is also rather different, with religion exerting widespread influence and imposing a strict moral code. The idea of young people having fun does not figure very prominently in religious priorities. Also, there is still a quasi-tribal attitude, with the Clan system still important – despite the dreadful mistreatments that have occurred within it over the past century or so. "Foreigners" are not readily assimilated into the social order, although their family connections have ensured that the Clyne children had no problems in that respect.

There are often meetings for children in the Church Hall at Boweremadden on Saturday mornings, to make sure that they're learning about the Bible etc. The Minister of Bower Parish, Dugald MacEchern, calls to Lena as she's leaving with the two boys after one of these meetings early in 1920.

"Lena, could I hae a wee word? The bairns can go on hame." Dugald is a kindly and highly educated man, but the Church is not to be trifled with in this part of the world. "I'm nae a harsh man, but I cannae have a couple of laddies playing conkers at the back o' the class when they should be learning their catechisms!"

"I understand, Minister, but it's very hard for them. Saturday mornings is one of the few times in the week when they can hope to get out and have a run around, especially in the winter."

"That's as may be lassie, but this is sacred ground and the Lord does'nae take kindly tae bairns playin' games here."

Lena's a spirited girl and the unfairness of this overwhelms her for a moment

"Is this Hall really consecrated ground, Minister? Anyway, they find it difficult to believe that God is on their side, having lost their brother and both parents. They weren't brought up to be strongly religious down in England. My mother was a marvelous woman, but she couldn't afford to spend a lot of time worrying about God – she knew that she was doing his work."

"Din'nae argue with me lassie. I ken well tha' yer family has had a verra hard time. God moves in mysterious ways and it's nae fur us to question them. Anyway, I'm sure that John Don would'nae stand for this if I were tae tell him. We ken each other verra well from our time in the Seaforths. He believes, as I do, tha' it's nae a gud idea tae spare the rod."

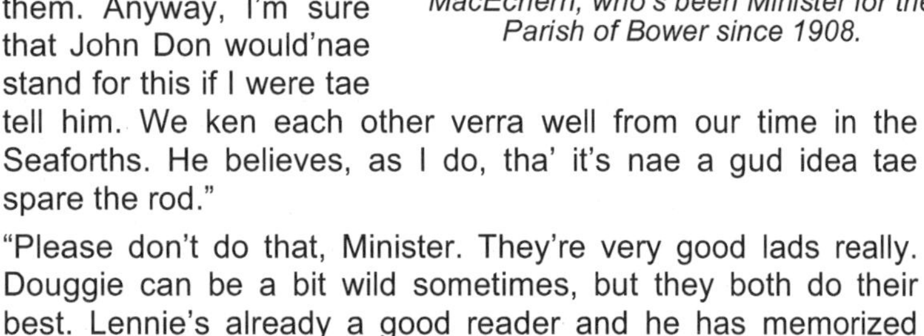

DUGALD MACECHERN, born Edinburgh, 25th Oct. 1867, son of Charles M., min. of St Mary's (Gaelic), Inverness, and brother of preceding; educated at Tiverton and Sangeen Schools, Canada, Edinburgh and Glasgow Schools, Raining's School, Inverness, and Univ. of Edinburgh; M.A. (1887), B.D. (1890); licen. by Presb. of Inverness May 1890; assistant at Birsay, Acharacle and Kyleakin; min. at Lochranza in 1891; ord. to Coll 20th April 1898; trans. and adm. 13th May 1908; bard to the Gaelic Society of Inverness, on nine occasions he won the Highland Mod prizes for Gaelic poetry; lieut. 5th Seaforth Highlanders, on special service under the Admiralty, and railway military officer on lines of communication, 1914-17. Marr. 3rd Oct. 1917, Margaret Louttit, only daugh. of John Baikie, Lochview, Bower. Publications — *Poems and Sketches* (Inverness, 1905); *Coll of the Waves* (n.p. 1907); *Clàrsach-nan-Gaidheal* ("Harp of the Gael"), with English Translation (Inverness, 1911); Poems, English and Gaelic in *The Celtic Monthly*; *The Angels of Mons* (Stirling, 1915); *The Sword of the North* (Inverness, 1923); *Place-Names of Coll* (*Trans. Gael. Soc. of Inverness*, xxix., 314).—[*The Sword of the North* (portraits), 503; Mitchell's *Book of Highland Verse*, 349.]

1908

Fig.6.19: Extract from Hew Scott's 1928 edition of "The Succession of Ministers in the Church of Scotland from the Reformation", concerning Dugald MacEchern, who's been Minister for the Parish of Bower since 1908.

"Please don't do that, Minister. They're very good lads really. Douggie can be a bit wild sometimes, but they both do their best. Lennie's already a good reader and he has memorized several passages from the Bible."

"Aye, that young lad may have the makings o' a scholar. I'll keep ma eye on him. But in the meantime, ye need tae tell them tae tighten up a wee bit in God's house. An' there's another wee thing, lassie. We dinnae want too many distractions here – an' there's a few young men around the place who cud' get easily distracted. Ye're nae longer a bairn yer'self. Perhaps ye cud wear yer hair a wee bit shorter, or put it under a bonnet?"

Fig.6.20: Dugald MacEchern, as a Lt-Col (the Rev.) in the Seaforth Highlanders, in 1916.

Lena bites back the response that first comes to mind. She does actually know that this Minister is an erudite man with good intentions, as well as a deep love of the area. She sees in a flash of insight that he has his own constraints and pressures. Anyway, falling out with him would be potentially disastrous.

"I'll do that, Minister. Lizzie is handy with the scissors and I'll sort something out with her. I'll also make sure that the lads are as good as gold in church tomorrow."

"That's bonny an' fine, Lena. I ken well that ye're a gud girl. If I were 40 year younger, I'd be interested in ye myself in a verra different way. We'll stay friends. An' I'll tell ye a wee secret. I do ken verra well the cost o' the Great War fur us in this part o' the world. I've started to write a wee book about it and I even have a title fur it – 'The Sword of the North – Highland Memories of the Great War'. The Clynes, an' also the Dunnets, are just twa o' the many families from these parts that paid a high price. I'm also pushing for a proper memorlal in Wick – we should all be verra proud o' those that fell."

Life is therefore far from easy for the three children, or indeed for most people in the area. Still, everything is relative. Sixty years earlier, Kier Hardic, who went on to found the Labour Party around the turn of the century, started work aged 7 - and by age 10 he was working down a mine in the Lanarkshire coalfields. His income of a few shillings a week was critical in keeping the family together, particularly when his stepfather was thrown out of work for 6 months in the Clydeside shipyards - in retaliation against the activities of workers who were trying to create a union. The family had to sell virtually all of their possessions, just to avoid starvation. Deprivation and exploitation on this scale is now mercifully rare, with unions being legal and increasingly strong - although hardly welcomed by the ruling classes. However, there's no escaping the fact that life is still hard for many people, including many children. Furthermore, it is considerably harder in certain other countries. Having defaulted on their reparation payments at the end of 1922, inflation in Germany during 1923 is such that a loaf of bread costing 250 marks at the start of the year is selling for 200,000 million marks by the end. The cost of printing even large denomination notes is greater than their value. Starvation is an issue for the majority of the population. That a proud and resourceful people, such as the Germans, will somehow find a way out of this, no matter how ill-advised, is self-evident. The Nazi Party is on the rise and, while the Munich Putsch of 1923 fails, and Adolf Hitler is briefly imprisoned, support for their extreme views and solutions is spreading.

Life is also moving on in other parts of the world. There is much complexity surrounding the redrawing of national boundaries by the Peace Conference, particularly in Eastern Europe, the Balkans and the Middle East. Significant mini-wars sporadically break out during the period from 1919 to the early 1920s, as nations or ethnic groups attempt to change the de facto situation on the ground. The victors now have far fewer troops under arms, so implementing their decisions by force is not so easy. Kemal Atatürk, who was a highly successful commander at Gallipoli, rallies the Turks to resist the complete dismemberment of the Ottoman Empire that is being proposed. He mobilizes a Turkish army and drives out the Greeks and Italians who were moving into various parts of Anatolia, creating a new Turkish state. Those in charge of the Peace Conference had a truly onerous task, with so many conflicting demands and expectations. Still, even allowing for this, much of what they eventually decide turns out to have disastrous consequences. The League of Nations is effectively stillborn – not even ratified by the US Senate, despite the fact that it was largely the brainchild of Woodrow Wilson. He does try hard to get approval, but his health is failing and there are various political issues. His term expires in March 1921 and he dies early in 1924.

Furthermore, not only are the Germans and Turks driven quickly into dire straits, but even some of those on the "winning" side are left very unhappy. Italy, for example, is frustrated about not gaining much territory; this contributes strongly to a rise in nationalist (fascist) sentiments in the country during the 1920s. Japan made rather few demands at the Paris Conference, but their request for a Racial Equality clause in the Covenant of the League of Nations is rejected – leading to them retreating again into an isolationist and nationalist attitude. Finally, China, which had sent many thousands of labourers to help the Allies during the last two years of the war, are treated in cavalier fashion, with Japan being awarded the hated concession in Shandong that had previously been held by Germany. Shandong, which is geographically important and the ancient home of Confucius, means a lot to the Chinese. There is huge unrest, particularly among the young, and the country becomes chaotic and disenchanted with the West. Mao-Tse Tung and Chou-En Lai are among the activists in the demonstrations. There is a move towards communism, encouraged by the Bolsheviks. All of these chickens will come home to roost within a fairly short period.

There are also serious problems in Russia. Many European countries are strongly antagonistic towards communism. They support the "White" Russians in their internal battles with the "Red" (communist) Russians, which drag on for a couple of years. The deprivations resulting from this, and from Russia's disastrous involvement in the war, are extreme. There is a terrible famine there in 1921-22, with 5 million dying of starvation. In addition to this, many millions are dying across various European countries from "Spanish Flu" – the death toll undoubtedly being raised substantially by the poor state of health and nutrition of many people, due to the aftermath of war. Another region in which chaos quickly emerges is Palestine. The Jews, whose case is put forward very ably at the Peace Conference by Chaim Weizmann, obtain support from Lloyd George and Woodrow Wilson for a Jewish homeland there. This is in accord with the Balfour Declaration, composed by the British Foreign Secretary, Arthur Balfour, in 1917. Weizmann is in fact a Russian-born chemist and, rather improbably, is able to assist the Allied war effort via his discovery in 1915 of an effective way to produce acetone, which is a key component in the manufacture of certain explosives. However, the objections of the Arabs already living in Palestine are neither properly understood nor taken into account and its period as a British Mandate during the inter-war years is increasingly turbulent. (Weizmann is destined to become the first President of the fully-fledged state of Israel in 1948.)

Nearer home, there is also turmoil in Ireland. After years of trouble, the Anglo-Irish Treaty is signed in December 1921, setting up the Irish Free State. Despite certain similarities between the ways that Irish and Scottish tenants have been mistreated over the last century or so, there is no strong drive for independence in Scotland. There are several reasons for this, including a different situation regarding religious divides, but the far north of Scotland is still in some ways a country apart. Life is clearly rather different in Caithness. Infectious disease is not much of an issue there and, while hunger is not uncommon, starvation is rare. The family in Bowermadden is not strongly impacted by the state of the British economy, but local unemployment, and the depressed state of the fishing industry, does affect everyone in the area. While Lena has a strongly maternal attitude to the two younger boys, she is thinking about her own future. She just can't imagine staying in the area after leaving school, which is now starting to loom up on the horizon. She's not the only one to be thinking in these terms and there is much talk locally about emigration. There are currently certain government-sponsored schemes to promote moving to the colonies, particularly Canada. In fact, links between Scotland and Canada have been strong for a while and Lena is seeing attractions in the idea of starting a new life there – perhaps when Douglas and Len are entering their teens and won't need her quite so much. They're already adventurous young lads, and the greatest of friends. She discusses this possibility with Minister MacEchern, who himself spent several years in Canada as a child. He and his wife have a strong influence in the area and, while none of the Clyne children are growing up to be strongly religious, the church pervades all aspects of local life, with the Minister being a key figure. Dugald MacEchern has a strongly paternal attitude to all of the children in the area. While he regrets the continual hemorrhage of bright young people via movement to the south or emigration, he has their interests at heart. He encourages Lena to think about Canada.

Meanwhile, the rest of the family is still in Kent, where life is also far from easy. The overall economic situation in the country becomes progressively more difficult in the 1920's, with many of the traditional industries struggling. There is rapid growth in some types of production, such as that of cars and of household goods - including electrical appliances – but shrinkage in many traditional industries and jobs. Much of the new activity becomes concentrated in the capital, which starts to expand quickly as new suburbs are created and the spaces between them are filled. The population of London is to increase by almost a million in the 1920's (and a further million in the 1930's). This tends to suppress developments in other parts of the country, with many energetic young people being drawn to the capital. The pressures on accommodation and employment are very high.

Frank is demobilized early in 1919, after which he marries Gladys Balchin (aged 20). He obtains a job as a skilled machine operator with Vickers and they settle in Dartford. However, Vickers is being forced to cut back sharply as military demands fall and he's made redundant shortly afterwards. They can't afford to stay in Dartford and they move to a house in Birmingham that is shared with three other families, one of which includes two children. In 1921, Frank (aged 23) is unemployed, despite having skills that should be in strong demand in an industrial society. As for millions of other workers, times are very hard for him and his young wife. (The chances of her obtaining employment paying anything significant are very small.)

When Herbert finally gets home at the end of 1919, he is demobilized and returns to St. Paul's Cray. He gets a job in a local paper mill (W Joyner Ltd.) and rents the family's old house in Green Walk (in which his father died). After his short period in Scotland, Harry returns to live with him. By 1921, Harry is aged 15 and has just completed his schooling in St.Paul's Cray. Shortly afterwards, he joins the Metropolitan Police – the only one of the family to follow in father's footsteps with regard to work.

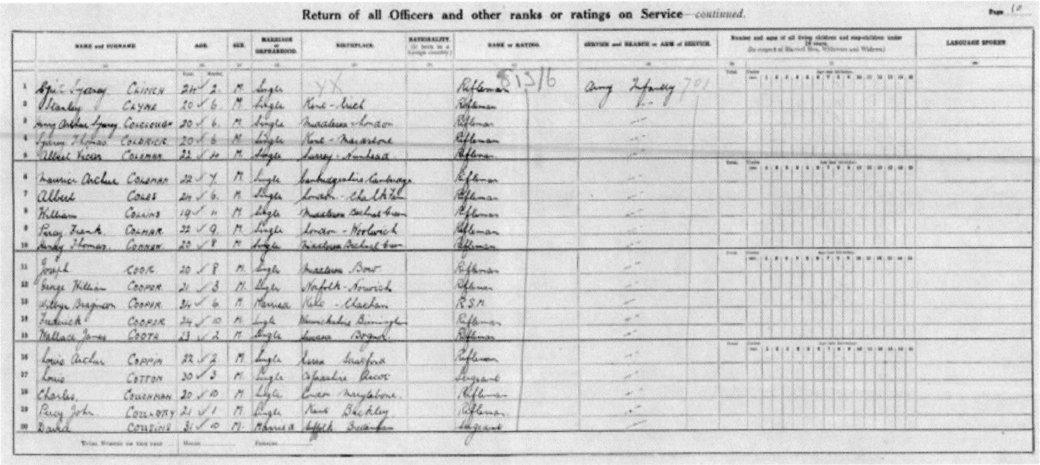

Return of all Officers and other ranks or ratings on Service—*continued.*

	Name and Surname		Age	Sex	Marriage or Orphanhood	Birthplace	Nationality	Rank or Rating	Service and Branch or Arm of Service
1	[illegible] George	CLINCH	24 2	M	Single			Rifleman	Army Infantry
2	Stanley	CAYNE	20 6	M	Single	Kent - [illegible]		Rifleman	
3	Harry Arthur George	COLECLOUGH	20 6	M	Single	[illegible] London		Rifleman	
4	George Thomas	COLDRICK	20 6	M	Single	Kent - Maidstone		Rifleman	
5	Albert [illegible]	COLEMAN	22 10	M	Single	Surrey - [illegible]		Rifleman	
6	Maurice Archer	COLEMAN	22 7	M	Single	Cambridgeshire Cambridge		Rifleman	
7	Albert	COLES	24 6	M	Single	London - [illegible]		Rifleman	
8	William	COLLINS	19 11	M	Single	Middlesex Bethnal Green		Rifleman	
9	Percy Frank	COLMAR	22 9	M	Single	London - Woolwich		Rifleman	
10	Henry Thomas	CONNOR	20 8	M	Single	Middlesex Bethnal Green		Rifleman	
11	Joseph	COOK	20 8	M	Single	Middlesex Bow		Rifleman	
12	George William	COOPER	21 3	M	Single	Norfolk - Norwich		Rifleman	
13	[illegible]	COOPER	34 6	M	Married	Kent - [illegible]		R.S.M.	
14	Frederick	COOPER	24 10	M	Single	Warwickshire Birmingham		Rifleman	
15	Wallace James	COOTE	23 2	M	Single	Sussex Bognor		Rifleman	
16	Louis Arthur	COPPIN	22 2	M	Single	Essex [illegible]		Rifleman	
17	Louis	COTTON	30 3	M	Single	Oxfordshire [illegible]		Sergeant	
18	Charles	COUCHMAN	20 10	M	Single	London Marylebone		Rifleman	
19	Percy John	COULTRY	21 1	M	Single	Kent Bexley		Rifleman	
20	David	COUSINS	31 10	M	Married	Suffolk [illegible]		Sergeant	

Fig.6.21: Part of the entry for the 1921 census, submitted by Major AA Ird, on behalf of army personnel based in Quetta.

Meanwhile, Stan had joined the army just before the end of the war (aged almost 17) and he elects to stay in the Army for a while. In 1921, he is a Rifleman stationed in Quetta (India). Mina comes back to North Kent in 1918, after her very short visit to Caithness, and stays initially with Stan - although he doesn't have a proper base and is himself staying with friends and neighbours at that point. She's in a particularly difficult position as she leaves school, faced with great difficulty in obtaining a job in the local area and having no family able to provide her with accommodation or support her financially – with Herbert not due to arrive back from India for almost another year. At the end of 1918, she takes a job as a scullery-maid in a school run by the Kensington and Chelsea Guardians, at 241 King Street, Hammersmith (the Kensington, Chelsea and St.Marylebone School). The school is one for poor children and orphans, although it's in a large mansion (later to become Palingswick House). Mina is keen to help such children, but it is poorly-paid, menial work -

quite unsuited to an intelligent girl such as her. However, it does include free accommodation in the school and she is at least living in a fairly salubrious area. By 1921, aged 17, she is doing her best in these new circumstances.

As the boys and Lena grow up, they accept the realities of their situation. They become known in the area, although Bowermadden is a very small place and they don't get into Wick or Thurso very often. One Saturday morning in the spring of 1924, however, the two boys (now aged 9 and 11) are on the quay in Wick, having come into town with John Don, Lizzie and Lena, who are looking for some bargains in the shops. Len is sitting on the quayside, dangling a length of string into the water, while Douglas has organized a race with some snails, having persuaded a few other young lads to bet their pennies on the outcome.

"What in God's name do ye think ye're up to, laddie?"

"Auntie Jessie – we're jus' havin' a wee bit o' fun."

"Ye're tryin' tae tak' money off o' these half-witted bairns, is what ye're up to! An' another thing – is it ye that has got por' little Lennie fishin' here, when the whole town kens that the little darlins' nivver come into the river or near the quay." The two boys both look a bit sheepish at this, with Len protesting that Douggie had promised him a big fish. "Gi' these bairns their pennies back – they've a lot tae learn yet."

Jessie grabs Doug by the ear and drags him, with Len in tow, a hundred yards up the road to a roundabout, where there's a large monument to Wick men killed in the Great War. It was opened 6 months ago.

"Do ye see the name of my poor Frank here? An' ye may notice that there are another five Clyne names here? Do ye think that ye're doin' yer family name proud hangin' round the quay, takin' pennies from wee kiddies? Does John Don ken tha' this is how ye spend yer time?"

"Nae, Auntie Jessie, but ye ken tha' there's nae much tae do round here. An' we did come in tae see this place being opened. I'm verra sorrie aba' ye losing Uncle Frank."

Fig.6.22: Photo taken at the opening of the Wick War Memorial, on 31st October 1923.

"Aye, well, it were almos' 8 year ago now, but I still miss him evra day. I ken tha' yer nae bad laddies really. An' another thing, Douggie, ye mus' do right by young Lennie – fur some reason he thinks the world o' ye. Come along an' I'll gi' ye both a cake in the teashop."

6.5 Douglas and Lena Depart

Any supplement to the diet in the Bowermadden household is welcome. Copious quantities of porridge and Scotch broth are attractive in some ways, but a bit of variety, particularly protein-rich food, certainly doesn't go amiss. Meat is in general very expensive, although mutton, and perhaps haggis, can be obtained at fairly reasonable cost. Also, they do sometimes splash out on a small barrel of salted herring, to use through the winter – slightly lower quality fish is sold quite cheaply. Of course, anything obtainable for free is of great interest. Poaching, however, is in general not a good idea. Firstly, there really isn't very much game in the area. Perhaps a few rabbits, but they're not easy to catch. Crows, mice etc are a bit beyond the pale. The Dunnets don't have a gun and in any event they wouldn't dream of doing anything illegal. There is, however, one potentially free source of tasty protein, which is birds' eggs. In particular, there are a lot of seagulls, and hence their eggs, in the vicinity. Taking the eggs of woodland birds is difficult, unlikely to yield much and frowned upon by locals, even if not actually illegal. Gulls, however, are different: there are lots of them (partly due to the fishing industry), they're not greatly loved by most people and obtaining their eggs at least doesn't require a treasure hunt or the climbing of trees.

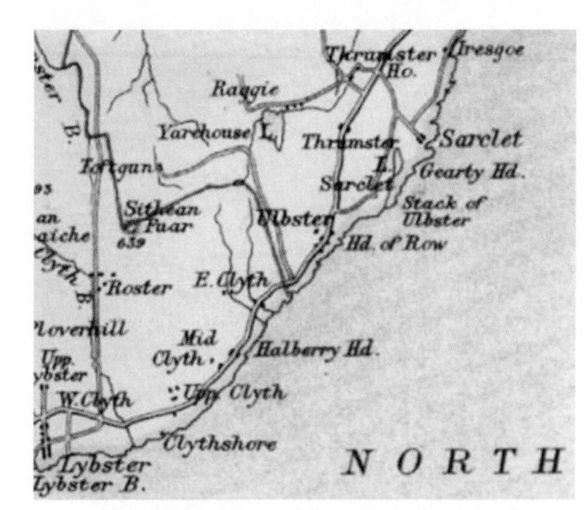

Fig.6.23: Map of the East Coast of Caithness, near Lybster.

However, that doesn't mean that they're easy to collect. Natural selection ensures that any gulls leaving their eggs in readily accessible locations don't procreate very successfully. They tend to lay them on inaccessible ledges and crevices in and around steep cliffs, of which there are quite a few in Caithness. This usually ensures that they're more or less safe from most of the natural predators, such as foxes or rats. However, they're not necessarily out of the reach of agile boys. The Dunnets certainly haven't encouraged the Clyne boys to supplement the household food supply in this way, but if Douglas, who is a very adventurous and athletic lad, brings back a bagful of gull eggs occasionally, they're not going to be thrown away.

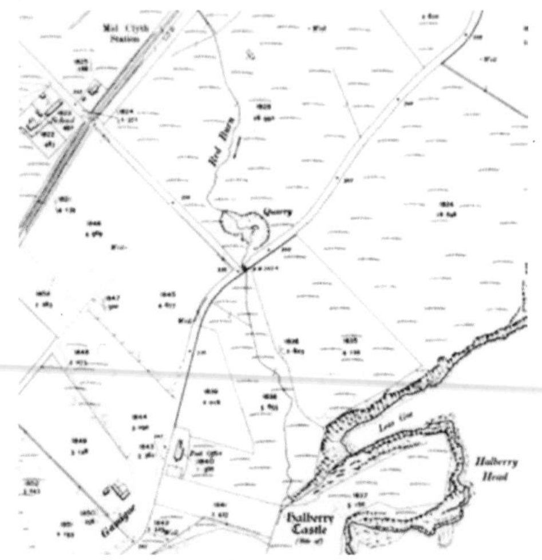

Fig.6.25: Map of the area between Mid-Clyth station and the cliffs.

To be fair, the Dunnets do warn the boys about the dangers, which are certainly real. One issue is that there aren't many good nesting sites nearby. The nearest coastline, at Dunnet Bay, is mainly composed of sand dunes. There are cliffs at Dunnet Head, but that's quite a long way and the roads are poor. In fact, the prime area for nests is along the East Coast a little further to the south – ie between Wick and Helmsdale. This is an extensive stretch (35 miles long) of weathered sandstone cliffs, towering up to 300 feet above the waves – later to become a highly protected site of special scientific interest and nature conservation. Moreover, the branch line from Wick to Lybster runs along the northern 13 miles of it.

Fig.6.24: Photo of a train at Lybster, waiting to depart for Wick, in July 1931.

There is a grapevine among adventurous young boys and, by the time that he has reached his teens, Douglas knows the locations of the best nesting sites in this area, and the closest railway stations. An 8-mile cycle to Bower station, followed by an hour's train journey to, say, Mid-Clyth and a further short walk to cliffs that are teeming with seabirds and their eggs, is a feasible day trip for a young boy on a summer Saturday, costing just a few pence. One of the best locations is at Halberry Head, where there are huge numbers of nests on a section of steep cliffs that are about 150 feet high.

The Dunnets do appreciate that places like this are genuinely dangerous. They forbid Douglas from going there. However, they can't put him under house arrest. The boys are naturally free to roam at weekends, or at least on Saturdays – there are in general more strictures about what can be done on the Sabbath. Being able to cycle around the area, and to take the train to Thurso or Wick occasionally, is not unreasonable. They do impress on Len that he must not go on the train with Douglas to places that have not been agreed in advance. They know that Len, although not yet in his teens, is very trustworthy, and that the two boys mostly do things together. However, Douglas can be headstrong and, on Saturday 30th May 1925, he heads for Mid-Clyth on his own, having told Len that he's off with a couple of his friends to play football. He may have been to that site once or twice before, but he's certainly not been to the area very often. He's never seen again by anyone from Bowermadden.

Fig.6.26: Cliffs at Mid-Clyth.

—Page 10.—

1925. DEATHS in the Parish of Latheron in the County of Caithness

No.	(1.) Name and Surname. Rank or Profession, and whether Single, Married, or Widowed.	(2.) When and Where Died.	(3.) Sex.	(4.) Age.	(5.) Name, Surname, & Rank or Profession of Father. Name, and Maiden Surname of Mother.	(6.) Cause of Death, Duration of Disease, and Medical Attendant by whom certified.	(7.) Signature & Qualification of Informant, and Residence, if out of the House in which the Death occurred.	(8.) When and where Registered, and Signature of Registrar.
28	Beatrice Elsie Fraser. Poorhouse Matron. Married to John Smith Fraser Poorhouse Governor	1925. July Seventh 7h. [illegible] Benefield House Latheron	F	24 Years	Hugh Montgomery Distillery Maltman. Elsie Montgomery M.S. Geddes	Tuberculosis (general) As cert. by John R Kennedy M.B.C.M.	J. S. Fraser. Widower (Present)	1925. July 16th At Latheron. Agnes McInnes Registrar.
29	Walter Douglas Clyne. Scholar	1925. Between 5 pm and 7 pm on 30th May At the sea-shore at Clyth Latheron Caithness. Usual Residence Mid Clyth in the Parish of Latheron Caithness	M	13 Years	William Clyne Detective of the Metropolitan Police. Alice Clyne M.S. Pollard	Probably accidental fall over Cliff on sea shore at Clyth Latheron Caithness. Body not recovered	Registered on the information of D. J. Henry Procurator Fiscal	1925. August 8th At Latheron. Agnes McInnes Registrar.

Fig.6.27: Parish entry recording the death of Douglas.

Of course, there are search parties and investigations. It's established that he did take the train to Mid-Clyth and he was seen going to the cliffs by some local people. He was clearly collecting eggs and he was seen making a pile of them and going back for some more. This was towards the evening. It was a lovely day and the last train back was not until an hour or two later. It's clear that he must have fallen. He was an excellent climber – agile and with a good head for heights. It will never be known exactly what happened – perhaps he was subjected to a particularly violent attack by some of the birds. His body is never found and his death is only recorded a couple of months later. Of all the blows that have fallen on Len during his life so far, this is probably the hardest.

The arrangements for Lena's emigration to Canada were fixed by early in 1925. She's due to leave in September. She moves down to London around Easter, staying with Mina in King Street, Hammersmith. Seeing how hard it is for Mina reinforces her feeling that she should leave. She's 17 years old at this point, while Douglas is 12 and Len is 10. She feels that they should be OK without her now. The death of Douglas, which has to be accepted as fact by mid-summer, comes as a terrible blow to everyone. She thinks long and hard about whether she should still go, recognizing that Len will now be on his own. She goes up to Scotland to talk to him about the situation.

"Look, Len, I can come back up here to stay with you for a while. I can't bear to think of you on your own here – I know how close you were to Douglas."

"You're such a kind girl, Lena – nobody could wish for a better sister, but you know that makes no sense. There's nothing for you here – there are no jobs, you can't go to school and there aren't even many men around here! You're doing the right thing. I was in Wick the other day with John Don and we passed by the station. He told me that the train pulling out was a special, just for young people emigrating to Canada! He said that there had been several periods in the past when this had happened, and that lots of people like you are shortly going to leave. If you withdraw, they may not let you go on this scheme later. The country is in a mess, even in England, but they're crying out for people in Canada. I'll be fine here – I've got friends at school and John Don and Lizzie look after me well. I'll probably stay for another 6 or 7 years and then go down to London. The situation will be better then and, who knows, you may come back and we'll set up house together there! In the meantime, we'll write regularly."

Fig.6.28: Photo of Wick station in 1912, with a special train for emigrants to Canada.

Lena knows that he's right, and that it would be crazy to stay, but that doesn't make this any less heartbreaking. She hugs him long and hard, with tears streaming down her face. Len's eyes are dry – he knows that he has to be strong – but this is so hard, now that he's to lose both of the people who have always been there for him, and whom he loves so much. Lena takes a last look at him – he's just a little boy, trying to be brave, but she does feel that he's going to be OK. Whether she is going to be OK is not so clear to her. It's less than ten years since they were both enveloped within a huge, happy family, but it seems an age ago now. She suddenly has a flashback, as sharp and real as if it were yesterday. It's the summer of 1915 and she's walking arm-in-arm with Mamma along the babbling

River Cray. Douglas is in front of them, chasing some ducks along the bank, while Len, just a year old, is toddling along behind him at high speed, chortling with pleasure. It's almost too much to bear. The vision disappears as suddenly as it came. It now feels to her as if both she and Len are finally being cast adrift from that idyllic life, but she can see no other choices. Maybe it will all be OK in the end.

Name of Ship Doric . Date of Departure 25th September 1925 . Where bound Quebec & Montreal
Port of Departure Liverpool. Steamship Line White Star

NAMES AND DESCRIPTIONS OF **BRITISH** PASSENGERS EMBARKED AT THE PORT OF Liverpool 5

S.O.S.B.W. PARTY

British Cash

Contract Ticket Number	Names of Passengers		Last Address in the United Kingdom	Class	Port at which Passengers have contracted to Land	Profession, Occupation, or Calling of Passengers	Age	Country of last Permanent Residence	Country of Intended Future Permanent Residence
109	Archer	Mrs E.	5 Claremont Road	III	Quebec	Wife	53	1	Canada
		Elizabeth	Windsor Berks			Dom	18	1	
37078	Mitcheson	Lucy W.	Horrelse Cottage Hattersley Mottram Cheshire				46	1	
39086	Park	Jeanie P.	48 Benfield Road			Wife	54	1	
		Jean	Clapham			Dom	34	1	
8	Jones	L. May	48 Frears Road			Wife	28	1	
		Edward W.	Bridgenorth Salop			Child	4	1	
39095	Hales	Bertha C.	63 London Road Staines			Dom	44	1	
310144	Brodie	Margaret	57 Cutter's Road Blackhill Co Durham			Cook	38	1	
310988	Draney	Margaret	23 Peel St. Birkenhead			Dom	25	1	
311461	Spencer	Jane	32 Radford St			S'Keeper	33	1	
		Betsy	Blackley			Busswoman	34	1	
319498	Stone	Florence	15 Kennington Park Place London S.W.			Milliner	28	1	
3153944	Smith	Emily R.A.	2 Westbourne Road Barnsbury			Dressmaker	55	1	
5	Lewis	Emmy P.	Caxton House Westminster			Wife	45	1	
7	Clyne	Lena A.	241 King St. Hammersmith London			Dom.	18	1	

Fig.6.29: Part of the passenger list (relating to unaccompanied females) for sailing of SS Doric from Liverpool on 25th Sept. 1925.

So when the SS Doric, of the White Star Line, sails from Liverpool on 25th September, bound for Quebec City – the oldest port in Canada, Lena is on board. There are about 500 passengers, most of them emigrants. Lena is listed as a "Domestic", as are many of the women. This just means that they don't have a recognized job – not necessarily that they work as domestic helps. (Wives are commonly described as domestics, although the designation of housewife is used in this passenger list.) The Doric is a comfortable ship, even for those (the majority) sailing in 3rd Class – although Lena does share a cabin with three other women. The voyage, however, is not entirely pleasant, since they encounter some North Atlantic storms and it takes almost 2 weeks. It's the last run of the year for the Doric, which is dedicated to emigration trips of this type, since the St. Lawrence Seaway will soon start to freeze up. Reception arrangements for dealing with the immigrants are in place on arrival.

Fig.6.30: Print of SS Doric, dating from about 1924.

Lena's emigration is part of a scheme stimulated by the so-called Empire Settlement Act of 1922. This created a framework for promoting emigration of British people to the colonies, providing assistance with the cost of the voyage, and helping with initial accommodation, finding employment etc. It is particularly aimed at single people, including young girls. There is a disproportionately high take-up by people from Scotland. She settles down to a new life, in a country where unemployment is low and there are clearly possibilities of growth as the huge natural resources are exploited. The winters are cold, but not so different from those in Caithness. Lena writes regularly to her siblings back in Britain, but visits (in either direction) are not really feasible and inevitably they're not in very close contact. She does create a new life for herself, and acquires a range of new skills and experiences, but she always feels a strong affinity with her homeland. She has several opportunities to marry Canadians during the coming years, but is reluctant to make a commitment that would probably mean that she would never return. As for many people during this period, her future is far from clear.

6.6 Life in the Late 1920's

As the 1920s evolve, life moves on in various parts of the world. The situation in the USA advances rapidly, with many industrial and economic developments and a rapidly rising standard of living for most people. Terming these years "The Roaring Twenties" is quite appropriate for them. The picture is less rosy in much of Europe, at least for most working people. Things are improving slowly is Germany, although there is still much resentment about their treatment after the war and nationalist feelings are rising. Italy also has problems and there is increasing friction between left and right in many countries, including Britain. The levels of general dissatisfaction here, and the economic stresses, lead to a General Strike in May 1926. This arises from the treatment being meted out to the miners. The coal industry in Britain is in crisis, with prices depressed (partly due to the fact that the war reparations imposed on Germany include an obligation to supply coal free to France and Italy). Other contributory factors include the reintroduction of the Gold Standard (by the Chancellor of the Exchequer, Winston Churchill) the previous year, which had the effect of overvaluing the pound and thus harming British exports. To maintain profit margins, the mine owners have driven down the weekly wage of the miners (from £6 to less than £4 over the previous few years) and also extended their working hours. The miners feel that they simply cannot survive on these reduced levels of pay and they decide that they must go on strike. By mid-1926, more than a million of them have been without income of any sort for several months, with the situation for them and their families becoming increasingly desperate.

A general strike in support of the miners is called by the Trades Union Congress, which has been in effective existence for about 5 years. There are concerns, both in the TUC and the Labour Party, that this could rebound badly on them, particularly in terms of communist elements taking advantage of the situation. The strike is therefore limited to just a few types of workers – those in transport, the steel industry, dockers, printers etc. Just under two million workers take part. The Prime Minister, Stanley Baldwin, is relatively sympathetic, as is King George V and the Prince of Wales (future King Edward VIII). However, the corridors of power also harbour much more hawkish views, including those of Churchill, who calls in the Army. In any event, the strike is unsuccessful, partly because various (middle class) "amateurs" step up to ensure that vital services continue. It is called off by

Fig.6.31: Photo of a bus, with a police escort and military monitoring, during the General Strike of 1926.

the TUC after just 9 days. The miners continue their strike for a few more months, but most are forced to return to work by the end of the year. Their pay and conditions are slowly improved over the coming years, partly as a consequence of further government enquiries and measures, but it continues for many years to be a dangerous industry in which to work, and it remains subject to various economic forces.

The Clyne family ceases to be entirely based in North Kent, although Herbert does stay in Green Walk, in St. Paul's Cray, for the rest of his life and Frank (and his wife Gladys) come back to Dartford in the mid-1920s, when he again gets a job as a machinist. Stan leaves the Army after a few years and returns to civilian life in the mid-1920s. He settles in Wandsworth (further to the west, just south of Fulham) and marries Annie McCarthy in 1926. A few years later, they move out to one of the new "garden towns" being created to relieve the pressure on accommodation in London. This is Welwyn Garden City (Hertfordshire) and Stan gets work there in a cereal factory. Harry, aged 20 in 1925, and now in the Metropolitan Police, is living in Twickenham (West London).

Just as the economic situation seems to be getting better in Britain, towards the end of the 1920's, the whole financial and industrial system is hit by a dramatic crash, leading to the so-called "Great Depression". The apparently limitless growth during the late 1920s had led to high levels of debt, as people and institutions borrowed in order to invest further in companies. The whole system is based on confidence that debts can be paid and, once this becomes doubtful, the tendency is for people to cash in their assets. If borrowing is at a level where the demand for repayment cannot be met over a short period, then a collapse in prices inevitably follows. A sharp drop in share prices starts in Britain on 20th September 1929 (partly due to uncovering of some fraud), but this spreads concern to the USA, where the levels of investment and debt are much higher, and the collapse there is much more dramatic. On 24th October ("Black Thursday"), shares fall in value by over 10% in a single day.

Over the following weeks, months and years, there is a progressive fall in the value of the stock markets around the world, and particularly in the USA. By mid-1932, the Dow Jones Index stands at just over 10% of its level before the crash. The repercussions are felt all over the world, in the form of reduced trade, protective tariffs, cuts in production, loss of wealth and increased unemployment. For example, in Britain unemployment rises over this period from about 7% to around 15%, with local levels much higher than this – particularly in regions of traditional heavy industry (such as steel production, shipbuilding, textiles etc). In areas such as South Wales, the North-east, the North-west, the Midlands and Northern Ireland, the situation is dire. London is hit slightly less hard, but life becomes difficult everywhere. A series of Coalition governments lurch from one crisis to the next. After Britain comes off the gold standard in September 1931, giving a boost to exports as the pound is devalued, the situation slowly starts to improve, but it's several years before unemployment falls to manageable levels.

6.7 Football above 58° North

Towards the end of the 1920s, Len moves on to Castletown School. It was built in 1875, by the School Board of Olrig Parish. It's not linked to any particular religion. The school in Bowermadden (in the Church) is rather limited, although he has learned a lot from Minister MacEchern. Castletown, on the other hand, is a good school (by the standards of the day), with committed teachers and good facilities. As well as taking his education to a higher level, and instilling a love of literature and history, it brings Len into contact with a wider range of people and he becomes more involved with the life of the town. This includes playing football for the town team.

There is a strong footballing tradition in Scotland. The first Scottish team, Queen's Park, was founded in 1867 – about the same time that many of the very early clubs were being formed in England. Matches between teams that could be taken to represent the two countries started in 1870. When the "British Home Championship" tournaments started in

1884, Scotland tended to dominate, winning most of them in the 1880s. The Scottish football league started in 1890 and, of course, fierce rivalries started to develop at club level from around this period. In fact, the league-winner has been one of the two Glasgow clubs, Rangers and Celtic, in all but a handful of the years since then. Support for them is highly partisan - mainly along religious lines. The population level in the far north is much lower, so that the resources available there for football (or almost anything else) have always been much more limited. However, the interest levels, and the rivalries between local teams, are nevertheless at similar levels of intensity, and have been since around the same time. Castletown Football Club, for example, was one of the pioneers in the area, being founded around 1892 and having had a very good ground since that time. There has, however, been quite a lot of infighting in the region, with various league and cup competitions being set up, and decisions about which teams are eligible for them sometimes being hotly contested.

Also, there has always been something of an issue about when the games are played. In the middle of winter, there are only about 6 hours of daylight in these latitudes, plus the pitches are often covered in snow and the danger of getting frostbite is not always negligible. Many teams have thus opted to shift their football season to the summer (early May to mid-August). That means that they're unable to take part in any national competitions, so some of the bigger teams, such as Wick and Thurso, have stuck to the normal seasonal timetable.

When a Caithness county league is set up, most of the "village" teams, such as Castletown, are excluded, so they form their own – the Caithness North East Rural Football League, in 1930. They also have a cup competition. The league is made up of Castletown, Halkirk, Mey, Watten, Wick Boy Scouts and Keiss, who were the first winners of both league and cup. These teams probably wouldn't beat Rangers or Celtic, but the standard is not so bad – this region breeds strong and athletic young people.

Fig.6.32: Photo of the Castletown football team of 1931. Len is second from the right in the front row.

At this point, Len is 16 years old. He's a good footballer, and he joins the Castletown team for the following (summer) season. This is the start of a long winning run for the team, who carry off both league and cup for several years. In fact, Len moves down to England after a couple of years, but he's a stalwart of the team as this run gets under way. He's spared the embarrassment of receiving the Clyne Bowl, which is presented by honorary league president Noss Clyne towards the end of the 1930s, and awarded each year. Noss is a prominent farmer in the region, with his father

Fig.6.33: Photo of the Castletown football team of 1936.

having been a butcher.

Len does feel an affinity with the area, but it has its limitations and constraints. While he is close to the Dunnets, they're not quite like parents to him. In a slightly similar way to his father, he is drawn to the south – although in fact he knows very little of his father's life – particularly the early part of it – and his memories of him are very hazy. However, moving is going to be a little easier than it was for his father, since he does have contacts there already, in the form of his remaining siblings. Sadly, he doesn't really know them very well – Lena and Douglas were the ones to whom he was close during his formative years – but of course they will help him to find his feet. Anyway, as was the case for his father, there is not much work in the far north. He has done well at school, so that going to University – perhaps one of the Scottish ones – would have been an attractive option, but that would require cash and there simply isn't any. Still, he's sure, just as his father had been, that he'll be able to make his own way down there. It's time to move on. He's now 18 years old.

Chapter 7: Return to the South (September 1932 – September 1939)

7.1 Farewell to Bowermadden

While Len has certain advantages in his move to the south, compared with the situation of his father half a century earlier, he also faces some similar problems. An obvious one is cash. The Dunnets do have some savings, but these are of the order of a few tens of pounds, rather than hundreds or thousands. They can't provide Len with very much, even as a loan, and there just hasn't been much opportunity for Len to earn anything himself – paper rounds are not common in rural Caithness. In relative terms, he's in an even worse financial position than his father – whose parents were reasonably prosperous, with other sons in the family who were already employed in the thriving fishing industry. The current cost of train travel has been stable for some time at about 1.5 d per mile, so, with 240 d to the pound, the Thurso to London ticket costs about £4 – possibly a bit less if he negotiates carefully in advance. However, the main problem is the cost of living in the south – particularly London, which is considerably higher than in the far north. He can go down with a few pounds in his pocket, but it's not going to last him very long.

Fig.7.1: Hoarding at Euston station in the early 1930s, advertising cheap fares offered by the LMS.

Although Len is a good scholar, with excellent reading and writing skills (and an outstanding mark in his Scottish Leaving Certificate), there is little scope for him to get a job in advance – the economy is still severely depressed and he obviously doesn't have the skills or technical qualifications that might have given him a chance of immediate employment. He simply has to go down on spec and hope to pick up something. He does have the important advantage, compared with his father, of several prior contacts (siblings) in the London area. However, while there are 5 of these (Herbert, Frank, Stan, Mina and Harry), he doesn't actually know them very well. His formative years were spent with Douglas and Lena. He barely remembers anything from the time in Kent. They're mostly much older than him. Of course, there has been some letter-writing, but not so much. It is very sad that, having been born into a large, thriving and happy family, his childhood has turned out to be very different from what might have been expected – particularly in terms of contact with his siblings. Also, those 5 do have problems of their own, with Frank and Stan trying to support their young wives in shared houses, competing in a difficult job market, Herbert also being in a shared house and Mina still living in limited accommodation provided by the school. Harry, however, who is closest to Len in age, does have a stable job in the Met and he lives in a nice cottage in Twickenham. He has agreed that Len can come and live with him. This is a vital step, since it does offer at least a measure of security. Harry has visited Bowermadden a couple of times over the past dozen years and Len is sure that they'll get on well - and that he'll soon be able to get a job of some sort.

He takes his leave of the Dunnets shortly after his 18th birthday (and the end of the local football season). He'll always be grateful to them. They're very nice people – happy in their own way to be living in an environment that they know very well, even though it has its limitations. John Don is a pillar of the local community, being a founder member of the Bee-keepers' Association that is destined to be an important part of his (long) life. He and his sister get on very well and it's clear that neither of them will marry. They've not done a bad job in bringing up Len, all things considered, and they're clearly going to stay in contact with him throughout their lives. However, it's also clear that this is going to be a parting of the ways, with visits (in both directions) inevitably destined to be quite limited – after all, 700 miles is quite a long way. Len also takes his leave of a number of good friends he has in the area – including the other members of the Castletown Football Club and the teachers in the School. They also know that they probably won't see him very often in the future, if at all.

Just before he leaves, he also goes to see the Minister of Bower Parish, Dugald MacEchern. Dugald is now about 65 years old, but still in very good health and still very active, mentally and physically. He has no plans to retire from the Ministry and everyone is very happy to see him stay as long as possible. He's taken a keen interest in Len over the past dozen or so years, even after he moved on from Bower School to Castletown. In fact, Dugald has to some extent replaced the father than Len lost so early, and that young John Don could never quite become. Len has not become deeply religious, but he has acquired a love of literature and of the general atmosphere of the area, which somehow incorporates the ethos of the Church of Scotland. He knows the Bible quite well and has also learnt to love a lot of the poetry associated with Scotland. He recognizes that some of this has arisen from his contact with Dugald.

"Well, Len, we're sad tae see ye go, but this is the way o' the world. We often lose our best people, ye an' Lena amongst them. Ye'll be back – John Don an' Lizzie will'nae leave an' ye'll be back tae see them from time tae time, I'm sure o' that."

"I will that, Minister – and also to see you. This is not a place that's easily forgotten. I need to make my fortune, though – if not in cash then in experience. There are things I want to do that I cannot do here."

"Ye go with my blessing, son. An', if I may make so bold, with God's as well."

Some of his friends and teachers come to the station at Thurso, to see him off. Unlike the situation when the 5 newly-orphaned children arrived, 15 years before, which Len barely remembers, he and the Dunnets are not dependent on an old horse and rickety cart for transport. There are now taxis available, and Len has a proper suitcase, containing a good suit. Everyone knows that he'll certainly give this his best shot.

7.2 Finding a Foothold

The train journey down is also rather different from the Jellicoe Express experience. It's less crowded and more relaxed, although not any quicker – Len has to change trains a couple of times and, to save cash, he doesn't take a sleeper. He does, however, get to see quite a lot of the sights, including some of the deprivation in cities and towns en route. He is impressed, however, by much of what he sees – things like the Forth Bridge and Waverley Station – and also the surroundings there, since he has to spend a couple of hours in Edinburgh. He really has only the haziest recollections of the original northward journey and he hasn't since been any further south than Inverness. He eventually arrives at Euston, where Harry is waiting for him. They take a couple of buses down to Hampton (near Twickenham), where Harry rents a cottage in Hampton Court Road. Len has his own room and the facilities, which include mains water and electricity, are very good – certainly compared with what's available in Bowermadden. It's also a very pleasant area, close to Bushy Park and places like Hampton Court Palace. Len is determined to take advantage of this situation, and repay Harry for his kindness and generosity.

Len quickly sets about looking for a job. This is not easy. Even in London, with its wide range of industrial and commercial activity, the level of unemployment is very high at this point. However, Len is presentable and has good literary and communication skills. Within a few months, he's offered the job of an assistant in a tobacconist shop in Holborn. Even for a job like this, with relatively low pay, there is a lot of competition, but Len comes across well at the interview and, as a policeman, Harry is able to provide a reference that carries weight.

Fig.7.2: Photo taken in 1934 of the tobacconist shop at 337 High Holborn, with Len (right) and the Manager, Don.

The hours are long, but the working environment is good and he sticks at it. He gets on well with the Manager, Don Horne. He has to travel in from Hampton every day, but of course the transport system in London is excellent. It's only a short walk from Harry's house to Hampton station, from where he can reach Wimbledon in less than half an hour. Switching to the tube, it's just another half an hour to get to Chancery Lane, which is immediately adjacent to the shop. He soon learns the ropes and, like any Londoner, works out how to manage travel and other day-to-day arrangements as efficiently as possible. Don soon realizes that he can rely on Len to perform well in dealing with customers, promoting sales, managing the stock and handling the accountancy side. He increasingly leaves Len in sole charge and, within a few years, he moves on, strongly recommending that Len should be promoted to Manager. The owners agree and, by 1936, still only 22, he's in charge. Len and Don will keep in touch for a number of years.

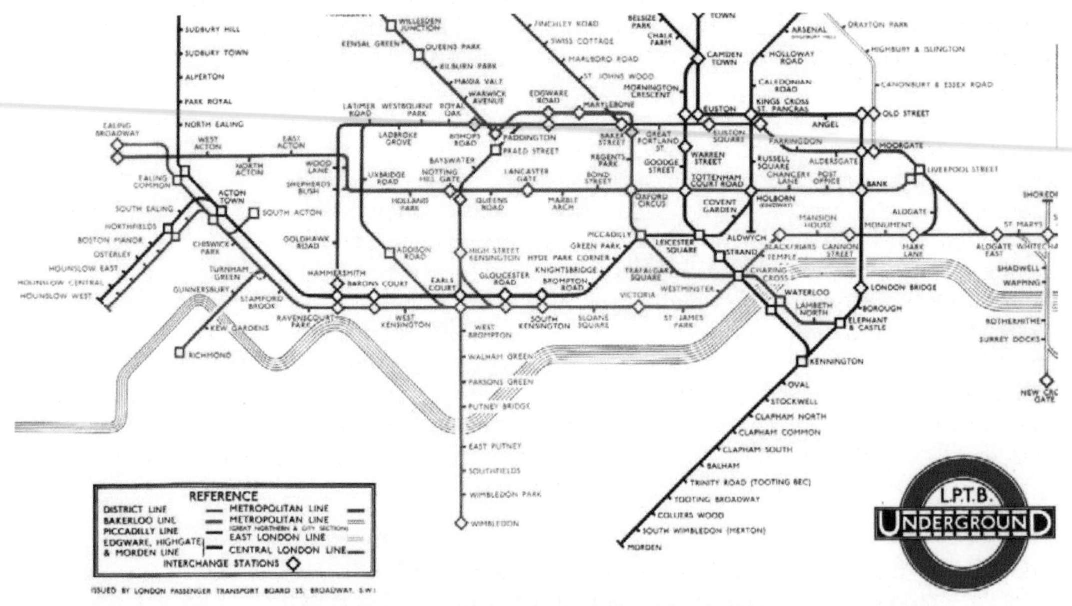

Fig.7.3: Part of the London Tube map of 1933.

Len is now on a commission arrangement and, with the shop doing very well (in a prime location), he starts to earn a good wage – up to £10 per week. He starts to save some money and he's also able to pay Harry something appropriate for his board and lodging. The arrangement is proving very successful and Len is now in a much better situation than most working class men in the country. In 1937, Harry (now aged 33) marries Grace Sibley. They move to a slightly larger house in Upper Sunbury Road – number 26. Len offers to move out, but both of them are keen for him to come and live with them. Len is very happy to do this and the 3 of them remain together in this house for a further period. He's getting to know the west and central part of London well, making new contacts and friends etc. His Scottish accent, which never became very strong - since he spent his most formative years (in Kent and Scotland) mainly with Lena and Douglas, starts to fade. He does, of course, have some contact with his other siblings still in the area – Herbert, Frank, Stan and Mina. Mina now has a partner (Frank Lunn) and has moved out of the school. They're shortly to be married. Only Herbert remains unattached, sharing the house in St.Paul's Cray with another family.

Fig.7.4: Photo of Len, taken in 1936.

7.3 Another Storm Brewing

A lot of things are happening in Britain, and in the rest of the world, as the 1930s unfold. The effects of the Great Depression linger on, creating dissatisfaction among working people in many countries. In the USA, President Roosevelt instigates his "New Deal", starting in 1933. These measures provide support for farmers, the unemployed, the young and the elderly. Constraints are imposed on the banking industry and federal funds are used for various public works and other activities that provide employment. It takes a while, but these initiatives do alleviate a lot of the worst suffering and by 1936 things have improved significantly in the USA. In Europe, however, while the Great Depression did not lead to such a sharp downturn as in the States, problems persist through most of the 1930s. In Britain, there is real deprivation for many people – out of work and with little cash being provided from anywhere. Many people depend on soup kitchens in order to survive. Desperate men engage in a series of marches from the North and Midlands down to London, to hand petitions in at the House of Commons and 10 Downing Street.

Fig.7.5: Photo of a hunger march passing through an English town en route to London, taken in 1935.

The political system in Britain is actually in chaos, with two national coalition governments being in charge throughout the first half of the decade, both headed by Ramsey MacDonald. He's a member of the Labour Party – having become the first Labour Prime Minister in 1924, albeit of a very short-lived minority Labour government. He takes over again in 1929, after a Labour election victory, but the Wall Street Crash leads to the formation of a coalition government, with him remaining at the helm. However, the policies adopted over the following years are very conservative – a long way from Roosevelt's New Deal – and do little to alleviate the situation for under-privileged people. Many Labour politicians and supporters become very frustrated with MacDonald and he is expelled from the Party in 1931, shortly after agreeing to lead a government that is notionally a coalition, but is now composed almost entirely of Conservative MPs. The whole episode is disastrous for both MacDonald and the Labour Party: his health suffers and he dies in 1937. The bottom line, however, is that the country goes through a very difficult period, largely due to failings of government.

Such problems are not confined to Britain and in some countries the long-term outcomes of their policies during this period are even worse. There is a tendency towards polarization between extreme left-wing (communist) and extreme right-wing (fascist) views, with violent clashes between them becoming widespread. In Germany, with resentment against the conditions imposed on them after the Great War still widespread, fanning nationalist sentiments, the outcome is a victory for fascism, imposed by Hitler in an increasingly dictatorial way. The Germans have something of a tradition for favouring strong, militaristic leaders and Hitler acquires support and powers that allow him to increasingly impose his extreme views. These include prejudice against other races – particularly the Jews – and against other political doctrines – particularly communism. Fascism also finds favour in several other European countries. Its initial rise can be traced back to Benito Mussolini becoming the Prime Minister of Italy in 1922. As an integrated country, Italy's history only stretches back to the 1860s. Dissatisfaction after the Great War was very high, partly because their hopes of obtaining more territory were largely frustrated. Mussolini capitalized on these strong nationalistic feelings. His initial creed didn't really extend to racial prejudice, although that did develop later. Hitler, and later General Francisco Franco in Spain, partly took their lead in the philosophy of fascism from Mussolini. Hatred of communism was a unifying thread.

As the 1930s unfold, Hitler becomes the strongest fascist leader, particularly after he is installed as Chancellor in 1933 and effectively stops any further democratic elections. Fascism, and Hitler's personality cult, attract adherents in many countries. These include Britain and France. In Britain, Ostwald Moseley emerges as the leader of fascism. Moseley is a complex character. From an aristocratic family, and a charismatic public speaker, he initially became a Conservative MP in 1918, aged only 21. However, he was strongly anti-war, and had much sympathy with working people. He left the Conservative Party after a couple of years and, after a period as an independent, became a Labour MP in 1926. However, he was very ambitious and became frustrated at lack of personal advancement in the national coalition government. He also felt that they were adopting the wrong policies to counter the Great Depression and left the House of Commons in 1932, to found the British Union of Fascists (BUF). Increasingly impressed by the progress Hitler was making in Germany, he starts to adopt similar tactics, creating his own militia (the Blackshirts) and coming into increasing conflict with both communism and Jewish communities.

At this point, the BUF has quite widespread support in the country, as indeed does communism. A particularly high profile clash occurs in October 1936, termed the "Battle of Cable Street. The BUF is given permission to march through the East End of London, into territory where there is strong support for communism, and also a large Jewish community. It is deliberately provocative. There are about 3,000 marchers, but many thousands of opponents take to the streets. It is clear beforehand that there is likely to be trouble and the authorities arrange for 6,000 Metropolitan Police - almost half of the force - to be there, mainly to protect the marchers. This is a reflection of the

Fig.7.6: Photo of police dispersing crowds that were attempting to disrupt a march of the British Union of Fascists in the Cable Street area on Sunday 4th October 1936.

sympathy for the BUF in the corridors of power. Violent clashes ensue, mainly between police and anti-fascist protesters. Almost 200 protesters are injured and a similar number arrested. Harry Clyne is appalled by what he and his colleagues are asked to do.

"You know, Len, this government is just a bloody mess. It's full of all sorts of factions and Baldwin has absolutely no idea how to control them. There are certainly a lot of very powerful people with fascist leanings, including much of the aristocracy and royal family. I just don't know where it's going to end, but letting that idiot Moseley go ahead with this march was mad – it was just a deliberate attempt to whip up trouble and it's the Met that has to somehow handle it. We're being made to act in the same way as Hitler's bloody private army!"

Fig.7.7: Photo of Ostwald Mosely in Millbank (London) on 4th October 1937.

"Well, you certainly can't refuse to obey orders," says Len, "but you're right that it's starting to look as if we're headed for serious trouble. The problem is that people just don't know which direction to turn – the Commies and Jews are getting the blame for everything, but the logical outcome for all this mad nationalism is war. Surely people can see that this solves nothing and that it's ordinary people who pay the price."

"Of course, but what are we all supposed to do? I've got mates in the force who say that the only way out of all this for ordinary working people is communism – and it's certainly true that there seems to be logic in what they say. Still, I'm sure that it wouldn't work here – and in any event people in the Army and Police are taking a risk just saying such things. We are in serious trouble, Len!"

Also prominent in the public mind in 1936 is the saga associated with the monarchy. King George V dies in January, with his son David becoming Edward VIII – it's common for names to be changed on accession to the throne. David is a charismatic and popular character – his sympathy with the plight of the miners in the previous decade - "Something must be done" - having gained him a lot of supporters. However, more recently he has shown signs of m oving much more to the right in political terms, visiting Nazi Germany several times and establishing various personal links there. Of more immediate concern is his determination to marry Wallis Simpson, an American socialite who is divorced from her first husband and in the process of divorcing her second. This is just not acceptable to most of the Establishment, particularly the Church. After a very public tug-of-war, he abdicates towards the end of the year, with his brother Bertie

Fig.7.8: Photo of Neville Chamberlain brandishing a copy of the Munich Agreement, as he arrives back in England on 30th September 1938.

reluctantly becoming King George VI. He's a less confident character than his brother, with a stammer that makes public speaking a trial, but he's to prove a much more reliable monarch than his brother would have been.

Len and Harry do take a close interest in these developments, along with the rest of the country. It's a topic of conversation for everyone. However, most people are becoming increasingly aware that a much more serious threat to normal life is developing in Europe. In October 1935, Mussolini's ambitions to expand the Italian Empire lead to the invasion of Abyssinia, in East Africa. As a member state, Abyssinia appeals for help to the League of Nations, but the response is minimal – an attempt at sanctions against Italy, but not taken seriously by anyone. The Italians complete the invasion within a year or so, and also leave the League. It's clear to all that it is ineffective and it soon virtually falls apart. Meanwhile, the other fascist nations of Europe are also increasingly using military aggression to achieve their aims. In March 1936, Hitler sends more than 20,000 troops into the Rhineland – a part of Germany that had been demilitarized under the conditions of the Treaty of Versailles. Again, there is no effective action from the League of Nations.

Aware that there is little international stomach for restraining him, and having eliminated internal resistance (partly via many assassinations in the "Night of the Long Knives"), Hitler goes strongly on the offensive. He expands the effective size of Germany over the next couple of years, via the "Anschluss" (annexation) of Austria and a similar takeover of the "Sudetenland" (Czechoslovakia). There is no military resistance to these, and German troops march in unmolested. The Austrians are mostly in favor. The Czech-speaking people (and the government) in the Sudetenland are not, but they are out-maneuvered politically, partly because there are also many German speakers there. Hitler sees this kind of thing as correcting the injustices of the Treaty of Versailles, but it's clear to all that his territorial and political ambitions have not yet been satisfied. The British and French try to restrain him, but unconvincingly.

The British and French Prime Ministers, Neville Chamberlain and Edouard Daladier, meet Hitler in Munich in September 1938 – at a conference arranged by Mussolini – and sign the "Munich Agreement", effectively accepting the annexation of the Sudetenland (on the understanding that the German expansion will end there). Chamberlain, who became Prime Minister just over a year earlier, knows that most people in Britain are still desperate to avoid war if possible. He returns proclaiming "Peace for our Time" – a message that people want to hear, but which is looking increasingly unlikely. This approach – perceived as "appeasement" of Hitler – may buy some time, but it clearly carries dangers.

In parallel with these ominous developments, there is a highly relevant battle going on in Spain. The country has been in a turbulent and chaotic state for well over a century. Its industrial development has been slow and it suffered badly during the Great Depression. The polarization between left and right has been more marked, and more evenly balanced, than in most other countries. The situation comes to a head in 1936, with its left-leaning government very unpopular and conflicts of various types springing up everywhere. The country is close to complete anarchy. There is a recent history of military coups and one now starts, under the leadership of Franco, which splits the country in a bitter and protracted civil war. The rebels, termed "Nationalists", are mostly drawn from supporters of the Catholic Church and the Monarchy, although their unifying theme is abhorrence of communism. Their opponents, termed "Republicans", are generally left-leaning, with the support of many ordinary working people. The army is split fairly evenly between the two sides. The balance of the war oscillates over a period of almost 3 years, with many atrocities committed and several other countries stepping in to fan the flames. Franco receives overt support from Mussolini and Hitler, who take the opportunity to try out their weapons of war. Germany sends the "Condor Legion" – ostensibly composed of individual volunteers, mostly from the Luftwaffe. Italy sends 50,000 troops. Franco also gets assistance from Portugal, whose leader (Antonio Salazar) has fascist leanings. The

Republicans are supported by the Bolsheviks (Soviet Union), although this is done a little more surreptitiously, and is not so effective. Individual volunteers also come into the country, mostly to fight on the Republican side, but, in military terms, their influence is small. Prominent among the atrocities is the bombing to virtual destruction of Guernica, by Nazi planes. This is a small town in the Basque region, held by the Republicans. Many hundreds of civilians are killed, illustrating the dreadful potential effect of the carpet-bombing of town and cities. A famous painting created shortly afterwards by Pablo Picasso makes this a high profile event. In April 1939, the war ends in victory for the Nationalists, with Franco installed as Head of State (although he had notionally held the title of Prime Minister since early in 1938). By this point, a much more widespread conflict is starting to look inevitable.

Britain is still heavily divided about fascism, with Moseley retaining a lot of support, but many recognizing the dangers of appeasement. The Conservative Party is badly split, with not only Churchill repeatedly warning about the dangers represented by Hitler, but many younger Tories also becoming strongly opposed to fascism. These include Edward Heath, whose parents met Alice and William in Crayford back in 1916. By 1938, Heath has already become active in (Tory) politics, being elected President of the Union in Oxford University and railing against the (supposedly Coalition) Government for its lack of resistance to Hitler and Franco. Heath has already travelled widely in Europe, attending a Nuremberg Rally and meeting people like Himmler, whom he later describes as "the most evil man I have ever met". Heath also spends a period in Spain with Republican forces, coming under machine gun and bomb attack, and narrowly escapes from Poland, with a Jewish friend, just before war is declared.

7.4 Preparation for War

The alarm bells have been ringing loudly in Britain, and in many other countries, at least since the middle of 1938. Hitler seems hell-bent on endless expansion (to create "Lebensraum" – space in which to live - for the German people), as well as on hounding the Jews and other "Untermenschen" (sub-human) races. He is also on a collision course with communism (particularly in the Soviet Union). Serious preparation for war starts in Britain late in 1938, although an increase in the manufacture of military products had been initiated a couple of years earlier – partly at the urging of Churchill. One concern, frequently expressed, is the vulnerability of London – a huge area containing a massive concentration of people and other resources that are likely to be vulnerable to bombing from the air. Hearing about the destruction of Guernica starts to concentrate minds in this direction.

People in London are starting to get genuinely concerned. There are also extended debates in the House of Commons. In 1938, the size of the British Army is below 400,000. This compares with around 600,000 for both Germany and France, while there are about 1,800,000 in the Soviet Army. Furthermore, Germany brought in conscription about 3 years earlier and the rate of increase of their armed forces is very high. Moreover, most of the British Army personnel are scattered over the globe, on garrison duty in various parts of the Empire. While the Soviets are perceived as some kind of safety net against German expansion – particularly since there is clearly a deep political divide between them – it's obvious that Britain is looking very vulnerable, particularly in terms of civilians (in London) being bombed. The Luftwaffe is building bombers at an alarming rate. In February

Fig.7.9: An Anderson shelter being assembled.

1939, the first Anderson Shelters (named for the Minister of Home Security, Sir John Anderson) are erected. These are distributed free to those on incomes of less than £5 per week and about 1.5 million of them are assembled in domestic gardens in London over the following 6 months.

Effort is also directed towards increasing the size of the British Army. Little has been done up to now, with most of the recent military expenditure having been on the Navy and Air Force. On 29th May 1939, the Military Training Act passes into law, introducing conscription for all single men aged 20 and 21 who are living in the UK. This is the first UK conscription in peacetime. People in certain occupations, including the police, are exempted, so it doesn't apply to Harry. It also doesn't apply to Len, who is now aged 24, although it certainly seems likely that it will soon expanded in scope and, as for his brothers a quarter of a century earlier, Len is inclined to step up. Of course, everyone is still hoping that this will all blow over. There are also many people in the country who are strongly anti-war, including a large contingent with communist sympathies. It's a time of great uncertainty, with none of the confidence that was so widespread in 1914.

The government also starts to implement other measures, some associated with Air Raid Precautions (ARP). ARP Wardens start to get appointed in 1938, together with various people who will help with first aid arrangements etc. There is also a flurry of planning aimed at moving children and other vulnerable groups out of London (and other large cities). One measure that causes great inconvenience, and consumes a lot of resource, is the requirement to carry and wear gas masks. There is great fear of poison gas being dropped by bomber aircraft and arrangements are made for everyone – particularly in London – to have a mask. They will also be obliged carry it at all times and to put it on if instructed. This terror of gas is one of several attitudes inherited from the Great War, during which it was used quite extensively on battlefields and caused a lot of lasting damage to throats, eyes and lungs, as well as killing many soldiers. It turns out there will be no use of gas in the co ming conflict, but that is in the future.

Fig.7.10: A mobile gas mask fitting unit in London in 1935.

As 1938 comes to a close, with few clear developments, hopes start to rise. The German Army marches into the Sudetenland, as agreed, and Hitler repeatedly states that he intends nothing further. There are, however, ominous signs. In November, there is a night ("Kristallnacht") of extreme violence against Jews and their property in Germany. Floods of Jews, and others, are fleeing Germany, with terrifying tales of Nazi atrocities and rapid increases in German military resources. The Spanish Civil War is dragging to a close, with the fascists victorious. As 1939 evolves, there are feelings of dread, although still mingled with hope. It also has to be recognized that there are still many people in Britain with fascist

Fig.7.11: London chorus girls rehearsing in their gas masks during 1939.

sympathies.

Suddenly, however, things come to a head. In August, the Germans and Soviets sign a non-aggression pact – the Molotov-Ribbentrop Agreement. Hitler and Stalin agree, not only to avoid fighting each other, but also to collaborate and increase their trading and other ties. This quickly becomes public knowledge, although some of the details of the agreement, such as an arrangement to carve up Poland and the Baltic States between them, remain secret. This is a bombshell for Britain and France. People had assumed that Hitler's hatred of communism, and of the Slavic peoples, would act as some kind of protection. Now, not only Poland, but also most of the rest of Europe, is in grave danger. The Wehrmacht is growing rapidly and becoming highly efficient, with capabilities for rapid movement and strong support from the Luftwaffe.

The dam bursts on 1st September, when the German Army invades Poland. The Polish Army is quite large, but it is antiquated and inefficient. The Polish troops fight bravely and well, but they are ill-equipped to face the "Blitzkreig" tactics of the Germans. Another lesson from the Great War, which again turns out to be wrong, is that defensive strategies are often best – to attack runs the risk of huge casualties, as men are exposed to machine gun fire from strong entrenched positions. This war is to be very different, with highly mobile units, often including many tanks and with air support, able to crash through defenses, so that huge swathes of land can be invaded and occupied very quickly. In fact, the Poles are caught in several pincer movements, some involving Soviet troops, who move in a couple of weeks later. It's all over by the end of the month. The numbers of Polish dead and wounded are not so great, but hundreds of thousands are taken prisoner. Many of these are killed – either executed or starved to death. Part of the country comes under German control and the rest is taken by Russia, which also moves into the Baltic States of Latvia, Estonia and Lithuania. Many Poles, including those in government, flee the country – mostly to Britain.

The response of Britain and France is one of shock and panic. They both declare war on Germany a couple of days after the start of the invasion, but there is little or no attempt to come to Poland's aid. French troops are mobilized in the area, but no significant attack is made. Little is done in Britain, except to implement pre-planned war preparation measures. Conscription is immediately raised to cover all men aged between 18 and 41. ARP is stepped up, particularly in London. These include complete black-outs every night, distribution of gas masks and evacuation of children to the countryside. There are attempts to create some public bomb shelters – for example in the basements of certain buildings - and the distribution of Anderson Shelters is stepped up. The authorities are initially against use of Tube stations in London as shelters, although this does happen quite extensively later. Anti-Aircraft Batteries are set up in open spaces – mostly in the public parks in London. While some parents refuse to let their children be evacuated from London, the levels of concern are such that well over a million of them are moved out during the first few days of September.

Fear that the Luftwaffe will start bombing London within days or weeks is palpable. In Hampton, about 15 miles from the Houses of Parliament, Len, Harry and Grace are aware that they could be in real physical danger. Herbert, and also Frank (with his wife Gladys and their daughter Betty), are even closer to the firing line in Dartford. Mina is now in Aldershot, and thus about 40 miles from London,

Fig.7.12: Photo of 3.7" Anti-Aircraft guns in Hyde Park, taken in 1939.

although, as a long-established military town, it is likely to be targeted. In fact, Mina gets married in September to Frank Lunn, with Len and Frank acting as witnesses. Stan, with his wife Annie, is now in Welwyn Garden City, which is about 25 miles from London. However, there are potential industrial and military targets in that area. In fact, virtually the whole country is in a state of fear and uncertainty. Moreover, there is still quite a lot of internal resistance to the UK going to war with Germany, particularly from those aligning with either the communist or the fascist causes. The former includes many working class people, while the latter encompasses a number in influential positions in the country. Moseley is still at large, and still advocating some sort of alliance with Hitler.

Chapter 8: London at the Epicentre (September 1939 – May 1941)

8.1 Joining Up

Declaration of war triggers a big change in the conscription rules, with all men between 18 and 41 immediately being obliged to register. Len joins up on 20th October, at the Acton recruiting centre. Partly because two family members (father and brother) had joined the Metropolitan Police, he is recruited into the Corps of Military Police (CMP), in the London Area Provost Company (LAPC) – the Army is very fond of acronyms, many of them rather impenetrable. This seems to be particularly true in the area of "Provost", which can be taken to cover the various issues of discipline and general support for army activities: the terms that Len now has to absorb include Provost Marshall (PM), Deputy Provost Marshall (DPM), Assistant Provost Marshall (APM), Supply of Services (SOS), Line of Communication (LC) and Vulnerable Points (VP). Entry to the CMP is a little tighter than for normal army units, with strict educational and physical examinations.

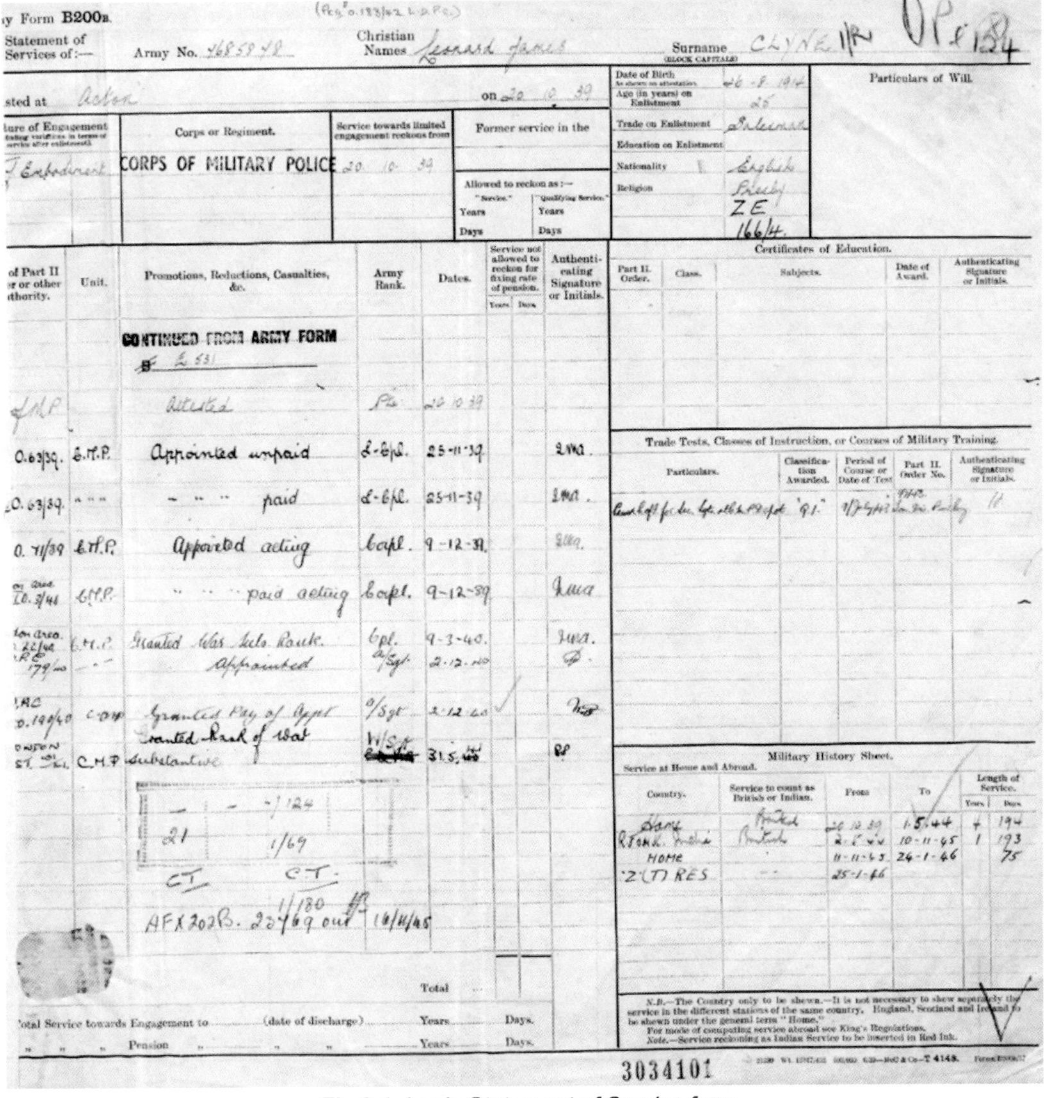

Army Form B200B.

Statement of Services of:— Army No. 7685948 Christian Names Leonard James Surname (BLOCK CAPITALS) CLYNE

Enlisted at Acton on 20 10 39

Date of Birth: 26-9-1914; Age (in years) on Enlistment: 25; Trade on Enlistment: Salesman; Education on Enlistment; Nationality: English; Religion: Presby

Particulars of Will.

Nature of Engagement	Corps or Regiment.	Service towards limited engagement reckons from	Former service in the
T Embodiment	CORPS OF MILITARY POLICE	20 10 39	Allowed to reckon as:— "Service." Years Days; "Qualifying Service." Years Days

Part II Order or other authority	Unit.	Promotions, Reductions, Casualties, &c.	Army Rank.	Dates.	Service not allowed to reckon for fixing rate of pension. Years / Days	Authenticating Signature or Initials.
		CONTINUED FROM ARMY FORM B 2531				
CMP		Attested	Pte	20 10 39		
O. 63/39.	C.M.P.	Appointed unpaid	L-Cpl.	25-11-39		
O. 63/39.	" " "	" " " paid	L-Cpl.	25-11-39		
O. 71/39	C.M.P.	Appointed acting	Cpl.	9-12-39		
O. 3/41	C.M.P.	" " " paid acting	Cpl.	9-12-39		
	C.M.P.	Granted War Subs Rank.	Cpl.	9-3-40.		
179/40	" "	Appointed	A/Sgt.	2-12-40		
O. 140/40	C.M.P.	Granted Pay of Appt	A/Sgt	2-12-40		
	C.M.P.	Granted Rank of War Substantive	W/Sgt	31.5.41		

AFX202B. 23769 out 16/11/45

Total Service towards Engagement to (date of discharge) Years Days.

Pension Years Days.

Certificates of Education.

Part II. Order.	Class.	Subjects.	Date of Award.	Authenticating Signature or Initials.

Trade Tests, Classes of Instruction, or Courses of Military Training.

Particulars.	Classification Awarded.	Period of Course or Date of Test	Part II. Order No.	Authenticating Signature or Initials.

Military History Sheet.

Service at Home and Abroad.

Country.	Service to count as British or Indian.	From	To	Length of Service. Years	Days
Home	British	20 10 39	1.5.44	4	194
	British		10-11-45	1	193
Home		11-11-45	24-1-46		75
Z (T) RES		25-1-46			

N.B.—The Country only to be shewn.—It is not necessary to shew separately the service in the different stations of the same country. England, Scotland and Ireland to be shewn under the general term "Home."
For mode of computing service abroad see King's Regulations.
Note.—Service reckoning as Indian Service to be inserted in Red Ink.

3034101

Fig.8.1: Len's Statement of Service form.

The concept of a "Provost" being in charge of discipline in the British Army goes back centuries, but having a sizeable and well-defined Corps of men with this responsibility is more recent. The CMP did exist during the Great War, but it was relatively small, and often proved inadequate for the various demands that arose. These included, not only general policing of misbehavior by individual soldiers, but also controlling military traffic, facilitating deployment of advancing or retreating units, handling prisoners of war etc. This time there is a determination to give these requirements a higher priority and the size of the CMP is raised from a few thousand to several tens of thousands within a few weeks of the start of war.

The relationship between the CMP and the rest of the Army is a slightly complex one. Unlike most soldiers, CMP Officers are always armed – they carry a small pistol. Moreover, they can in principle issue orders to soldiers of any rank, and even have them arrested. In practice it's very rare for a CMP Corporal to reprimand a General, even if he's clearly drunk and disorderly, but such authority is needed if the system is to work coherently.

Fig.8.2: New recruits to the Corps of Military Police, together with their instructor, at Mytchett in 1940. Len is on the left in the front row.

Len's uniform includes a cap with a red band. The esprit de corps of the "Redcaps" is very high. There is intensive training at the large camp in Mytchett, near Farnborough, lasting several months. Promotions follow in short order – these always tend to be quick in wartime, but there is also a feeling that military police need to have authority – in fact, there are no Privates in the CMP. Len becomes a Lance-Corporal immediately and a Corporal in early December. Further promotions, to Sergeant and then to (Company) Sergeant-Major (a Warrant Officer) are to follow within 18 months. This is quite rapid, although not unusual under wartime conditions.

Herbert, who is now aged 42, also joins up at the same time, but he naturally rejoins his old regiment, the Royal West Kents, and the same Battalion, the 1/4th – also following the footsteps of William and Stan. It is made clear to Herbert that, at his age, he will probably not be sent to any combat zones. Frank, who is 41, tries to rejoin the Seaforth Highlanders, but he's told that he should defer until the course of the war becomes a little clearer. Stan, who has a daughter (Betty) aged 6, is in a category that is at present exempt. This also applies to Harry, since the police are exempted.

8.2 The Phoney War

Everyone is braced for imminent attack, including the bombing of London, but the days and weeks go by without anything of this type happening. In fact, most civilians don't see or hear anything for many months. The blackout, which is strictly enforced, and the obligation to carry gas masks, start to feel unnecessary, as well as onerous. Some parents bring their evacuated children back to London. There is in fact some military activity during this period, but most of it doesn't impinge on everyday life, at least in Britain. A British Expeditionary Force (BEF), comprising about 150,000 soldiers, together with supplies and military vehicles etc, is quickly sent to France. A contingent of about a thousand CMP is included, most of them recruited from the Automobile Association (AA). Their role is seen as predominantly related to traffic control, ensuring that troop movements take place smoothly. Len and most of the other recent recruits are under training in Britain. The London area Company (LAPC), where Len is based, is already facing challenges, with a lot of activity taking place in the capital.

In fact, the BEF does very little there in the following months, apart from helping the French to dig defensive earthworks, although there are demands on the CMP, some of them involving cooperation with French authorities. There again seems to be an implicit assumption that this war will be similar to the last one, so that a lot of trenches will be needed. In October, Hitler offers peace terms to Britain and France, again indicating that his plans for expansion are now complete, but this is rejected. He no longer has any credibility with the Allies.

After invading Poland, the German military machine does very little for some time. The Soviets, on the other hand, do make a move. After taking over the Eastern part of Poland, and the Baltic States, the Red Army attacks Finland at the end of November, starting what becomes known as the "Winter War". Their justification for this is that some important parts of Russia, particularly Leningrad, are close to their Western border, and hence could be vulnerable to later attack by the Germans. This sounds a bit strange, although there is widespread recognition that the Soviet-German "alliance" may not last very long. More likely is that Stalin is attempting to seize another opportunity to expand the Soviet Empire by taking over all of Finland. They certainly expect to move in quickly, having a huge numerical advantage over the Finns in men and weaponry. However, it doesn't work out that way, with the Finnish resistance being strong, the severe weather causing problems for the invaders and the Red Army turning out to be far behind the Germans in efficiency and organization. This is duly noted. Hitler, in particular, forms a low opinion of Soviet military capabilities.

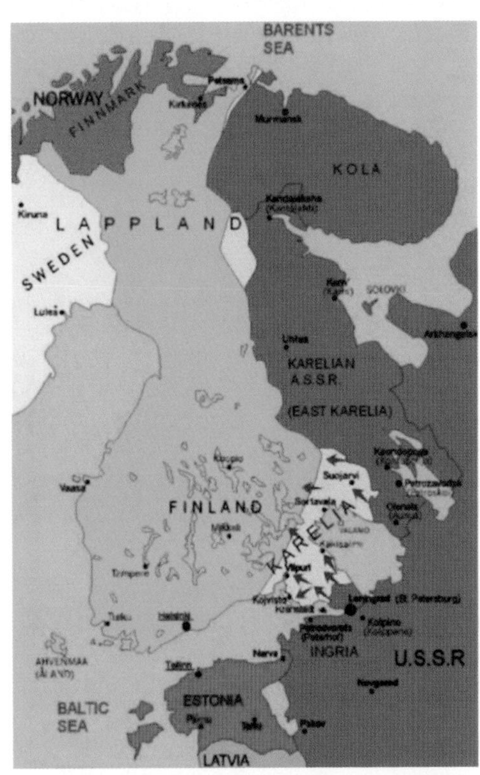

Fig.8.3: Map showing the areas in which Russia attacks Finland in the Winter War.

There is much sympathy in Britain for the Finns and an attempt is made to assemble an Army to assist them. On the other hand, there are many voices in the UK advising against attacking Russia. In the event, before any such assistance can become tangible, the Russians make peace with Finland (in March 1940), having taken possession of some small parts of the country, claiming that this was always their intention. Their loss of several hundred thousand men, against less than a hundred thousand Finns, is probably the real reason. Meanwhile, the Germans and British have been attacking each other, but mainly at sea, and in a limited way. Britain tries to impose a blockade on Germany, as it had done so successfully in the Great War, but this has little effect, partly because of trade between Russia and Germany. A couple of major British warships are sunk by U-boats, while a British task force traps the German cruiser Admiral Graf Spee in the harbour of Montevideo – Uruguay being a neutral country, where it is scuttled by its captain. A couple of daytime British bombing raids are undertaken on military targets in Germany, but these are unsuccessful, with heavy losses, and are discontinued. Some people propose bombing raids on German cities, but there is a fear that this will provoke retaliation in kind. Furthermore, soon after the start of the war, President Roosevelt had implored all sides to avoid the bombing of civilian populations and, at that point, Britain, France and Germany all agreed to this.

Among the other measures that Britain contemplates is sending troops to Norway – in fact, sending the force that had been assembled to assist the Finns. The objective here is to stop the supply of resources going from Norway to Germany – particularly iron ore coming originally from Sweden. However, the Germans hear of this and decide to invade Norway themselves, partly to obtain naval and air bases from which to attack Britain. At this stage, their decision-making and actions are much quicker and more effective than those of Britain and France. By the time that the British force has reached the Northern parts of Norway, Germany has already invaded from the South, taking over Denmark en route. The "lightning war" tactics of the Germans seem irresistible. By early summer of 1940, the Germans are in complete control of Norway, with a puppet government installed - later to be headed by Vidkun Quisling. His name becomes a byword for collaboration with the Nazis.

It's clear to all that both the French and the British responses to Hitler are dithering and ineffective. There are still people who are advocating an alliance with him, but it's obvious to most that he cannot be trusted and that he is in fact a megalomaniac. He has been through a lot of trauma in the earlier part of his life, but he's just totally unsuited as a character to being a national leader. Both British and French governments are now in crisis. Chamberlain is unwell and clearly cannot take any kind of control of the war. This is evident by April, with the fiasco of the Norwegian affair being the last straw. He resigns on 10th May 1940. The government is reorganized, still along national coalition lines, with Churchill taking the helm. There is frustration in the country, although it is also combined with a feeling that the war has actually amounted to very little so far. The term "Phoney War" starts to get bandied about and there is humorous reference in British papers to a "Sitzkreig".

However, this suddenly changes, on the same day that Churchill is installed as leader, when the German Army starts an invasion of France (and also Belgium, Luxembourg and Holland). As with their previous moves, this is well-planned, dynamic and highly effective. Within a few short weeks, they are crashing through the various defensive formations set up by the French, Belgians and British.

Fig.8.4: Map showing Allied defensive lines in 1939.

In fact, there had been extensive discussions within the German military (and with Hitler) during the previous 6 months about how and when to attack, with many changes of plan. There had been no initial intention to delay for so long, but it does mean that, when it finally comes, it is very well-prepared. A total of 3 million men are mobilized for the attack, including nearly a million in the hugely expanded Luftwaffe.

This force has deficiencies and limitations, but the attack – partly through the forests of the Ardennes, which had been discounted as impossible by the Allies – has a large element of surprise, with Panzer tank divisions moving at high speed, and it is spectacularly successful. The German Wehrmacht generals, such as Erwin Rommel and Heinz Guderian, show great initiative and flexibility. By the middle of June, it is all over – Paris falls and the French surrender unconditionally. Much of the British Expeditionary Force manages to make it back to England, after a frantic evacuation from Dunkirk, although they have to abandon virtually all of their equipment. During this operation, the small CMP contingent is suddenly thrown into a totally unexpected situation, becoming critical to the retreat. It's a nightmare scenario, with most of the roads suddenly blocked by huge numbers of civilian refugees and the Luftwaffe dominating the skies above them. The CMP personnel are faced with terrible problems in trying to find routes to the sea and somehow funnel the demoralized and disorganized troops along them. They're also faced with trying to facilitate embarkation into the hundreds of small and large ships in the vicinity of Dunkirk. Towards the end, they're among the last to abandon Calais and to finally get off the beaches, forming an important part of the rearguard. There is much heroism, but there's no escaping the fact that the whole episode is extremely chaotic. Many lessons have to be learned, including the potential importance of the role of the CMP. It clearly needs to be expanded and its training and organization overhauled.

The Germans are now in complete control of almost the whole of mainland Europe, and they have acquired huge resources - including many airfields and ports within easy striking distance of Britain. Mussolini, after keeping a watching brief for a while, decides that he can see which way the wind is blowing, and that there could be rich pickings. Italy therefore declares war on Britain and France in early June. Franco decides that Spain will remain neutral, although it's clear that his sympathies are with the Axis powers.

These rapid and catastrophic developments come as a terrible shock to the British people. They know that the gloves are off, and that Hitler's undivided attention is now going to focus on their island. Londoners, in particular, brace themselves for what is likely to come in the near future. Flat-out efforts are now being made in training of men and women – with the latter now making major contributions in many areas, and in creating huge stocks of armaments, explosives etc. This period is a busy time for Herbert. While he doesn't go to France with the BEF, where part of the Battalion is posted, and hence doesn't get caught up in the subsequent retreat from Dunkirk, he does go to Lincolnshire, to defend the coast there.

In November, he is moved nearer home, to the south coast of Kent, where they take responsibility for defending the section between Dungeness and Hythe. There's a lot of work to be done in building up defensive structures, since this is one of the prime sites for invasion. They're billeted in houses in Littlestone, next to New Romney. It's a very quiet place and, for recreation

Fig.8.5: An armoured train on the Romney, Hythe and Dymchurch railway in Kent.

in the evenings, they usually go into Hythe on the famous (miniature) Romney, Hythe and Dymchurch Railway, which has been requisitioned by the Army. In fact, this railway even has armoured trains, on which guns have been mounted. Of course, the real hub of social activity is still London – in fact probably even more so than before the war. It's a very lively scene, with both Londoners and various visitors keen to forget their worries for a few hours occasionally.

8.3 London under Siege – the Blitz Starts

With the German takeover of Europe virtually complete, the war as far as Britain is concerned is evidently not going to be a phoney one any longer. Hitler has a clear plan for the invasion of Britain, to be completed within a month - perhaps two if there is more resistance than expected. This involves gaining control of the air, partly via attacks on airfields and aircraft factories, followed by a quick seaborne invasion in many small boats. It's also planned that ports on the south coast will be attacked during the initial phase, weakening British naval power in the vicinity. Any kind of overall supremacy at sea is considered unlikely, but dominance of the air is expected to be sufficient to ensure that most of the landing craft get through during a quick, surprise crossing. Both gaining control of the skies and the subsequent invasion are each predicted to take just a couple of weeks or so. In view of recent events, it looks like a good plan. Of course, looks can be deceptive.

Fig.8.6: Photo taken on 9th September 1940, at Harrington Square, Mornington Crescent.

The air battle ("Battle of Britain") starts in mid-July, with bombing attacks by the Luftwaffe on ports and coastal airfields, plus night raids on aircraft production factories. At this point, the RAF and the Luftwaffe have broadly similar numbers of aircraft (~2,000), with technical capabilities that are not too dissimilar. The numbers of pilots on the two sides are also in the same ball-park, although the RAF is being reinforced by influxes from Poland and from British Empire countries. German pilots do have more combat experience, gained in the Spanish Civil war as well as in the recent invasions, but the assurances to Hitler from Hermann Göring, the Head of the Luftwaffe, are evidently optimistic. His main ambitions are to gain ascendancy for the Luftwaffe, and for himself, over the other military powers in the Nazi regime.

It soon becomes clear, however, that the RAF will be far from a pushover. Even if the rough numerical parity was no guarantee of this, there are further factors that favour it. One is the rapid development of radar in Britain, dramatically raising the efficiency of interception. Another is that, while lacking combat experience, the RAF pilots, and also the ground support crews, perform outstandingly well. A third is that most of the fighting is taking place in UK airspace: German planes, particularly fighters, often have insufficient fuel to do much very before they need to head for home. Finally, the rate at which aircraft are being produced in the UK does not fall significantly as a result of the bombing campaign. Nevertheless, it's a bitter and hard-fought battle.

After about 10 weeks of attacks on airfields and ports, dog-fights above Kent, hundreds of daytime bombing raids and frantic efforts on both sides to train more pilots, build more aircraft and refine various technical procedures, the Germans decide to change tack. Their attrition rate – for example, losing about 800 aircraft during August (compared with about half that number for the RAF) – is unsustainable. The invasion plans are put on hold. They decide to focus instead on night bombing of cities – mainly London. They anticipate lower losses at night, plus far less difficulty in ensuring that their bombs do damage. With the main objective being to intimidate Londoners, and seriously disrupt the many important activities taking place there, virtually anywhere in the huge city will do. Also, the characteristic shape of the Thames, which is usually quite readily visible, even at night, provides a useful landmark. The focus shifts during September, and the Blitz now starts in earnest. This is the first of a long string of poor military decisions for which Hitler is primarily responsible.

Fig.8.7: A couple demonstrating the use of a Morrison shelter.

Although it has been expected for a year, the concerted bombing attack on London comes as something of a shock. Suddenly, the bomb shelters, public and private, come into serious use. It has already become clear that the Anderson Shelters are not ideal – they often become cold and damp, if not completely waterlogged. Spending long periods at night in them can be extremely unpleasant. Moreover, not all houses have gardens in which they can be located. At around the start of the Blitz, some simpler set-ups are distributed, for use inside houses. These Morrison Shelters (named for the current Minister of Home Security, Herbert Morrison) are in the form of a simple steel frame, within which a bed can be located. They are provided free, in kit form, to households with annual incomes below £400. Half a million are in use by the end of the Blitz. They're capable of protecting people against even very heavy impacts from falling masonry etc and they save many lives.

Fig.8.8: Aldwych tube station being used as a bomb shelter in 1940.

Still, it's clear to all that home-based shelters cannot protect against direct hits. Many people, particularly those close to the centre of the city (and in parts of the East End, close to the docks that are particular targets) start to focus on deep public shelters. These include tube stations, although the government is not keen on their use: this is sensible enough, since they do want to keep the transport system operational and buses are obviously very susceptible to road damage. However, the raids are almost all at night, so use of tube stations starts to look like a good idea to some Londoners. The authorities eventually give way on this. In fact, the Aldwych branch, which is on a short spur from

Fig.8.9: Herbert Mason's famous photograph of St.Paul's Cathedral, surrounded by fire, during the air raid of 29th December 1940.

Holborn and is not so heavily used anyway, is closed to trains and given over to use as a shelter. Some others are also quite extensively used. Generally, they are safe, but uncomfortable and difficult to tolerate night after night. They're not very heavily used.

The raids quickly become relentless. There are attacks almost every night for the two months following the start in early September. On Sunday 15th September, about 1,500 Luftwaffe aircraft attack London for the whole of the day. They hope to inflict heavy losses on the RAF as they are forced to defend the city. It fails, partly due to thick cloud, and they switch after this to night raids, which are to persist until the following May. Life becomes a daily struggle for Londoners, with little sleep and constant fear. Large swathes of the city are virtually flattened. Fighting fires, repairing bomb damage, dealing with unexploded bombs, rehousing people, treating the injured and, somehow, continuing to live and work constitute major challenges for everyone. The local authorities bear much of the burden - arranging ARP wardens, fire fighters, stretcher bearers, first aiders, volunteers providing soup kitchens and other services – in fact a myriad of tasks are needed to keep the city functional under these conditions. There is no parallel in previous history for such a sustained onslaught on a city.

On 14th October, 380 bombers come over and about 200 people are killed. Only two planes are shot down. The next night, incendiary bombs are heavily used and about 900 fires are started. The London docks, and also the railway system, are heavily targeted. By the end of October, about 13,000 civilians have been killed and 20,000 badly injured. Nevertheless, morale remains high and the defences against air attack are gradually being improved. As the end of the year approaches, it's clear that Christmas will be a little different this year, but Londoners are determined to see this through.

Len's first year in the Army is thus an extremely challenging one. The first 6 months for the enlarged CMP is dedicated to training of various types, with some lessons being learned from the several hundred members of the Corps who came through the disastrous BEF venture and managed to escape via Dunkirk. However, particularly for the London Division, the Blitz suddenly brings a whole new series of challenges. To say the least, London is faced with many problems and a lot of these relate to discipline and control of the various military forces in the city. These include contingents from France, Poland, Norway, Canada and a number of other countries. In general, these soldiers do not have their own military police. From the summer of 1940 and into the winter, Len and his new colleagues are faced with many demands as the government and Army authorities struggle to create order in the chaos. Extensive liaison is needed with the Metropolitan Police and many other civil authorities. London is now a cauldron of people and the normal peacetime measures for its management are breaking down. These people include deserters, spies, fifth columnists etc as well as many bona fide refugees of various types. Trying to ensure that people have identity papers is a major administrative headache. Although the primary role of the CMP concerns discipline within the Army, they're also faced with many other tasks, including control over the high levels of military traffic in and around the city, which becomes nightmarish as the bombs start to fall.

8.4 New Friends and Another Family History

The statistics of surviving the Blitz are worthy of note. At first glance, the chances don't look so good, with bombs raining down virtually every night for about 8 months. In fact, about 30,000 fall on London (and explode) during this period – this doesn't include the many incendiary devices that are also dropped. However, the huge area of Greater London (about 60 miles^2 or 160 km^2) is relevant here. People in the immediate vicinity of an impact site are likely to be killed or seriously injured. However, while damage to property can extend for hundreds of yards, this "direct hit" zone typically has a radius of only about 20 yards, or an area of about 1,000 m^2. Moreover, while certain locations, such as the Port of London, are more heavily targeted than others, these 30,000 impact sites are in fact distributed fairly evenly over the whole city. With an average of about 100 bombs exploding every night, the aggregate area in which people are likely to be killed or badly injured during a particular night is thus about 100,000 m^2, or around 0.01% of the total area of the city. This is therefore the statistical chance of being killed or injured on any given night. The chance of surviving 250 nights of this is actually $(0.9999)^{250}$, or about 97.5%. Of course, that still leaves a 2.5% chance of suffering a direct hit. With 6 million people living in the city (down from about 8 million before the war), this corresponds to about 150,000 people being killed or badly njured during the Blitz, and indeed this is more or less what happens.

Of course, Londoners aren't in a position to make such estimates. However, it does start to become clear to many of them that it doesn't really make very much difference where they spend their time. Undoubtedly they are safer in a deep shelter, such as a tube station, but spending every night in such places is going to make life almost intolerable: in fact, on any given night, there are only a few tens of thousands at most in such shelters. If people are equally safe (or unsafe) in a dance hall or a pub as they are at home, then they might as well spend some time enjoying themselves. Being out on the streets at night for any length of time might not be a good idea, but the transport system is still functional, so there's no need to walk very far. This is at least part of the explanation for the lively social life in London throughout most of the war, including the Blitz period. There are other effects. One is that it's now an even more cosmopolitan place than ever. Many Canadians and Poles are now in the country, plus there are diplomatic contingents and refugees from many other countries. The American presence becomes huge, although mainly after the end of the Blitz, once the USA has entered the war. London is a magnet for all such people. On top of this, people need an occasional escape from the relentless pressure of trying to live under these conditions. Of course, socializing does cost money, and going to the restaurants and nightclubs in Hotels like the Ritz, Savoy, Claridge's, Dorchester etc is mainly for the well-heeled. However, there are plenty of places that are not expensive, but nevertheless offer great entertainment.

One example is the Palais at Hammersmith. This was the first "Palais de Danse" - opened soon after the Great War. It is huge and it attracts, not only large numbers of customers, but also some of the best dance bands – such as Oscar Rabin's and Alf Kaplan's. It stays open throughout the war. It often gets a bit lively, with many off-duty servicemen there – most of them in uniform. The CMP therefore has a regular presence, trying to keep the lid on anything a bit too boisterous. On the evening of Saturday 14th December 1940, Len is on duty, doing the rounds with a couple of Corporals. They come across a bit of a fracas, with a couple of lads throwing some punches, egged on by their mates. It's clear that a largish group is already the worse for wear, although it's all quite minor compared with many of the incidents that require the attention of the CMP. It looks as if this incident might be related to fraternization with the fairer sex – a common source of friction, since there is a small group of young women trying to edge away.

Fig.8.10: Photo of Pamela Fullbrook, taken in 1940, when she was 18.

"OK, lads, break it up. What's going on?"

"Look Sarge, I was just talking to this young lady and this Irish oik butted in and started offering her a drink. You can't let 'em get away with that kind of nonsense. Anyway, he's probably a spy."

"To be sure, that's a load o' blarney. The girl was just trying to get away from this drunken oaf. She'll tell you this herself."

The girl concerned, who's with a small group of friends, clearly is trying to get away from the whole scene, but she quickly confirms that she's not interested in any further contact with either of these men. The lads start to disperse, with the two miscreants deciding that it's probably best to wind this one down and perhaps have a drink together.

"Look Sergeant, this is nothing to worry about – they've just had a few drinks too many. You don't need to do anything."

"Well, we do feel responsible for any unpleasantness caused by soldiers."

He has a quiet word with his two Corporals.

"OK, lads, carry on with your rounds, and I'll just make sure that this young lady is OK – she's probably in a state of shock."

They exchange grins and quickly move off, omitting to comment that she doesn't actually look as if she's in a state of shock, although they can see why she has attracted the attention of the squaddies.

"Look, the Army does try to maintain good relations with civilians. It'll cover the cost of a drink on the house. What would you like?"

Fig.8.11: Photo of troops constructing sandbag defences around GOGGS, at the corner of Horse Guards Road, Great George Street and Birdcage Road, in May 1940.

"Why Sergeant," she says with a smile, "From my experience of the Army, the paperwork would be a nightmare for doing something like that. Are you sure that you have the authority to do this?"

This is not quite the response that Len expected. He looks at her a little more closely. She's certainly an attractive young girl, but she also seems to know quite a lot.

"OK," he says, "I admit it – I'd be doing this in a private capacity, although I can't have a drink myself while I'm on duty. Perhaps I could arrange to see you some other time, so we can both have a drink?"

This is a bit of a gamble, since they met just a minute or so ago, but it pays off. Pam Fullbrook also makes a snap decision and they do meet again a couple of days later. Pam is just 19, but Len soon realizes that she's a little different from many of the young girls who go along to the Palais. She's a working girl, but "work" turns out to be in the Treasury. She's a secretary, but working in the Treasury is not a run-of-the-mill job. She was recruited at the start of the war, when a trawl was made to find a number of bright young women to work there. Moreover, the vetting was not only of their shorthand and typing skills. It also included background checks of various types, and an obligation to sign the Official Secrets Act, an updated version of which was passed through Parliament at the start of the war. She's in an Army family, which made this operation a little easier.

Fig.8.12: Façade of the GOGGS building.

The reason for the security concerns is that the Treasury is in fact at the nerve centre of the whole

British war effort. The Government Offices at Great George Street (GOGGS), located at 1, Horse Guards Parade, is not only where the Treasury operates, but it is also the location of the Cabinet War Rooms and the Downing Street Annex. It is where Churchill spends both working and sleeping hours. The same building also houses the Joint Intelligence Chiefs and the Air Ministry Photographic Department. The basement, which is frequently used during air raids, lies under a large concrete slab. Unlike the Bank of England, which has hundreds of clerks, and has largely moved out to Hampshire, the Treasury is involved in important decision-making related to the war. Pam doesn't actually reveal any of this during her initial chats with Len, although those arrangements are not a secret. Inevitably, however, she does during her work come across information that is very sensitive. She never discusses such details with anyone. Nevertheless, it's clear to Len that she is doing important work.

As they quickly become committed to each other, they do, of course, discuss a lot of other things. These include famiiy histories. While the recent history of Len's family is rather unusual and complex, that of Pam's is a little more straightforward. Nevertheless, as with many families through these turbulent times, its story is interesting. Pam's father, Ernest Ralph Fullbrook, who has always been called Ralph, was born in 1889, in Denmark Street, Wokingham (Berkshire). His father was a (journeyman) carpenter – the term meaning intermediate between an apprentice and a master craftsman.

At the outbreak of the Great War, Ralph was thus 25 years old. He was tall and well-built, but had, and still has, a gentle disposition. He was essentially a pacifist, in the sense that he felt that wars were destructive and created barbarism, but he was also patriotic. He therefore joined up at the start of the war, but became a member of the Royal Army Medical Corps (RAMC). He already had some useful skills and was quickly promoted to Sergeant. Unlike most of the new recruits (Territorials), RAMC personnel were likely to be drafted into the front line rather quickly – presumably on the grounds that they didn't need to acquire familiarity with weapons or become hardened to the idea of killing people.

Fig.8.13: Royal Army Medical Corps officers in France in 1914. Ralph Fullbrook is second from the left in the back row.

Many of them became stretcher-bearers on the Western Front. Needless to say, the task of venturing into the "No-man's Land" between opposing trenches, and somehow getting wounded men back to (relative) safety, is an horrendous one. In principle, there is an understanding that stretcher-bearers should not be targetted, but in practice this is often ignored. Also, even if machine-gunning is restrained, there is a constant danger of being inadvertently hit by shells fired from behind the lines. Furthermore, the physical effort required to transport a wounded man hundreds of yards through muddy ground, pock-marked with shell-holes, is enormous. There are usually just 4 stretcher-bearers to each Company (~120 men). In bad conditions, all 4 are often needed to move one man.

The demands placed on stretcher-bearers are therefore onerous in the extreme. Ralph was moved to the Western Front in 1914 and was involved in several of the major battles, including that at the Somme in 1916. While there are no records about this, it's thought that the stretcher-bearer carrying a wounded man on his back in the frame from the film of the Somme shown in Chapter 4 is Ralph. He was certainly there and it certainly looks like him. Surviving the war was clearly an achievement for a stretcher-bearer involved in several such battles, although of course all such achievements are largely a question of luck.

Pam's mother, Bertha Burt, also made a contribution during the Great War. She was born in 1892, in Brooklyn Terrace, Eastbourne (Sussex). Her father was a (journeyman) tailor. She was thus 22 at the outbreak of war. She became a nurse at that point and was involved in caring for wounded soldiers throughout th e war. She met Ralph while he was on leave and they got married in Christchurch towards the end of the war. They decided that he should remain in the Army (RAMC) after the war and become a chef – he'd always had culinary interests and of course the Army always has requirements for feeding soldiers, irrespective of the level of military activity.

Fig.8.14: Photo of a "coach party" headed from Bournemouth to the New Forest, around 1910. Bertha Burt is on the nearside of the group of three girls at the back.

By 1920, they were living in Grosvenor Road, Westminster, attached to Millbank Barracks. They had two children, Charles Ralph (who is very tall and has always been known as Jum(bo)), born early in 1920, and Pam, born towards the end of 1921. Shortly after this, the family moved (with the RAMC) to India, where they remained for 4 years, based in Barian (Kashmir) and Quetta (Baluchistan) – both near the N W Frontier.

Fig.8.15: Photo of a group of nurses in Wokingham, taken during 1915. Bertha Burt is 4th from the right in the back row.

They returned to England in 1925, moving first to married quarters in the Queen Alexandra Military Hospital in Cosham (Portsmouth). That hospital started to be transferred to civilian usage shortly afterwards, at which point the family moved to the large military hospital at Tidworth Camp, on Salisbury Plain. Shortly afterwards, late in 1927, they moved again, this time to the famous Cambridge Military Hospital in Aldershot (which took the first contingent of wounded soldiers in the Great War). By this point, Ralph had become a Master Chef. He stayed in Aldershot for several years, but another promotion came in the mid 1930's, with a move to the Royal Hospital at Chelsea (RHC) – an even more prestigious establishment.

Fig.8.16: Pam Fullbrook and her father, in Barian (India) in 1925.

Fig.8.17: Photo of a class (of 45) and their teacher at an Infants school in Aldershot, taken in 1927-8. Pam Fullbrook (aged 6) is second from the right in the third row from the front.

Fig.8.18: Christmas 1929, in the Cambridge Military Hospital. Ralph Fullbrook is in the centre (with knives).

They returned to England in 1925, moving first to married quarters in the Queen Alexandra Military Hospital in Cosham (Portsmouth). That hospital started to be transferred to civilian usage shortly afterwards, at which point the family moved to the large military hospital at Tidworth Camp, on Salisbury Plain. Shortly afterwards, late in 1927, they moved again, this time to the famous Cambridge Military Hospital in Aldershot (which took the first contingent of wounded soldiers in the Great War). By this point, Ralph had become a Master Chef. He stayed in Aldershot for several years, but another promotion came in the mid 1930's, with a move to the Royal Hospital at Chelsea (RHC) – an even more prestigious establishment.

Fig.8.19: Pam Fullbrook (aged 8) with her mother, at Fisherman's Walk, Bournemouth, in summer 1929.

The RHC has a rich history, having been founded in the late 17th Century by Charles II. The idea was to provide a quiet refuge for deserving ex-soldiers in their final years, particularly when old and infirm. Pensions as such were rare in those days, but a place in the RHC would ensure comfortable board and lodgings for "Chelsea Pensioners" for the rest of their days. In fact, creation of the Royal Hospital was part of a larger scheme set up to help old soldiers, benefitting many more of them than just those actually living there – although it took a while before this became fully established and many disabled veterans of the Napoleonic Wars, for example, did not fare so well.

The distinctive red uniforms of the "In-Pensioners" living in the RHC date back to the early days. The buildings were laid out on a grand scale, to a design of Christopher Wren. There is accommodation for almost 500 old soldiers. In addition to the Pensioners themselves, various other people also live and work on the site, including gardeners, cleaners, clergy, administrators, those involved in maintenance, medical staff and, of course, those providing the meals.

Fig.8.20: Bird's eye view of the Royal Hospital at Chelsea. Pam Fullbrook and her family are living in West Court (on the right).

For those in major posts, such as Head Chef, accommodation is also available for their families. It's a very pleasant place for the Fullbrook family to live. This is where Pam is living when she meets Len. It's centrally located and convenient both for work in the GOGGS building and for social trips to places like the Hammersmith Palais (and indeed the slightly more up-market places in the West End).

Fig.8.21: Pam and Jum Fullbrook in the RHC, in April 1939.

8.5 London Endures

As the new year of 1941 unfolds, everyday living for Londoners continues to be hard and hazardous. However, life does go on. ARP systems are becoming well-developed, as are various social support measures. It's a war of attrition, but this applies to the Luftwaffe, as well as for the people of London. Anti-aircraft fire is intense and both planes and aircrew are being lost during every attack. In fact, they're losing an average of about 10 aircraft per day, and 15 aircrew. Neither can be replaced at quite that rate.

Londoners, and also the many people visiting the city, continue to mix socially at all levels. This is very successful and serves a useful purpose in raising morale. There are, however, some bad incidents. One such takes place in early March, at the famous Café de Paris – between Piccadilly Circus and Leicester Square. It's one of the most popular (upmarket) nightclubs in London, with the famous jazz band of Ken "Snake-hips" Johnson performing every night. Earlier performers at the club include Marlene Dietrich and regular devotees over recent years include the (then) Prince of Wales, Cole Porter and the Aga Khan.

Fig.8.22: Photos taken in the Café de Paris, before and after the bomb strike of 8th March 1941.

It's actually a bit less exclusive now than it was before the war, with lowered entry prices. It's now popular with members of the armed forces on leave. It's a very lively scene. The club is located in a basement and is felt to be fairly safe. On the evening of 8th March, however, soon after the band has started to play, disaster strikes in the form of a string of bombs falling in a line ending at the club, with the last two going down a ventilation shaft and exploding right in front of the stage. The result is terrible carnage, with around 35 people killed and about 80 injured, many of them very badly. Almost every member of the band is killed, along with many staff and guests. The club is forced to close, although many others continue to operate.

Fig.8.23: The cloister and members' lobby in the Palace of Westminster, after the air raid of 10th May 1941.

This is a very testing time for Len and his CMP colleagues. Some of their efforts are directed towards controlling military traffic, but there is also much to do related to misbehaviour of troops - which can range from the usual late night boisterous incidents to serious crime. A thriving black market is building up as rationing starts to bite and people in the military often have opportunities to exploit their position in various ways. Controlling this is critical in terms of maintaining morale in the city, and in the country as a whole. Len often patrols the streets, with two or three colleagues, checking on various locations, following up tips and assessing whether action is needed. Doing this without causing resentment among the rank

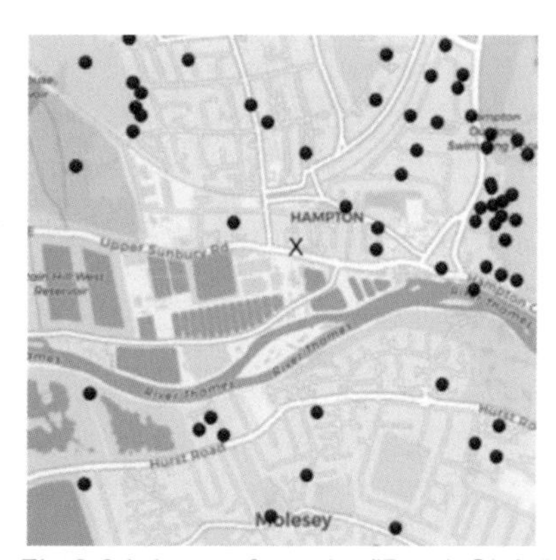

Fig.8.24: Image from the "Bomb Sight" Project, showing bomb explosion locations in the Hampton area between 7th October 1940 and 6th June 1941. The house where Harry and Grace (and Len) live, at 26 Upper Sunbury Road, is marked with an X.

and file of soldiers is a difficult balancing act. Len also has his own motorcycle and often uses this to patrol up and down motor convoys, check on bottlenecks etc. These often take place at night. Under blackout conditions, with many lorry drivers complete novices and bomb craters everywhere, the role of the CMP is crucial in keeping the city operational.

Britain and Germany are now locked in a bitter battle - the outcome of which still hangs in the balance. There is no other opposition to the Nazi regime, which is now oppressing many communities in occupied countries, using slave labour extensively and starting an inhuman campaign of cold-blooded murder against certain ethnic groups, and also against anyone who opposes them in any way.

For those remaining in London, the bombing campaign continues to bring daily trauma and stress. However, for most Londoners, including Pam and her colleagues in the Treasury, there is never any thought of doing anything other than continue to somehow get into work every day. They know that their work is vital. They're in good company. Churchill never considers the option of moving out of London. Neither do the King and Queen, with Buckingham Palace just a stone's throw away. The House of Commons, which is even closer, is hit several times and in fact it's virtually destroyed during the worst raid of the entire Blitz, which takes place during the night of 10th May 1941. This raid is a terrifying experience for the whole city, with a full moon and a very low ebb tide (making it difficult to obtain water for fire-fighting). Almost 600 sorties are flown by the Luftwaffe, who focus during this raid on dropping huge numbers of incendiary devices. Over 2,000 fires are recorded and around 1,500 people are killed.

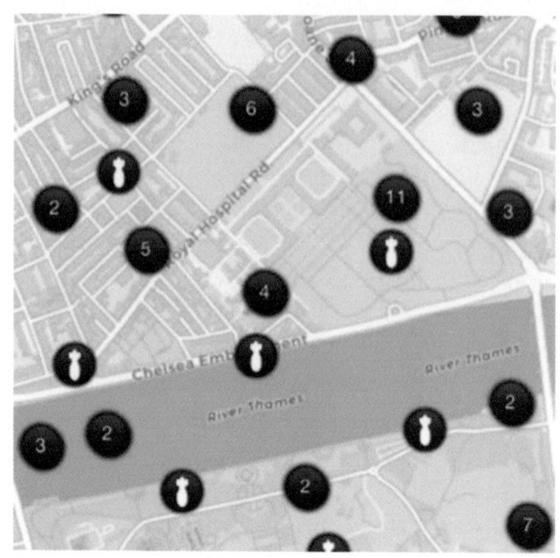

Fig.8.25: Image from the "Bomb Sight" Project, showing bomb explosion locations in the Chelsea area between 7th October 1940 and 6th June 1941. The Royal Hospital is near the centre of the map.

Almost everyone is in danger during intensive raids such as this one. This includes people like Harry and Len, both of whom are commonly called on to help in various ways during and after such events. Sadly, one of the problems associated with the wide-ranging destruction is that of looting. Of course, many people are in desperate straits in terms of their living conditions and the temptation to take items from ruined houses and shops is sometimes too great to resist. Also, London does attract deserters from the army and others living outside the law, or at least not wholly within it. Both the Metropolitan Police and the London Division of the CMP are pivotal to maintaining a semblance of law and order, with liaison between them being of critical importance. Len and Harry often discuss the challenges involved. They're also often on the streets at night, where there are many physical dangers. Even when they're home at night, they're as endangered as anyone else living in London in terms of their house suffering a direct hit. In the event, while

Fig.8.26: A group of Royal Scots Fusiliers at Ploegsteert in Belgium in 1916. In the centre is Lieutenant-Colonel Winston Churchill, while seated to his right is Major Archie Sinclair.

several bombs fall within a hundred yards or so, it comes through the Blitz unscathed.

In fact, that very heavy raid of 10th May heralds the end of the Blitz, with the bombing campaign against London (and other British cities) coming to a virtual halt within a month or so, as Hitler decides to shift the direction of the war. Over a million houses and flats are destroyed or seriously damaged during the Blitz. The Royal Hospital at Chelsea is quite central. It's unlikely to be specifically targeted, but much of the bombing is indiscriminate and it's quite close to several places that might be. A number of bombs, and many incendiaries, land in or close to the grounds. During the raid of Wednesday 16th April 1941 – one of the largest of the Blitz, an aerial mine explodes in the Infirmary in the East Wing. Thirteen people are killed, including 8 Pensioners and 4 nurses. Pam knows several of them very well. In general, however, the RHC escapes quite lightly (although there is more to come later).

During this period, Churchill takes the reins very effectively. His broadcasts to the nation focus everyone's efforts and raise levels of morale and determination. Also, he does have a very good set of people around him, including the War Cabinet. Churchill has had a strong say in its composition. Just to give a single example, he brought in Archie Sinclair, whom he has known since they were in the Royal Scots Fusiliers together during the Great War (in 1916, after Churchill's fall from grace due to the disaster at Gallipoli).

Fig.8.27: The coalition War Cabinet of May 1940. Standing, left to right, are Archibald Sinclair (circled), A V Alexander, Lord Cranborne, Herbert Morrison, Lord Moyne, Captain Margesson & Brendan Bracken. Seated, left to right, are Ernest Bevan, Lord Beaverbrook, Anthony Eden, Clement Attlee, Winston Churchill, Sir John Anderson, Arthur Greenwood & Sir Kingsley Wood.

Archie is an interesting character – charismatic and principled. He was born in 1890 in Caithness, into a prominent branch of the Sinclair Clan. Both of his parents had died by the time he was 5 years old, although the similarities to Len's history don't persist much beyond that. He was educated at Eton and Sandhurst and he became the 4th Baronet of Ulbster in 1912. He was elected as Liberal MP for Caithness and Sutherland in 1922 and always retained a deep affection for the far north of Scotland. As a strong supporter of Lloyd George, he rose quickly through the Liberal ranks, although the fortunes of the party were then starting to wane (as Labour grew stronger). In fact, he became its leader in 1935, although by this time the party was down to 20 MPs. Archie was one of the (relatively small) group, centred around Churchill, who, from an early stage, opposed Hitler, and appeasement. He was appointed Secretary of State for Air in the War Cabinet created in May 1940, and immediately played a key role in coordinating the Battle of Britain.

Both the cabinet and many military leaders are spending a lot of time in GOGGS. These are virtually all middle-aged men, whereas the secretaries in GOGGS, with whom they have quite a lot of contact, are all bright young women. There's inevitably a certain amount of flirtation, although not f rom Archie – who's an attractive man, but one with good morals and a very strong marriage. Nevertheless, he somehow discovers that Pam's fiancé was brought up as an orphan in the far north, and is part of the Sinclair clan, and occasionally finds time for a brief chat with her.

Meanwhile, it's around the time of the end of the Blitz that Len gets promoted to (Company) Sergeant-Major. He's now a Warrant Officer, with his own Company. The size of a Company can vary significantly, but in the CMP they're usually relatively small and Len's comprises only about 50 men. Nevertheless, it's a big responsibility for a young man in his mid-20's. The fear of invasion is now receding and thoughts are turning to how the war is now likely to evolve. For soldiers in general, and for the CMP in particular, it's starting to be understood that their services will in due course be required overseas. In fact, such demands have already arisen by this point. The BEF's move to Europe, and its ignominious retreat in May 1940, are already history, but the entry of Italy into the war in June 1940 created a crisis in the Mediterranean, with the Suez canal coming under immediate threat. There were already British and British Empire troops in Egypt, with their own small Provost Company, but it soon became clear that reinforcements would be needed. In fact, initial Italian advances were limited and easily repulsed, but during the early part of 1941 the arrival of a German contingent strengthened the Axis forces considerably and British troops were sent out to North Africa from the UK. These reinforcements included a CMP representation. They are already finding that they are playing a key role in a fluid and demanding set of battles.

In any event, as it becomes clear that the Blitz is over, the people of London start to understand that they have played a major role in winning a battle of epic proportions and importance. Of course, they also understand that the war is a very long way from being over. Nevertheless, what happens next offers real grounds for optimism.

Chapter 9: A Worldwide Struggle (June 1941 – February 1943)

9.1 The War Explodes

As Hitler starts to appreciate that neither invading Britain nor forcing it into some kind of negotiated peace are going to be achievable in the near future, his attention turns to the East. He is driven, not only by the attractions of capturing land (Lebensraum) and resources, but also by his demonic views about race superiority and inferiority. He actually admires the British, whom he views as largely Aryan and therefore almost on a par with the Germanic race. His hatred of the Jews is well-known, but he also regards the "Slavs" to the East (in the Soviet Union) as sub-human. He is driven by a desire to wipe them out, and also to destroy the detested concept of communism. He also has a low opinion of the Russian Army, which he regards as poorly equipped and lacking in good military leaders. He took careful note of the difficulties they had with the Finns in the "Winter War". He feels that the Wehrmacht is likely to sweep across the Western part of Russia in a similar way to that of the invasion of Western Europe a year before. While some of his generals are not so sure, many of them are reluctant to argue too much with him. He therefore orders the long-planned "Operation Barbarossa" to be launched on 22nd June 1941, soon after the Blitz of London has been stopped.

For the British, this offers enormous relief – not only will they no longer be alone, but they understand that the Russians will be no pushover. Moreover, it brings the various strands of opinion in Britain into much closer alignment. There is quite strong support for communism, and for Russia, within Britain. Up to now, many communists in Britain have been somewhat reluctant to fight Hitler, in view of his pact with Russia. Their views now swing heavily against him. Furthermore, the fascists in Britain now realize that supporting Hitler is no longer possible. Mosley had been imprisoned a year before, as soon as Churchill took power, and now anyone voicing support for Hitler is seen as a traitor. The man is clearly mad – although he's a very dangerous madman.

For the Russians, the attack comes as a shock. Stalin never actually trusted Hitler, but his assumption had been that switching focus from Britain wouldn't happen until it had been subjugated in some way. Stalin is no angel. He's as likely as Hitler to use mass murder and starvation as stock-in-trade. He's also almost as keen as Hitler to expand his empire, although he does already have a huge area of unexploited land and he'd really prefer people to become converted to communism (and then be absorbed into the Soviet sphere of influence). In any event, Russian preparation for the German invasion, which starts without any formal declaration of war, is very limited. The Red Army is large, but it's not prepared for this onslaught. Raids by the Luftwaffe in the first few days are particularly devastating, with thousands of Russian planes destroyed - many of them on the ground. As with the Battle of France, the Wehrmacht makes rapid advances along a very wide front, with the armies of both Rumania and Finland assisting

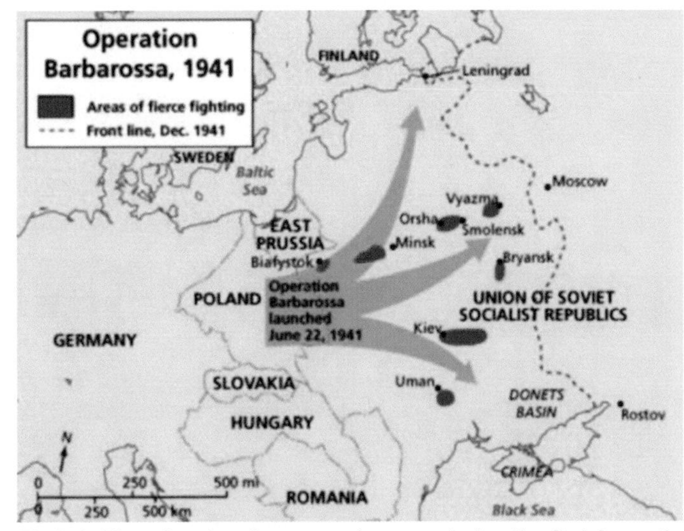

Fig.9.1: Map showing German advances during the first 6 months of the Barbarossa attack on Russia.

them in parts of it. The Russians suffer huge losses of men and materiel during the first few weeks. However, this is not Western Europe. Russian resources and resolve are deeper, and the challenges of weather and sheer distance are greater. This attack will turn out to be a terrible mistake. The Russian and German Empires start to engage in a conflict of relentless carnage on both sides, which is to last for the next four years.

As 1941 progresses, the rate of advance of the Wehrmacht starts to slow. There is a series of battles, and the Russians suffer crippling losses – with many soldiers being taken prisoner (and subjected to terrible treatment). However, the Russian people fight back – working out how to impede German advances, moving resources (including complete factories) back into their huge hinterland and stepping up their rate of production of tanks, aircraft and other military resources. Virtually every able-bodied citizen becomes deeply involved with these activities. It's a Herculean effort by many millions of people, who have a deep love of their Motherland. Furthermore, the weather starts to play a key role. It turns out to be the worst winter in living memory. The Germans are not prepared for this – they expected the whole thing to be over by the autumn. By the end of the year, their advance has ground to a halt. They occupy huge areas of Russia, and they have reached the outskirts of the key cities of Moscow and Leningrad, but their supply lines are stretched, they're starting to run short of fuel, their tanks and lorries are giving trouble in the intense cold and their troops are exhausted. The Luftwaffe no longer controls the skies. A tipping point is being approached.

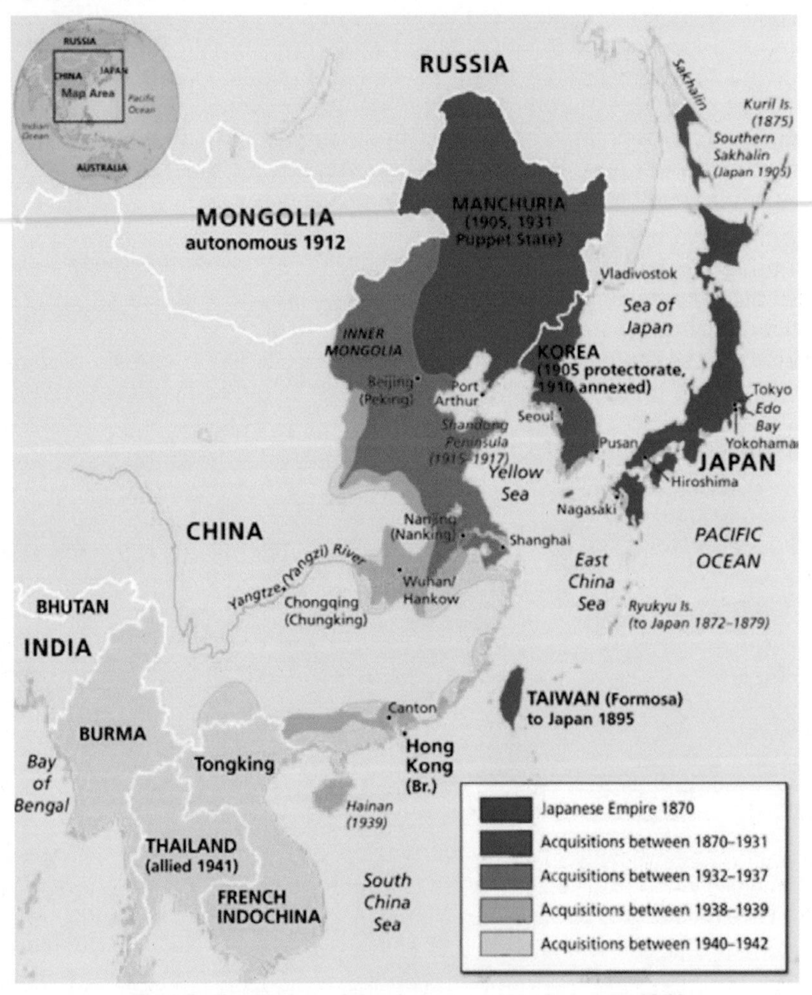

Fig.9.2: Expansion of the Japanese empire up to 1942.

Meanwhile, on the other side of the world, further momentous events are starting to unfold. The Japanese have also been expanding their empire. Like many other countries, they suffered during the Great Depression, losing some of their markets to China – particularly in textiles. Factions inside Japan, including Emperor Hirohito, have been pressing for expansion for several years, to secure access to raw materials and markets. This has particularly related to China and there has been much friction between the two countries. In fact, the Japanese invaded Manchuria in 1931. The simmering mutual resentments exploded in July 1937, with a full-blown invasion of China. The Japanese captured the major cities, such as Shanghai, Peking and Nanking – the Chinese capital – and committed many atrocities during this period. There has been an uneasy stalemate since then, with many of the Chinese retreating into the huge interior of their country, moving their capital further up the Yangtze River to Chungking. The Japanese have been unable to penetrate into these interior regions and there has been strong Chinese guerilla resistance, supported by Russia, and to some extent by the USA. Belligerence between America and Japan has thus been building up for a while and this comes to a head when the Japanese decide to make a pre-emptive strike – again with no prior declaration of war – a tactic they appear to have picked up from Hitler.

The Japanese attack on Pearl Harbor, the main base of the American Pacific Fleet, on Sunday 7th December 1941 thus comes with virtually no warning. There have been various attempts to resolve the disputes between Japan and the USA, but these negotiations are still going on when the Japanese mount an air attack with several hundred planes, launched from aircraft carriers some distance away. They sink a number of large battleships, destroy hundreds of planes on the ground and kill over 2,000 people (including civilians), but the damage is not really so great. As it happens, the three American aircraft carriers are not there. Also, since the water is shallow, most of the battleships and destroyers that are sunk can be salvaged fairly easily. Other resources in the base, such as fuel stocks and facilities for repair etc, are largely undamaged. American sea power in the Pacific will return to its previous level within a matter of months. The attack is already looking like a serious mistake.

Of course, war is immediately declared between Japan and the USA. There is an alliance, or at least a pact, between Japan and the European Axis powers of Italy and Germany: they also immediately declare war on America. The Japanese and the Nazis make strange bedfellows: the Japanese have done this partly due to resentment at the racism practiced against them, while Hitler is the one of the most racist leaders in history. Still, this is where events have led and the idea is presumably that they will carve up the world between them, without coming into conflict. In any event, this news is very welcome in Britain, and in fact Churchill declares war on Japan before Congress has ratified the American decision. China also declares war on Japan – although in reality there has already been a state of war between them for several years. Almost immediately, however, there are ominous warning signs of Japanese power and intentions in the Pacific, with the news that the Royal Navy Battleship Prince of Wales and the Battlecruiser Repulse have been sunk near Singapore by long range Torpedo Bombers. The importance of aircraft at sea is

Fig.9.3: Pam with friends from GOGGS, in August 1941. These are, from left to right, Sylvia, Mary, Eve and Pam.

becoming very clear. It also leaves Britain with little or no sea power in the area and with the dawning realization that their Empire in that part of the world is in serious danger.

Fig.9.4: Pam and Len, walking with Sylvia and Roy, late in 1941.

Nevertheless, the overall feeling is one of optimism. In the GOGGS, there is frenetic activity as America becomes an ally, and arrangements are rapidly made for a meeting between Churchill and Roosevelt. This is to start in Washington on 22nd December 1941 and run for three weeks. Pam gets involved in the flurry of communications, as do many of the Secretaries in GOGGS, and the place is a hive of activity. Important decisions must be made about prioritizing the various objectives. This meeting is not to become public knowledge – it's given the codename Arcadia, so various security measures are imposed. There is extensive sleeping accommodation in GOGGS, so some people hardly ever leave the complex during this period.

Roosevelt broadly agrees that beating Hitler in Europe has to be the immediate aim. This is exactly what Churchill wants. Despite the warning signs from the Far East, he naturally feels that the more pressing concerns are nearer home. It is also a logical decision for Roosevelt, since Hitler's war machine is highly developed, and most of Europe is already occupied, whereas the Japanese are certainly not in a position to launch any kind of attack on America. Their Pearl Harbor strike was clearly aimed at stopping the Americans from interfering too much with their expansion in the Pacific – particularly in the Philippines and Dutch East Indies, where the supply of oil is crucial to their plans. It could be argued that the Russians are already keeping Hitler fully engaged, but there's no doubt that the Americans are wary of Europe falling largely under Soviet control – the hatred of communism is strong in the USA. In any event, Roosevelt and Churchill get on well and a host of arrangements are made. These include plans for joint operations, the establishment of American air bases in Britain, a unified American-British-Dutch-Australian (ABDA) Command in the Far E ast and many other operational details. Churchill is able to sleep well at night for the first time in 18 months.

Although the Arcadia conference is held in secret, everyone in Britain naturally knows that America has joined forces – against Hitler as well as against the Japanese. This completes the transformation of their hopes, which started 6 months earlier with the entry of Russia. It is surely inconceivable that Hitler can prevail against the combined might of Russia, America and Britain. The atmosphere as Christmas approaches is therefore quite different from that of the previous year, when London was under nightly attack and the fear of invasion was palpable. There are, of course, still many privations and hardships. Most types of food, and many other items, are rationed, travel is restricted, blackouts still apply, many ships are being sunk – mostly by German submarines, air raids still take place and there are many places around the world where British troops and bases are at risk. Nevertheless, Pam and Len's second Christmas together is a hopeful time. They attend several lively parties. Places like the

Fig.9.5: Ralph Fullbrook (centre) in charge of the sampling of Christmas puddings in the RHC, in mid-December 1941.

RHC are still able to obtain provisions and the traditions of Christmas, including the Christmas pudding, are still upheld.

As the New Year starts, there is good news from Russia. It has been a terrible time for huge numbers of Russians, and also for the invading German army. Casualty numbers are mounting to levels of many millions. The Germans have made repeated efforts to capture Moscow, urged on by Hitler – who is increasingly demanding the ultimate sacrifice and refusing all requests by his Generals for any type of strategic withdrawal. By early January, however, it becomes clear that Moscow is not going to fall. The defensive arrangements are strong, the Russians are producing huge number of tanks and other armaments and they are also dominant in the air. Hitler is forced to accept defeat in this region, although he still intends to continue on the offensive in Russia, switching the attack to other areas – particularly in the South, where the oil-fields of the Caucasus Mountains are a valuable prize. It is nevertheless a clear defeat for the Wehrmacht – its first of the war. Their aura of invincibility is starting to fade. They are also hemorrhaging men and resources at an alarming rate. A sensible leader would cut their losses and retreat to a strong defensive line much further to the West. It's evident to all by now that Hitler is not a sensible leader. There is much more carnage to come on the Eastern Front.

Fig.9.6: Factory workers digging anti-tank trenches around Moscow in 1941.

9.2 The British Empire in Turmoil

The era of empires is coming to an end. Ironically, this is happening at a time when attempts are being made to create several more. Hitler's dreams of a "1,000-year Reich" are also reflected in the aspirations of Hirohito and Stalin, and even of the Americans. Churchill's powerful oratory, including the phrase "..if the British Empire and its Commonwealth last for a thousand years, men will still say 'This was their Finest Hour'…", delivered in the House of Commons on 18th June 1940, is highly effective in rallying the people of Britain, but it misjudges the drift of history. The British Empire is under immediate threat from the expansionist aims of others, but the forces that will bring it to an end are internal, and rapidly growing. Improving levels of education and communication throughout the world will ensure that no community or ethnic group will in the future accept long-term subjugation, and the idea of diversity will be celebrated, rather than crushed.

Nevertheless, the danger of immediate military collapse in their spheres of influence and control looms large in British minds in the early 1940's. When Italy declared war, in June 1940, one of their first actions was to attack the British bases in Egypt, from their adjacent colony of Libya. This was logical, in the sense that there were important strategic prizes there, in the form of the Suez Canal and the many oilfields beyond, in the Persian Gulf area. Furthermore, the British were heavily preoccupied at the time with German invasion activities and plans in Northern Europe. The plan had Hitler's full approval and in fact he assured Mussolini that Germany would have invaded Britain by the time that the Italians moved into Egypt. Of course, that didn't happen, but there's also no escaping the fact that the Italians have a very patchy record in terms of military prowess and achievements – at least unless one is prepared to go back to the era of the Roman Empire. While the British certainly were distracted and stretched at the time, they still had powerful naval and air bases in the Mediterranean, at Gibraltar and Malta. They could also call on resources from British India. The Italian attempts at invasion were so unsuccessful that they have to be regarded as a fiasco.

After several delays, the Italians started what they expected to be their decisive move on 9th September 1940. They had assembled a relatively large army in Cyrenaica – the province in Eastern Libya named after the famous city of Cyrene, which had been a great centre of learning during the time of the Greek and Roman Empires, but had effectively disappeared since then. They had originally planned to seize the Suez Canal, but their immediate objective was reduced to taking Sidi Barrani, a small port on the coast about 50 miles inside Egypt. They achieved this within a week or so, after only very limited contact with British forces, and started to consolidate there, bringing in supplies and starting to improve the road heading deeper into Egypt.

The Italians were not well prepared for desert warfare. Much of their equipment was obsolescent, and also lacked the special air and oil filters needed on vehicles and aircraft to combat the effects of dust storms. Their troops also had little experience of these conditions, whereas the British (Commonwealth) forces, and also those of the Free French in North Africa, were familiar with these issues and were relatively well equipped. The Italians remained in Sidi Barrani for some time, which was clearly a dangerous thing to do. By mid-September, the British had started to retaliate, attacking several places on the coast of Libya, as well as Sidi Barrani, both by sea and by air. In early December, under the leadership of General Archibald Wavell, the British launched a coordinated attack on Sidi Barrani, with tanks and infantry, as well as air and sea support. Despite having far fewer troops, the attack was completely successful, not only destroying the Italian Army, but also pursuing the remnants all the way along the Libyan coast, as far as Benghazi and the Gulf of Sirte. Of the 25,000 or so in the British force, less than 10% were killed or wounded. Italian (and Libyan) casualties were also relatively low, but over 130,000 surrendered and were taken prisoner. A large number of tanks, guns and aircraft were also captured. It was good news during a time of great stress back in Britain, but what follows now is far less comfortable.

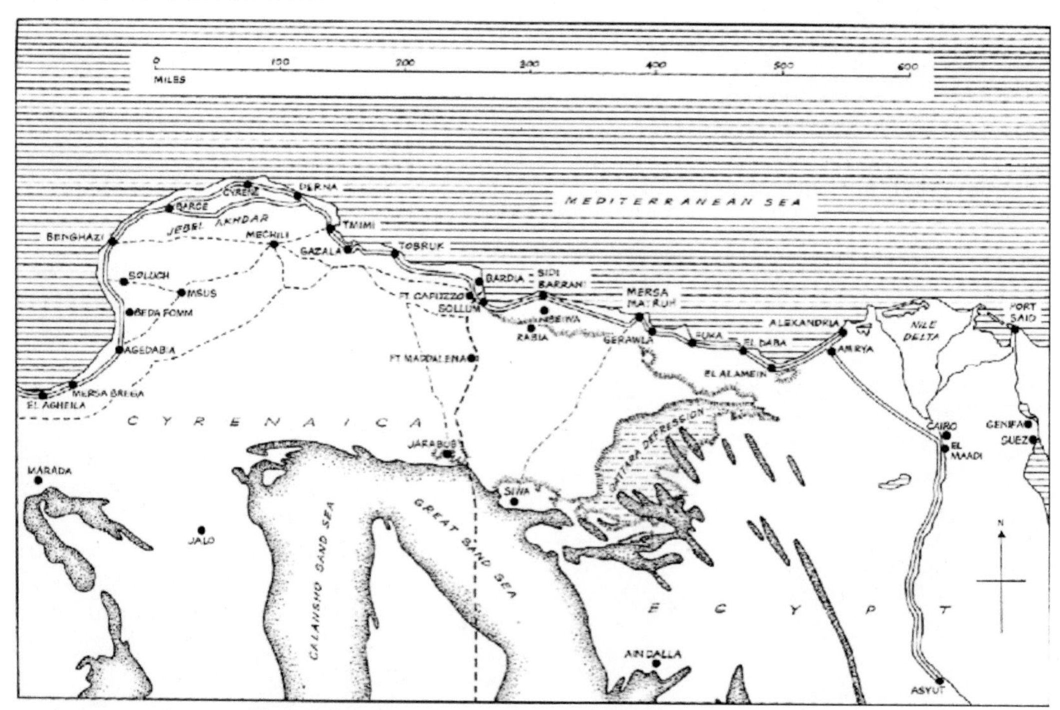

Fig.9.7: Map showing part of North-West Africa, in 1940.

Mussolini is furious with the outcome, and Hitler is certainly not pleased. Hitler does feel, however, that there is potential in the idea of capturing the Suez Canal, and he is also very focused on supplies of oil. He therefore agrees to send a small number of Panzer Divisions to North Africa, under the command of one of his best Generals, Erwin Rommel. In fact, there is an argument for regarding Rommel as the best military tactician since Napoleon Bonaparte. He arrives in early February of 1941 and rapidly reorganizes the Italian forces, while the German troops and equipment that come with him are of a high standard. There are parallels here with the Gallipoli campaign in the Great War, when a relatively small number of German troops and commanders played a key role in transforming the Turkish troops into a formidable fighting force, although in fact the Germans continue to regard their Italian allies as highly unreliable. Nevertheless, having regrouped to the West of Benghazi, Rommel starts to push the British back towards the East, with characteristic rapid maneuvering and outflanking tactics. Benghazi is quickly taken and the large garrison in Tobruk is eventually encircled. There are protracted battles over a period of many months, stretching along an extended length of coastline.

The small CMP contingents, some from Egypt and some recently arrived from Britain, find themselves in a nightmarish situation. Extensive movements of troops and military resources are needed along the coast, mostly along roads that barely exist and in some places are perched on cliff-sides. They are faced with a need to devise and embed signs that will allow lorries and tanks to follow these routes without getting hopelessly lost. The frequent sandstorms make this an almost impossible task, concealing signs and causing frequent breakdowns. The CMP people must keep these routes open, often requiring them to take decisions about abandoning vehicles – sometimes pushing them off the roads and into the sea. On steep, dangerous cliff-side routes, experienced CMP officers sometimes have to take over from novice lorry-drivers petrified by the situation. Tanks and tank transporters also have to be moved along roads that are totally unsuitable for such traffic. Mobility is key to these battles and the CMP people are central to this as the British forces try to cope with Rommel's tactics. The numerous minefields, planted by both sides in many locations, make the task even more demanding. On top of this, the CMP are also responsible for captured Italian prisoners, of which there are a huge number in this campaign. The standard arrangement they are forced to adopt is that groups of 500 prisoners are guarded and shepherded by just 5 CMP soldiers, creating major challenges. Fortunately, they appear to have little inclination to escape, but the logistics nevertheless present some huge problems.

Tobruk is finally captured by Italian-German forces in June 1942 and they penetrate into Egypt as far as El Alamein – only about 50 miles from the key city of Alexandria. Their advance is stopped there in a major battle, partly because their supply lines have become over-extended. Still, at this point, the situation is very precarious from an Allied point of view. Rommel, known by now as the "Desert Fox", has out-smarted a string of Allied commanders – who are repeatedly replaced by an increasingly frustrated Churchill. In fact, Churchill has been partly responsible for the situation, since he gave instructions, just before Rommel's arrival, for much of the British and British Empire forces to be moved to Greece, where their presence turns out to be largely wasted.

In August 1942, command of the Allied forces is passed to General Bernard Montgomery. From this point, the tide starts to turn. Montgomery, who is unquestionably an abrasive and demanding character, certainly does manage to improve the morale and performance of the embattled army facing Rommel, but the gradual turnaround that follows is also due to several other factors. In November 1942, a coordinated set of Allied landings (Operation Torch) is carried out further West, in Algeria and Morocco. This is a joint Anglo-American operation, bringing US troops into direct contact with German forces for the first time. The American commanders include Dwight D Eisenhower and George S Patton. These forces, which meet little opposition, move to the East in a pincer operation on the

Italian – German army. Support from both sea and air is becoming increasingly influential. Axis attempts to take Malta fail.

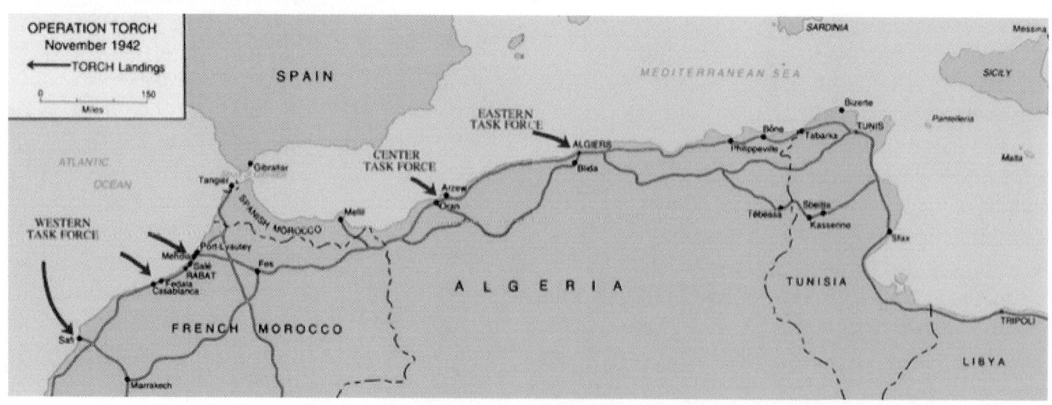

Fig.9.8: Map showing the landings of Operation Torch, in November 1942.

After much initial confusion, the Free French forces, which are quite strong in Algeria, work in tandem with the Allied forces, while the Vichy French, fighting on the Axis side, are defeated or decide to disengage, or potentially to change sides. On hearing about this, Hitler orders the invasion of Vichy France, although the French do manage to scuttle most of their remaining warships before they can be requisitioned by the Nazis. Also, despite Rommel's best efforts, his beleaguered forces are starting to struggle. He has received very little in the way of reinforcements. At about the time of the Torch landings, a second battle is fought at El Alamein between Rommel and Montgomery, which results in the Italian – German forces starting a retreat to the West. This is effectively the first British victory in the war (albeit with some American help) and church bells are rung throughout the country in celebration.

Fig.9.9: Australian troops disembarking from HMT Johan Van Oldbarnevelt at Singapore on 15th August 1941.

Meanwhile, The Japanese are rampant in the Far East. In early February of 1942, they attack Singapore – the foremost British military and economic base in the Far East. About 85,000 Allied troops are in place, including a substantial number brought in from Australia and India over the previous 6 months, but they are poorly prepared for this attack. In fact, the Japanese have been on the move for some time, having formed an alliance with Thailand

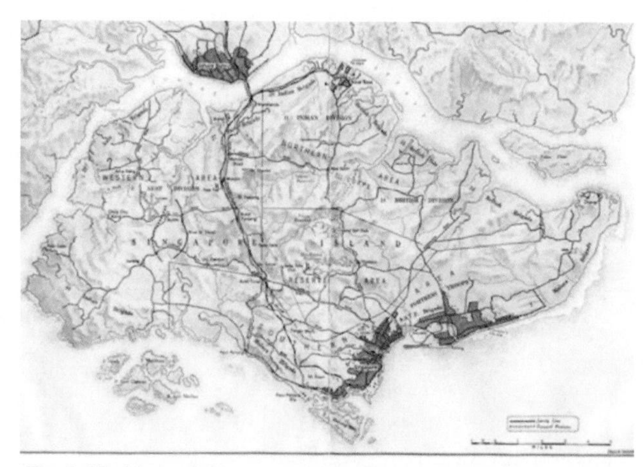

Fig.9.10: Map of Singapore island, showing the disposition of troops prior to the Japanese invasion.

at the end of 1941. A Japanese army, under General Tomoyuki Yamashita, had started to move from there down the Malayan peninsula towards Singapore at the start of the New Year. Part of the Japanese strategy in the area is to foment rebellion of local populations against British (and French) dominion, promoting the idea that they will become independent after the British have been expelled. This is done in Malaysia, French Indo-China, Burma and India, and with some success – military organizations that will fight alongside the Japanese are being formed in all of these countries.

The British consider the jungle in the Malayan peninsula to be impassable, but Yamashita's army soon shows that this is wrong. They move partly down the western coastline and, where they do pass through the interior, they use bicycles (taken from locals) to pass rapidly along native paths. They are also dominant both in the air and at sea. It should have been obvious that they intended to take Singapore in the near future; however, not for the first time, British military commanders in the field turn out to be complacent and incompetent.

The force that Yamashita commands is in fact a relatively small one – about 30,000 troops, although it is certainly an efficient and well-trained one. Its size, however, is not clear to the commander of the garrison in Singapore, Lieutenant-General Arthur Percival. Furthermore, he makes several tactical errors, misjudging where the attack will come and failing to ensure good communications. The Japanese overwhelm the small Australian force defending the point of attack (in the North-West of Singapore island), despite their heroic efforts. There are echoes of Gallipoli here in terms of Australian troops feeling that they have been badly let down by British military incompetence at higher levels.

The Japanese take control of the water supplies to the city of Singapore, to which about a million local people have retreated. Partly to spare these people the deprivations of a siege, Percival surrenders to the Japanese – despite having been instructed by Churchill to fight to the last man. In fact, since casualties during the initial attacks have been limited to just a few thousand, he is surrendering an army of 80,000 men to an attacking force of less than half this size. This is virtually unprecedented in military history – at least in British military history. Furthermore, those taken prisoner face severe mistreatment by the Japanese, and about a third of them will die in captivity. There are some mitigating circumstances to the decision to surrender, but this defeat does untold damage to

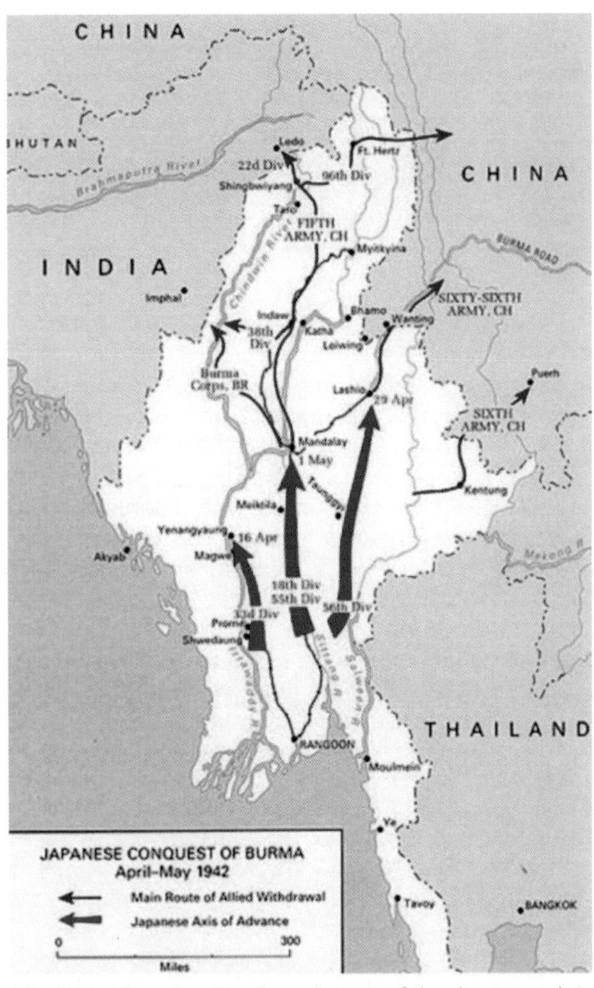

Fig.9.11: Map showing the advance of the Japanese into Burma in 1942.

Britain's reputation and standing.

Worse is to come. The Japanese quickly realize that, while in principle they are opposed in this part of the world by the British, the French, the Chinese, the Americans and the various indigenous populations, in practice there is very little serious resistance. They have several incentives to invade Burma, such as cutting the recently-opened Burma Road, by which supplies are reaching the Chinese Nationalist government under Chiang Kai-Shek. They are very keen to gain control of the oilfields in central Burma. They also see potential for moving on into India. While Burma is rather sparsely populated, with a lot of dense jungle, India is still the Jewel in the Crown of the British Empire. However, resentment at British rule among the indigenous peoples of India has been steadily growing - arguably since the Indian Mutiny of almost a century ago and certainly since the Massacre of Amritsar soon after the Great War. The Japanese can see that, if they manage to penetrate into India, there is a very real possibility that there will be an uprising against the British, making the task of complete invasion much easier.

Their initial take-over of Burma is certainly rapid and decisive. Starting early in 1942, it is virtually complete by the summer – in fact, by the start of the monsoon season in May/June (after which any kind of military movement or attack is virtually impossible). The Japanese 15th Army, formed in late 1941 under Lieutenant-General Shojiro Iida, surges to the west and north, driving the Allies (mainly British and British Indian divisions) before them. They are supported by the newly-formed Burma Independence Army, which grows rapidly during the advance. The Japanese quickly establish air superiority and subject the capital of Rangoon to severe bombardment. The city falls in early March, leaving no route in for Allied reinforcements. The Allied troops retreat to the North in complete disarray, together with many civilians – mostly Anglo-Indian and Anglo-Burmese people fearing reprisals from both the Japanese and the Burma Independence Army. There are at least half a million refugees of this type, turning the retreat from what is already a rout into a chaotic nightmare. The terrain is terrible – mostly dense jungle that is oppressively hot and humid, but with obstacles in the form of mountain ranges and torrential rivers. Diseases and illness are rife. Many people die.

While the size of the invading force is again relatively small at about 30,000 troops, and the total number of Allied soldiers is well above that, the difference in levels of preparation and organi zation is dramatic. Despite some attempts to destroy oil wells and bridges as they retreat, much equipment has to be abandoned: the Japanese use these resources very effectively. General Archibald Wavell, in overall command, tries several times to establish defensive lines, but they are repeatedly out-maneuvered and forced to retreat again in disarray. The Burma Corps is under the command of Lieutenant-General William Slim and in the end he does well to ensure that a substantial number of troops do make it back to defensible locations in India, such as Imphal and Dimapur. Nevertheless, the whole campaign has been a shambles from the Allied point of view. There is now an opportunity during the monsoon to regroup and reinforce, although this is somewhat hampered by the complex political situation, involving the Americans, the British, the Chinese and (British) India. However, at least this disaster promotes a focus on the Far East back in London and Washington. Some drastic action is needed.

9.3 Titanic Battles

Even while Japanese armies are surging towards India, incurring minimal losses and with their enemies in complete disarray, and the Philippines and Dutch East Indies are also occupied, there are ominous signs that they are shortly going to be faced with much more formidable forces. The Pacific is huge, and mainland USA is a very long way from where the Japanese are expanding their empire, but it soon becomes clear that American reach and resources are extensive. On Saturday 18th April, the USA launches the audacious Doolittle Bombing Raid. A total of 16 B-25 Mitchell bombers, modified to extend their range, take off from the aircraft carrier USS Hornet, venturing 3,000 miles from its base in

Pearl Harbor. The plan is for them to bomb Tokyo, about 750 miles away. In order to remove the need for the carrier to stay in the vicinity, they will continue after the bombing to China (outside of the area of Japanese occupation), a further 1,500 miles or so away. It is clearly a hazardous undertaking, if only because the range of these aircraft is less than 2,400 miles – even with the extra fuel tanks and reduced weight. All of the pilots and crew are volunteers. The leader is Lieutenant-Colonel Jimmy Doolittle, who has been centrally involved in all of the planning.

The raid is successful, with most of the bombs hitting targets of some sort in the Tokyo area, and most of the airmen surviving. However, it is not an entirely smooth operation, since all of the planes but one are lost – either being abandoned in mid-air over China as fuel runs out or crash-landing. The one that survives diverts to Vladivostok, in Russia. This is nearer, but, since Russia is not formally at war with Japan, the men and their plane are interned. (They are, however, later allowed to return home surreptitiously.) In fact, the damage in Tokyo is minimal and the Japanese impose terrible reprisals on the area of China where assistance was given to the American airmen in their escape. Since all of the planes were lost, Colonel Doolittle fears that he will be court-marshaled on his return. In fact, he is feted as a hero and all of the airmen receive medals. The psychological value of the raid is enormous. In Japan, there is panic and fear among the civilian population, as it becomes clear that the assurances of their military authorities are worthless. In the USA, morale is given a huge boost. Some of these effects contribute to subsequent errors by the Japanese military leaders.

Fig.9.12: Photo of the B25 piloted by Jimmy Doolittle, taking off from USS Hornet on 18th April 1942.

About 6 weeks later, on 4th June, a major sea battle is fought, turning the tide of the war in the Pacific. Partly because of the Doolittle raid, the Japanese – particularly their influential Admiral Isoroku Yamamoto, decide to invade Midway Island. This is a remote atoll, about 1,300 miles North-West of Pearl Harbor, serving as a US outpost base for both naval and air-force operations. The Japanese feel that they must expand their line of control eastwards, to stop further American incursions, and they are keen to engage and sink American ships – particularly carriers. They send a strong force and this turns into a major battle between two large fleets, with air power playing a key role, spread over 3 days and hundreds of miles of sea. Both sides have about 25 ships and 250 carrier-based aircraft. A further 130 American aircraft are based at Midway. American breaking of Japanese coded messages gives the US Admirals, led by Chester Nimitz, a crucial advantage in a giant game of hide-and-seek. The result is a crushing victory for the Americans. The Japanese lose all 4 of their carriers, while, of their 3 carriers taking part in the battle, the Americans lose only the USS Yorktown. It was damaged in a battle a month before, but emergency repairs allow it to join the battle, in which it plays a key role. The Japanese lose all of their aircraft, plus 3,000 men, while only 150 American aircraft are lost, and 300 men are killed. There are strenuous Japanese efforts to conceal the outcome from their own people, but this battle means that their control of the sea in the Far East is irrevocably lost.

In Britain, news of these events takes a while to filter through, and indeed little detail is released of the Japanese advances on land. It does, of course, become known that Singapore has fallen, and that Prince of Wales and Repulse have been sunk. It's evident to all that this is a disaster for Britain. Conscription is expanded dramatically at the start of 1942, to cover all men aged 18-51 and all unmarried women aged 20-30. Pam, now aged 20, thus becomes eligible for call-up, but it's rapidly made clear to her that the people working in the Treasury will not be released. Still, this is a rapid expansion of the conscription net, although in practice many of those now covered have already volunteered for one of the armed service, or are engaged in work relevant to the war effort. In particular, many women – married or single – are already working in factories or on the land. Nevertheless, the size of the Army is progressively rising and reaches about 2 million by mid-1942. The number of places where they're needed – in North Africa, India, South Africa, Persia, Malta etc - is also increasing. The sinking by German submarines of British and American ships, bringing much-needed food and war materiel across the Atlantic, continues inexorably. Success stories for British forces are thin on the ground.

There is excitement for the Fullbrook family, and for the other RHC residents and workers, on Monday 25th May 1942. King George VI and Queen Elizabeth are the guests of honour for Founders' Day, taking part in the Oak Apple Celebrations. They have been to the RHC previously, but this is the King's first visit as monarch. The RHC Governor and his wife, Sir Henry Knox and Lady Knox, act as their hosts and everyone stays for the various proceedings and activities on the lawns. The King gives a short speech, congratulating the Pensioners on their splendid turnout and thanking them for their contributions in previous conflicts. There is also reference to the current struggle, and confidence is expressed about ultimate victory. They also visit the ruins of the Infirmary, which was destroyed towards the end of the Blitz (during the raid of 16th April 1941). They're both very warmly welcomed and there is great appreciation of their decision to stay in London – they are just a couple of miles away. In fact, Pam decides not to take time off work for this occasion, and both Len and her brother Jum are away with the Army, but her parents, Ralph and Bertha, are centrally involved. Ralph is in charge of all of the catering and everyone agrees that he and his staff have done an outstanding job, despite the various limitations and the effects of rationing. It's a cheerful event during a time of stress and extensive difficulties.

Meanwhile, there are further developments in the titanic struggle between German and Soviet forces in Russia. Hitler has largely switched his focus towards the South. The main reason for this is that a shortage of fuel is starting to become critical for the German forces and obtaining control over the

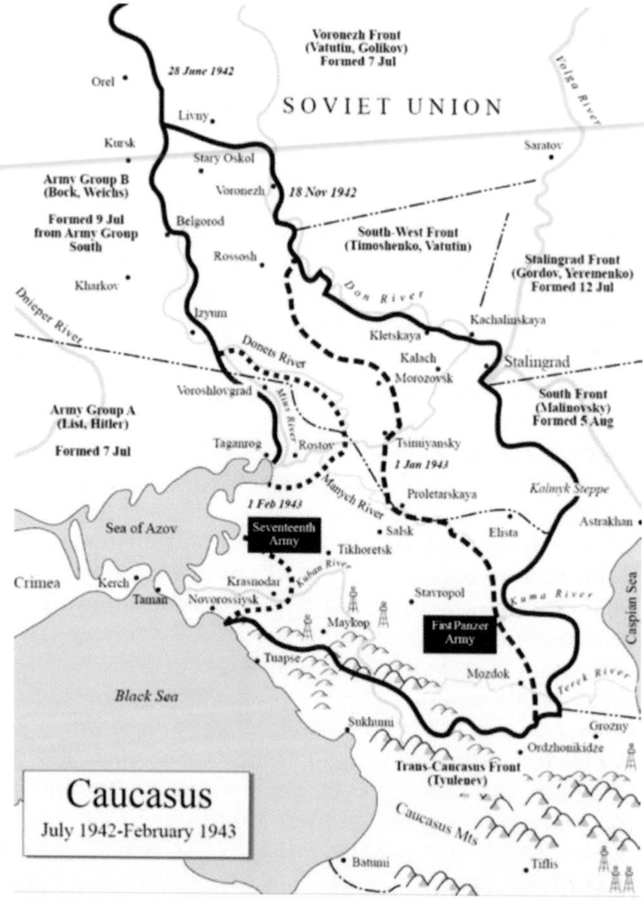

Fig.9.13: Locations of the battle front between German and Russian forces during late 1942 and early 1943. Various oil fields in the Caucasus range are also shown.

oilfields near the Caucasus Mountains is a crucial objective. The German forces, supported by armies from Rumania, Italy and Hungary, make rapid progress in the summer of 1942, capturing some oilfields and pushing the Russians back over a wide front. However, the Russians resist strongly, particularly as winter starts to set in again. Even this far South, winters can be very harsh. The battle starts to focus on Stalingrad, a strategically important city located on a bend in the Volga River. A bitter conflict develops, with casualties mounting horrifically on both sides and hand-to-hand fighting continuing in the city even after it has been reduced to rubble. Huge numbers of reinforcements pour in on both sides. Both Hitler and Stalin are determined not to retreat from this confrontation. Eventually, the Russians encircle a large German army of 300,000 men (commanded by General Friedrich Paulus). They achieve this partly by penetrating the flank of a large salient, which is being defended by the Rumanians. A German attack aimed at relieving them, led by General Erich von Manstein, almost succeeds, but fails because of Hitler's insistence that Paulus must not try to meet them, since this would involve retreating from Stalingrad. He has forbidden any sort of retreat and insists that fighting must continue to the last man. In the end, virtually the whole of that army is obliterated. Paulus eventually surrenders in February 1943, but only a few thousand of his troops actually survive. It is a clear victory for the Russians, and for Stalin. Many of his Generals, such as Georgy Zhukov, have performed heroics and the resilience of the Russian people has been a revelation.

Overall, the carnage during what can be regarded as the Battle of Stalingrad is unprecedented. The Axis Armies lose about a million men, plus 1,500 aircraft, 1,500 tanks and 10,000 guns. On the Russian side, losses are even greater, at well over a million troops – a significant proportion of them women, 3,000 aircraft, 4,000 tanks and 15,000 guns. However, this is far from a German victory. The Russians continue to produce armaments at a high rate, and can also replenish the personnel. They have regained control of the air. The German armies remaining in the area are exhausted and short of virtually everything. There is no prospect of any substantial reinforcements reaching them. What they are faced with now is a long, slow retreat back to the West, pursued with ever-increasing vigour by the Red Army. The German military, and also most of the German people, can see that they have made terrible mistakes, many of them due to the demands of an increasingly unstable and manic leader. It is becoming clear that they are likely to be on the defensive for the rest of the war, which is now one that they cannot possibly win. They are faced with a terrible dilemma. Many realize that they should somehow get rid of Hitler and attempt to make peace. However, this is far from easy, since he has surrounded himself with intensely loyal henchmen. On the other hand, they are a proud and patriotic people. If their homeland is attacked, their instinct will be to defend it to the death. Whatever happens, they are faced with further nightmares. In mid-1942, Hitler orders the building of an "Atlantic Wall" of defences all along the

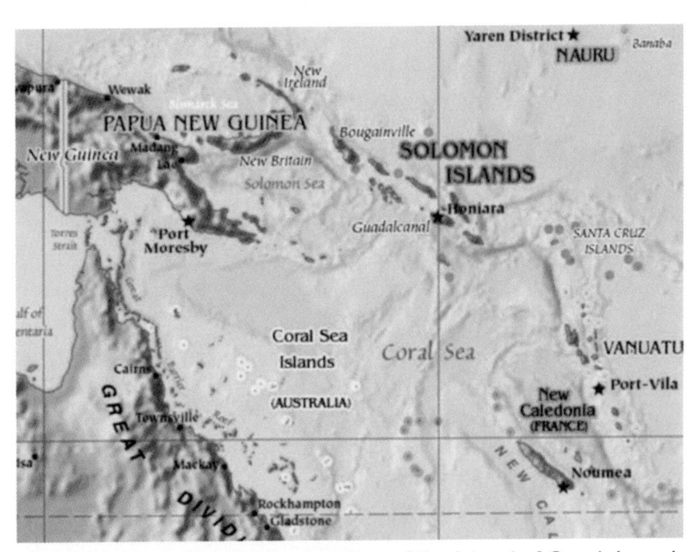

Fig.9.14: Map showing the location of the island of Guadalcanal, off the North-Eastern coast of Australia.

seaboard facing Britain. The prospect of invading the UK is fading and the idea of protecting what they hold is starting to take its place.

The American focus is mainly on Europe, with large quantities of men and materiel now being shipped across to Britain. However, they also start to go on the offensive against the Japanese in the Pacific area. At around the time that the Battle for Stalingrad is starting, they attack the Japanese-occupied Solomon Islands – particularly the group of islands that includes Guadalcanal – the name that becomes associated with the battle. The Chief of Staff of the US Army, George Marshall, gives his support to the plan, although most of the responsibility falls on the US Navy, under Admiral Nimitz. The assault begins in August, as 3,000 US Marines land on two small islands near to Guadalcanal. The Americans achieve complete surprise. These islands are defended by fewer than 1,000 Japanese troops, who are quickly overwhelmed. A larger force of Marines then invades Guadalcanal, which is taken very easily. The Japanese do regroup to attack the islands and there is a protracted series of battles in the area, mostly at sea and by air. This continues for several months, but by February 1943 the Japanese concede and withdraw from the area. The Americans are gradually wresting control from the Japanese over the whole Pacific area, including the various island groups between Australia and the mainland of Asia. However, this still leaves the Japanese in almost total control of the huge landmass of South-Eastern Asia and it's clear that this problem will have to be addressed soon.

In January 1943, a conference is held in Casablanca (Morocco), involving Roosevelt, Churchill and General Charles de Gaulle (representing the Free French). Stalin is invited, but he declines in view of the situation in the ongoing Battle of Stalingrad. However, the focus is mostly on Europe, and a decision is made that nothing less than the unconditional surrender of the Germans will be accepted. This is certainly a change from the position a year or so before, and is due in large part to the events in Russia over the past 6 months. De Gaulle is naturally pushing strongly for plans to invade Europe from Britain. While Stalin is not present, he has been making it clear for a while that there is a desperate need for something along these lines to be done, so that the Germans will be unable to focus exclusively on the Eastern Front. Nevertheless, while the intention to invade is made clear, no detailed plans are developed. There is concern about the situation in North Africa, and there is also the possibility of attacking Italy – the "soft underbelly" as Churchill refers to it. It's difficult to avoid the conclusion that the British and Americans are happy to see the Russian s bearing the brunt of the task of wearing down the Wehrmacht. To be fair, however, a major amphibious invasion is always risky, with a serious danger of being driven back into the sea during the early stages. The British still bear the scars of the Gallipoli fiasco in the Great War. They want to prepare very carefully for such an invasion. The decision is made that there will be no invasion of Northern Europe this year, but an attempt will be made to attack Sicily and Italy. This is, of course, highly confidential information, and strenuous efforts are now made to confuse Hitler about Allied intentions. This includes various attempts at misinformation, such as ensuring that the Spanish authorities find a dead body washed up on their coast, with documents suggesting that the main attack will be on Greece – the so-called Operation Mincemeat.

Chapter 10: The Balance Tilts (March 1943 – June 1944)

10.1 Battles in the Atlantic and the Mediterranean

Arguably the longest battle of the war is that being fought in the Atlantic. Right from the start, surface warships of the British and German fleets seek each other out. Unlike the Great War, in which this engagement was mainly in the North Sea area, these are fought in many places. Following on from the Great War, the British attempt to blockade Germany. However, this is not very successful. The Germans are much less dependent now on goods coming in via the North Sea. As they take over much of Europe, the focus shifts largely to the Atlantic. They now control many ports and airfields around the French Atlantic coast. The blockading is now of Britain, which is highly dependent on goods being brought in by sea, mainly from North America. This happened even before the USA entered the war at the end of 1941, but by 1942 there is a huge tonnage of ships engaged in bringing food and matériel across the Atlantic.

Initially, the German Navy carried out most of their attacks (on both warships and cargo ships) using their surface raiders, such as the Bismarck, Scharnhorst and Tirpitz. However, this was not so successful, with many of these powerful ships eventually being sunk. By the end of 1941, the German strategy had become almost entirely oriented around submarine warfare. This was given a huge boost by the occupation of France, and by the entry of Italy into the war – requiring Allied marine resources to be diverted to the Mediterranean. By early in 1943, this strategy has become highly successful, with developments both in the technology of the U-boats and in the tactics employed. They are now hunting in packs, spreading out so as to detect convoys efficiently and then homing in on them in large numbers, making it difficult for the escorts to protect the cargo ships. Hundreds of ships, adding up to many hundreds of thousands of tons, are being sunk every month.

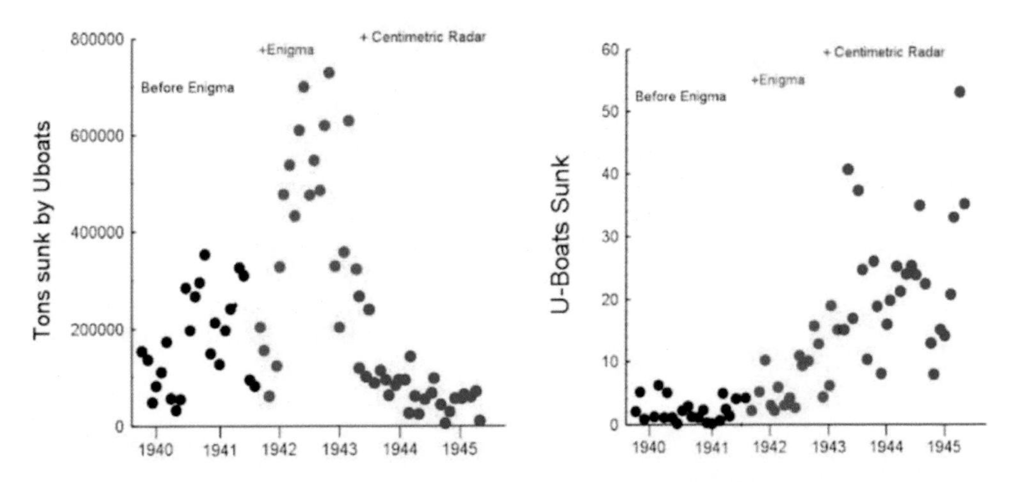

Fig.10.1: Monthly tonnage of Allied shipping sunk by U-boats, and number of U-boats sunk, during the war. "Centimetric radio" refers to equipment for using radio signals from submarines to find them.

However, the tide now starts to turn. A contribution to this comes from deciphering German (Enigma-coded) messages that involve submarines, but in fact, while both British and German code-breakers have some success, this is not really of critical importance. Much more significant are the various developments in the technology of hunting and destroying submarines. There are several strands to this, from use of high intensity searchlights (Leigh Lights) on planes to dramatic improvements in the technology of Sonar to detect and track nearby submarines. Finding them from further away is made easier by the development of High Frequency Direction Finding equipment, picking up the HF radio signals by which submarines communicate with shore.

Fig.10.2: Photo of a High Frequency – Direction Finding receiver, on HMS Belfast.

Relevant here is the phenomenon of diffraction - essentially the "spreading" of waves as they pass the edge of an obstacle, which occurs on a length scale of the order of the wavelength. Light, with a wavelength around a micron – a thousandth of a mm – thus casts a sharp shadow, whereas sound, with a wavelength of the order of a metre, can be heard around corners. Ordinary radio waves have wavelengths of tens or hundreds of metres, so they can be detected behind walls, or even multiple sets of walls. This is good for picking up signals, but not for establishing where they originate. High frequency radio waves, however, have wavelengths in the mm range, giving them good penetration for long range communication, but also making detection of their source easier. Furthermore, the increasing range of certain types of aircraft, such as the USAF B-24 Liberators, means that there are no parts of the Atlantic in which submarines cannot be hunted by air. As a result of these developments, there are now sharp rises in the rate at which U-boats are being sunk, and associated falls in loss of merchant ships. By early 1944, the Battle of the Atlantic has effectively been won and the flow of men and cargo to Britain is reaching new highs. Many of these resources will shortly be used in a massive operation.

As 1943 unfolds, it becomes clear that the Allies are going to prevail in North Africa. Large shipments of aircraft and other resources, both British and American, come in via Gibraltar. American paratroopers are also dropped, having been brought over from Cornwall - although this operation does suffer from logistical difficulties. The invading Allied forces move inexorably Eastwards along the coast, while Montgomery's forces pursue the retreating Axis army to the West. The trap closes and Rommel's forces are driven out of North Africa. This process is completed by May.

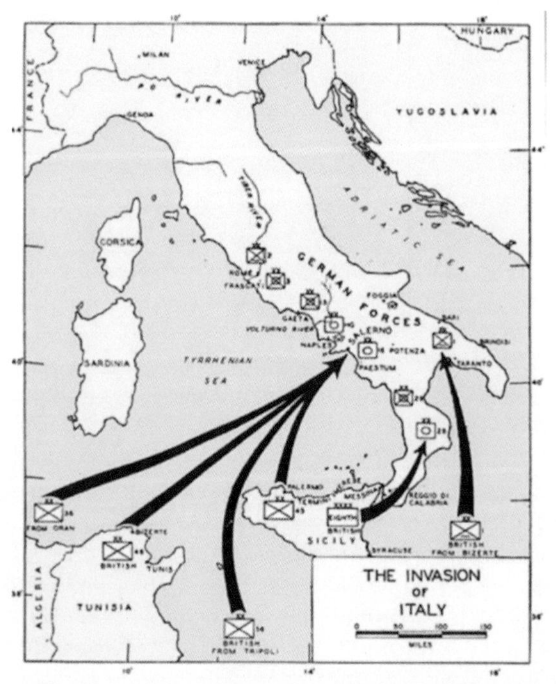

Fig.10.3: Map showing the points of invasion of Italy by Allied forces in September 1943.

The attention of the Allies now switches to Italy, with Sicily as the immediate target. Hitler is now increasingly alarmed about the threat from the Mediterranean. As it becomes clear that Sicily is about to be attacked, he starts to switch resources from his main engagement area, which is still in the East with Russia. This can therefore be regarded as some sort of response to Stalin's repeated request for a Second Front. The Russians are now pushing the Germans back to the West, with several major battles taking place. These include the epic tank battle at Kursk, about 300 miles South-West of Moscow, which takes place in July and August of 1943. It starts with a German attempt to counter-attack, but ends with a sweeping Russian victory. Casualties, and material losses, are again enormous on both sides. The Russian losses are again higher than those of the Germans, but again they can more readily absorb them. While the battle is going on, Hitler orders a retreat from Kursk and directs to Italy a mass of reserve troops in France that were earmarked for the Eastern Front. After the battle, the retreat and pursuit continue unabated.

The Allied attack on Sicily starts in July, initially with about 150,000 troops – although this is quickly built up to about 450,000. The invasion is completed in just over a month, with minimal losses. Casualties are also relatively light on the Italian side, although they again surrender in large numbers – with over 100,000 taken prisoner. Their heart is clearly no longer in this war. There are about 50,000 Germans on the island, but most of them escape to the Italian mainland (with a lot of equipment). There are recriminations that this should not have been allowed to happen, and indeed their presence in Italy turns out to be important in allowing the Axis forces (soon exclusively German) to resist subsequent invasion of the country very stubbornly.

Nevertheless, the writing is now on the wall as far as the Italians are concerned. Mussolini is deposed towards the end of July, although he escapes the immediate wrath of the Italian people by going into hiding and manages to avoid being held to account for almost a year. The Allies start to invade Italy early in September and Italy surrenders a few days later. However, the Germans bring in reinforcements and resist the landings strongly. Nevertheless, by late September, the Allies are established in Southern Italy. However, progression up the country is hard and slow, with the Germans fighting a strong rearguard action. By early 1944, they have retreated behind strong defensive lines in Northern Italy. There is bitter fighting still to come in this area.

10.2 Important Decisions

In autumn of 1943, the Allied leaders take stock of the overall situation. The crucial battles in Stalingrad, Guadalcanal, North Africa, Kursk and Sicily have all been won. The Italians have surrendered. Both the Germans and the Japanese are far from final defeat, but the tide is turning inexorably against them. However, there are many issues to be resolved between the Allies, concerning both short- and long-term objectives. One of these is to somehow minimize the further slaughter before the war is over. Others relate to the subsequent reshaping on the world order, and the aims of the individual Allies on this may well be conflicting. There are therefore important decisions to be made. Churchill, now aged almost 69, is still physically active and is always keen on travelling, and meeting up with other power brokers. He is reveling in his renaissance over the past 3 years, from a situation in which many regarded his career as being over. Roosevelt, on the other hand, while only 61, is not at all well. He has been paralyzed from the waist down for over 20 years. He has coped well with this, and has already been President for 10 years, but he is also a chain-smoker and he has high blood pressure and coronary artery disease. Nevertheless, he is a highly principled and conscientious man and he recognizes the value of face-to-face meetings in the current situation, with a lot of negotiation and horse-trading being required. Stalin is different again. He has effectively been in charge of Russia ever since Lenin's death in 1924, and certainly since the start of the 1930's. He is being increasingly admired in the West, and is often referred to as "Uncle Joe". Aged 65, he is in reasonably good health, despite a fondness for alcohol, but he refuses to travel by air – apparently because a number of prominent Russians died in air crashes during the 1930's. He is a ruthless and suspicious man, but also determined to protect the Russian people, and to somehow reduce the slaughter to which they are still being exposed on the Eastern Front. He is understandably keen to ensure that the British / Americans open a "Second Front" against the Germans. He asks for a summit meeting at which this will be the main item on the agenda.

Roosevelt, on the other hand, wants a meeting focused on the Japanese. It's clear that the situation on land in the Far East has been neglected. The British Empire is under serious threat, although neither the Americans nor the Russians see any need to prop it up. What Roosevelt does see is a strategic interest in China, which has suffered heavily at the hands of the Japanese over the past decade. He wants to involve the leader of (Nationalist) China - Chiang Kai-Shek. Attempts are in hand to coordinate Allied activities in the area, by setting up the South East Asia Command (SEAC), involving Chiang, as well as Louis Mountbatten and Joe Stilwell, respectively representing Britain and the US. Friction is already mounting between Stilwell and Chiang. Unsurprisingly, there is turmoil inside China, with the Government having been forced to move its capital a long way up the Yangtze River to Chungking. Moreover, there are many factions among the embattled Chinese, including a number that embrace communism. As ever, one of the main preoccupations of America, and indeed Churchill, is to fight the menace of communism, so support for Chiang is part of this strategy. This does have its downsides, particularly since corruption is rife amongst Chiang and his Chinese supporters. The US is trying hard to get resources of various types to them, so that they can fight the Japanese, but a substantial proportion of these tend to disappear en route. Stilwell doesn't think much of Chiang, and isn't too enamored of the British either. Also, resentment within China about this corruption is promoting support for communism amongst ordinary Chinese - many of them just poor peasants. Roosevelt wants the Russians to declare war on Japan, but they're reluctant to do this – they have enough on their hands already and they perhaps recall their heavy defeat to the Japanese in the war of 1904-05. Furthermore, Stalin is not keen on Chiang and his sympathies are more with the communists in China. He refuses to take part in a summit meeting about this.

Chiang has his own objectives. These naturally include protecting the Chinese people from further suffering at the hands of the Japanese, and reclaiming the country from them. He does also have to deal with a lot of internal disagreement about the best way forward for China, which of course has been suffering for a long time at the hands of a string of predatory foreign powers, including the British. He has been involved in many campaigns and has a lot of personal military experience – in fact, he's commonly known as the "Generalissimo". He's relatively young, at 56, and he has a high profile, attractive wife, Soong Mei-ling. She's usually known as Madame Chiang and she tends, not only to accompany her husband on his various trips etc, but also to take an active part in negotiations.

Fig.10.4: Cairo meeting in Nov. 1943. Seated, from the left, Chiang Kai-shek, Roosevelt, Churchill and Madame Chiang. Others include two future UK PMs, Anthony Eden (talking to Roosevelt), and Harold MacMillan (two to his right), and US Ambassadors to Egypt and Russia, Alexander Kirk and Averill Harriman (3rd and 2nd from right).

It's therefore a complex situation and the upshot is that two summit meetings are set up, both in late November. The first, to be held in Cairo, will involve Churchill, Roosevelt and Chiang, while the second, immediately afterwards, will be in Tehran, with Churchill, Roosevelt and Stalin present. There is frantic activity in GOGGS, with many telegrams and highly confidential documents flying backwards and forwards. Strong bonds are being formed between all of those working in the building, including Pam and the other 30 or so Secretaries entrusted with handling much of this vital paperwork.

Churchill, Roosevelt and Chiang finally sit down together in the opulent residence of Alexander Kirk, the US Ambassador to Egypt, on the afternoon of Tuesday 23rd November

1943. It's been made clear to Chiang that his wife cannot take part, despite the fact that she has spent most of 1943 on a speaking tour of the USA, to gain support for the Chinese cause, and is also very busy networking at this meeting. These three do at least have common ground in the form of a hatred of the Japanese and it's clear that the main outcome of the summit will be a condemnation of them and a determination to drive them out of mainland Asia, accepting nothing less than their unconditional surrender. However, that still leaves a lot of tactical detail to be sorted out, even if most of it probably won't appear in the final communiqué. Roosevelt starts the ball rolling:

"Chiang, we're keen to help you, but Joe Stilwell keeps telling me that you and your crew spend most of your time lining your pockets from the stuff we send you, and also your troops are often a bit sl ow to actually engage with the Japanese. We do feel that the main thrust has to be to drive the Japs southwards out of Burma and we need Chinese help with this."

Chiang naturally bridles a bit at this, although in fact he is very pleased to have been invited to this "top table" and he's keen to be as diplomatic as possible. His English is not as good as that of his wife, but he is able to express himself reasonably well.

"General Stilwell is a fine man, but he can be a little difficult and I'm not sure that he fully understands all of the problems that face us."

Actually, Joe Stilwell understands the situation rather well, and he knows that Chiang's main preoccupation is with fighting his communists opponents in China, and also that he and his friends are certainly corrupt; on the other hand, Stilwell can undoubtedly be outspoken and it's not for nothing that he's known as "Vinegar Joe". Roosevelt is aware of this, but of course he does want to somehow make this SEAC operation work.

"Well, we are prepared to pump a lot of resource into the area, which mainly means into bases in North-East India, and to continue to get materiel from there across to you in China, but we must be confident that it will be well used. As you know, we're not charging you for any of this."

At this point, Churchill feels that he has to take centre-stage – after all, those bases are mostly British and it's British, and British-Indian, troops that have had to bear the brunt of the Japanese penetration into Malaysia and Burma.

"We naturally expect to play a central part in all of these actions and, in Louis Mountbatten, I've put an excellent man into the key liaison role."

Roosevelt, while a very good diplomat, and an admirer of Churchill in some respects, finds this a little difficult to swallow. It's well known that Mountbatten is a notorious social climber, while also having proved disastrous as a naval commander. This was certainly the case when he was a ship's captain, but he was also responsible for planning of the ill-conceived Dieppe Raid the previous year, for which the Canadians have never forgiven him. His royal connections, however, are extensive. Moreover, he's known to be a favorite of Churchill, who is himself a strong exploiter of family and social links. Roosevelt feels obliged to say:

"Accepting that Joe can be a little harsh, his opinion of Mountbatten is, if anything, worse than his feelings about Chiang. A 'popinjay', is, I believe, his summary."

This is greeted by a period of silence, followed by some very strong demands for Stilwell's removal, but in fact all three of them realize that the SEAC structure, having been just set up with a lot of fanfare, cannot be dismantled now. They just have to make sure that it does in fact function reasonably well. Both Stilwell and Mountbatten are in Cairo, so there is scope for various conciliatory meetings. In any event, the real organizational details tend to be worked through at slightly lower levels and some good people will be involved on all three sides. These include General William Slim, who at least managed to extricate most of the British and British-Indian troops from Burma during the chaotic retreat from the Japanese. He does now have valuable experience of conditions on the ground in Burma, which can certainly be very difficult.

In any event, the key agreements are reached, which include a commitment to increased levels of resource, particularly aircraft, and to the main immediate focus being to drive the Japanese out of Burma. Of course, this does commit large numbers of Allied soldiers to having to fight in the nightmare conditions of the Burmese Jungle, but this is all-out war. It's also agreed that the Japanese will be forced to give up all of the regions they have invaded, including Korea, Manchuria, Formosa, Indonesia, Malaysia, Indo-China etc. It's recognized that this is likely to be a long and difficult process, but the commitment is made. This doesn't appear in the communiqué, but it's hoped that the Russians will be able to assist with this, once the war in Europe has been completed and they are no longer engaged in a death-struggle with the Germans. This is one of the items on the agenda for the second key summit, to follow immediately. In fact, while the summary announcements are simple, an enormous amount of work is done behind the scenes at these meetings. This includes the compilation of much detail concerning military and economic issues, transport, communications etc – these are below the level at which the leaders hold their discussions, but are essential when it comes to implementation of decisions.

So immediately after the Cairo meeting, Churchill and Roosevelt move on to Tehran – still in the Middle East, but well over 1,000 miles away. In the end, Stalin does fly to Tehran – it's a long way from Moscow overland, but in an American plane, and with an escort of 40 fighters. This is in fact the first time that Roosevelt has met Stalin, although Churchill has already seen him in Moscow several times. There was an Anglo-Soviet invasion of Iran in 1941, which required extensive collaboration between them. That was partly aimed at securing oil supplies, but the focus now is simply on putting increasing pressure on the Germans, hopefully enough to finish the war with them by around the coming summer.

Fig.10.5: Stalin, Roosevelt and Churchill in Tehran.

There is agreement from the start that the Western Allies will indeed attempt an invasion of Northern Europe in the near future. It's clear that the German defences at the Northern end of Italy, using the Alps, could be virtually impregnable. Anyway, there is enormous pressure to liberate France and the Low Countries as soon as possible. It has been delayed for too long. It is mostly Churchill who has prevaricated, partly through a feeling that the Wehrmacht is a fearsome opponent. Still, the Russians have shown that they can be beaten, and there's no doubt that the battles on the Eastern Front have damaged German military capabilities considerably. With American resources pouring across the Atlantic, and the Russians moving in from the East in huge numbers, this really shouldn't be so difficult. The communiqué certainly involves a strong commitment to the opening of a "Second Front", although it provides few details. The unwritten expectation is that it will start fairly early in 1944, but of course there will always be issues about exactly how much preparation will be needed, the vagaries of weather etc – ventures involving sea and air always tend to be subject to these. There is nothing relating to the possibility of Russia attacking Japan after the defeat of the Germans, although there has been a lot of discussion about it.

10.3 Slim Steps Up In Burma

The campaign in Burma is strongly influenced by terrain and weather. During the monsoon season, which typically extends from May/June to October/November, movements on the ground are almost impossible in much of the country. It's also unpleasant to be anyw here but in solid, waterproof buildings during this period. Even outside of the monsoon season, the danger of disease is high in many areas, with malarial mosquitos, and also other hazardous wildlife - such as venomous snakes, poisonous spiders and blood-sucking leeches, widespread. It's also hot – even during the notional winter. The difficulties experienced by armies in maintaining sanitary conditions in the field also mean that dysentery is often rife. Native peoples do live in these jungles, but their adaptation to the conditions is naturally much better than that of soldiers from other parts of the world.

Around the start of 1943, the expectation is that the Japanese will renew their penetration to the North and West, into India. In fact, they do not do this, preferring instead to consolidate their position in Burma, while also encouraging the native peoples of the whole area to revolt against British rule. There is fertile ground for this, particularly in India. There is certainly a lot of disaffection in the Eastern provinces of India, such as Bengal, where there is a disastrous famine – with 2-3 million people dying of starvation. The Indian National Army, led by Rash Behari Bose, is formed late in 1942, partly from British-Indian troops captured by the Japanese in Malaya and Singapore. They fight alongside the Japanese, together with the Burma Independence Army, and these two armies constitute a significant force.

The British, on the other hand, under Bill Slim, would have been inclined to attack the Japanese during the 1942-43 season, but they are denied the necessary resources. With the focus very much on Europe and North Africa, they become the "Forgotten Army", stuck in what is regarded as a backwater of the war. Early in 1943, there are some minor incursions into Japanese-held territory, led by Major Orde Wingate. He's an eccentric character – in fact, verging on the mentally unstable, but his claims that great things can be achieved by small parties of highly trained commando-style troops, operating behind enemy lines, attracts the support of both Wavell and Churchill. These groups are termed the "Chindits" and they do manage to cause a few minor problems for the Japanese. In general, however, despite their achievements being publicized quite widely, providing some positivity back in the UK during a very uncertain period, these activities, and some further attempts early the following year, are abject failures – costing valuable resources and with a very high casualty rate – mainly from disease.

It takes the decisions of the Cairo Conference towards the end of 1943 to galvanize the Allies into focusing properly on this theatre of the war. Mountbatten may have his limitations, but he is very good at PR and he makes sure that the profile of the Burma Campaign is raised, while the Americans now focus in earnest on the situation on land in the Far East. It's therefore during the 1943-44 season that the counter-attack is to be made. Unfortunately, this is also

Fig.10.6: Len and the Fullbrooks' dog, Bonnie, in the grounds of the Royal Hospital, in 1943.

the season that the Japanese have earmarked for their big push into India. It's true that 1942-43 was relatively quiet in this part of the world, but it's evident that 1943-44 is going to be very different. In fact, while the British are planning a "March on Rangoon", the Japanese have in mind a "March on Delhi".

Meanwhile, Len and his CMP colleagues in London have been kept very busy. The city is now thronged with military personnel, including large numbers of American troops and airmen. The influx of US military into the UK over the 18 months since Pearl Harbor is building up rapidly – by summer of 1943 the number is approaching half a million (and a further million will arrive over the next 12 months). They do have their own military police, but there is scope for friction with such a high concentration of adrenaline-fuelled young men brought together under stressful conditions. In fact, the thoughts of both the troops and the CMP officers are moving towards the likelihood of their services being required abroad in the near future. Experience in North Africa, as well as at Dunkirk, has shown that relatively large CMP presences are going to be needed once invasions get under way, both in mainland Europe and in South-East Asia.

Although Herbert has stayed in the UK, the 4th Battalion of the RWK has been on the move. In May 1942, it was shipped out to North Africa and became involved in the first battle of El Alamein. They stayed in the area until early in 1943, when they were transferred to the 5th Indian Infantry Division in North East India. The Japanese are now firmly established in southern Burma. Their experiences there so far have been very positive and they have little respect for the opposition. Their confidence that they will continue to call the shots is high. However, the organization of the British and British-Indian Armies has been greatly improved, with Slim doing an outstanding job. They are better equipped than before, with many more tanks. These are mostly American Stuart and Lee light and medium tanks, which are proving very successful. It's a measure of the power of the American industrial economy that, within just 2 years, thousands of complex pieces of military equipment like this have been designed, manufactured and shipped half-way round the world. It's a major factor in determining the course of the war.

British tanks have in general not been a great success, but British and British-Indian troops – and indeed Chinese forces to the east – are now using American tanks very effectively. Tanks have to be handled carefully in jungle terrain, but they are potentially a powerful resource, and the Japanese have very few. The morale of the Allied troops has been raised considerably by changes in equipment such as this, and by improvements in provisioning and training. High quality reinforcements, such as the 4th Battalion of the RWK, are also helping. Despite being new to the area, they are an effective and coherent fighting force of about 600 men, with many outstanding, highly experienced officers. They arrive at the port of Chittagong in late October 1943. From there, they move by train to the railhead at Dohazari. A shortage of lorries means that they then have to march down to the encampment at Bawli Bazar – a distance of some 120 miles, which takes about a week. This is not an easy journey. It's hot and humid, with a lot of (malarial) mosquitos active in the evening and at night. The Arakan area is made up of jungle-covered hills, with mangrove swamps and paddy fields in the lower-lying regions near the coast. There are also mountain ranges running north-south and deep, dry stream beds (chuangs) running east-west, which become raging torrents during the monsoon. These are often hundreds of feet wide and, outside of the monsoon season, they are tidal. They're one of the many natural hazards and barriers.

In early February, the RWK Battalion, and a number of others in the Arakan region, are taken by surprise as the Japanese suddenly launch a major counter-attack, attempting to encircle them. This is the kind of thing that the Japanese have done many times before in Burma and they expect the Allies to either surrender or try to escape to the North. This time they do neither. They hold their ground and, crucially, they are supplied by air, so they can continue fighting long after such a siege would normally have made this impossible. In fact, this attack, while certainly substantial, is really a feint by the Japanese, who hope that it will bring Allied troops down from the major bases of Imphal and Dimapur, thinking that this is a major assault on India, through Chittagong. In fact, it is through Imphal - further to the north-east - that the Japanese plan to make their main attack, capturing the massive stockpiles of Allied supplies there and at the railhead of Dimapur before starting their "March on Delhi". They have decided, partly in view of their declining power in the Pacific, that an invasion of India - leading to complete collapse of the British Empire – is their best strategy for building a pan-Asian Empire of their own.

This siege goes on for most of February. The Japanese take the Ngakyedauk Pass – dubbed the Okidoke Pass by the British - a track through the range of hills just to the south of Chota Maunghnama, which has been improved by Allied engineers. Several isolated British-Indian groups continue to resist, with water, food and ammunition being dropped by air to them every day. One of these is in the so-called Admin. Box, which is less than a mile in diameter, but contains about 8,000 men from the 7th Indian Division. Their tanks are proving very effective against attacks in situations such as these. The Japanese, on the other hand, are running short of ammunition and food. Eventually, on the verge of starvation, the Japanese stop their sieges and retreat to the south. This is the first time that a Japanese force on the ground has been beaten in this war. While the withdrawal might not have happened if the Japanese had not had this plan for an all-out attack elsewhere, it certainly raises the morale of the Allied troops. Although there are no American troops on the ground, the US Air Force is making a major contribution to these airdrops that are proving so crucial.

The Japanese launch their attack on Imphal immediately after withdrawing from around Maungdaw. Slim recognizes the dangers and moves quickly to reinforce the area. The 5th Indian Division is to go, but there are logistical challenges in moving 15,000 men and their equipment – the 161st Brigade is just one of more than a dozen in the Division. In view of the urgency, it's decided that the move will be made largely by air. This is the first time that such a large body of men had been airlifted in this way and it's something that the Japanese never expected. They fly in Douglas C47 Dakotas, sometimes called the "Skytrain". It's a very reliable and robust plane. It has a payload of almost 3 tons - about 25 men, with their basic kit. Also, they do take some equipment, including jeeps. Loads are carefully calculated, taking the maximum on each flight.

Fig. 10.7: Troops of 5th Indian Division loading a jeep into a Douglas Dakota Mark III of 194 Squadron RAF, during reinforcement of Imphal in March 1944.

Dimapur is an enormous encampment, with huge stockpiles of supplies – being brought in continuously via trains from the West. Transport links – particularly by rail, road and air, are crucial in this conflict. Supply lines, and the mobility of troops on the ground, are the keys to success. The rail links from Calcutta and Chittagong to Dimapur and Ledo, and beyond by air into China, are precarious in many ways, but are central to the needs of the Allies. Airlifting supplies to the Chinese army of Chiang Kai-Shek has to be done over a part of the Himalaya Range – the so-called "Hump". Not only does this involve flying over peaks above 15,000 feet, but also the weather conditions are often extreme. It is very hazardous and hundreds of planes are lost. The rail link is also difficult, with a change of gauge requiring manual transfer of goods between trains and also a difficult river crossing. The men keeping these links operational, including many working in the Assam Tea Plantations, are playing roles as important as those of the fighting troops. The Americans have several "Railway Operating Battalions" in the area, and there has been an influx of American locomotives. Various measures raise the original line capacity of about 500 tons per day by a factor of more than ten. These supplies are absolutely critical for Slim's 14th Army, and also for Chiang Kai-Shek's Chinese forces.

The area to which the 4th Battalion is now moving lies in hill country, and is thus at least a little cooler than the steaming coastal regions of the Arakan. Imphal, which is in the middle of a large plain, is at about 2,500 feet, while Kohima is a small hill station, lying at about 5,000 feet. Dimapur, on the other hand, is at about 500 feet. This area is the most accessible way into India – better in many ways than the shorter coastal route through Chittagong, which has barriers in the form of paddy fields and swamps. There is a good (recently improved) road between Imphal and Dimapur, which passes though Kohima. The Japanese are now starting to launch a massive attack on Imphal and Kohima, intending to use captured resources at Imphal in a subsequent drive down to Dimapur. They know that, if they could take Dimapur, then the British-Indian, American and Chinese fighting capabilities in South-East Asia would collapse. The way to India would be clear.

The defence of Kohima, with the 4th Battalion of the RWKR playing a central role, is to enter into the annals of the history of the Second World War. It is a desperate action, spread over a period of about 2 weeks, with many thousands of Japanese troops repeatedly hurling themselves at the few hundred soldiers dug in around Kohima. They are desperately short of water. On the other hand, the Japanese supply lines are totally over-stretched are they are short of both food and ammunition. Supplies are repeatedly dropped by US planes, some of them falling in the small area between the two sets of troops - leading to desperate attempts by both sides to retrieve them. The Japanese repeatedly attack, showing incredible courage and belief in their cause. There are many casualties on both sides, although the Japanese certainly lose far more men. There hasn't been much trench warfare in the whole of this war, but conditions here are worse than almost anything experienced in the Great War. The Japanese, while having more freedom of movement, are beginning to starve – many of them have eaten nothing for weeks. They're also being hit hard by disease – of course, under-nourished men are more susceptible to this. Their repeated, fanatical attacks have resulted in many being killed by machine gun fire or grenades.

In the end, relief does reach the defenders of Kohima before they can finally be overwhelmed, although it's a very close-run thing. Reinforcements in Dimapur had been gathering force for a while and the breakthrough finally comes on 18th April. Of the 500 soldiers of the 4th Battalion who had arrived in Kohima 2 weeks before, about 70 have been killed and 125 wounded. Still, the survival rate of the Japanese attackers will turn out in the end to be very much lower than this. Nevertheless, the Japanese forces around Kohima, and indeed around the bigger encampment at Imphal, aren't about to give up. In fact, they carry on fiercely contesting both places for a further month or two. The tide of the battle, however, is turning against them, with more Allied resources and reinforcements flowing in from the West, while the strain of their long supply lines from the South tells increasingly against the Japanese. In June, Sato starts to withdraw his Division, ignoring Mutaguchi's frantic instructions to continue pushing to the North and to, if possible, to attack Dimapur. Sato knows that this is not possible and that all he'd be doing would be to ensure that they all die of starvation and disease. Nevertheless, it's clear that the Japanese are not going to abandon Burma, or indeed the other countries that they occupy in the region. They're going to have to be driven out yard by yard. The Allied commanders envisage at least a further year of warfare here, and quite possibly two years. There's then likely to be the enormous challenge of subsequently invading Japan. The need for troops on the ground here is clearly going to continue for some time. Moving back through the testing terrain and climate of Burma, retracing their steps of 2 years earlier, will present a huge challenge.

Back in the UK, awareness of these events is starting to spread, although everything in Asia is still seen in Britain as something of a sideshow to the main event, which is the upcoming invasion of France. Many of the CMP people know that they will shortly be going abroad as part of this – it's quite clear that there will be enormous logistical demands as the invading army establishes beachhead and then moves into the interior of France, Belgium, Holland and Germany. In parallel with this, it's recognized that, as this huge evacuation of military personnel from Britain takes place, the need for the Redcaps there, and particularly in London, will be reduced. However, it is also clear that extended movement will now be needed through Burma. If anything, the job of the CMP there will be even more difficult than in Europe. In April, Len learns that he, together with his Company, will shortly be moving to India for this purpose.

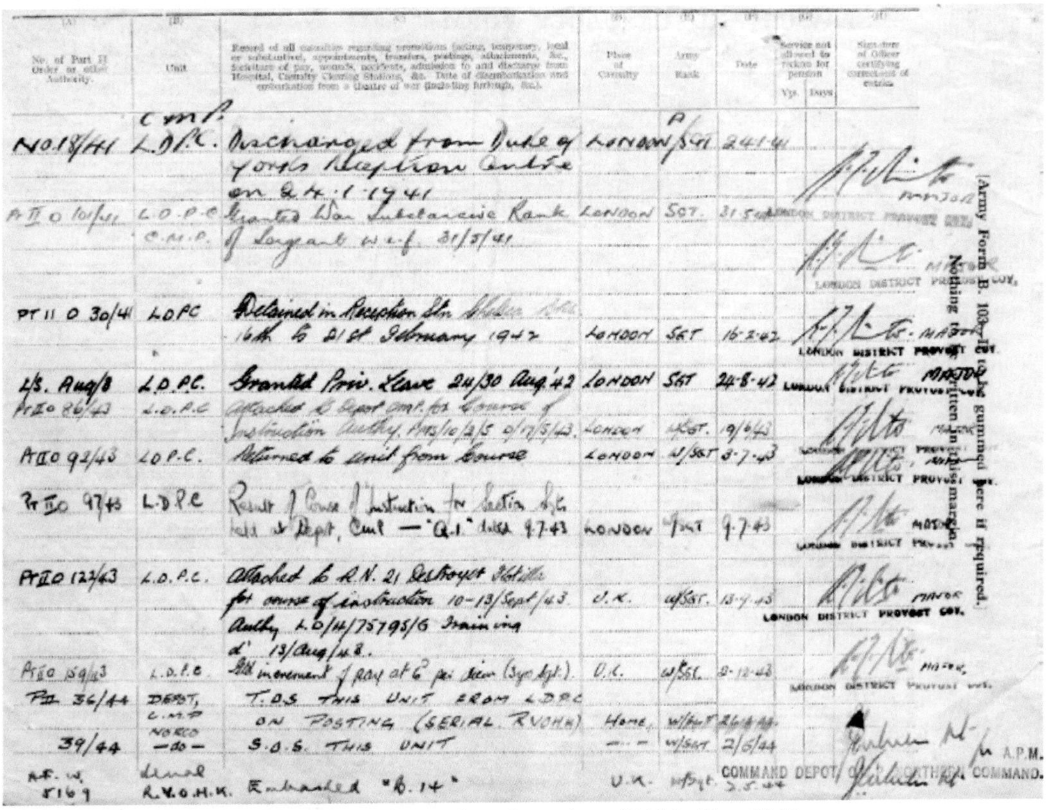

(A) No. of Part II Order or other Authority	(B) Unit	(C) Record of all casualties regarding promotions (acting, temporary, local or substantive), appointments, transfers, postings, attachments, &c., forfeiture of pay, wounds, accidents, admission to and discharge from Hospital, Casualty Clearing Stations, &c. Date of disembarkation and embarkation from a theatre of war (including furlough, &c.)	(D) Place of Casualty	(E) Army Rank	(F) Date	(G) Service not allowed to reckon for pension Yrs. Days	(H) Signature of Officer certifying correctness of entries
NO.18/41	CMP L.D.P.C.	Discharged from Duke of Yorks Reception Centre on 24.1.1941	LONDON	A/SGT	24.1.41		[illegible] Major
Pt II O 101/41	L.D.P.C. C.M.P.	Granted War Substantive Rank of Sergeant w.e.f. 31/5/41	LONDON	SGT.	31.5.41		[illegible] Major, London District Provost Coy.
PT II O 30/41	LDPC	Detained in Reception Stn [illegible] 16th to 21st February 1942	LONDON	SGT	16.2.42		[illegible] Major, London District Provost Coy.
L/S. Aug/8	L.D.P.C.	Granted Priv. Leave 24/30 Aug.'42	LONDON	SGT	24.8.42		[illegible] Major, London District Provost Coy.
Pt II O 86/43	L.D.P.C.	Attached to Depot CMP for Course of Instruction Authy. [illegible] d/17/5/43.	LONDON	A/SGT.	19/6/43		[illegible] Major
Pt II O 92/43	LD.P.C.	Returned to unit from course	LONDON	A/SGT	3.7.43		[illegible] Major, London District Provost Coy.
Pt II O 97/43	L.D.P.C.	Result of Course of Instruction for Section Sgts held at Depot, CMP — "Q.1." [illegible] 9.7.43	LONDON	A/SGT	9.7.43		[illegible] Major, London District Provost Coy.
Pt II O 122/43	L.D.P.C.	Attached to R.N. 21 Destroyer Flotilla for course of instruction 10–13/Sept/43. Authy LD/14/75795/G Training d/ 13/Aug/43.	U.K.	A/SGT.	13.9.43		[illegible] Major, London District Provost Coy.
Pt II O 159/43	L.D.P.C.	[illegible] increment of pay at 6d per diem (Sgt. [illegible]).	U.K.	A/SGT.	8.12.43		[illegible] Major, London District Provost Coy.
Pt II 36/44	DEPOT, C.M.P.	T.O.S. THIS UNIT FROM LDPC ON POSTING (SERIAL RVOHK)	Home.	W/SGT	26.4.44		[illegible] for A.P.M.
39/44	NORCO —do—	S.O.S. THIS UNIT	— —	W/SGT	2/6/44		
A.F. W. 5169	[illegible] R.V.O.H.K.	Embarked "B.14"	U.K.	W/Sgt.	3.5.44		COMMAND DEPOT C.M.P. NORTHERN COMMAND

[Army Form B. 103 [illegible] to be gummed here if required. Nothing to be written in this margin.]

Fig.10.8: Len's postings from Jan. 1941 to May 1944.

Len has a chat with Ralph, Pam's father, shortly before he leaves.

"Well, Len, so you're off shortly. There's been a lot for you to do round here over the past 5 years, but people like you are going to be in big demand abroad now. Do you know exactly where you'll be going?"

"They've just said India, but I think it's clear that it's going to be Assam, with a view to invading Burma."

"We never got over to the eastern side while we were there, although a lot of north India is fairly similar. You do know that it's going to be very hot Len, especially at the time of year that you'll be arriving. The only escape is to get to higher altitudes, so aim for some hill stations if you can!"

"I don't think that we'll get a lot of choice, but I'll bear it in mind! What about the rain and the mosquitoes etc?"

"The rain does get to you, although it's only really bad for a few months in the summer. The mossies are a real pain, but they're only active in the evenings and at night. You must keep your net in good shape, so take a needle and thread. Keep your arms and legs covered up in the evenings, and also your neck – they go for any fleshy parts, but they're not so keen on hands or faces. There are also sprays and creams – use anything that's available and take it seriously – you really don't want to get malaria. We do need you to come back, Len – we don't want a suicidal daughter on our hands."

"Don't worry, Ralph – I'll be back."

Taking leave of Pam is, as for millions of other couples over recent years, a traumatic business. They meet up at the RHC in the afternoon before Len is due to leave. Len thought it would be better if Jum were there as well, so he suggested that they all meet up for a game of tennis. Of course, Pam is worried sick about what might now happen.

"Why on earth do you have to go? There's plenty of policing still needed round here. These Yanks have no inhibitions at all."

"I'm sure they don't, although they've got their own CMP. Anyway, we all know that this place is shortly going to become almost deserted. The action is going to move on and we all have to go. Look, as I've explained before, I cracked all this a long time ago. I spotted at the start of the war that, while the CMP do a very important job, they don't actually get shot at as much as the poor bloody infantry. Of course, we all need to get a little closer to the action now, but I'll be much better off in Burma than acting as a Beach-master in France, with a lot of Krauts taking pot-shots. I won't see any Japs in Burma."

"You're such a stupid bloody idiot! Don't you realize that most of the soldiers killed in Burma didn't get shot – they died of disease. Do you think that your bloody red cap will protect you from malaria?!"

Both Len and Jum are taken aback slightly – she doesn't normally swear, but also this rather sounds like a very rare example of her revealing what might be restricted information.

"At least, that's what some people seem to think....", she finishes lamely.

"Look, Pammie", Len says gently, "You surely know that we don't get any choice about these postings?"

"Of course I do. You've just got to promise to come back in one piece. I'll go out there and kill you myself if you don't!", she says, hammering on his chest. "Also, where's that photo you promised?"

"Here it is", he says.

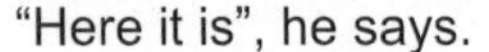

Fig.10.9: Photo of Len from 1944.

"And make sure you don't lose mine!"

"I'll carry it everywhere, even if it falls to bits. Look, you know very well that we'll meet again, even if we don't quite know where or when. It might even be a sunny day!"

They try to keep it light, but it's not easy.

"What about this game of tennis?", asks Pam.

"Well, I'm not sure that's a good idea. I know you get annoyed when I beat you, but I couldn't let you win and leave you crowing indefinitely."

Actually, Pam usually wins, since Len has only just started playing.

"I'll give you a game, Len.", says Jum.

"You must be joking, Jumbo, how can anyone beat an elephant at tennis? Anyway, I do actually have to go now. We have a briefing this evening."

They both watch him walk away.

"He'll be fine, Pam. I wouldn't like to face him in the jungle and the Japs are half his size. He's a tough lad."

"He's not so tough and he doesn't like hot weather or confined spaces. He'll get a lot of both out there. Anyway, if he doesn't come back, I'll die too."

Len and his company travel by train to Liverpool on 2nd May 1944. They spend a couple of days in the city before joining the SS Stratheden when it sails on 5th May. It's a sizeable and fairly upmarket ship, built about 7 years ago, although it's seen a lot of service as a troopship over the past 4 years. There are just over 3,000 troops on board, crammed in a little more densely than the 1,000 or so paying passengers it used to carry before the war as a P&O ship. Len's CMP Company is in charge of discipline among the soldiers on the ship.

They move out of the Mersey and join a large convoy (KMF-31) that had left the Clyde earlier in the day. This is Len's first experience of a troopship, although he did spend a few days in the North Sea last year, with a Destroyer Flotilla. That kind of attachment, designed to widen experience, is fairly common for CMP personnel. In fact, the weather had been quite rough then, and Destroyers are relatively small, so it took him a while to get his sea-legs.

Fig.10.10: SS Stratheden at Southampton in 1938.

Vessel	Pdt.	Tons	Built	Cargo	Notes
ALMANZORA (Br)	12	15,551	1914		DETACHED OFF GIBRALTAR FOR FREETOWN
ANTENOR (Br)		11,174	1925		GIB TO PT SAID
ARUNDEL CASTLE (Br)	62	19,118	1921		ALGIERS
BAZELEY					ESCORT 06/05 - 18/05
BENTINCK					ESCORT 06/05 - 18/05
BOISSEVAIN (Du)		14,134	1937		GIB TO PT SAID
BURGES					ESCORT 06/05 -
BYARD					ESCORT 06/05 - 18/05
CALDER					ESCORT 06/05 - 16/05
CAPETOWN CASTLE (Br)	53	27,000	1938	916 TROOPS	ORAN
CHIDDINGFOLD					ESCORT 16/05 - 18/05
CITY OF LINCOLN (Br)	44	8,039	1938		BOMBAY
COTTON					ESCORT 07/05 - 12/05
CROOME					ESCORT 13/05 - 19/05
DART					ESCORT 18/05 - 19/05
DELHI					ESCORT 13/05 - 15/05
DRURY					ESCORT 06/05 - 18/05
DUCHESS OF BEDFORD (Br)	13	20,123	1928		DETACHED, DATE ESTIMATED, FOR LAGOS
DUCHESS OF RICHMOND (Br)		20,022	1928		GIB TO PT SAID
EMPRESS OF AUSTRALIA (Br)	31	21,833	1914	4236 TROOPS	NAPLES
EXMOOR					ESCORT 13/05 - 19/05
FELIX ROUSSEL (Fr)	23	17,083	1930	1018 TROOPS	DET OFF GIBRALTAR FOR W AF
FRANCONIA (Br)	63	20,175	1923	225 TROOPS	ORAN
HMCS PRINCE ROBERT (Br)	11	6,982	1930		
HMS AMEER (Br)	43	11,420	1942		TRINCOMALEE
JOHAN DE WITT (Du)	22	10,474	1920	352 TROOPS	BRIEF REPAIRS AT GIBRALTAR
LEDBURY					ESCORT 13/05 - 19/05
MOOLTAN (Br)	61	20,952	1923		EMPTY TO ALGIERS
NAIRANA					ESCORT 11/06 - 19/06
NEA HELLAS (Br)	42	16,991	1922		E AFRICA VIA SUEZ
NIEUW HOLLAND (Du)		11,066	1927		GIB TO PT SAID
ORBITA (Br)	21	15,495	1915	191 TROOPS	DET OFF GIBRALTAR FOR W AF
ORDUNA (Br)		15,507	1914		ORAN TO PT SAID
ORION (Br)	52	23,371	1935	3135 TROOPS	
ORMONDE (Br)		14,982	1917		GIB TO PT SAID
PEGU II (Br)	33	7,838	1943		GIBRALTAR
PRINCE ROBERT					ESCORT 07/05 - 18/05
RANCHI (Br)		16,738	1925		ORAN TO PT SAID
SAMARIA (Br)	32	19,597	1921	4511 TROOPS	NAPLES
STRATHEDEN (Br)	51	23,722	1937	3132 TROOPS	.
STRATHMORE (Br)	41	23,428	1935	3309 TROOPS	
WHEATLAND					ESCORT 14/05 - 19/05

Fig.10.11: Ships of Convoy KMF-31, leaving Britain on 5th May 1944.

Even as they move into the choppy waters of the Irish Sea, the motion of this ship, with a displacement of almost 24,000 tons, is entirely sedate by comparison. On the other hand, they're certainly crammed in tightly and a few of the soldiers do start to suffer.

In the convoy as a whole, there are about 21,000 troops, bound for various places in the Mediterranean and Far East. There are about a dozen escort ships, which also come and go as the convoy progresses. A strong escort is certainly still necessary. While the Bay of Biscay and the Mediterranean are less dangerous than they were, there are still German submarines on the prowl. As they move down into the Atlantic and start their long voyage, Len is not really aware how closely he is following in the footsteps of William, his late brother. It's symptomatic of how thoroughly the family was broken up that the knowledge of exactly what happened to William has largely been lost. His older brothers, Herbert, Frank and Stan, were in contact with William for a while, but it was their mother who kept in the closest touch with him and Len lost her at a very young age.

In any event, his voyage around Portugal and Spain, through the straits of Gibraltar and across the Mediterranean to Port Said, which is reached on 19th May, is a close reflection of William's trip of 30 years ago. There are, however, one or two differences. For example, these ships are larger and slightly faster than those of the 1914 convoy, although the overcrowding is at least as bad. Perhaps a more significant difference is that most of the troops in the earlier voyage thought at the time that they were off on a great adventure, with little physical danger, although that was to change sharply within a year or so, as the horrors of Gallipoli and many other places became known. In contrast to this, none of the troops on the 1944 convoy are under any illusions about the potential dangers. Many are bound for Italy, where the invasion is well under way, and most of the rest are headed for Bombay and then across India to Burma. In both cases, while they will be on the front foot, they know that they will be facing fanatical, well-organized and resourceful enemies (Germans in the case of Italy). Nobody doubts that there will be many more casualties on all sides.

Fig. 10.12: Photo of the SS Mooltan, one of the group of ships from convoy KMF-31, in the Suez canal, on 22nd May 1944.

The convoy breaks up at Port Said, with a certain amount of redistribution of troops between ships. The SS Stratheden, and several others from the convoy, now move (unescorted) into the Suez canal. In fact, a further thousand troops join the Stratheden before it leaves Port Said, bringing the number up to about 4,000. All of the ships moving down the canal are now heavily over-crowded. Also, it's getting very hot. The daily routine becomes even more stressful for everyone on board. Inevitably, there is some friction, although the CMP Company manages to maintain reasonably good order without too many problems. As the ships move slowly through the canal, there is very little to do and the daily routine is quite stressful. Soldiers must get up at 6am, roll up their bedding and have breakfast (tea, bread and oatmeal) at 6.30. Boat station drill is at 10am and lunch at 11.30, followed by an evening meal at 5.30. These are usually tea, bread and some kind of meat and potato. The quality is poor and the portions small. It's so hot inside the ship that everyone strips down to shoes and shorts for meals and the perspiration runs in streams off everyone's body. This diet is sufficient to ward off illness, but it's certainly not pleasant. For Len, his childhood in Bowermadden has prepared him quite well for dietary hardship, if not for the heat and overcrowding. He has always much preferred open spaces to confinement.

As they move down the Red Sea towards Aden, with the temperatures still very high, there are certainly some disciplinary issues. Len and his CMP colleagues are obliged to patrol around the ship, normally in groups of 2 or 3. Some of the problems relate to enforcement of the blackout that applies after 8.30pm.

"I'm afraid that you'll have to put those fags out, lads", says Len to a bunch of soldiers on deck at the back of the ship.

"Give us a break, Sarge. It's like an oven down below and we're gasping. Anyway, what's the point of this blackout – the Eyeties are out of the war now and there are no Jerries for hundreds of miles!"

"You're probably right, but we don't make the rules – we just have to enforce them. That's how the Army works. Anyway, we'll shortly be moving into the Arabian Sea, where the Japs still have plenty of ships, including one or two carriers. In any event, it only takes one stray Stuka or Zero. We currently have no defences at all. Just imagine what would happen if we were dive-bombed."

Looking around the crowded deck, it doesn't take much imagination to get a feel for the carnage that would result. They throw their fags over the side.

"We're all gasping, lads, but this trip won't last forever. We'll get a bit of a break at Aden, where we'll become part of a new convoy. We should be a bit safer then."

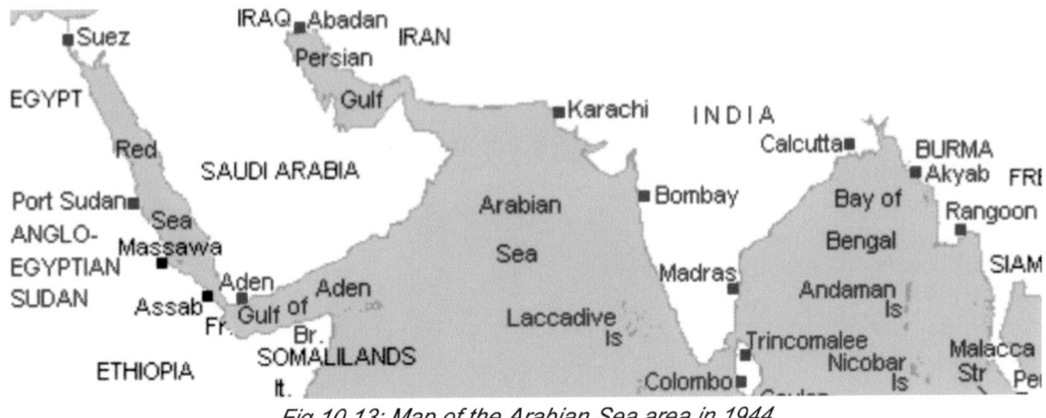

Fig. 10.13: Map of the Arabian Sea area in 1944.

They reach the port of Aden on the evening of 25th May. They spend a couple of days here, taking on water and other provisions. They also refuel, with some of the soldiers watching fascinated as a connection is made to one of the floating buoys that have oil pipelines connected to them. They're all marked as the property of the Anglo-Iranian Oil Company (AIOC), following the Shah's request to drop the word "Persia" from the name. The value of having secured the oil fields in the Persian Gulf, and built pipelines to places like this, is clear to everyone. The soldiers are also fascinated to watch the many porpoises that are cavorting happily around the ships. Aden is a very small settlement – there are only about 50 buildings here, surrounded by steep escarpments – but it has great strategic importance and its existence is entirely built around (British and British-Indian) military activities. The population is largely made up of Arabs, but they're very much second class citizens. The place is now a (British) Crown Colony. The troops are allowed to spend some time ashore now, although there isn't very much for them to do or see.

Army Form B-103.
Part II.

SERVICE AND CASUALTY FORM, PART II.

Regt. CMP. Army Number 7685878.

*Sub. Surname CLYNE Christian Names LEONARD JAMES.

*Acting, L al Rank

*To be entered in acilitate alteration.

(A) No. of Part II Order or other Authority.	(B) Unit.	(C) Record of all casualties regarding promotions (acting, temporary, local or substantive), appointments, transfers, postings, attachments, etc., forfeiture of pay, wounds, accidents, admission to and discharge from Hospital, Casualty Clearing Stations, etc. Date of disembarkation and embarkation from a theatre of war (including furlough, etc.).	(D) Place of Casualty.	(E) Army Rank.	(F) Date.	(G) Service not allowed to reckon for fixing the rate of pension. Yrs.	Days.	(H) Signature of Officer certifying correctness of entries.
10.283 7/44	CMP(I) DEPOT.	Disembarked India. proceeded to CMP(I) DEPOT.	India	Sgt.	2.6.44			for Rec. Offr.
9/14.11.44	HQ DEPOT	[illegible] to CMP(I) & granted [illegible] 20.6.44	"	"	20.6.44			Rec. Offr.
20/20.6.44	62 L(CP)U	[illegible] TOS w.e.f. 9.10.44	"	Sgt	9.10.44			
CRO 69/1 of 44	Depot	[illegible]			30.9.44			
02E 87-22/3/45	Depot CMP(I)	appointed [illegible] P/A/WO II	India	[illegible]	11/2/45			

Fig.10.14: Len's postings from June 1944 to March 1945.

A new convoy (AB 40A) is now being assembled. This includes a number of British warships. Len isn't really aware of this, but its composition is very different from that of William's convoy from here, which was escorted by several powerful Japanese cruisers and battleships. There are now several such ships somewhere the Arabian Sea, although fewer than earlier in the war, and it's unlikely that they will attack a strong convoy. They have, however, sunk a couple of unprotected merchant ships in the area recently. Their reputation for mistreatment of prisoners is growing all the time and nobody wants to contemplate ending up in their hands. In fact, the 5-day voyage to Bombay, a trip of almost 2,000 miles, is completely uneventful. The weather is still hot, although, with the convoy averaging a brisk 15 knots, there is always a pleasant breeze.

Fig.10.15: Photo of the Bombay (Victoria Terminus) station.

They arrive on Thursday 1st June. They disembark the next

day, taking in the various sights of the area. One of these is a large area of smouldering ruins near the docks – the aftermath of a huge explosion of an ammunition ship about 6 weeks ago. There are other, more uplifting sights, such as the towering gothic cathedral that is the main railway station in Bombay. On the other hand, there is the dirt, poverty and disease, for which none of the warnings have really prepared them. They're now entering a malarial region - in fact this applies to virtually the whole of India and Burma, and there are strict instructions that legs and arms must be covered from the evening onwards. This is a major pain in such hot, humid conditions. There are also anti-malarial tables to be taken by all soldiers. There is resistance to this, partly because of rumours about side-effects (including impotence). Most of these have little or no substance, but in any event it's not easy to enforce this kind of thing. In fact, anti-malarial precautions are being strongly enforced in Burma, where Bill Slim fully understands the damage that malaria can do to a fighting force. Implementation of all such rules falls squarely on the shoulders of the CMP.

Len and his Company, together with thousands of other disembarked soldiers, are now faced with a long train journey across India. They're headed for Dimapur, the main Army supply base in North-East India, which is about 1,600 miles away by train. It's a long journey – twice as far as William's trip to Jubbulpore in 1914 – and it's going to take at least 6 days. The section to Calcutta could be done by sea, but that route is well over 2,000 miles and would itself take 6 days, with a further 2 or 3 days for the tortuous rail trip onward to Dimapur. There's also still danger from Japanese warships and submarines. Going overland the whole way is logical, although it does mean that the troops are subjected to a very long, hot and overcrowded journey – worse in many ways than the sea voyage that they've just endured. Still, British soldiers do tend to be long-suffering, and to put up with a lot without too much complaint. At least they'll be safe from attacks by the enemy on this journey, if not by various insects and diseases. They're not fully aware of this yet, but avoiding serious illness is now going to be a major challenge for everyone. Life is going to get a lot harder over the coming weeks and months.

Fig.10.16: A heavy goods train on the Thull Ghaut incline, just beyond Kalyan Junction on the line from Bombay to Jubbulpore Powerful locomotives are at the front, in the middle and at the end of the train.

The journey is certainly not a joyride, with all of the compartments full, no facilities on the train (unless one counts the holes in the floor at the end of each carriage) and progress generally very slow. The locomotives themselves are not so primitive – there have been strenuous efforts recently to improve the railway system in India – but much of the track is in poor condition, there are a number of single track sections and there are some fearsome gradients. For example, the Thull Ghaut incline, which has to be tackled on the first day, runs for ten miles with a gradient throughout of about 1 in 40. The challenging sections in the UK system pale into insignificance by comparison. Double heading, possibly with a banking engine as well, are often used – and even then the speed frequently drops to little more than walking pace. Furthermore, there are often civilians on these trains – riding on the railway is a national pastime, often without tickets, and over-crowding is just accepted as normal. These include young urchins who play the trick of jumping on a train, crawling under seats to steal anything they can find, throwing it out of the window and then jumping off themselves. Tempers can get frayed, but of course some kind of control, and even tolerance of local customs, has to be maintained.

Len comes across one such incident on the Thull Ghaut incline, with a terrified-looking child in the grip of a burly Corporal.

"Put him down, Corporal - what the hell do you think you're doing?"

He turns on Len with a face like fury, only the sight of the red ribbon in Len's cap causing him to step back a pace.

"This little runt has just thrown my kitbag out of the window, Sarge. There are dozens of the little buggers doing this – I'm going to teach him a lesson he won't forget in a hurry." There are mumbles of assent from his mates.

"Well, it won't get your kitbag back. Was there anything precious in it – a photo of your sweetheart?"

"No sweetheart exactly," he says, reddening slightly, "I keep a picture of my parents and kid brother here in my pocket."

"OK, well the bag's gone. You don't really need it on this train. Here' a chitty for a new one and some gear – you can pick it up when we get to Fort William camp in Calcutta – and here's a packet of fags for your trouble. Meanwhile, just throw this kid off the train. He's probably learnt his lesson. Actually, I'll do it myself – I don't want you waiting till we speed up or you spot a really nasty patch of brambles."

Len takes the kid to the end of the carriage and pushes him out of the door. They're only going at just above walking pace and it's a fairly gentle push. The lad understands only a little English, but he knows that he's had a narrow escape and he flashes Len a grateful smile. Whether he'll stop doing this kind of thing is another question, but Len feels a pang of guilt as he notices that the lad has nothing on his feet and his clothes are just a couple of rags. He's probably about 6 years old. Life in this country is not easy.

They reach Calcutta on 6th June. It's very hot, although the monsoon season has started. The rains are welcome in some respects, since they do gives some respite from the heat, but it now becomes very difficult to keep dry. Also, there was a terrible famine in this area (Bengal) the previous year, with at least 2 million deaths. There were several causes, including the loss of the usual rice imports from Burma (due to the Japanese invasion), but much of the blame was put on the British, and it's true that the response of the authorities here, and of the UK government, was very poor. There was extensive requisitioning of rice for war-related purposes, with the needs of the local peasantry being largely ignored. There is still extensive resentment, and terrible poverty, here. Len and his colleagues spend a day or so in the city, appalled at the scenes of deprivation in the streets.

Eventually, after a short break in the base at Fort William, they start the difficult journey over the last part of the route, through Bengal and Assam to Dimapur. Improving the transport links in this region never had a high priority for the (British-controlled) authorities. The only traffic considered to be of much significance was the trade associated with production of tea in the Assam province and, indeed, the existing rail links are largely the result of pressure from the Assam Tea Association. However, rapid transit was never a high priority and the network is slow and inefficient. In fact, a large contingent of US engineers have improved it significantly over the past 6 months or so, importing powerful locomotives and revising various practices that were limiting the speed and capacity of trains. It's still, however, frustratingly slow for the thousands of troops now in transit – partly because there are many heavy freight trains and partly because the rivers in the area are now in flood, as the monsoon rains have their effect.

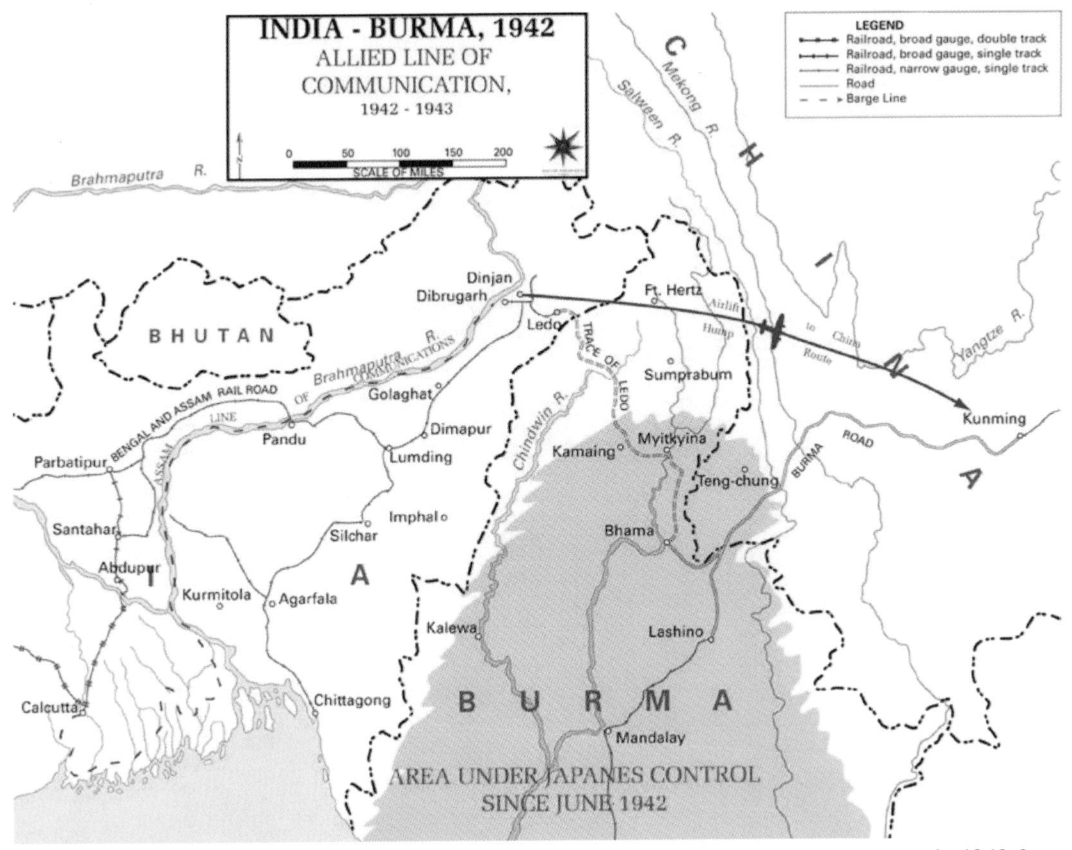

Fig. 10.17: Map showing Allied lines of communication in the India-Burma border area in 1942-3.

The first stretch of a hundred and fifty miles is not too bad, on doubled, broad (5' 6") gauge track. However, the route is then single track for the next hundred miles, causing a lot of delays. Then, at Parbatipur, a switch is needed onto a narrow (metre) gauge line, requiring passengers and, more problematically, goods, to be moved across to a different train. This also is initially double track, but soon reduces to single track for a further hundred miles or so. The real barrier here is the Brahmaputra river. It has to be crossed, but there is no bridge anywhere in this region. At Amingaon, the

Fig. 10.18: Trucks being shunted onto the ferry at Amingaon, on the Brahmaputra river, in 1944.

carriages or trucks are laboriously shunted onto a ferry, which crosses the river to Pandu. This turns out to be particularly slow, with the river close to bursting its banks. There is very little at Amingaon, to say the least, but they have to spend a day of two there as the backlog of trains is slowly cleared.

Finally, there's another two hundred miles of single track between Pandu and Dimapur, again with many trains needing to wait in the few passing places. They don't arrive until 13th June. It's been a nightmare journey. Dimapur is not London, but it's a large encampment and there are many facilities here, even if they're fairly basic. The place is awash with people, including many British, American and Indian military personnel, and also a number of refugees from Burma. It's an administrative and disciplinary nightmare. Len and his men are welcomed with open arms, since CMP people are very thin on the ground.

Fig.10.19: Dimapur station in 1944.

However, it's clear to all that the plan now is to move to the south en masse, driving the Japanese out of Burma. Everyone knows that this will be far from easy, but at least there's an opportunity here for a few days rest, a shower or two, some clean, dry kit and some reasonably good food. The rain, however, is a constant plague and, during the evenings and night, the mosquitoes swarm everywhere, many of them malarial.

10.4 An Amphibious Gamble

The Allied invasion of North Europe has been in the offing for some time – in some ways since early in 1943, but definitively since late in 1943 (following the Tehran Conference). It is to be the largest seaborne invasion in history and, even with the German military system under considerable stress, it's clear that it will need to be very carefully planned if it is to succeed. Being driven back into the sea before strong beachheads can be established is an obvious danger.

The nerve centre for this planning is Norfolk House, in St.James' Square – just across St.James' Park from the GOGGS complex. In fact, this planning started in March 1943, when Lieutenant General Frederick Morgan was appointed Chief of Staff to the Supreme Allied Commander – the role taken up by Eisenhower at the end of 1943. The key people meet up there in early February 1944. Various landing sites are considered, but the Normandy area is finally chosen. Keeping this a secret, and even disseminating misinformation indicating that it will be elsewhere, is a key objective over the next few months. The weather will be a critical factor, with clear skies and calm seas essential to the planned amphibious and airborne activities. Late Spring or early summer is the target. Other requirements include a full moon – giving good visibility for an attack at dawn - and a high tide on arrival, minimizing the exposure of troops on large areas of beach.

Churchill is keen to be deeply involved – his Gallipoli experiences apparently forgotten, but the Americans give this fairly short shrift, and Roosevelt quietly advises him to keep a low profile. Nevertheless, there are extensive communications between GOGGS and Norfolk House. Pam and her colleagues are kept very busy with production and handling of a huge range of documents. In the country as a whole, it's fairly clear that something big is afoot, with the movement of troops and equipment hitting new heights. In December, there are about three-quarters of a million American GIs in the country, but this number is going to double over the next 6 months. They're particularly concentrated in London.

Eisenhower is keen not to spend all his time in the centre and he sets up house in a cottage in Bushy Park, very close to where Harry and Grace live. In fact, Bushy Park itself becomes a huge encampment for American serviceman, with large numbers of temporary barracks created in it. The West End of London is now thronged with GIs, who are taking advantage of the local amenities and attractions. There is something in the claims of comedians that they're "...over-paid, over-sexed and over here". They're certainly better-paid – upwards of £15 per month, which is about twice that of British equivalents. It's a lively time, although nobody really knows what awaits these young men in a few months. Len and his CMP colleagues are kept busy trying to deal with excessive socializing, and with occasional incidents between British and US troops. Pam and her friends are in great demand, although Pam herself is only personally concerned about Len, whose posting to the Far East is confirmed in April 1944.

The preparations are meticulous. They include a full rehearsal of one of the planned landings (on "Utah" Beach). This is to take place in late April (about 6 weeks before the actual assault), at Slapton Sands - a resort in South Devon with a similar layout to the one in Normandy. It's to be as realistic as possible, with a range of landing craft being used, about 30,000 troops (mainly from the 4th Infantry Division) involved and a pre-landing barrage employed, with live shells. Eisenhower is heavily involved in the planning. He wants the troops to experience almost exactly what will happen on the day – a long sea crossing, sea-sickness, the effects of shells landing in the area just before they arrive etc.

Fig.10.20: American landing craft LST-289 arriving in Dartmouth on 28th April 1945, after being torpedoed off Slapton Sands.

The idea is perhaps not a bad one, but the exercise turns out to be an absolute disaster. While the convoy is assembling (well out in the bay) during the night of 27th April, it is spotted by a small squadron of German E-boats (torpedo boats). They have been alerted by the extensive radio traffic. Several of the craft, including some relatively large LST (Landing Ship – Tanks) vessels, are torpedoed. Some of them sink and others are damaged and set on fire – of course, there is a lot of fuel on these ships. Many of the soldiers drown, partly because they've not been told how to put on lifejackets - which is difficult with their large back-packs. Moreover, there is very poor communication between the convoy and the British warships that are there to protect it, and also to lay down the barrage. The time of the landings is changed at a late stage and this information does not reach this escort. The outcome is that many soldiers are killed by the barrage as they move onto the beach.

The total number killed is not clear, but it's around 1,000 – far more than are to die during the actual landings on Utah Beach. Eisenhower is both mortified and furious. There are recriminations all round, but the whole saga is kept highly secret – even extending to relatives of the dead being given no information about what happened. The survivors are told that they must say nothing to anyone – on pain of being court-martialed. The high command is terrified that the episode may have alerted the enemy to details of the planned invasion – dates, locations etc. They even consider making major changes to the plans, but it's really too late for that now – so much of the hugely complex machinery needed to carry out this invasion is already in motion. At least the incident leads to urgent steps being taken to improve communications between British and American forces, and also to reduce the chances of troops drowning if a landing craft sinks. Ferocious efforts are made to eliminate as many E-boats as possible from the Normandy area.

The invasion finally takes place on 6th June 1944 – the "D-Day" of subsequent legend. It's naturally not without hazards, mistakes – even minor disasters, but it is successful. Penetration on the first day is less than planned, but over 150,000 troops are landed and strong beachheads are established across the whole front. Over 5,000 vessels are involved in the attack. However, experiences are very different in the five areas. After their horrific time at Slapton, the 4th Infantry Division meets little resistance on Utah beach. About 20,000 land on the first day, with just a couple of hundred casualties. About 15,000 paratroops landed in the area behind the beaches during the previous night, and casualties among them are higher, but overall they progress with few problems.

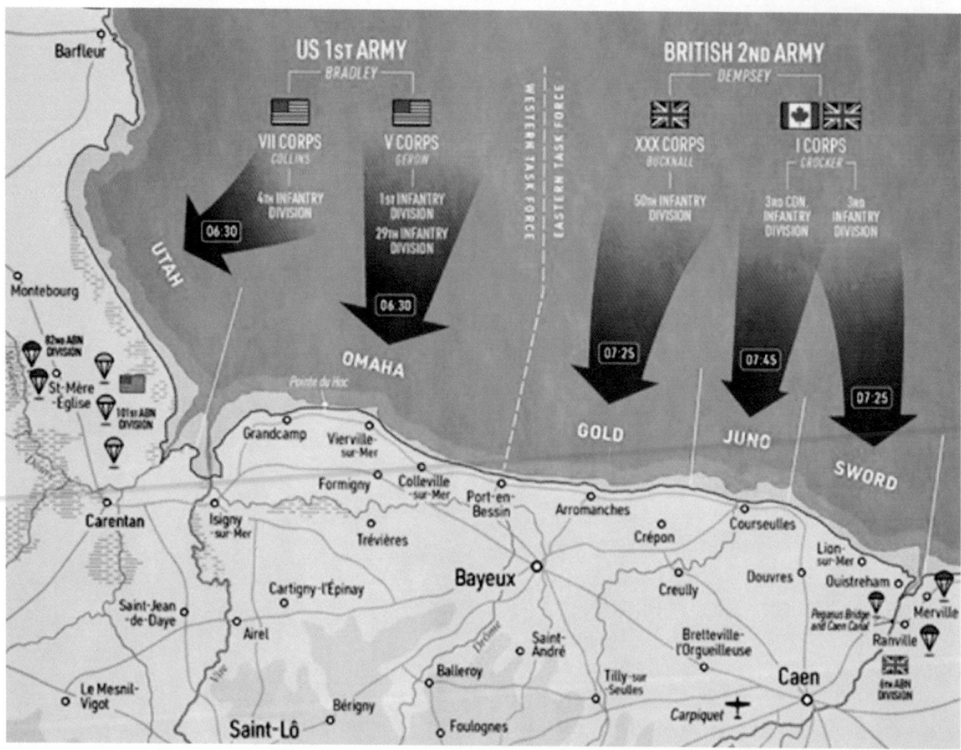

Fig. 10.21: Map showing the landing areas for the D-Day invasion.

On Omaha Beach, the story is a different one, with it being much more strongly defended. About 40,000 troops are landed here, but they meet horrendous conditions. Well over 2,000 are killed on the beach during the early stages. Rommel has been given the job of organizing the defences along the Channel coast - reinforcing the "Atlantic Wall" – and, as ever, he has done an outstanding job. He has insisted on strong defences being created close to the beach – he is convinced that the best chance of stopping this invasion will be to prevent troops from getting off the beach. On Omaha Beach, this is almost achieved, with wave after wave of attackers meeting withering machine gun fire, as well as various obstacles on the beaches. A decision to abort the landings here is almost taken.

Fortunately for the Allies, Rommel is himself in Berlin on the day, pleading with Hitler for more Panzer divisions in this part of France. The commander of the only Panzer Division in the area, Edgar Feuchtinger, is also away – the Germans did not think that an attack was imminent, in view of the very poor weather that has been forecast: indeed the seas are rough, which has been a problem for the invading forces. This is the 21st Panzer Division. It comprises over 100 tanks, and has a formidable reputation. It does counter attack the forces moving inland late on D-Day, and on the following days, but they're trying to stem an irresistible tide. However, if the Germans had known the time and place of the invasion beforehand, and a number of Panzer Divisions had been lined up behind these beaches, the outcome might have been different.

The central beach of the five, Gold, is another that is not so strongly defended. About 25,000 British troops are landed here, with fewer than 1,000 casualties. The bombardment (from both air and sea) is particularly effective. The one next to this, Juno, has been allocated to Canadian forces, who perform particularly well. While not as strongly defended as Omaha, the opposing forces and gun emplacements here are formidable. The Canadians, however, have a number of DD (amphibious) tanks and these turn out to be very successful during the early stages of the landings – the Americans do not have these. About 20,000 Canadian troops land during the first day, with around 1,000 casualties. There is also relatively little resistance on the most easterly beach of Sword. About 30,000 British troops land here, again with fewer than 1,000 casualties.

Fig.10.22: Omaha beach on 9th June 1944. Several LSTs are in the middle distance. A "half-track" convey is being assembled in the foreground.

Overall, the invasion is highly successful. Both sides lose about 10,000 men on D-Day, but this is out of a total invading force of 150,000, whereas there are only about 40,000 German soldiers in the area. The Allies also have total control of the skies and adjacent seas. Not only are the landings well-planned, but the way in which troops and resources flow in through the beachheads during the following weeks is impressive – with many technical innovations being employed. These include the floating "Mulberry" Harbours, the pipeline on the ocean floor for pumping fuel across, the machinery for creating passageways from the beaches for heavy vehicles and many other infrastructural developments. During the two months following D-Day, about a million Allied troops and around a million tons of supplies are shipped into Normandy – mostly without using established port facilities. Hitler's Atlantic Wall has not proved insurmountable, but the resources employed to overcome it have been titanic. Of course, the war is not yet over, but, for the Germans, the writing on the wall is clear for all to read. Towards the end of July, there is a concerted attempt (at Rastenburg) to assassinate Hitler, but it fails. For most of the German population, all that is left is prayer for this nightmare to end.

Chapter 11: The Final Phase (July 1944 – June 1945)

11.1 Spiteful Blows against London

Londoners experienced little in terms of direct attacks during the 30 months between mid-1941 and early in 1944. At that point, however, this changed with the launch of another strategic bombing campaign by the Luftwaffe, mainly aimed at London. This can be linked to the concerted bombing offensive against German industrial cities initiated by the RAF and the USAAF in November 1943. Hitler orders another attack on London in retaliation. With German resources at a lower level than previously, and the London air defence system more highly developed, this has much less impact than the campaign in 1940-41. It is thus commonly termed the "Baby Blitz". It is an abject failure from the German point of view. Many Luftwaffe planes are shot down and a lot of the bombing is haphazard. About 1,500 civilians are killed over a period of about 5 months – far fewer than the 40,000 killed during the Blitz. There is also damage to thousands of houses, but again this pales into insignificance compared with the more than 1 million homes damaged or destroyed in 1940-41. The campaign is abandoned in May 1944, when it becomes clear that the Allied invasion of Europe is imminent and Hitler is finally persuaded that these resources should not be wasted on futile attempts to bomb London.

At the time, Londoners have a slightly different perspective. For people like Pam, trying to go to work every day and to deal with the general requirements of living in a damaged city, a further set of air raids, or at least the threat of them, is stressful - even if many of them turn out to be minor or false alarms. There are still 500 bombers dedicated to this task. Nevertheless, London people are by now very stoical and take it largely in their stride. However, they are shortly to be subjected to an ordeal that is in many ways even more terrifying than repeated conventional bombing.

Whatever else might be said about wars, they do tend to promote rapid scientific and technological advances. This is certainly true of World War 2, during which the areas of major innovation and development include radar, Sonar, jet engines, the basics of computing, nuclear physics and rocket science. British, American and German scientists all play important roles in these developments. The Germans are certainly pioneers in rocketry – that is, the propulsion of flying objects via backward expulsion of the products of chemical reactions. The reactants are all carried as fuel, so that there is no need to ingest air, and indeed rockets can function in a vacuum (space). There is, however, a lot of scope for things to go wrong.

Fig.11.1: A V1 Flying Bomb being dragged into position for launching.

Flying bombs sound like a good idea – a pilotless plane in which up to almost half of the total weight is the explosive. There is no need for any of the normal requirements to accommodate a pilot. Provided they are cheap and easy to build, having a lifetime of one flight is acceptable. It is in fact the precursor to many later generations of guided missile, as well as space travel. However, the technology needed just to get it into the air, and to fly it automatically in the right direction, is revolutionary. Accurate control of where it ends up is beyond what is achievable at this time. It therefore can't be aimed at specific military targets, and its range is inevitably limited. The objective is to hit London, and possibly one or two other cities in the South of England. Hitler, by now beyond all reason or humanity, sees it as a weapon of revenge (for the bombing of German cities), and indeed the V designation stands for Vergeltungswaffe (Vengeance Weapon).

Actually, the V1 is not rocket-powered – it is propelled by a pulse jet, ingesting air and injecting atomized fuel in pulses, 50 times per second. This pulsing generates a characteristic buzzing noise, such that it is referred to as a "buzz bomb" or "doodlebug" (after the common name for some flying insects). Guidance is via two gyroscopes and a magnetic compass, while power for actuating the controls etc comes from a compressed air system. The propulsion system is cut out when the distance travelled, measured via a rotating vane, reaches a set value, after which it crash dives. The V1 flies at an altitude of only about 2,000 – 3,000 feet and it's clearly audible from the ground for miles around. Londoners come to dread the sudden stopping of the buzzing, since this means that it's shortly going to hit the ground and explode somewhere nearby.

Fig.11.2: Werner von Braun, with a number of prominent Wehrmacht officers, at Peenemünde on 21st March 1941.

These weapons have in fact been under development for a number of years, partly motivated by the progress that a number of German scientists made in this difficult technological area. Prominent among them is Werner von Braun, who completed a doctoral thesis on rocketry in 1934. His studies were certainly built on pioneering work by others, but he did show a lot of aptitude and initiative. There are many areas of technical challenge in designing and building rockets and he certainly required a large team with a range of technical skills. This was provided for him by the German State from the mid-1930's. He has a major operational base at Peenemünde, in the North-Eastern tip of Germany. He is involved in the creation of the V1 Flying Bomb, although his main interest is in genuine rockets, such as the subsequent V2 weapon.

Launching of V1s at London starts in mid-June of 1944 – just a week or so after D-Day. The first lands in the East End, killing 6 people and doing severe damage to buildings. Over the next few weeks, hundreds more start to arrive. About 30,000 V1s are made in total, of which about 10,000 are fired at England – mostly aimed at London – over the following 4 months. Only about 2,500 hit London, killing over 6,000 people and injuring many more. There are several reasons why only a quarter of them arrive. Some fail technically during flight, but most of the failures are due to British counter-measures. These include being intercepted by aircraft. Spotting them is relatively easy – they can be picked up by radar, they make a loud, distinctive noise and their exhaust is highly visible. Destroying them, however, is not easy. Their altitude during the flight is quite low – typically about 3,000 feet, but their speed is high – around 350 mph. Most British planes simply

Fig.11.3: A Hawker Tempest Mark V being refueled and rearmed at Newchurch (Kent) on 12th June 1944.

can't catch them.

However, the Hawker Tempest, recently introduced and representing just about the final development of propeller-driven fighters, can manage 390 mph at these low altitudes. There are two ways in which these planes can destroy the V1s. One is with cannon fire, although they need to get quite close in order to hit them and, if the warhead explodes, then the plane could be in serious danger. The other is to fly alongside and tilt them over sharply with the plane's wingtip. This usually disrupts the guidance system enough to ensure that it crashes, although it requires skilled airmanship and it's hazardous. Nevertheless, many V1s are intercepted en route in this way. One Tempest pilot, Squadron Leader Joseph Barry, accounts for 59 of them. Others are hit by Anti-Aircraft fire, although their high speed and low altitude makes tracking them from the ground difficult. Some hit barrage balloons.

Fig.11.4: Photo showing a Tempest about to tip a V1 Flying Bomb, taken in July 1944.

Nevertheless, "Doodlebugs" are a plague for the long-suffering Londoners. There is no time for air raid warnings and, in any event, they are coming over too frequently. There are multiple occasions every day when one can be heard and, if the buzzing suddenly stops within earshot, people know that, within the next minute or so, there could be a major explosion close to them. There is no possibility of taking any evasive action. It is harrowing. Pam and her friends have to put up with this all the time - at work, while travelling and at home. This campaign has little or no military value and the resources being expended on manufacturing and launching them are enormous. This is purely a tactic of terror, aimed at breaking the spirit of Londoners. However, this is not going to happen.

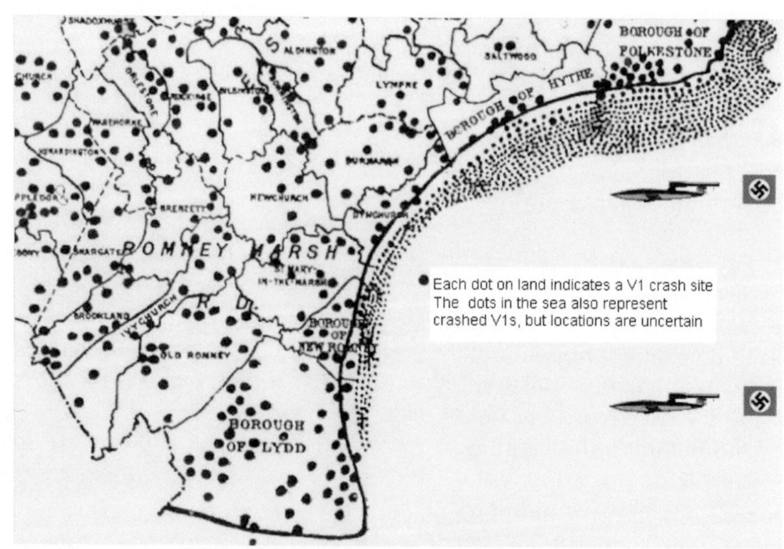

Fig.11.5: Locations near the Kent coast where V1 Flying Bombs crashed, mostly due to RAF actions.

The V1 attacks on London stop in October, because the launch sites - which are all near to Calais in view of their limited range - are being over-run by the invading Allied Armies. However, this period during which death can descend out of the blue is not yet over for Londoners. The reason for this is that a much more highly developed weapon – the V2 – has now become available. This is a big advance on the V1. Firstly, it is a genuine rocket, capable of generating huge levels of thrust that can lift it to great heights – and indeed into space. Secondly, it is much larger – about 13 tons, which compares with about 2 tons for the V1, although the warheads are of similar size at about 1 ton. Finally, its range is greater than the V1, and it doesn't require a long, inclined launch pad. Not only is it launched (almost) vertically, but also the pad can be relatively small and potentially moveable. There is no defence against this weapon. It ascends to a height of around 50 miles (~260,000 feet) – effectively at the edge of space - and then descends in free fall, reaching speeds of up to about 3,000 mph. The exact figures don't matter: the bottom line is that it is literally a bolt from the blue – there is no warning of any sort, just a huge explosion on the ground, followed by a sonic boom. The penetration tends to be deeper than for the V1, endangering gas and water mains, and possibly tube lines, but often destroying slightly fewer houses at ground level. Nevertheless, the danger of death or injury is high for anyone in the vicinity of an impact site.

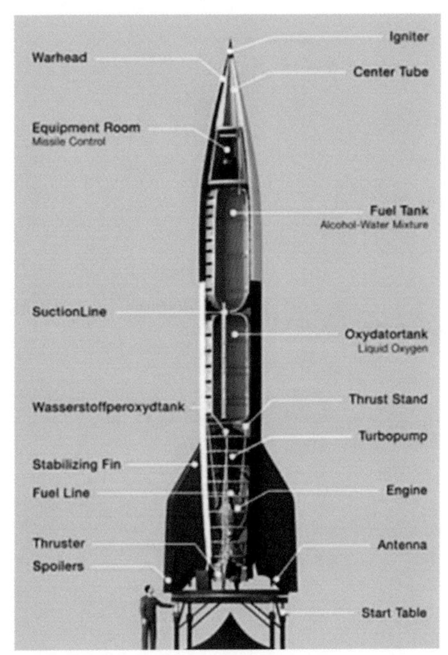

Fig.11.6: Technical drawing of the V2 rocket.

Fig.11.7: Damage at the Royal Hospital in Chelsea, caused by a V2 bomb on 3rd January 1945.

The first V2 attacks on London come in September, just as the V1 campaign is stopping. About 3,000 V2s are made. They are far more expensive to produce than the V1s and the expenditure of resource is enormous (although costs are minimized by using slave labour, and indeed many thousands of prisoners die working on this project). Over the next 6 months, about 1,500 are aimed at London (and a similar number at Antwerp in Belgium, which is liberated by the Allies in early September). About 3,000 people are killed in London by V2 rockets, with another 6,000 injured. These numbers are smaller than the corresponding figures for the V1, and much less than those of the Blitz, but nevertheless these attacks are a further protracted trial for the beleaguered people of London.

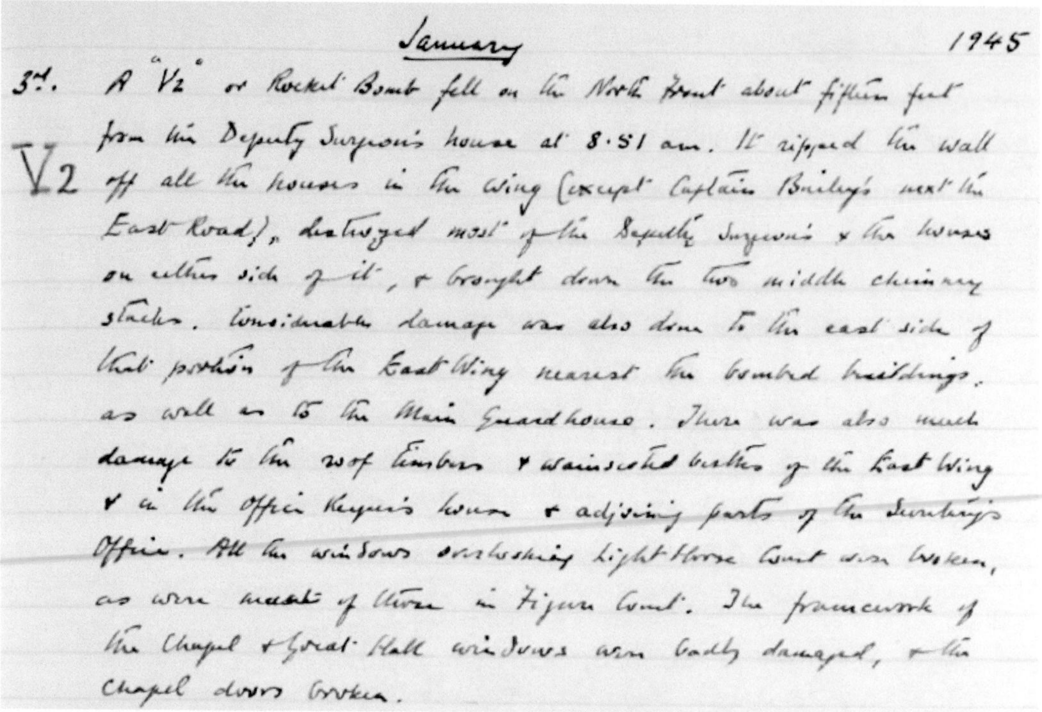

January 1945

3rd. A "V2" or Rocket Bomb fell on the North Front about fifteen feet from the Deputy Surgeon's house at 8.51 am. It ripped the wall off all the houses in the Wing (except Captain Bailey's next the East Road), destroyed most of the Deputy Surgeon's & the houses on either side of it, & brought down the two middle chimney stacks. Considerable damage was also done to the east side of that portion of the East Wing nearest the bombed buildings, as well as to the Main Guardhouse. There was also much damage to the roof timbers & wainscoted berths of the East Wing & in the Office Keeper's house & adjoining parts of the Secretary's Office. All the windows overlooking Light Horse Court were broken, as were most of those in Figure Court. The framework of the Chapel & Great Hall windows were badly damaged, & the Chapel doors broken.

V2

Fig.11.8: Written report of damage caused by a V2 hitting the RHC on 3rd Jan. 1945.

For Pam and her friends and family, there is again serious risk. In fact, early in January, a V2 hits the North-East Wing of the Royal Hospital, completely destroying the Wing and damaging surrounding buildings. Five people die and about 20 are injured. It arrives just before 9am, an hour or so after Pam has left for work. She hears about it there and rushes back in a state of dread. A scene of devastation greets her, but her parents are unharmed - their living quarters are on the West side of the site. However, she knows several of the dead and injured. Most of the Pensioners are quickly moved to Sloane Gardens or evacuated from London. Having lived through the Great War, and also had plenty of this kind of thing during the Blitz, they're used to such scenes. Still, this huge explosion in their idyllic home, with no warning, is a new experience for them. In fact, this is the last of about 30 bombing incidents at the Royal Hospital, which in total result in 21 deaths and 33 injured. This is a lot in a relatively small community, but it's a microcosm of what has happened to London as a whole.

11.2 Converging on Germany

The final stages of the liberation of the lands to both east and west of Germany, and then the invasion and occupation of Germany itself, have an aura of inevitability. The Germans are beaten and leaderless. Their enemies are now implacable. The Wehrmacht still has some good generals and the military machine is still operational, but their situation is hopeless. There's not even enough spirit or organization for another attempt to assassinate Hitler – now recognized by all sides to be a megalomaniac who has lost all trace of reason and compassion. Of course, as he retreats to his bunker, simply getting physical access to him becomes very difficult.

Fig. 11.9: Cologne from the air on 25th April 1945. The huge cathedral, or at least its shell, has survived. The main station, located between it and the Rhine, has been obliterated, as have the bridges over the river. Virtually all of the buildings are skeletal.

Nevertheless, these invasions are far from easy. With apparently no option for an overall surrender, all that the German soldiers can do is to fight for every yard of ground – perhaps hoping that their individual generals will in the end save at least some lives by surrendering – although this will inevitably have to be done against Hitler's specific instructions. The civilians in the liberated countries are mostly ecstatic – although perhaps with much more mixed feelings if they might be perceived as having collaborated in any way. The civilians in Germany, on the other hand, are all in terror of what is to come – mainly just hoping that they will somehow survive, and that their country might be able to recover in due course – if it is to be permitted to exist at all. Some of the things that have been done in their name are such that their rights to anything may be hanging in the balance.

As the Allied armies move towards Germany, attacks on the country by air are intensified. This applies particularly to bombing by the Western Allies. The Red Army is approaching Germany more quickly than the move in from the West, but it's the RAF and USAAF that are now doing most of the bombing. In fact, many German cities are being progressively laid waste, particularly in the north and west of the country. The figures are stark. In 1942, the RAF dropped about 50,000 tons of bombs on Germany, and the Americans practically none. In 1943, these figures had risen to 150,000 and 50,000. In 1944, however, they are 500,000 and 400,000 tons respectively. This may be compared with about 12,000 tons dropped in total on London. There is no scope for fortitude, or the spirit of the Blitz, in a city such as Cologne – one of the closest to the Allied airfields. There are no services left – no water, no sanitation, no electricity, no gas, no food – nothing. The firestorms suck all of the oxygen out of basement areas. To stay in the city is to die. In fact, whole populations of German cities evacuate to rural areas. Moving into 1945, bombs are being dropped onto deserted wastelands. The Americans do insist on at least trying to hit only military targets, whereas the British, under the command of Arthur Harris, openly recognize that destroying civilian homes reduces the capacity of the enemy to fight. In practice, the difference in approach is not so great – most bombs don't fall very close to their targets. The slight difference in attitude is perhaps understandable – after all, the British have been subjected to bombing of their civilian areas for years, and this is now being repeated with the Baby Blitz and the V-weapons. Hitler seems to have no understanding of the consequences of his actions. In any event, many German cities are being completely obliterated.

The practical effect of the bombing on the German population is horrendous. The figures again speak volumes. British civilian deaths from bombing are now winding down, but they will end up at around 60,000. In fact, rather more French civilians than this die during British and American air raids on French cities. The number of German civilians killed by bombing is subject to more uncertainty, but it is at least half a million. Many millions more are now homeless. About 50,000 Italian civilians are killed during bombing of the north of the country, most of them during the period after Italy itself has surrendered.

There are other figures that give pause for thought. The commitment of the British and American Allies, and the deep impact of the war on the two countries, are beyond any kind of question, but their total dead – civilian and military, from all war-connected sources - is "only" about 400,000 each. The Russians losses, on the other hand, are probably upwards of 30 million, about 10 million of them in official military roles – although this distinction is a blurred one in their case – such is the total immersion of the Russian people in this war. This is about 15% of the total population. Several million of these people are women. The Germans are to lose about 5 million military personnel, plus another 2 million or so civilians. It's particularly difficult in their case to give exact figures: for example, Germans murdered by their own government – Jews and other races – are not included in these figures. In any event, their cities are being reduced to rubble, even before the country is invaded.

Fig.11.10: Russian advances during the 2nd half of 1944.

The drive to the west and south by the Red Army is inexorable. It accelerates as 1944 grinds on, with the Russians using Blitzkreig tactics as effectively as the Germans ever did, and various other factors working in their favour. For example, when Rumania is invaded (early in August), the pro-Nazi government of Ion Antonescu is toppled by an internal coup (led by the deposed King Michael I). Suddenly, the Russian troops entering places like Bucharest are welcomed with open arms. Not only do the Rumanians immediately make peace with Russia, but they also declare war on Germany and their Army starts to pursue the German troops out of the country. The Russians don't really need much help, but they accept the assistance of their new "Allies" and the fuel from the Rumanian oilfields is certainly welcome. Something similar happens in Bulgaria and Hungary, although there were variations in the degree to which different countries had resisted Nazi pressure earlier in the war. Bulgaria, for example had never formally declared war on Russia. Of course, the populations of all such countries in the "Eastern Block" had been suffering badly from various effects of the war, and from their treatment at the hands of the Nazis. At great cost to themselves, the Russians really have been the salvation of the people in this part of Europe – in fact, arguably in the whole of Europe. This naturally has various long-term consequences.

Fig.11.11: Red Army tanks entering Bucharest on 31st Aug. 1944.

While the Russians push on into the Eastern part of Germany at the beginning of 1945, the Western Allies are still moving through France and the Low Countries. It's clear that the Russians are going to win this "race", at least into most of Germany, and in particular in taking the key "prize" of Berlin. De Gaulle had insisted on a "detour" to liberate Paris. He's a hero to most of the French, but he has a remarkable facility for irritating the other leaders – not only Churchill, but also Roosevelt and Stalin. His speech at the service of thanksgiving in Paris at the end of August gives the distinct impression that the city has been liberated almost entirely by (Free) French troops: while there are certainly a few around, this is a grotesque distortion of how the Germans are actually driven out Paris, and indeed the rest of France. Irrespective of exactly how it is liberated, Paris comes close to being laid waste. Around 22nd August, with it becoming clear that the city cannot be defended, Hitler gives instructions for it to be destroyed. Various explosive charges are laid around the city, but they are not activated – perhaps due to General Dietrich von Choltitz disobeying Hitler's order (as he is to claim) or perhaps just due to

Fig.11.12: Charles de Gaulle and his entourage on 26th Aug. 1944, walking down the Champs Elysees to Notre Dame, to attend a service of thanksgiving for the liberation of Paris.

chaos among the demoralized Germans. In any event, de Gaulle readily takes umbrage at perceived slights from the other national leaders – and there are a few genuine ones, such as Churchill's jibe about him looking like "..a female llama who has just been surprised in her bath.." and, rather more significantly, being excluded from several important conferences. De Gaulle certainly harbours a grudge during his subsequent extended period as French President. This doesn't have much effect as far as Russia and America are concerned, but he's definitely not an Anglophile and this is to become apparent in many of his policies.

It's completely clear by this time that the Allies are going to win the war – at least in Europe. The German Army is in complete disarray and the Luftwaffe has almost ceased to exist. In the Far East, the Japanese are also in full retreat, but there is a concern that invading the island of Japan could be extremely difficult. They evidently do not intend to surrender and they have proved to be fanatically brave during various encounters with US forces in the Pacific. Roosevelt fears for the loss of huge numbers of American lives during an invasion of their homeland and he is very keen to bring the Russians in to help – they have still not declared war on Japan. What Roosevelt has in mind is use of Russian airfields for a massive bombing campaign, much as is now being waged against Germany. This is an item on the agenda for another summit meeting with Stalin and Churchill. This is fixed for February 1945, to be held in Yalta – on the Crimean peninsula. Stalin is still reluctant to fly and, while Yalta is about 1,000 miles from Moscow, it's only a day's travel by train. The route no longer goes through any areas of active conflict.

One of the reasons that Roosevelt is keen to push for a meeting is that he is not well. His health has been deteriorating for some time and the stresses of the war have certainly not helped. He knows that he is dying and, indeed, he only has another couple of months or so to live. He feels that he must do his best to sort out a few vital issues while he can. Prominent among these is the shape of Europe after the war – redrawing of national boundaries, government systems, spheres of influence etc. It's fairly clear that this was not done well after the Great War and there is universal recognition that, this time, it really is essential to ensure that another war like this cannot happen. In fact, there has already been a meeting between Churchill and Stalin, about 5 months previously, in Moscow. This meeting, which was somewhat unofficial, was focused on "carving up" various European countries in terms of the degree to which they would be under the influence of East (Soviet) or West (British, plus possibly a bit of French). It's not an edifying concept. In fact, one of the outcomes of Yalta is a clear statement that all independent countries should be encouraged to set up democratic structures and be free to decide their own policies. However, as at the Paris Conference of 1919, it's inevitable that there will be a lot of horse-trading, since the three main powers do not have identical long-term aims and priorities.

To be fair to Stalin, his feeling that the West owes Russia an enormous debt is entirely justified. If they had capitulated, or come to some compromise arrangement with Hitler, then the whole of Western Europe would almost certainly have fallen under Nazi rule. Also, even given an absolute political determination to resist, only the incredible courage and sacrifice of the Russian people has ensured that they have prevailed. The Western Allies, particularly Britain, have dragged their feet on opening up a "Second Front" and this has probably translated into even more Russian lives being lost. In common with the French, the Russians feel that they have repeatedly been exposed to crushing military attack by Germany, and they want to ensure that this cannot happen again. They feel that, at the least, there should be some kind of buffer zone, which is under their control – rather similar in concept to what the French demanded after the Great War.

There is also the issue of ideology. Stalin feels that it is the fellowship fostered by communism that has allowed them to come through this, and that a capitalist society would never have been able to endure in the same way. There may be something in this, but it could also be argued that the American capitalist system has certainly delivered the necessary military resources. "Lend Lease" planes, tanks, ships etc have been sent out in huge quantities from the US, not only to Britain, but also to Russia, China, India and other countries. Also, America has been fighting the Japanese, as well as the Germans. Furthermore, it could be argued that the capitalist system has delivered a better average standard of living for its citizens than communism, although at the cost of much more inequality. In any event, the vehement opposition of the Americans to communism, and of the Russians to capitalism, is deeply ingrained. The concept of letting every country choose its own way forward sounds sensible, but life is not so simple. There is also the issue of what to do about Germany itself. Should it be allowed to exist in its current form? The possibility of breaking it down into several smaller entities, or even handing it out in bits to surrounding countries, is being seriously considered at Yalta.

The communiqué from Yalta does emphasize this principle of self-determination. It also makes clear that the Nazis will be held accountable for their crimes, and Germany will be completely demilitarized. No clear decision about the long-term future of Germany is taken, but it is stated that the country will be divided up into four zones of control – increased from the initial three after bitter complaints from de Gaulle, with a French zone being carved out from those originally allocated to Britain and the US. Berlin, which will be in the Russian zone, is itself to be divided up into four zones of occupation. Russia is also to take over a part of Eastern Poland, with the Poles gaining a part of Eastern Germany in compensation. Stalin makes a commitment to Poland becoming self-governing. He also makes a pledge to declare war on Japan 3 months after the surrender of Germany.

Roosevelt feels that they have done a good job, and both he and Churchill have confidence that Stalin will keep his word. It may be that he intends to, but there is always the danger that events will evolve so as to change situations. Meanwhile, the Red Army is flooding into Germany, converging on Berlin, where Hitler is determined to fight to the last – or put another way, he has no compunction about needlessly sacrificing his people. Perhaps he still harbours hopes of some kind of turnaround, or at least thinks that he may possibly be able to escape to some impregnable fortress in Bavaria. He is, of course, literally mad. In fact, he even thinks that the death of Roosevelt, which occurs on 12th April, may give him some kind of opportunity to exploit confusion amongst the Allies. Needless to say, nothing of the sort is going to happen. The Vice-President, Harry Truman, smoothly takes over the reins and nothing changes in the military or political situation. The Russians are now battering Berlin, where bitter street fighting is taking place. The Western Allies crossed the Rhine in early March and they are now starting to move across Germany.

Fig.11.13: The Yalta conference in early February of 1945, with (left to right) Churchill, Roosevelt and Stalin (seated), and Ernest King, William Leahy, George Marshall, Laurence Kuter and Aleksei Antonov

During these early months of 1945, both sets of Allied Armies become aware of the scale and depravity of the atrocities that have been committed in the concentration camps in Germany and Poland over the preceding years. These horrors are not made fully public at the time, but they become widely known among military people and political leaderships. Attitudes towards the Germans harden significantly. Hitler finally commits suicide in his bunker in Berlin on 30th April and Germany surrenders on 7th May. The following day is declared "Victory in Europe" day, with widespread celebrations. There is now much to resolve, on both short and longer timescales. Another major summit conference is to be held - this one in Germany, during the summer.

11.3 Reversing the Tide in Asia

Len doesn't hear many details about the developments in Europe. Pam knows much more, but most such information cannot be put into letters and there is no possibility of communicating by phone. Everyone does know that the Normandy landings were successful and that the Russians are pushing rapidly westwards, but the British and British-Indian troops in India and Burma during the second half of 1944 have their own preoccupations. By the start of the monsoon season in June, the Japanese advance has been halted, but driving them out of Burma, and the other occupied countries, is a daunting task. Slim decides to start this process without waiting for the monsoon season to finish towards the end of 1944. There is some logic in this, since the Japanese forces in Burma are clearly exhausted, and their supply situation is dire, but doing anything on the ground during monsoon rains is very difficult.

The duties of Len and his CMP colleagues are now shifting in emphasis. In London, their main activities were oriented around misbehavior of soldiers – anything from fairly low key brawling and drunkenness to more serious issues such as pilfering of Army supplies, and perhaps setting up large scale operations involving their selling on the black market, often in collaboration with civilians. Stealing petrol for sale in this way is endemic. There is a Special Investigation Bureau (SIB) branch of the CMP that investigates serious cases requiring detective work, but Len and his Company have dealt with many such activities. There's looting in bomb-damaged areas, some of it by soldiers. Also within their scope are cases of desertion. This is not uncommon in England - particularly in London. It also occurs in certain places abroad, such as Cairo and Alexandria in Egypt and Durban in South Africa – a common port of call for convoys coming around the Cape.

However, their role is now changing. It's unlikely that anyone will desert in Burma, or even in India. Stealing for the black market is also minimal – soldiers don't normally have contacts among the local population. There might still be drunkenness, and perhaps mistreating of locals, but there's not even much scope for that near the front line – and that's where Len has now arrived. The main role of the CMP here is actually even more important – it's facilitating the advance into enemy territory. The logistics of this – of moving through alien country, via poor roads in difficult terrain – are horrendously difficult. There are engineers to improve roads, set up (Bailey) bridges etc, but it's the CMP who are charged with controlling the traffic, signposting, deciding about the optimum routes, and also finding and removing bottlenecks along the way. Len has his own motorbike, as do most of his men, and this will be the main way in which they'll monitor and control these movements. They're also in charge of any prisoners of war that are taken – less onerous in terms of numbers when fighting the Japanese than, say, the Italians, but still a significant challenge, particularly with long lines of supply and communication.

After spending a couple of months in Dimapur, during which time Len is hospitalized for a week with a severe bout of amoebic dysentery, he and his Company are moved in late July to the large encampment at Imphal. On this road, they pass through the village of Kohima, recently the scene of the heroic defence by a few hundred British and British-Indian soldiers against a complete Japanese Division of 15,000 men. It's a wasteland to rival anything from the Great War. The decisive battles of Kohima and Imphal having just been won, the British and British-Indian troops are now starting to move south.

However, the roads in this whole area are something of a nightmare. They're now carrying heavy traffic as the Allied Armies move deeper into Burma, but the monsoon season is in full swing and everywhere is awash with water and deep mud. It's Bill Slim's decision to move before waiting for the end of the rains in November. It makes sense in terms of giving the Japanese no time to regroup, and reinforcements and supplies are now arriving from the north in a constant stream, but it's still asking a lot of these men to move under these conditions.

Slim and Mountbatten meet up in July 1944, to plan for the invasion of Burma.

"Are you sure that this is a good idea, Bill? It's absolutely pissing down all the time now and moving through this jungle looks like a nightmare to me. I still think that a seaborne invasion to the south looks more sensible."

"You don't need to tell me about this jungle, Louis – I know it's a nightmare, particularly during the monsoon. Nevertheless, we need to hit the Japs while they're reeling. They were banking on capturing our supplies and, now that they've failed to do this, they're in desperate trouble. They're starving and short of ammunition - we mustn't give them time to regroup. Anyway, it sounds as you've been told that you can't have the resources needed to attack by sea?"

"Unfortunately, that is true. Look, Bill, I'm happy to let you make most of the tactical decisions. As you say, you know the situation on the ground here. I see my role as being primarily to liaise with the Yanks and Chinks, and to clear things at a higher level. Joe Stilwell is an awkward character, as is Chiang, but I've got Winnie's ear, and he and Teddy are bosom buddies. What do you really see as the measures needed to make this work?"

"OK, well there are a few points about fighting in this dreadful place. One of them is that, despite the hand-to-hand stuff, and the Japs being very brave – not to say lunatics – nearly all of the casualties are caused, not by bullets or bombs, but by disease. It's malaria that's the real killer and, even if people don't die, they're completely incapacitated and getting them back to hospital takes up valuable resources. Dysentery is also an absolute bugger and that's mainly down to sanitation, getting some rest, having the right medication and general health. Trust me, you don't want half your platoon with shit running down their legs all the time. The Japs don't bother and, whether it's disease or wounds, they just let their men die. Needless to say, we can't and won't do this. However, we can cut right back on malaria if we enforce the taking of Mepacrine and a few other measures. We also need to keep them well fed and well supplied. The key

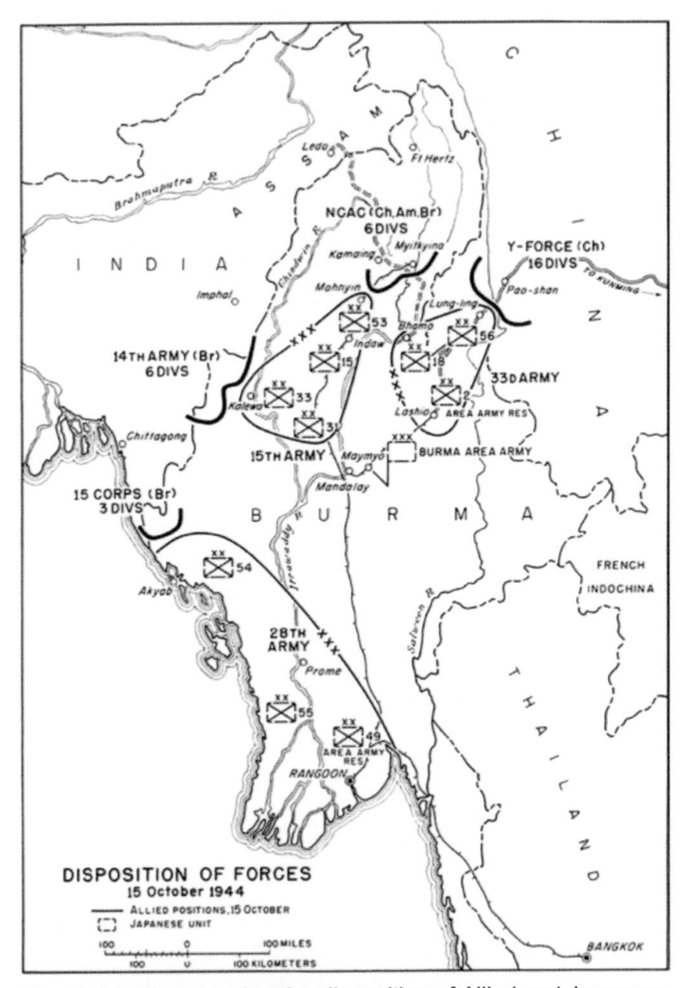

Fig.11.14: Map showing the disposition of Allied and Japanese Armies in Burma, in October 1944.

issues will actually be logistics and discipline. We need the Yanks to keep supplying us by air and we also need really good discipline and organization among the troops and concerning movement through the jungle, crossing of rivers etc. We must have a lot of CMP people moving along with the invading force."

"OK, well, as I say, you can look after all of these details – just let me know if you want me to pull any strings. Of course, I will keep abreast of everything and I'll be making plenty of visits to the troops etc."

And you won't forget your camera crew, will you Louis, adds Bill mentally, although he doesn't actually say this.

There are many complications on the ground. British troops are fighting alongside Indians from various cultures and religions, many of them with mixed feelings about the British Raj. They recognize the benefits that British rule has brought, and in general they are loyal, but they share the view of most of their peoples, which is that the time is ripe for them to become an independent nation. Most of them understand well the motivations for the formation of the Indian National Army (INA), which is now led by Subhas Chandra Bose. He's a charismatic leader, although tainted by extensive collaboration with the Nazis, as well as with the Japanese. It's hard for the British-Indian troops to be fighting their fellow-countrymen, although in truth the INA has never been a very significant military force and they're certainly starting to lose heart now – with the Japanese in evident disarray.

Overall, however, the feeling that the British should leave India soon is strong. In any event, the bonds of respect and friendship being forged between the British and British-Indian troops fighting alongside each other in Burma are likely to assist in the promotion of mutual understanding. Nevertheless, there are many in the British "Establishment" who will not be easily persuaded that it is time to leave the sub-continent.

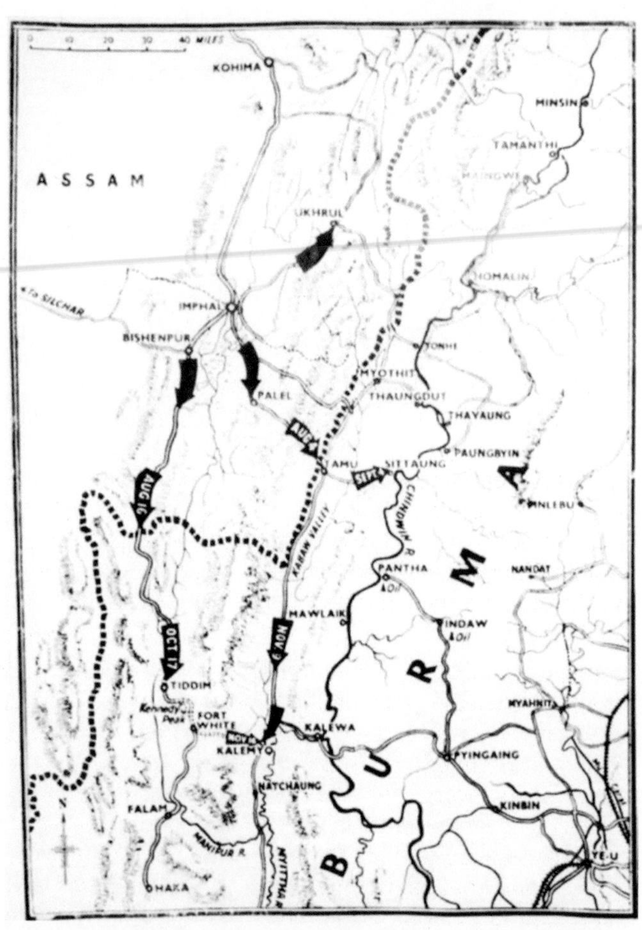

Fig.11.15: Map showing the route from Imphal to Kalemyo, and the dates in 1944 of advances made by the 14th Army. The dotted line is the India-Burma border.

These operations continue for some time, with many challenges for the pursuing troops, but relatively few casualties. They're being supplied by air, with the Allies in complete control of the skies. The retreating Japanese, on the other hand, are very short of food and are suffering badly from disease. Malaria in particular is taking a heavy toll, but more disciplined use of Mepacrine starts to hold it in check among the Allies – it is effective, although there is resistance to its use from some soldiers. (Supplies of the established medication of Quinine have dried up, now that the Japanese have control of the parts of Indonesia and the Philippines where it is produced.) The responsibilities of the CMP include enforcement of the taking of Mepacrine, and also other measures against disease - such as covering arms and legs at night and encouraging good sanitation procedures. None of this is easy in the jungle.

The main task for the CMP at present, however, is to keep the troops and equipment moving along these terrible roads. These include tanks and resources such as the pontoons for "Bailey bridges", which are going to be needed for crossing the major rivers. Such things clearly can't be dropped by air and there are very few usable airfields. Anyway, a Lee tank weighs 30 tons and the load capacity of a C47 is 3 tons. There are no railways. These things have to be moved by road. This sometimes involves winching a tank up a muddy, precipitous incline. There are several Companies of Royal Engineers engaged in improving bits of road and providing tools, but it's often the CMP people who are faced with somehow keeping the show on the road.

Len's Company leaves Imphal, heading for Tiddim, in mid-August. They're just a couple of weeks behind the advance guard, which is faced with continual sniping from the retreating Japanese. A second group, which included the 4th Battalion of the RWK, had left Imphal a month earlier, heading south-east. The plan is for these two Armies to meet up further south, at Kalemyo, and then cross the huge Chindwin river at Kalewa. The road to Tiddim is probably the worst of all. It includes the notorious "Chocolate staircase", a steep and tortuous section, where the mud is particularly bad. The CMP Companies reach this part in mid-September and Len patrols up and down it on his motorbike many times during the next month or so. There are many places where men and machines are in serious danger, and indeed a lot of lorries are lost over steep cliffs. Nothing could have prepared their drivers for these conditions.

Most of the troops are on foot and getting up the staircase takes a whole day (in the hot sun, carrying full kit). It can't be done at night – the danger of mosquito bites would be too great, as would that of slipping off the road down steep escarpments. With most of the men already in poor health for one reason or another, it's a big ask. Len spends a lot of time dispensing water and encouragement. In cases of complete collapse, soldiers can be put into jeeps or lorries, but hard lines have to be taken if this is to be kept within reasonable limits. Fortunately, these troops have a lot of pride, but conditions here are extreme.

Fig.11.16: Photo of part of the "Chocolate staircase" leading up to Tiddim – an 8-mile stretch of road, rising 3,000 feet and with 40 hairpin bends.

There is just the occasional distraction. It's also worth noting that, while conditions are certainly bad, not all of the troops are keen to push on as fast as possible – after all, they do know that there are still plenty of Japanese in the jungle ahead.

"What's going on here?" asks Len, as he skids to a halt next to a melee of soldiers, with a long backlog of jeeps and lorries building up behind. It soon becomes clear that they're all scoffing Hershey bars and other treats.

"Sorry Sarge, but we can't let these go to waste!"

"What's wrong with him?" – pointing to a soldier lying on the road, moaning gently.

"Oh, he's with the Worcesters. I think that this lot might have landed on him. He doesn't seem very hungry!"

"All right, the party's over. Get back into line, and back into your lorries. You – get this lad up in the cab with you – I think he might have dislocated his shoulder – and make sure that a medic sees him this evening. Also, take the rest of this pack and give it to your CO. I'll be checking with him later today." A 100 pound pack, dropped without a parachute, can do a lot of damage, even if it's full of chocolate bars.

At 5,000 feet, the temperature is lower in Tiddim and the air clearer. Some welcome rest is available there, if only for a day or two. For the Japanese, however, there is no respite. They're in full retreat, being pursued along several routes - including some in the eastern part of Burma, where Chinese divisions are moving into the south of the country in large numbers. These manoeuvres are jointly coordinated by Joe Stilwell and Chiang Kai-Shek. There is still some friction between them, but these troops have received a lot of training and supplies from the Americans, and they are an effective fighting force. USAAF pilots are still flying over the "Hump", as well as supplying many groups on the ground. They're proving to be absolutely crucial in the whole Burma Campaign. There are also many RAF squadrons in the region now, harrying the retreating Japanese, as well as dropping supplies. The whole process accelerates as airfields, supply dumps and other resources are overrun. The Japanese try to destroy these, but they're now in complete disarray – individual soldiers are still fighting bravely, but they're short of virtually everything. It's a mirror image of the retreat of the British and British-Indian forces two years before.

Fig.11.17: Jeeps of the 5th Indian Division on the Imphal to Tiddim Road, in July 1944.

For Len and the rest of the CMP contingent, it's a demanding time. Racing up and down the roads on their motorbikes, dealing with various bottlenecks, clashes between different units, a continuous threat from Japanese snipers, in heavy rain and with venomous insects and snakes everywhere, it's not an easy task. It's a nightmare scenario for everyone, but the CMP have a particular responsibility to keep the show on the road. The rivers, large and small, present a serious problem. They're now in spate, swollen by the monsoon rains. Getting men and equipment across even small tributaries is a slow and hazardous operation, while the large ones constitute major strategic issues. There were never many bridges and now there are virtually none. The retreating Japanese have destroyed them all. In particular, the huge Chindwin river now represents a major barrier to the advance.

Donald Bailey, a civil servant in the British War Office, had first proposed the idea of a portable "kit" bridge in 1936, but little was done until the war was well under way. In 1941, some trials were carried out and a prototype tested in Christchurch. The design involves a number of floating pontoons, bolted to a roadway running over them. The idea is simple, but, with no foundations in the river bed, and rigidity coming only from the connections between the pontoons, there's clearly a danger of the whole thing being washed away – particularly if it's fairly long. Also, the pontoons need to be very buoyant, to support both the roadway and things like tanks running over it. It's already been shown that the idea is workable, and several have been successfully built and used during the ongoing invasion of Northern Europe, but the logistics of this particular operation are mind-boggling. The components were manufactured in the USA, Britain and India, and had made their way by various sea routes to Calcutta, from where they were transported via the tortuous rail link to Dimapur, crossing the Brahmaputra en route, and thence down through Imphal and Teddim in dozens of lorries. They arrive at the town of Kalemyo, and thence to the river at Kalewa, in late November.

Fortunately, the monsoon season is now coming to an end, so the assembly is not hampered by torrential rain. In fact, the weather is very good. Nevertheless, the river is in full flow and at this point it's over 1,100 feet wide – this is to be the longest Bailey Bridge constructed so far. Nevertheless, some British "sappers", now expert in assembling these bridges, put this one up in record time. Sections are assembled in Kalewa and then towed by boat to positions on the river. These are then assembled into a bridge in 28 hours of strenuous effort. It works perfectly straight away – even with a stream of tanks and lorries going over it. The whole operation is an engineering and logistical triumph. In fact, the Japanese abandon the East bank just before construction begins, although a number of Zeroes attack it throughout. However, this doesn't stop it going ahead and in fact two planes are brought down by anti-aircraft fire. The Japanese had at least expected a respite before the river was crossed, but in practice they're given none.

Fig.11.18: Photo of the Bailey Bridge over the Chindwin, taken shortly after its completion on 10th December 1944.

Len and his Company arrive at Kalewa just as the bridge is being completed. He's there during a visit by Mountbatten, which is quite short and is mainly a photo opportunity. Some videos are taken, showing a couple of jeeps with his entourage on board, driving across the bridge at quite high speed. Len doesn't get to speak to him, but he does spend a while talking to some of the troops from the 11th East Africa Division, which is the first to reach Kalewa. These troops are amongst the first to march across the bridge. They're coping with the heat and flies somewhat better than the British soldiers, but they're also impressive in terms of general discipline and stoicism. Len notices that Mountbatten doesn't pay them much attention and it's difficult to avoid the conclusion that there's a strong element of racism in the British Army. It also applies to some extent to the Indian troops, although the British military are at least familiar with their culture and feel that they have a working relationship with them. Len rather fears that these African troops may be somewhat airbrushed out of the history of these turbulent events. Meanwhile, they're certainly presenting no problems in crossing the bridge: they don't actually have many vehicles.

Len also has a chat with a few of the sappers before they leave.

Fig.11.19: Louis Mountbatten inspecting a small group of Royal Engineers at Kalewa on 12th December 1944, shortly after they had finished building the Bailey Bridge over the river Chindwin.

"Well, Len, we've got to move on now, but perhaps you could stay here for a few days – there's a lot of traffic building up in Kalemyo and this bridge will need to be used carefully. Of course, it's all going to be moving in the same direction for a while."

"That's fine", says Len, "but what do you think it will take? Do we need to limit the weight on it at any one time and will there be any warning signs if it's under stress? Is it possible that a few bolts could break, sending a section downstream with a tank or two onboard?"

"Well, that might be one way to make some progress south, but perhaps not the best way. To be honest, we don't really know how it might fail, since this is the longest one we've built so far, and there's quite a strong current here." They look at the noticeable curve in its shape, even with no traffic on it.

Fig.11.20: Troops of the 11th East African Division, about to cross the Bailey Bridge at Kelawa on 11th December 1944.

"Just keep your eye on it and play it by ear. Perhaps best to have no more than one tank on it at a time, maybe plus a couple of lorries or jeeps. With a limit of just one vehicle, things would be slowed down quite a bit. However, they should all drive slowly, even jeeps – it's actually rather bumpy, particularly if it's hit by a floating log or two – and make sure that nobody hits the sidewalls, even a glancing blow – they're quite flimsy. Also, no traffic at night – it's tempting, but it's not worth the risk. It certainly won't last forever, and there could be some fatigue failure of a few bolts eventually, but in a month or two it will have largely served its purpose. To answer your question, if a vehicle does come off, then we think that the bridge might well rupture, and then the whole thing will come to bits: remaking it doesn't bear thinking about."

"I think I've got the picture." says Len, "We'll make sure that there are a couple of CMP people here day and night. It won't be much fun here at night, but you never know when some cowboy might come tearing along, thinking that he's on the A1!"

The Christmas festivities, while naturally a little different from back home – where spirits are rising rapidly as the war in Europe continues to go well – are thus rather positive for the "Forgotten Armies" in Burma. However, there is no time for extended relaxation. Slim, and also Stillwell and Chiang, keep forcing the pace, determined to give the Japanese no time to regroup or establish a strong defensive line. Slim is clear that he must drive them completely out of Burma before the start of the next monsoon season in May. The final objective is Rangoon, capture of which will surely eliminate any possibility of them retaining a foothold in the country, but the immediate target is Mandalay. It's a beautiful old city – previously a royal capital of Burma, full of golden pagodas, and with some romantic imperial associations. These are captured in Rudyard Kipling's famous poem of the same name ("On the road to Mandalay, Where the flyin'-fishes play, An' the dawn comes up like thunder outer China 'crost the Bay"), but current thoughts are focused solely on how to drive the enemy out of what is at present an important strategic location.

Mandalay lies on the Irrawaddy river, about 70 miles upstream from its confluence with the Chindwin at Myingyan. The Japanese are very strong in the vicinity of Mandalay, having retreated there from various positions to the north. There are rail links between Mandalay and Rangoon, and also between these two and Myingyan. Slim decides that the best strategy is to cut off the vital link between Mandalay and Rangoon. The most

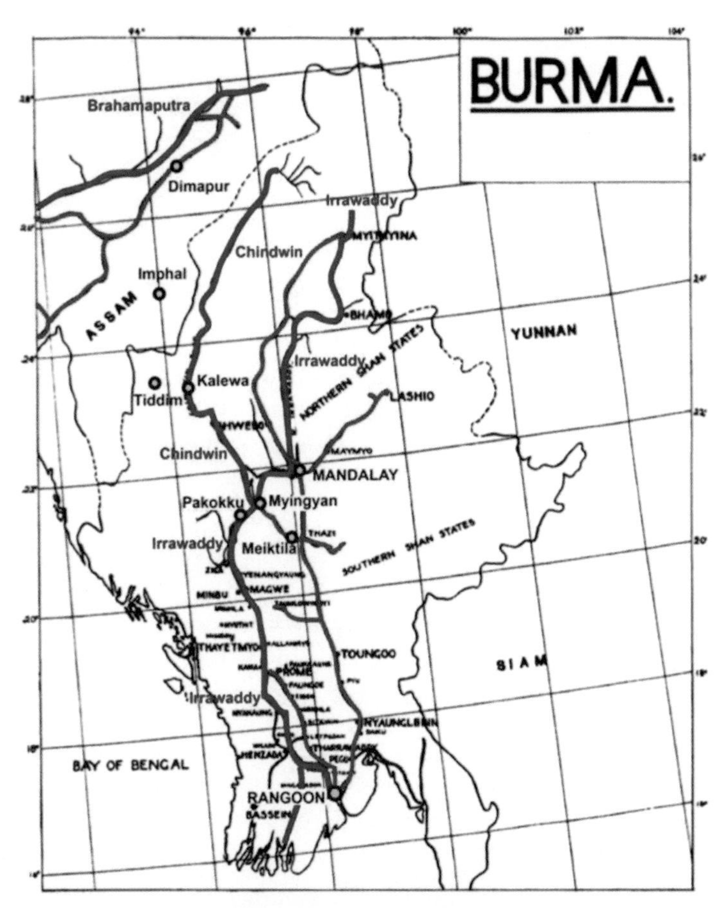

Fig.11.21: A map of the main rivers and railways in Assam and Burma, in the 1940's.

decisive battles of the "re-invasion" of Burma are about to take place.

As British and British-Indian units cross the Chindwin, at Kelawa and also at another Bailey Bridge further upstream, they start to move east, hoping to catch the Japanese in disarray in the plain between it and the Irrawaddy. (In fact, it's British-Indian troops that predominate now, plus some African units, with a number of the surviving British battalions finally being allowed to retire northwards, having in some cases been fighting continuously in Burma for a year or more.) However, it soon becomes clear that the Japanese don't intend to make a stand here – they're retreating en masse to the area around Mandalay. Slim seizes the opportunity to attack the key town of Meiktila, which is about 90 miles south of Mandalay. If this can be taken, breaking the rail link between Mandalay and Rangoon, then the supply situation for the embattled Japanese troops in central Burma will become hopeless.

Fig.11.22: A Lee tank being loaded onto a pontoon ferry by British troops, to cross the Irrawaddy near Pakokku on 28th February 1945.

Slim therefore implements a feint, attacking Mandalay, but also switching a major part of his forces in a wide detour to the West, swinging around to cross the Irrawaddy at Pakokku (using boats and floating pontoon ferries) and then attacking Meitkila. A series of hard-fought battles ensues around both cities during February and March, with the Japanese defending fanatically and making a series of counter-attacks in both places. They make a protracted stand in the massive Fort Dufferin in Mandalay. Their position, however, has become very difficult, partly because the Allies now have complete control of the skies, supplying the troops on the ground and continually harrying the Japanese. By the end of March, both Mandalay and Meiktila have been taken and secured. Many Japanese have been killed (and only a few taken prisoner). Some escape south to Rangoon, but the position in the capital is becoming nightmarish, with almost continuous bombing, virtually no functioning services, law and order breaking down, food in very short supply and the Japanese uncertain whether they have any hope of holding out. They're repeatedly urged by the Japanese High Command to make last ditch stands, but this is looking increasingly hopeless (and is reminiscent of Hitler's demands in Russia and Europe). Unlike the Germans, however, the Japanese have a chance of retreating to their island home and making it virtually impregnable. They debate

Fig.11.23: A British soldier sharing tea with a Burmese family in Meiktila on 10th March 1945.

frantically about whether they should now do this.

Len and his Company move south from Kalewa early in the New Year. Their services are continually in demand as the Allied armies flood in behind the advance guard, with many traffic control and resource supply demands. However, while the situation for the retreating Japanese is getting increasingly desperate, that of the pursuing troops is easing somewhat. Firstly, the weather is now relatively good – little rain and not yet intolerably hot. The terrain is also getting better – less jungle, flatter and with better roads - and also with fewer insects and snakes. They still have to deal with fanatically brave Japanese troops, but they're well-supplied and well-equipped. Len and his men spend most of April in and around Mandalay. They're able to sleep in reasonably good buildings, although much of the city, including many beautiful old pagodas, has been damaged or destroyed. A few Japanese prisoners are taken. Moving them north to the detention camps in India is a logistical nightmare, but this is done, with a couple of CMP personnel accompanying each group.

The logistics of moving men and equipment to the south again becomes a central issue. There is an immediate focus on the rail link from Mandalay to Meiktila and from there to Rangoon. There is a lot of damage in Mandalay, with many beautiful building lying in ruins. However, Len can see how it became famous in the folklore of the British Empire. He now understands that the "Road to Mandalay" (from Rangoon) is the mighty River Irrawaddy. The city is on a huge bend and inlet of the river, called Mandalay Bay. It's easy to see how Kipling was inspired to write about dawn coming up out of China to the east and rising over the bay. In any event, the rail line going south from Mandalay is still in fairly good shape and the rolling stock hasn't been completely destroyed. However, there are no civil authorities and certainly nobody around to operate the railway. It was being run entirely by the Japanese.

"OK, Smithers," says Len, "so you think you might be able to drive this thing?" They're in a siding near the remains of Mandalay station, on the footplate of a battered-looking locomotive, which has a roaring fire and steam issuing from various places.

"Well, Sarge, my dad's a driver with the LMS. He used to drive the 'Coronation Scot' regularly. He's always been keen for me to become a railwayman and he used to take me along in the cab of a few goods trains and show me the ropes."

"Well, that sounds promising, but what about this thing – it looks as if it's Japanese, from these little labels. We don't want you blowing yourself up."

"Yes, well that's not impossible, but the main controls, and the safety valves etc, do seem to be working OK. Steam engines all work in pretty much the same way. I think I can handle it. Most of the other locos seem to be damaged, although there are plenty of trucks around that still seem to roll. There's a Company of sappers going over the track itself now."

"Good man – well, we'll give it a whirl. You might be able to have a go with a first train within a day or two. I'll let you have a strong lad as fireman. We'll also set up a system for controlling who and what goes on it, and rig up a few machine guns along the train. Even in these battered trucks, everyone will want to get on board – it'll be a lot better than walking or being crammed into these lorries. What about signaling, switching of points etc?"

"I don't think that there'll be many other trains to worry about. We'll just jump down and sort out any points ourselves. There seems to be plenty of coal and wood around. I'm more worried about water – we probably can't rely on any water tanks being operational along the way. We should load a couple of wagons up with water containers."

"That sounds like a good idea. Let's just get a first run down to Meiktila under our belt. I'll aim to come with you on this one. It's less than a hundred miles, and we can take our time – we just need to get it done in daylight."

Taking Rangoon by the start of the monsoon season in May is now the key objective. Nobody wants to repeat the horrors of the previous summer – the rainy season is really not a time to be undertaking military activity in this part of the world – but it's also seen as important to give the Japanese no time to regroup. A fierce competition now develops between Mountbatten, who has a long-cherished plan for a joint invasion of Rangoon by sea and air, and Slim, who is determined to push on down from central Burma with his Army. Mountbatten wins this race, with thousands of seaborne soldiers and paratroopers entering the city at the beginning of May, just as the rains start. However, there is no battle – the Japanese abandon the area towards the end of April. Many leave on ships that are sunk soon after reaching the open sea. Some do escape along the notorious Bangkok to Rangoon railway, which had been completed about 18 months before (using PoWs and other forced labour, with many deaths and atrocities). It had been intended to serve as an important route for supplying Japanese armies as they pushed through Burma and invaded India. Of course, this never happened and the main legacy of the line is its label of the "Death Railway". It's shortly to be closed and it's not destined to survive as a through route between Thailand and Burma.

Some INA troops are left in Rangoon (to keep some sort of order and to defend Indian nationals from reprisals by local Burmese), but they surrender to the Allied armies as soon as they arrive. The city is in complete chaos, but they're able to move in without resistance. Now that it can be supplied by sea, it becomes a little easier to bring some order, and to feed the starving local population. While it remains to drive the Japanese completely out of Burma, the situation is now starting to return to some semblance of normality (after more than 3 years of terrible conflict and deprivation for everyone in the country).

Len's Company reaches the city in early May. There is a desperate need to establish some order, cut down the looting etc and they contribute strongly to this operation. However, a decision is soon made to fly them back to India. They've now been on the move, through terrible terrain and conditions, for almost a year. Fresh reinforcements are arriving in large numbers from India, and also from Europe. The war there is now over and it's recognized that the focus must be switched firmly to the Far East. At this point, it's far from clear how long it might take to complete the operation, but it's expected to be a protracted and difficult job. Places such as Singapore, Hong Kong and Malaysia remain firmly in Japanese hands and invading Japan itself looks likely to be a mammoth task.

Fig. 11.24: Len's Company in India, in June 1945. He's in the centre of the second row from the front. The location may be Fort William, near Calcutta.

Those arriving in Rangoon include large contingents of CMP and nobody in Len's Company is going to argue with the idea that they deserve some R&R. There are now many aircraft available and the Company is flown to Calcutta in a couple of Dakotas in mid-May. It's a first flight for most of them, and it's not an easy one, through pouring rain and thunderstorms. It's about 600 miles by air and the trip only takes about 3 hours, but it's a rough one, with a lot of airsickness. Still, it's a lot better than their journey down, and certainly a lot quicker. They know that they may well be called upon to resume operations soon, but in the meantime they can relax and recover. Spirits are high and there's even time for some football matches. Len, now in his thirties, is still playing, although he's not as quick as he used to be and he has switched position to become a centre-half of the old school. He tends to give the centre-forward an early "reducer", as Martin Keown (ex-Arsenal defender, subsequently a prominent pundit) will refer to the technique decades later, so playing against him is not such an attractive prospect for opposing forwards.

Fig.11.25: The Company football team in June 1945. Although Len does play in the team, he's not wearing his kit here.

11.4 Home Fires

In Britain, the realization is slowly dawning that the war is soon going to be won – at least in Europe. Less is known about exactly what is happening in Asia. It is becoming clear that many German cities are being pounded to rubble, but there is little sympathy for the Germans. The policy of indiscriminate carpet bombing, which is being promoted by "Bomber" Harris, has quite widespread support, including that of Churchill. Archibald Sinclair opposes it, but he's in a minority within the War Cabinet. It's now relatively rare to see Luftwaffe planes over the UK, but the V-weapons continue to cause anxiety in London and there is a general feeling that the Germans must be made to understand exactly how much misery and fear they have caused over the past 5 years.

Fig.11.26: Pam and bike, taken in 1944.

Within the Clyne and Fullbrook families, the stresses are

starting to ease. Of course, Pam has been in terror of hearing bad news from Asia. Len's letters have downplayed the horror of conditions there, but she's well aware that there are many casualties in that part of the world – both from disease and from the ferocity of the conflict. She also knows that, while the worst period is probably over now for Allied troops, there's certainly still a lot of danger. Moreover, she's aware that, while the Japanese are now in full retreat, many Allied soldiers are likely to be required to stay in the area until the enemy can somehow be forced to surrender, which could take years. She has little idea how long it will be before they can meet up again.

For her and her parents, however, life in the Royal Hospital is now slightly less stressful. The bomb damage has not yet been repaired, but their housing situation is better than that of many people in London. Pam was very concerned that Jum might get involved in the Normandy landings and it's aftermath, but he's still based in the UK and the requirement for more troops on the continent is now starting to drop off. On the other hand, the V2 rocket bombs continue to be launched at London. In fact, the last one falls on Vallance Road (Bethnal Green) on 27th March 1945, killing 130 people. As it happens, Jum's fiancée, Annie Clark, lives in Coutts Road, which is not far away. This area has already suffered a lot of bomb damage, and it's also a rather rough and ready neighbourhood – the Kray Twins have lived in Vallance Road throughout the war and that vicinity is sometimes known as "Deserters' Corner".

Thoughts are starting to swing towards the situation after the Germans have surrendered, and the logistical challenge of bringing large numbers of soldiers and others back into the country - and the even bigger challenges of rebuilding the infrastructure and finding work for people. The UK is now desperately short of cash, having borrowed and spent huge sums of money. The rethink actually goes deeper than this, since many things have been fundamentally changed by this war. The Labour Party is perceived as more in tune with the times than the Conservatives. While the appetite for communism is not widespread, it's certainly felt that the Russians have achieved a lot. There's also a strong consensus that the old ruling elite has let the country down. Their attitude to war has always been fairly cavalier, but the burden of wars on ordinary people is no longer sustainable. It's also being recalled that many on the right in the UK were actually supportive of fascism. While Churchill is universally admired for the way that he has pulled the country through, there is a growing feeling that a "New Deal" is needed. A General Election is scheduled for the summer. Many people are openly saying that the old system must be swept aside.

The atmosphere in GOGGS is also starting to change. There is great pride in what has been achieved, and many close bonds have been formed between those working there – at all levels. However, as events move towards some sort of denouement, everyone is starting to think about their lives after this war has ended. Most of the Secretaries feel that simply carrying on in this kind of role is likely to be something of an anti-climax after the pressures and excitement of the past 5 years. Also, many of them have formed attachments and, while marriages have been almost out of the question until now, the idea of a stable home and a family is starting to look attractive. Of course, the politicians and the military people are also starting to think about how their

Fig.11.27: Revellers in the Strand on VE Day.

careers are likely to develop after this is all over. It's a time of great uncertainty everywhere in the country, but perhaps particularly in the corridors of power.

When the announcement of Germany's surrender finally comes through, Churchill immediately declares a public holiday: VE Day is Tuesday 8th May 1945. There is an enormous emotional release in the country, although of course people have seen this coming for several weeks now. The celebrations are certainly riotous, if a little constrained by the fact that so many servicemen (and a few servicewomen), plus a number who were prisoners of war, are still overseas. Also, the situation in the Far East is now starting to attract much more attention. Most of the colonial territories are now more secure, but Singapore and Hong Kong are still under Japanese occupation and don't look likely to be liberated any time soon. Moreover, while there us a lot of uncertainty about their fate, it is known that the Japanese have taken well over 100,000 prisoners, and none of them have been released yet.

Fig.11.28: Two young girls in Battersea on VE Day.

Chapter 12: A New Life (July 1945 – March 1952)

12.1 A Fresh Start for Britain and for the World

The general election in the UK is scheduled for 5th July 1945 - the expiry of 5 years since the coalition government was formed coinciding neatly with the end of the war in Europe, although it's actually been ten years since the last general election. In the event, the result is not officially announced until 26th July, allowing time to count the votes of the many people still serving abroad. The result is a landslide victory for Labour. Conservative seats fall from almost 400 to fewer than 200, while Labour goes from about 150 to almost 400. The Liberals, who have been in disarray for about 15 years, are virtually wiped out.

The result comes as a shock to Churchill. The Conservatives oriented their campaign largely around him, and his personal rating remains high, but the confidence of the electorate in the Conservatives is now low, whereas Labour has a clear plan for dealing with the serious economic and industrial challenges facing the country. It involves extensive nationalization of several areas of industry and the creation of a National Health Service. Clement Attlee, who has been Deputy Prime Minister through most of the war years, is perceived as a capable and hardworking man. It certainly looks like a logical decision on the part of the electorate, since radical change is clearly needed.

Churchill is an interesting and exceptional character. He's a talented writer and artist, as well as being highly charismatic and a powerful orator. On the other hand, he certainly believes in privilege and the concept of being born to rule. He's also headstrong and arrogant. The early parts of his career are peppered with poor decision-making, although also with prodigious levels of hard work and effective networking. The rise of fascism – with which he certainly had some sympathy originally, and in particular the rise of Hitler, gave him the opportunity to crown his career in a way that looked unlikely earlier. He has taken it with both hands. His standing is such that he remains leader of the Conservatives, despite the catastrophic nature of the defeat. In fact, he is destined to take up the reins one more time, although there is probably an argument for saying that it might have been better all round if he had graciously stepped down at this point. In any event, the immediate future of the country is firmly in the hands of the Labour Party. There are visions of a completely new social and economic order.

The timing of these events is somewhat fraught – certainly from Churchill's perspective. The long-planned summit conference, at which many important decisions will need to be taken, starts in Potsdam (near Berlin) on 17th July. Churchill represents Britain at the start, although he must have at least an inkling that he may be about to be removed from office. A short postponement of the conference might have been sensible, although it was planned a couple of months previously and a change would not have been easy to make. For everyone in

Fig.12.1: Group photo at Potsdam on 1st Aug. 1945, with (left to right) a front row of Clem Attlee, Harry Truman and Joe Stalin and a back row of William Leahy (Truman's Chief of Staff), Ernest Bevan (UK Foreign Minister), James Byrnes (US Secretary of State) and Vyacheslav Molotov (Soviet Foreign Minister).

GOGGS, there are several layers of complication as preparations are made. For example, should Atlee be involved in putting the various documents together? Churchill is adamantly opposed to this, and takes the line that there is no real prospect of defeat in the election. Many of the people in GOGGS, including Pam and her colleagues, feel that this may be unduly optimistic, but of course they're unlikely to tell Churchill this. In any event, the announcement of the election result, ten days after the start of the conference, creates chaos. While it is not completely unexpected within the UK, it comes as a shock to the Americans and Russians. Churchill can't possibly continue to lead the negotiations, and Atlee immediately flies out to take over. Having worked under Churchill for several years, he knows all about his rather swashbuckling style, but it's clear to all that this has been badly handled. In contrast to this, Truman is well-briefed and of course Stalin is an old hand. They're both fairly clear about what they want to get from the conference.

The main outcomes of Potsdam are in fact fairly predictable – largely along the lines roughed out at Yalta. Germany is to be partitioned and the Nazis held accountable for their war crimes – the first time that such a procedure has been carried out (with multinational judges and much new legislation required). The trial is to start at Nuremberg in October. Stalin also makes a commitment to declare war on Japan shortly. Among the other positive outcomes is confirmed support for the formation of the "United Nations" organization, which is formally created in October 1945. There is widespread recognition that the League of Nations was unsuccessful – mainly because support for it was lukewarm and it was poorly resourced. Nevertheless, it's clear to all that a forum for international discussion and arbitration, with the power if necessary to act positively, is desperately needed. The United Nations is to be well-resourced, with strong support from all of the major countries.

More problematic for the Potsdam participants are issues surrounding the "spheres of influence", particularly in Eastern Europe. America isn't really interested in "colonizing" Europe in any way, but it is desperate to limit the spread of communism. As events start to unfold on the ground, the trust being placed in Stalin's word is starting to unravel – Truman, Churchill and Atlee are all starting to have doubts. Much of this focuses on Poland, where his pledges to allow an independent, democratic government are looking doubtful as a "caretaker" communism system takes over. Poland is looking to the West for support, but there are big issues at stake here and the animosity between the Americans and the Soviets is building up. Britain is starting to look like a minor player, with their concerns about retaining the Empire looking increasingly irrelevant – it is starting to unravel anyway. The French are looking even more marginalized, with de Gaulle becoming apoplectic, but still being largely ignored.

There are, however, still common aims among the Allies. Prominent among these is to obtain the quick surrender of Japan. There have been developments behind the scenes. The Americans have already started to build up their conventional bombing campaign against the island of Japan, but their "Manhatten Project" - initiated in 1939 and gathering momentum over the past couple of years, is about to deliver the first nuclear weapon. During the conference, Truman has a quiet word with Stalin about a new super bomb that he is ready to use against Japan (unaware that Stalin already knows the details – in fact, became aware of them before Truman – as a result of Russian espionage activities). Stalin is supportive of its use.

Nobody is really aware of exactly how destructive these weapons might be, and there is certainly very little understanding of the long-term effects of radiation released by them. On the other hand, the basic principle behind a nuclear weapon, and indeed nuclear power, has been clear for a little while. Einstein's famous $E = mc^2$ equation was put forward 40 years ago. Since the speed of light, c, is a huge number, this equation indicates, not only the equivalence of energy (E) and mass (m), but also that an enormous amount of energy is released by the "disappearance" of a very small amount of mass. Mass does not disappear during ordinary chemical reactions – the atoms involved may recombine in various ways, but the same atoms are present before and after, and their mass has not changed. Nothing happens to the nuclei of the atoms. Any energy released is just due to changes in the energies of bonding between atoms.

Nuclear reactions are different. They're of two basic types – fission, which is large atoms breaking down into smaller ones (with net loss of mass), and fusion, which is small atoms (particularly hydrogen) combining to form larger ones, again with net loss of mass. The latter type of reaction powers all of the stars in the universe. It's difficult to control, and so presents a major challenge for power generation (on earth), although uncontrolled reactions (an explosion) are relatively easy to create. The focus of the Manhatten Project, however, is largely on fission. The concept of a chain reaction, in which small nuclear particles are released during the atomic splitting, and go on to strike other atoms, causing them in turn to split, is well understood. One problem is that such a reaction only becomes self-sustaining if the piece of fissile material is relatively large – ie a critical mass is required. This is often of the order of a few tens of kg – ie quite a lot. Much of the challenge actually lies in assembling such a mass, particularly since such materials do not occur naturally in large quantities. Much of the initial focus is on uranium, but, not only is it relatively rare, but in its natural form the unstable isotope, U^{235}, constitutes only a very small proportion of the total (mostly U^{238}). Separating them is very difficult, since that small difference in mass is all that distinguishes them. Nevertheless, after the injection of enormous and intensive levels of technical and scientific effort, successful methods are devised. Triggering the explosion is commonly achieved by firing sub-critical pieces together to form a critical mass.

That the Americans do drop two nuclear bombs on Japan (Hiroshima on 6th Aug. and Nagasaki on 9th Aug.) becomes a major, and a controversial, historical event. Accurate estimation of the number of dead is difficult, but it's probably about 200,000 - mostly civilians. Both cities are literally razed to the ground. Some people regard it as a war crime, but there are many factors that should be taken into account. Firstly, dreadful as these deaths are, the numbers are not out of line with those caused by conventional bombing – now completed in Germany, but still building up on Japan. The only real difference is that it happens more quickly, although the effects of lingering radiation are only just starting to become apparent. If these bombs had not been dropped, then the probability is that far more Japanese would have been killed in the end, plus, of course, large numbers of Allied troops – since it seems likely that there would have been no surrender without an invasion. It is important to understand just how intransigent – or, looked at in another light, brave and patriotic – the Japanese actually are. It can certainly be argued that they have committed war crimes that are on a par with those of the Nazis, and include systematic large-scale genocide. However, while many Germans have become aware of the depravity of the crimes carried out in their name, and deeply abhor them, Japanese society is more homogeneous and unquestioning, instinctively deferring to those in charge. Hirohito blithely ignored Truman's warning concerning what was about to happen, and indeed still insisted after Hiroshima

Fig.12.2: Hiroshima shortly after dropping of the bomb. The name in the corner is that of the pilot of the plane from which it was dropped.

that there would never be any surrender. However, after Nagasaki, it finally dawned on those in charge that there was a serious danger of their society being wiped out. Hirohito actually used the declaration of war on them by Russia as the main reason for capitulation, although it's difficult to believe that it wasn't actually the bombs that forced this decision on him.

Finally, there is another argument that should be borne in mind. The images of the aftermath, particularly those showing what had happened to individual people, shock the world. Such horror was almost unimaginable previously, even amid the many horrors of conventional war. This is surely going to have a major effect on future decision-making about use of nuclear weapons, particularly since the destructive power of these two bombs will be dwarfed by future capabilities. It can't be argued that the Americans had this "benefit" in mind, but it's nevertheless a point that is worth taking into account when balancing the pros and cons of this momentous decision.

Irrespective of the political and technological background, the surrender of Japan (on 15th August, declared as VJ day) comes as a huge relief to many people around the world, and probably to at least many of the Japanese themselves. For people like Len, waiting in India for what could well have turned out to be further horrendous conflict, it's a cause for celebration. Suddenly, they can expect to go home almost immediately. Of course, that's not quite what happens. There's a shortage of ships and a lot of troops hoping to be repatriated from the Far East, including about 100,000 prisoners of the Japanese who are now released. Some of these people are in urgent need of hospitalization, or at least some kind of rehabilitation back in Britain. Also, many troops have now been in the Far East for several years. Len and his Company, who've only been here for just over a year, are not at the front of the queue. Nevertheless, they don't have to wait very long. After a couple of months in Calcutta, with the rain still pouring down for much of the time, they're told in early October that they'll soon be on the move.

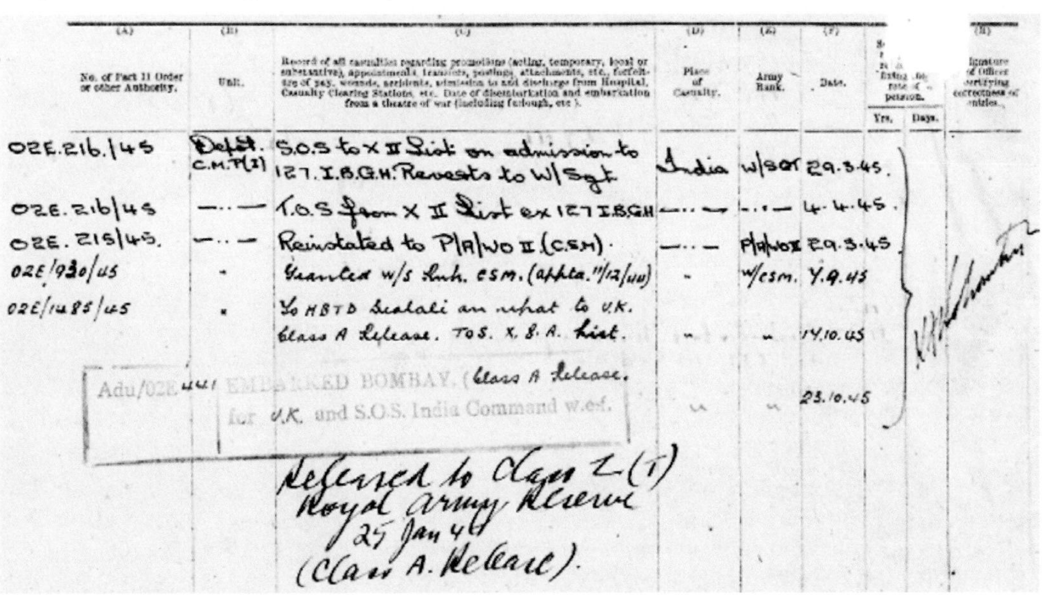

No. of Part II Order or other Authority.	Unit.	Record of all casualties regarding promotions (acting, temporary, local or substantive), appointments, transfers, postings, attachments, etc., forfeiture of pay, wounds, accidents, admission to and discharge from Hospital, Casualty Clearing Stations, etc. Date of disembarkation and embarkation from a theatre of war (including furlough, etc.).	Place of Casualty.	Army Rank.	Date.	Yrs.	Days.	Signature of Officer certifying correctness of entries.
02E.216./45	Depot. C.M.P.(I)	S.O.S to X II List on admission to 127. I.B.G.H. Reverts to W/Sgt.	India	W/Sgt	29.3.45.			
02E.216/45	— " —	T.O.S from X II List ex 127 I.B.G.H	— " —	— " —	4.4.45.			
02E.215/45.	— " —	Reinstated to P/A/WO II (C.S.M).	— " —	P/A/WO II	29.3.45			
02E/930/45	"	Granted w/s Rank. CSM. (appta. 11/12/44)	"	W/CSM.	7.9.45			
02E/1485/45	"	To HBTD Sealdah on repat to U.K. Class A Release. TOS. X. 8. A. List.	"	"	14.10.45			
Adu/02E.441		EMBARKED BOMBAY. (Class A Release. for U.K. and S.O.S. India Command w.e.f.	"	"	23.10.45			
		Released to Class Z (T) Royal Army Reserve 25 Jan 46 (Class A. Release).						

Fig.12.3: Last page of Len's Army records relating to postings, promotions etc.

They take the train across to Bombay in mid-October and embark on the RMT Otranto on the 23rd. This is a very different trip from the one in the reverse direction a year and a half ago. For one thing, it's cooler and the rains have eased off. Perhaps more importantly, they know where they're going and what awaits them there – hopefully a return to more or less normal life. Thirdly, the trip is much more relaxed – no blackouts, no fear of torpedoes or other attack by air or sea. It's still a bit crowded, and the food is still not great, but there's less need for discipline or strict adhering to rules. Most of them are not sorry to be leaving India and Burma, although they do recognize that they're been through a life-changing experience and they've made many close friends within the Army and the other armed services. They also understand well the major contributions to the war effort made by many of the indigenous peoples of the Empire – particularly those from India. There is real sympathy for them and an understanding of how hard life is for many of them, even without a war. There is a feeling amongst most of the troops that they deserve to run their own countries, particularly India.

Christmas is passed in the Suez Canal, with the rules about alcohol being somewhat relaxed and a good dinner provided. Spirits are high, although everyone is naturally wondering just what life is going to be like in peacetime, and how their lives will change. Some are thinking that they might want to stay in the Army, but most can't wait to get out and enjoy some freedom. The voyage passes without incident and the Otranto docks at Southampton in late January. Of course, as the ship moves into its berth, the quayside is thronged with family and friends of the arriving troops. Pam is naturally among them – things aren't quite so hectic now in GOGGS, but in any event there is nothing that could have kept her away. She does know that he's basically OK, but she also knows that few of the soldiers who spent time in the Burmese jungle have come through it totally unscathed, mentally or physically. She doesn't really know what to expect.

They catch sight of each other while he's still on the ship – and still fulfilling CMP duties for controlling the disembarkation. He's actually one of the last down the gangplank and they're certainly one of the last couples to wander off from the quayside, arm in arm. While he does look slightly different – perhaps a little thinner – it's clear that he's actually in quite good shape. Pam is overjoyed.

"I told you I'd be back, and I also said that I couldn't promise you that it would be on a sunny day", he says, as they look at the rain bucketing down. "Also, just as I told you, I never did see a Jap – at least a live one".

This is only stretching the truth a little – he's certainly seen some live Japanese, although most of them were prisoners. He may have been fired at a few times by snipers that he couldn't see – it's often difficult to be sure about this.

"And I suppose you were also never ill", says Pam, trying hard to stem the flow of tears. "I suppose that stuff was all made up and the place was just like a holiday camp, but with no need to spend any money?"

"I'll tell you all about it sometime soon, while you tell me all about the various excitements round here, but we've got more important things to think about now – we have lots of people to meet up with and a fair amount of partying and other activities to catch up on! We also need to start thinking about cash – weddings, honeymoons, houses etc!"

Fig.12.4: Photo of George Marshall, taken in July 1946.

Len is discharged from the Army there and then (25th January), taking leave of the many members of his Company whom he now knows very well. Payments are made to troops being demobilized, although these are not huge amounts. None of them now have much cash in their pockets and they're surprised at how prices seem to have risen since they left, although a lot of food and other goods are still rationed or just not available.

For Pam and Len, and for many other reunited couples and families across the UK and USA, the focus is now on future domestic planning. However, momentous events, and decision-making that will have lasting and fundamental consequences, are in motion in various parts of the world. One of these relates to the rebuilding of Europe. Most European countries, both victors and defeated, are on their knees – economically, industrially and in terms of infrastructure. Enormous investment is needed and the global financial system is still in place. Cash has to be found and redistributed and the only country that has plenty of it, and has suffered virtually no internal damage, is America. Among the people who recognize this is George Marshall, who has been US Army Chief of Staff throughout the war. Marshall is one of the (relatively) unsung heroes of the war. He has been behind many of the important strategies and decisions, deeply impressing, not only Roosevelt and Truman, but also Churchill and Stalin. He has always been an extremely safe pair of hands – too valuable to be spared for commanding armies in the field. He's also prominent now in planning for the peace. He's convinced that all of the countries in Europe need to be given urgent assistance in rebuilding and restructuring, including those of the Axis forces. His name is attached to the "Marshall Plan" for this. He subsequently moves smoothly into the peacetime administrative system, becoming Secretary of State in 1947 and Defense Secretary in 1950.

Simplifying somewhat, and blending the Marshall plan with one or two others, about $30B is transferred over the 8-year period immediately after the war, followed by about $8B annually over the next 10 years. This should be seen in the context of a US GDP of about $260B shortly after the war. These sums are part loan and part gift. In fact, the lion's share goes to the UK, although sizeable sums also go to Germany, Italy and Austria, as well as France. It has to be recognized that all of this is in the long-term economic interests of the USA, both because these are partly loans and because rapid recovery of European economies will create further demand for American goods and services. Furthermore, as tensions between the Russians and Americans continues to ramp up, and the "Cold War" gets under way, this financial aid is seen as a way of guiding countries away from Soviet influence. Nevertheless, this is an enlightened policy, in stark contrast to the punitive aims of most of the victors after the Great War. It will be pointed out later that the UK economy and industrial capacity recovers more slowly after the war than Germany's, despite the lower levels of aid that the Germans received, leading some economic "hawks" to suggest that it might have been healthier in the long term to have let market forces control the recovery. However, there's no real doubt that this aid will turn out to be crucial in assisting the people of Europe to recover relatively quickly from the ravages of war (although conditions in Germany certainly remain extremely hard for several years).

Both Britain and America also focus on the Far East, now that the Japanese have surrendered and been expelled from all of the occupied territories. American interest is largely oriented towards China. Their support for Chiang throughout the war doesn't pay dividends. The communists take over China, with Chiang's "Nationalists" being forced to retreat to the island of Formosa, which becomes Taiwan. American attempts to "defeat" communism in the Far East is destined to cause decades of conflict and frustration.

Britain's concern, however, is mainly with India and the other colonies. Things are coming to a head in India. The British have effectively promised them independence and it's becoming clear that this promise will have to be kept. The role of Mahatma Gandhi has been critical. Now aged 76, he has been advocating non-violent resistance to British rule for many years. This has been increasingly successful, and a valuable counter-point to many Indians concluding that only violent overthrow is likely to be effective - which almost came to pass during the war when the Indian National Army sided with the Japanese.

There are also religious complications, with friction building up between Hindus, Moslems and Sikhs. Gandhi is, however, a unifying force, with a huge personal standing, particularly among poorer people, and a consistent message that violence is no solution. The British are naturally in favour of this, but many are still determined to hang on to "The

Jewel in the Crown". Churchill, in particular, has hated Gandhi for many years, describing him as "...a seditious Middle Temple Lawyer, posing as a fakir of a type well known in the East." However, the views and stances of Churchill are slowly passing into history. It's now clear, not only that this type of colonialism is no longer defensible, but that the internal demand for change in India cannot continue to be suppressed. The objective of the British now is to orchestrate the transition to independence smoothly and efficiently. Sadly, they don't do well in this final duty to the sub-continent.

While Churchill might have tried to hang on as long as possible, which would almost certainly have ended in armed insurrection, Atlee has always taken an interest in India and is strongly in favour of its independence. However, there is a lot of complexity, with the rising tension between religious groups becoming a prime concern. The Hindus are represented by Jawaharlal Nehru, while the Muslim leader is Muhammad Ali Jinnah – who is increasingly calling for a separate Muslim state to be formed. A small Cabinet Mission is sent out, arriving in New Delhi on 24th March 1946. They report that it would be best for the unity of the country to be preserved. This has the support of the Viceroy (Archibald Wavell), Nehru (and his mentor, Gandhi) and Attlee. However, it soon starts to become clear that the Muslims will not accept this and attempts to set up an interim government lead to voting by the electorate entirely along religious lines and a complete lack of cooperation from the Muslim members of this government. Levels of violence between religious groups in various parts of the country start to rise. The British government loses confidence in Wavell and in February 1947 he is replaced as Viceroy by Louis Mountbatten, now elevated to Lord Mountbatten of Burma.

Fig.12.5: Mahatma Gandhi (right) and Jawaharlal Nehru at an All-India Congress meeting in Bombay, on 6th July 1946.

The British government now indicates that transfer of power should be completed by July 1948. Mountbatten moves to New Delhi to oversee this operation.

To say that Mountbatten doesn't have a deep understanding of India and its culture is something of an understatement. His main skills have always been those of a social climber within the British Establishment. He arrives in Delhi with his wife, and they have always been a somewhat flamboyant and irresponsible couple. Edwina's penchant for extra-marital affairs is notorious and she decides to have one with Nehru, which becomes

Fig.12.6: Lord and Lady Mountbatten, with Mahatma Gandhi, in 1947.

very widely known. This is hardly helpful and stokes the resentment of Jinnah and the Muslims. Mountbatten's main reaction is that the whole place is starting to look like a powder-keg and it would be best if the complete British Establishment, including himself, were to get out as soon as possible.

He therefore presides over a very hasty drawing up of plans for a partitioning of the country into two states – one Muslim and the other Hindu, with one or two tweaks to take account of the interests of the Sikhs – and announces on 3rd June 1947 that this operation will be carried out on 15th August – ie just over two months later. The idea that such a momentous undertaking can be planned and implemented over this timescale is shocking. However, the British government feels that it has to go along with the plan. The job required a statesman, an expert diplomat and a brilliant administrator, but it has been given to a dilettante. It's certainly possible that he was duped into taking on this onerous task. In any event, while it was always going to be a very difficult operation, it degenerates into a disaster of almost unprecedented proportions. Mountbatten himself has a few distractions at the time, such as orchestrating the marriage of his nephew, Prince Philip, to Princess Elizabeth (in November 1947) – thus cementing his relations with the British Royal Family for the foreseeable future.

India at this point comprises about 280 million Hindus, 30 million Muslims and 6 million Sikhs (plus about 7 million Christians). The main cultural clash is between Hindus and Muslims. The Muslim state of Pakistan is to be created in two parts, one East and one West, over 1,000 miles apart. People finding themselves in a state having the "wrong" religion are just expected to somehow migrate. No assistance of any kind is provided. As it turns out, not migrating is likely to result in their death. Over the following couple of years, about 7 million Muslims move into one of the Pakistans and a similar number of Hindus move out of them. Large scale, systematic assassinations become endemic, with reports of atrocities by one side leading to reprisals by the other in an escalating cycle of appalling proportions. Many of the migrations are on foot and large groups of people moving slowly along roads with their possessions are systematically ambushed and slaughtered by the other side. Similar attacks are even made on (ludicrously overcrowded) trains, which arrive at their destinations with blood still dripping out of the carriages.

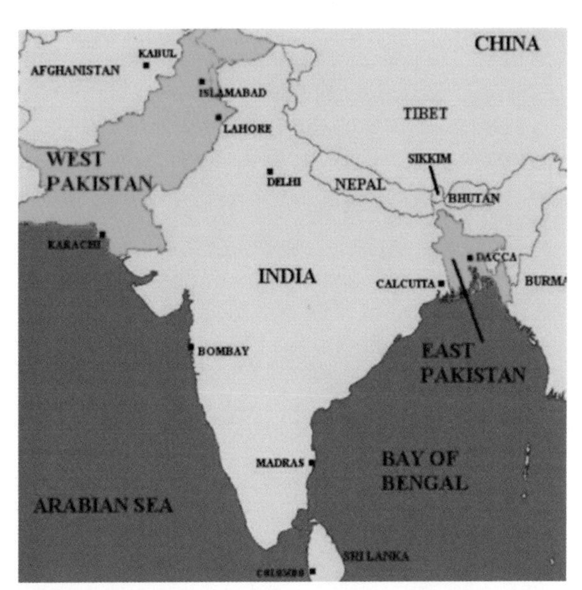

Fig.12.7: Map showing the partition of India in 1947.

Estimates of the number killed are difficult to make, but mostly lie between one and two million – more than the combined total of Britons and Americans killed throughout the war. The mistrust and hatred engendered will persist for generations. The British, meanwhile, move out very quickly, and with no interference. Mountbatten's prior assurances that they would stay and oversee the migrations, and the setting up of new civil structures, turn out to be entirely hollow. There is no independent policing of the operation or attempts to control the criminality. It is the most blatant abdication of responsibility, and a cause for lasting shame. In January 1948, Mahatma Gandhi is assassinated (by a Hindu nationalist). Gandhi had, of course, been deeply saddened by the events of the preceding 6 months, but he continued to plead for non-violence. His death does at least bring the country together for a period of mourning, but this is all too brief and there is little reconciliation.

There are many ironies here. For example, men such as Len, and indeed his brother William (who was present at his birth, but left home soon after, never to return), were sent out to the East to fight for an Empire that was in any event about to implode. That the main colony would then be hastily abandoned, leaving chaos for many millions of indigenous peoples previously under British "care", only throws this into sharper relief. In reality, for most of these volunteer or conscripted British soldiers who return alive, it probably doesn't figure so prominently in their thoughts at present. Their focus is on the future, with hopes that everyone can now move on to something better. The country to which they're returning has already changed substantially – certainly in terms of attitudes towards various issues, although physically there is now much that needs to be repaired and rebuilt. The country will be a very different place in the years to come. Something similar could also be said about most other countries around the world. The other British colonies will virtually all acquire independence over the next few decades. These transfers of power are mostly carried out fairly smoothly, and with a reasonable level of dignity, although there are certainly problems with some of the African ones. One of the most important achievements of the new Queen, who is to accede in 1952, will be to foster some sort of bonding, and various cultural links, between the UK and the countries that were formerly part of the British Empire, with the idea of a "Commonwealth" emerging as a positive concept. Her sound instincts and cultural skills will lead to a rare example of a modern monarch making a valuable political contribution.

The rebuilding in the UK does start quickly, with Atlee and his team rapidly setting the wheels in motion in a number of areas – railways, power generation, water supplies, social and health services, state pensions, mining etc. He may have chosen the wrong man to oversee the end of the British Raj, but here in the UK a lot of talented, competent and visionary people are becoming available and being drawn into national planning. Several of the incoming Labour government played valuable roles in the War Cabinet, while the new generation of MPs includes many whose experiences during the war have given them valuable insights into how the country must now change. Enormous effort is now going into the financial and organizational details of how to implement the various new administrative structures being created. There are also various issues to resolve concerning technological development – the burgeoning aerospace industry, the completely new concept of nuclear power generation, the explosion in car ownership and many other areas. The role of government in all such activities is undergoing a fundamental rethink.

Fig.12.8: Sir Archibald Sinclair on the footplate of the "Battle of Britain" class Bulleid Pacific locomotive named after him, during the naming ceremony at Waterloo station on 24th Feb. 1947.

Of course, old habits die hard. There are those who see the hard-earned victory as a vindication of the old system, allowing the *status quo ante* to be quickly re-established. They're in a minority, but they retain influence. Also, to be fair, it is often difficult to view the present day in an historical context. Britain has been an industrially and economically dominant nation for so long that it seems difficult to believe that this won't necessarily continue. The railways offer an illustration. They were developed in

Britain and, for well over a century, British designers and manufacturers have been at the forefront, exporting the technology all over the world. The railways in Britain are now on their knees, and the "Big Four" private companies were in any event starting to lose money before the war, largely due to the competition from road traffic. The nationalization, implemented at the start of 1948, is certainly necessary – railways are in any event a good example of a resource that should be centrally coordinated and provided as a national service. There is recognition of this, and also a willingness to invest. However, while countries such as Germany, France and Japan push ahead with new technologies, particularly concerning Diesel locomotives and electrification, the emphasis in Britain remains on steam, with (excellent) new steam locomotives being designed and built for another dozen years. It's perhaps part of an (attractive) British leaning towards nostalgia, and it will result in Britain at least becoming world-leading in the (not insignificant) industry of "heritage railways", but pioneering (and profiting) in railway technology now starts to be dominated by other countries.

12.2 Moving on – Weddings, Homes and Jobs

By the time that Len returns, in late January 1946, various plans are already being implemented in the Fullbrook household. Jum had never left the country and he and Annie have already fixed their wedding date for May. The Royal Hospital is still partly in ruins, but the remaining buildings are quite spacious and, compared with much of London, there is still a fair amount of good accommodation available. The RHC authorities are very understanding and Annie has already been able to move in – her parents are living in temporary accommodation in Stepney, where conditions are still very bad. Harry and Grace have stayed throughout the war in his house in Hampton, which has come through it more or less unscathed.

Fig.12.9: RHC Bowls team in 1946. Ralph is 4th from the left in the back row.

Fig.12.10: Wedding of Jum and Annie, on Saturday 11th May 1946. Pam and Len, and also Ralph and Bertha, are to the left of the couple. The identities of most of the others are unknown.

The wedding of Jum and Annie goes ahead on 11th May 1946, in St. Luke's Church, Chelsea. Ralph and Bertha, and also Pam and Len, are centrally involved in the planning. Len is Jum's Best Man. It's a relatively small, but very happy, event. The clean-up of the city has barely begun, so there is much war damage still evident in the streets. Rationing of many things is still in place. Nevertheless, the Reception, held at the RHC, is lavish by the standards of these austere times, and greatly enjoyed.

Len and Pam are already clear that they too want to get married as soon as possible. Of course, a key issue for the many couples in this situation is where they will then live. Fortunately, it's agreed that adjoining sets of rooms will be made available within the RHC for all three couples – ie for both Jum and Pam, and their partners, as well as Ralph and Bertha. This is very generous, but many authorities are being encouraged to do all they can to help with what is now becoming a full-blown housing crisis in London. Ralph's prominent position in the Hospital helps with this, but so does the fact that Len and Jum have been in the Army, plus the point that both Pam and Annie stayed in London throughout the war. The housing crisis is being caused, not only by so much property having been damaged or destroyed by the bombing, but also because many of the 2 million or so people who left the city early in the war now want to return. In many cases, these are relatively affluent people who owned houses in London, but also had relatives or other property to which they could move. Their London properties were in most cases requisitioned by the government – some to be used for official purposes, but others to be made available – often at very low rent - to people who were determined, or obliged, to remain in the city. The authorities are reluctant to evict them too quickly.

Fig.12.11: Wedding of Pam and Len on Saturday 14th September 1946. Ralph and Bertha are to the right of the couple, Jum and Annie are behind them and Lena and Don are to their left. Most of the others are unknown, although the two on the far right may be there to ensure that there are no breaches of the Official Secrets Act.

Pam and Len fix their date for 14th September – at the same church as was used by Jum and Annie. One of the guests is to be Lena. She has been keen to get back to the UK for several years, having decided a little while ago that she didn't want to make her life in Canada, but it has just been impossible throughout the war years. However, she manages this early in 1946 and she meets up with Len shortly after he gets back in the country. She's now aged almost 40, but she's still an attractive woman. (In fact, she is to meet Andrew Melville shortly, and they are to get married in two years time.) She hasn't seen Len for 20 years, although they have corresponded regularly throughout this period – and they continue to do this for many more years. Len does manage to visit his other siblings, now somewhat scattered around London and the surrounding areas, but they're unable to make the wedding.

The day itself is rather wet and windy, but everything goes off well. There is a good turnout, although in these straitened times not everyone they'd like to be there is able to make it (and the cost has to be kept within limits). Only a few of Pam's many friends from the Treasury are able to come (4 of them as bridesmaids), although a number of the others club together to send her a nice gift – and a card, which turns out to be one of the few surviving documents in the "family archives" that provides any information about them. On Len's side, a lot are missing. The ones uppermost in his thoughts include Douglas and his parents. There's nobody here from Bowermadden. It's such a long way and travel is still very difficult. Perhaps Dugald MacEchern might have tried to come, but he is now very ill and in fact he dies the following month, aged 79. Harry is also unable to make it, but Len is so pleased that Lena is here, and also Don Horne, who has kept in touch since his time at Brumfit's before the war.

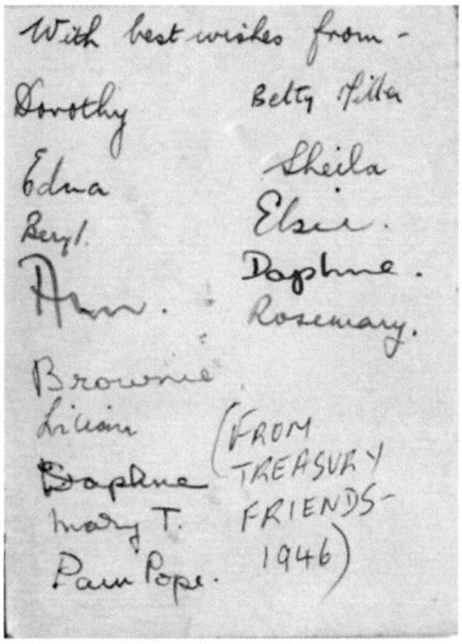
With best wishes from -
Dorothy Betty Pilla
Edna Sheila
Beryl. Elsie.
Ann. Daphne.
Rosemary.
Brownie
Lilian (FROM
Daphne TREASURY
Mary T. FRIENDS-
Pam Pope. 1946)

Fig.12.12: Wedding card note from Treasury friends of Pam. Details of their identities are unknown.

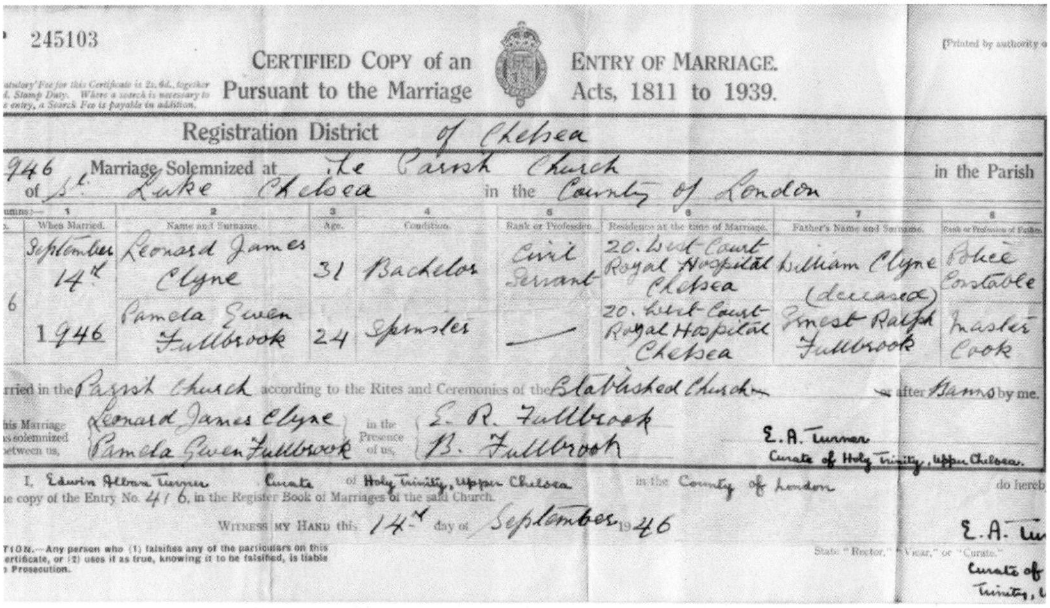
245103

CERTIFIED COPY of an ENTRY OF MARRIAGE.
Pursuant to the Marriage Acts, 1811 to 1939.

Registration District of Chelsea

1946 Marriage Solemnized at The Parish Church in the Parish of St. Luke Chelsea in the County of London

No.	When Married.	Name and Surname.	Age.	Condition.	Rank or Profession.	Residence at the time of Marriage.	Father's Name and Surname.	Rank or Profession of Father.
6	September 14th 1946	Leonard James Clyne	31	Bachelor	Civil Servant	20. West Court Royal Hospital Chelsea	William Clyne (deceased)	Police Constable
		Pamela Gwen Fullbrook	24	Spinster	—	20. West Court Royal Hospital Chelsea	Ernest Ralph Fullbrook	Master Cook

Married in the Parish Church according to the Rites and Ceremonies of the Established Church after Banns by me.

This Marriage was solemnized between us, Leonard James Clyne, Pamela Gwen Fullbrook; in the Presence of us, E. R. Fullbrook, B. Fullbrook. E.A. Turner, Curate of Holy Trinity, Upper Chelsea.

I, Edwin Alban Turner, Curate of Holy Trinity, Upper Chelsea in the County of London do hereby certify that this is a true copy of the Entry No. 416, in the Register Book of Marriages of the said Church.

WITNESS MY HAND this 14th day of September 1946. E.A. Turner, Curate of Holy Trinity, U…

Fig.12.13: Marriage certificate of Len Clyne and Pam Fullbrook.

Len and Pam do manage to fit in a honeymoon – in the Channel Islands. They take the train from Waterloo to Weymouth, from where there are now once again regular sailings to St. Helier, in Jersey. The ferry itself, the "St.Helier", has acquired something of a history. She was one of the "stars" of Dunkirk – making 7 round trips and evacuating over 10,000 troops and 1,500 refugees (leading to the award of medals to the captain and officers). She also saw extensive service transporting prisoners of war to the Isle of Man and was then converted to an assault ship for the D-Day landings. The Channel Islands were only liberated in May 1945 and normal sailings have been taking place for less than a year. The atmosphere in the Islands is thus still a bit strange, although the islanders are certainly keen to get the tourist trade up and running again. In fact, the crossings experienced by

Pam and Len are very rough, with many of the passengers suffering rather badly from sea-sickness. Still, Jersey is an attractive place and this is a welcome return to the idea that normal life is now a possibility.

There's clearly an issue now regarding jobs, and making sure that they have some cash. With the end of the war, the arrangements in GOGGS start to change. Atlee is now based in 10 Downing Street, as normal, and his Chancellor, Hugh Dalton, occupies number 11. The Treasury starts to operate more conventionally and of course it is focused on the economic situation in the country, which is a state of ongoing crisis. Pam's bosses are keen for her to stay on, but there is a big turnover of secretarial staff, with many of these talented young women now opting to move on with their lives. Pam stays for the moment, but makes it clear that she expects to leave shortly – hopefully to start a family.

Fig.12.14: Photo of TSS St. Helier in Weymouth harbor on 13th July 1936.

Len, on the other hand, clearly needs to find a job – along with millions of other demobilized servicemen. He decides that he needs to move into a suitable profession and opts for teaching. The government is setting up schemes for training of teachers, and generally investing quite heavily in education. Also, people are now returning to London, including a number of evacuated children, and there will clearly need to be an expansion in the provision of schools. While London is certainly faced with many difficulties, Pam and Len decide that they want to stay after they're married. Len therefore joins a training scheme for teachers, which starts in October 1946. These are accelerated schemes, involving short stays in a number of schools. He does get paid during the training, although it's not very much. Still, the rent that they pay at the RHC is small, and Pam is still getting her salary at present, so their financial position is not too bad. The country as a whole, however, is very short of cash, as the Labour government struggles to set up various new systems and structures.

Fig.12.15: Pam and Len during their honeymoon in St.Helier.

If life is now slowly starting to get back to something approaching normality, that doesn't mean that most people in the UK are comfortable. In fact, the winter (1946-47) turns out to be the worst in living memory. Starting early in the New Year, it stays below freezing for very long periods, with huge snowdrifts building up and almost every aspect of life being disrupted. Cross-channel ferry services are suspended due to pack ice off the Belgian coast. Transport of coal to the power stations becomes difficult and many are forced to shut down. Electrical power to houses is cut, typically being available for less than 20 hours per day. Many houses are still in poor condition and just keeping warm becomes a major challenge for most people.

Disillusionment with the government starts to build up and these problems get associated in people's minds with the concept of nationalization, and also with a reluctance to challenge the miners – part of the scenario is that domestic production of coal is well below predicted levels. Stockpiles of coal become frozen solid and cannot be moved. Many activities are stopped, raising unemployment levels, and food rations are cut to levels lower than those during the war. The worst of the weather only lasts for about 2 months, but there is a sense of crisis. In fact, the severe weather, and the associated deprivations, are even worse in some countries in Europe - including Germany, but this does little to reduce the levels of dissatisfaction in the UK.

Fig.12.16: A London bus in a snowdrift in February 1947.

Meanwhile, Len has started on his teacher training scheme. These are accelerated courses, of a year's duration, to be followed by an appointment in a school - with a 2-year probationary period. These courses have largely been set up as a consequence of the Education Act of 1944 (authored by Rab Butler), which in turn was largely based on the McNair report published in May 1944. It was clear by that point that, not only was a crisis looming in terms of educational resources and the effects of the war, but also the whole system was in any event in serious need of overhaul. The proposals are for raising the school leaving age to 15, reducing class sizes, expanding nursery education and making the teacher training system more formal and efficient. It is evident that a huge increase is required in the number of qualified teachers. A scheme was initiated in June 1945, open to all men and women who had served at least a year in HM Forces, or in a war industry. By December of that year, 5,000 applications were coming in every month.

A large number of college places were clearly required and, by the time that Len starts his course (late in 1946), over 50 new Colleges have been opened – based in various types of building – and about 13,000 people are being trained in them. The vast majority of people on these courses are returning from military service and in fact most of them are men who have recently been demobilized as soldiers. Ages range from 20 to 50 and backgrounds are also very disparate. Despite the "emergency" nature of the system, it produces a large number of very good teachers. Many of them start work in newly-created "secondary modern" schools. There are now no fees to be paid for state-funded education. It's a major change and in general the new system has the support of all of the political parties, and of the general public.

Len is paid a termly grant of about £40 during this year of training – not a lot, but certainly better than nothing. This jumps up to about £400 pa once he actually starts teaching, in September 1947. His first appointment is at Ackmar Road School, next to Eel Brook Common. This is just a couple of miles from the Royal Hospital at Chelsea – a pleasant daily walk, partly along the Thames Embankment. Len settles in well there, teaching children from the area in the 11-15 age range. The intake covers various backgrounds, ranging from the affluent and fashionable along the Chelsea riverfront to the much more deprived from parts of Fulham and World's End. Len teaches a range of subjects, but specializes in history and physical education. The members of staff are also a rather eclectic mix, although several of them are recently demobilized soldiers. Parent-staff evenings provide lively discussions and there is a general feeling that things are moving forward.

There is certainly progress in the UK as the 1940's draw to a close. Most of the nationalization and restructuring is complete by around 1948, with the National Health Service operational and a range of social welfare arrangements set up. Centralization of services such as electricity generation, water supply and railways starts to create various benefits. Generally speaking, people are appreciative of these changes, but the country is hamstrung by shortage of money. Moreover, rationing is still in place and National Service is introduced in 1947 – all able-bodied men between the ages of 18 and 30 are required to serve in the forces for 18 months, raised to 2 years in 1950, during the Korean War. Those conscripted in this way often end up on garrison duty in various places around the world – both in Empire outposts and as occupying forces in Germany and Japan. It does rather disrupt young men attempting to move on in their careers and in general it's not popular – most people have had enough of wars and deprivation.

The government gets the blame for many of these problems. At the general election held in February 1950, there is a big swing away from Labour and back towards the Conservatives. Labour hold on, but their majority drops from about 150 to just 5. Much of the swing is probably attributable to the Tories promising to scrap rationing, which is very unpopular. Labour finds it difficult to govern with such a small majority and they call a snap election just 20 months later, in October 1951. However, this backfires badly. While Labour still polls more votes overall than the Tories, they actually lose about 20 seats to them. This leaves the Tories with a small, but workable, majority of 17, so they take power, with Churchill again becoming Prime Minister (at the age of 77). Four months later, King George VI dies, so that Elizabeth becomes Queen at the age of 25.

12.3 New Life

Both Annie and Pam do become pregnant fairly soon after their weddings. Lindsay Leonard is born to Pam in November 1947, with the birth being a little prolonged. She is, however, in a good place for this, since he is born in St.George's Hospital, at Hyde Park Corner. (The building is later to become the Lanesborough Hotel, with the Hospital being transferred in 1980 to a larger site in Tooting.) That the birth is in such a place is a reflection both of the strong move away from home births over the past couple of decades and the effect of state provision of health services – since a Hospital such as this would previously have been used mainly by the affluent.

There are therefore two growing families in the rooms at the RHC, in addition to Ralph and Bertha. It's a happy arrangement, and the grounds are excellent for young children. However, it obviously can't continue for very long. Both Len and Jum do now have jobs and, while Pam and Annie have stopped working, the idea of finding separate places for each family is starting to look financially viable. There is, however, still a housing problem in London, with the rebuilding going slowly and a number of people wanting to return to the city. After a couple more years, Len and Pam move out into No. 34, Cheyne Place. While it's a relatively small house, it's in an affluent part of Chelsea, near to the river. However, some assistance with rents is being provided by the local authority, particularly to people who stayed in London and/or served in the armed forces during the

Fig.12.17: Bill Clyne, aged about 4 months.

war, so they are able to afford it. On the other hand, this is a temporary arrangement and they'll probably have to move on from there fairly soon.

Pam and Len have a second child in March 1952, also born in St.George's. This is Trevor William, who'll be known as Bill throughout his life. Two children is becoming more or less the norm – certainly child mortality rates have dropped dramatically over the past half century and family planning is now much more widespread. On the other hand, there has been a huge spike in births since the war - commonly known as the "Baby Boom", as couples finally have the stability and confidence to start families. In any event, Pam and Len feel that their family is now complete. For couples like them, there is a decision to be made about whether to remain in London. The capital has many attractions and in fact it could be argued that the UK has become too London-centric, to the detriment of other parts of the country. Furthermore, its rate of recovery from the war is slow.

Fig.12.18: Piccadily Circus (in the middle of the day) in December 1952.

One of its problems has always been with high levels of pollution, partly caused by the presence of many industrial operations and now made worse by the growing motor traffic. Also, most domestic heating is still by coal. The idea of "pea-souper" fogs in the London area extends back at least a century, but if anything it's getting worse. In December 1952, a combination of unusual weather conditions and heavy emissions from coal fires and industrial activities creates dense smog that lasts for weeks. It's so serious that it's considered to be the cause of thousands of premature deaths. It's the kind of thing that persuades many Londoners, particularly those bringing up young families, that moving to somewhere with cleaner air and open countryside nearby might be a good idea. While Jum and Annie decide to stay, Len and Pam start to look elsewhere and they do move away from London a year or two later.

Fig.12.19: Len and Bill Clyne on Bognor beach, in summer 1953.

12.4 A Footballing Legacy

One of the pupils taught by Len at Ackmar Road School was a certain Ron Springett, who was born in 1935. He was evacuated during the war, but returned in 1945 and attended the school between then and 1950. Ron was a keen footballer from an early age and, as the member of staff in charge of games, Len spotted his talent and encouraged him in this direction. Although he was never tall, only reaching 5' 10" at maturity, Ron's preferred position was in goal. He more than compensated for his lack of height via remarkable levels of agility, timing and fearlessness.

He was to become England's first choice goalkeeper between 1959 and 1964, playing over 30 times for his country. He was in the 1966 World Cup squad, but he never played in the finals, being the understudy to Gordon Banks by that point. Regulations at the time precluded players in his situation, which included Jimmy Greaves, from receiving World

Cup winner's medals, but these were finally awarded in 2009, presented by the Prime Minister (Gordon Brown).

Fig.12.20: The England football squad of 1966. Ron Springett is in the centre of the back row.

Ron joined Queen's Park Rangers in 1953 and moved in 1958 to Sheffield Wednesday, where he stayed for 9 years, playing for them almost 400 times. Wednesday was consistently one of the best teams in the country during the early to mid-1960's. Ron kept in touch with Len during much of this period. Len had been a Sunderland supporter since the 1930's, having seen them win the FA Cup in 1937. However, his younger son had been attracted by Wednesday's style of play from an early age and this allegiance was cemented (aged 9) when Ron heard this and sent him (unsolicited) a set of autographs of the Wednesday team on headed notepaper. This was typical of Ron, who has always had the reputation of being a kind and modest man, despite his fame.

SHEFFIELD WEDNESDAY
FOOTBALL CLUB LIMITED
Hillsborough
SHEFFIELD-6

Fig.12.21: Autographs of the Wednesday team of 1961. Ron Springett's is at about 1 o'clock. Others of Wednesday stalwarts who were household names at the time include those of Peter Swan, Colin Dobson, Johnny Fantham, Bobby Craig and Gerry Young.

Of course, genuine football allegiances are always forged for a lifetime. As it happens, Wednesday fans tend to be particularly loyal. This is just as well, since, while Wednesday have always had a reputation for playing attractive football, have one of the great grounds in the country and have a tradition that stretches back to the foundation of the Football League, the vicissitudes in their fortunes over the past 60 years have been rather trying for their supporters. In 2022, Wednesday met Sunderland in the play-offs for promotion to the second tier. Like two heavyweights who've seen better days, they slugged it out in a two-leg cliff-hanger in front of huge capacity crowds. Sunderland prevailed and perhaps they'll now move on to recapture some past glories. Perhaps Wednesday will follow them.

That's football and one never quite knows what's around the corner. Rather appropriately, Ron's own personal allegiance was always to QPR. In fact, exceptionally, he continued to live in London and train with QPR throughout his period with Wednesday. He returned to QPR in 1967 and completed his career there. Many people at both clubs still have very fond memories of him.

12.5 Postscript

While both Len and his father had spent their formative years in the Far North, followed by an extended period in London that involved coping with the rigours of war, the final parts of their lives turned out to be very different. Len returned to the Celtic fringes, although at the other end of the country. In 1954, he relocated to a small town by the sea in Cornwall, taking up another job as a teacher in the local school and moving the family into a pleasant house with a view over a beautiful estuary. Len and Pam lived out the remaining 50 years of their lives in that house, both of them having many friends and acquaintances in the town – a lot of them ex-pupils of Len's. Pam taught shorthand and typing in a College of Further Education. It can readily be argued that they deserved a period of peace and contentment. That it came to them, and also to many others (in the UK and abroad) who lived through that tumultuous period of history, is surely a happy ending – although of course it's not an ending, because life goes on. Lessons have been learned, and history lessons are among those that must never be forgotten.

Appendix: Timelines

Month	Family Events	External Events
Feb. 1869	23rd: Birth of William Clyne, to George & Williamina, Latheron, Caithness	
Mar. 1869		4th: Ulysses Grant (47) becomes US President
Apr. 1870		22nd: Birth of Vladimir Lenin, Ulyanovsk
July 1870		19th: Start of Franco-Prussian war
Jan. 1871		18th: Creation of the nation state of Germany
May 1871		10th: End of Franco-Prussian war
Feb. 1874		20th: Benjamin Disraeli (70) becomes UK PM
Apr. 1874	12th: Birth of Alice Pollard, to Thomas & Frances, Powick, Worcestershire	
Nov. 1874		30th: Birth of Winston Churchill, Blenheim Palace
Mar. 1876	17th: Birth of Francis William Clyne, to Lachlan & Isabella, Pultneytown, Caithness	
Mar. 1877		4th: Rutherford Hayes (55) becomes US President
Dec. 1878		18th: Birth of Joseph Stalin, Gori, Georgia
Jan. 1879		Incandescent electric light first demonstrated (by Thomas Edison)
Apr. 1880		23rd: William Gladstone (71) becomes UK PM
Sept. 1880	22nd: Birth of Herbert Ernest Pollard, to Thomas & Frances, Powick, Worcestershire	
Mar. 1881		4th: James Garfield (50) becomes US President
Sept. 1881		19th: Chester Arthur (52) becomes US President
Mar. 1885		4th: Grover Cleveland (48) becomes US President
June 1885	1st: William Clyne (16) starts at Singer Factory in Glasgow	23rd: Marquess of Salisbury (55) becomes UK PM
Jan. 1886		29th: Carl Benz patent, leading to first automobiles
Feb. 1886		1st: Gladstone (77) becomes UK PM
July 1886		25th: Salisbury (56) becomes UK PM
Mar. 1889		4th: Benjamin Harrison (54) becomes US President
Apr. 1889		20th: Birth of Adolf Hitler, Braunau (Austria)
May 1889		Opening of first central electric power station (at Deptford)
June 1889		12th: Armagh rail disaster
Oct. 1889	22nd: William Clyne (20) interviewed for Metropolitan Police	
Nov. 1889	11th: Willian Clyne (20) starts work for Metropolitan Police	
Dec. 1889	13th: Birth of Ernest Ralph Fullbrook (RALPH), Denmark Street, Wokingham	
Mar. 1892	6th: Birth of Bertha Burt, 10 Brooklyn Terrace, Eastbourne	
Aug. 1892		15th: Gladstone (83) becomes UK PM
Mar. 1893		4th: Grover Cleveland (56) becomes US President
Mar. 1894		5th: Earl of Rosebery (49) becomes UK PM
Jan. 1895		5th: Lt.-Col Alfred Dreyfus (35), French Army, convicted of treason
June 1895		25th: Salisbury (65) becomes UK PM
Feb. 1896	8th: Marriage of William Clyne (26) & Alice Pollard (21), Woolwich	
May 1896	3rd: Birth of William Thomas Clyne (WILLIAM), to William & Alice, 59 King Street, Woolwich	
Mar. 1897		4th: William McKinley (54) becomes US President
June 1897	1st: Birth of Herbert George Clyne (HERBERT), to William & Alice, 3 Brewer Place, Woolwich	
Nov. 1898	9th: Birth of Francis Cecil Clyne (FRANK), to William & Alice, 3 Brewer Place, Woolwich	
Mar. 1899		27th: First radio signal transmission across the Channel (by Guglielmo Marconi)
Oct. 1899		11th: Start of Boer War, South Africa

Mar. 1900	13th: Birth of Alice Minnie Clyne, to William & Alice, 56 Eglinton Road, Plumstead	
Jan. 1901		22nd: Death of Queen Victoria (81), at IoW: Accession of King Edward VII (59)
Sept. 1901		14th: Theodore Roosevelt (43) becomes US President
Jan. 1902	16th: Birth of Stanley Clyne (STAN), to William & Alice, 19 Stanmore Road, Erith	
May 1902		31st: End of Boer War, South Africa
July 1902		12th: Arthur Balfour (54) becomes UK PM
Jan. 1903	21st: Death of Alice Minnie Clyne (34 months), Erith (typhoid)	
Feb. 1904		8th: Start of Russo-Japanese war, Manchuria
Aug. 1904	15th: Birth of Willimina Maud Clyne (MINA), to William & Alice, 95 High Street, Erith	
Sep. 1905		5th: End of Russo-Japanese war, Manchuria
Nov. 1905	27th: Birth of Harry Clyne (HARRY), to William & Alice, 95 High Street, Erith	
Dec. 1905		5th: Henry Campbell-Bannerman (49) becomes UK PM
Aug. 1907	27th: Birth of Alice Lena Clyne (LENA), to William & Alice, 95 High Street, Erith	
Apr. 1908		8th: Herbert Asquith (56) becomes UK PM
Mar. 1909		4th: William Howard Taft (52) becomes US President
Mar. 1910	31st: Birth of Alec Norman Clyne (ALEC), to William & Alice, 20 Hearns Road, St. Pauls Cray	
May 1910		6th: Death of King Edward VII (68), at Buck. Palace: Accession of King George V (44)
Jan. 1911		3rd: Sidney Street siege, London
June 1911	22nd: Death of Alec Norman Clyne (15 months), 20 Hearns Road, St. Pauls Cray (typhoid)	
Apr. 1912		15th: Sinking of RMS Titanic, Atlantic Ocean
July 1912	29th: Birth of Walter Douglas Clyne (DOUGLAS), to William & Alice, 20 Hearns Road, St. Pauls Cray	
Mar. 1913		4th: Thomas Woodrow Wilson (57) becomes US President
June 1914		28th: Assassination of Archduke Franz Ferdinand, Sarajevo
Aug. 1914	26th: Birth of Leonard James Clyne (LEN), to William & Alice, 20 Hearns Road, St. Pauls Cray	4th: Britain declares war on Germany
Sept. 1914	8th: William Thomas Clyne joins Royal West Kent Regiment, 1/4th Battalion, at Tonbridge	
Oct. 1914	29th: William Thomas Clyne leaves Southampton on *RMT Grantully Castle*, for Bombay	
Nov. 1914		1st: Battle of Coronel, off the coast of Chile 5th: Britain declares war on Turkey 25th: War Council meeting - Dardanelles raised (by Churchill)
Dec. 1914	5th: William Thomas Clyne arrives at Jubbulpore, India	8th: Battle of the Falkland Islands, South Atlantic
Jan. 1915		28th: Decision at War Council on Fleet action in the Dardanelles
Feb. 1915		19th: Naval attack starts on outer forts at entrance to Dardanelles
Apr. 1915		25th: Gallipoli Landings (Cape Helles and Ari Burn)
May 1915		7th: Sinking of *HMS Lusitania* by German U-Boat 22nd: Quintinshill rail disaster 25th: Fisher and Churchill sacked
Aug. 1915		10th: 2/4th West Kents arrive at Suvla Bay
Sept. 1915		26th: Death of Kier Hardie (59), Glasgow
Nov. 1915		26th-27th: Blizzard at Gallipoli
Dec. 1915		13th: 2/4th West Kents leave Suvla Bay
Feb. 1916	7th: Death of William Thomas Clyne (19), Butaniyah, Mesopotamia	

Apr. 1916		24th: Easter Rising, Dublin 29th: Surrender of British Garrison at Kut
May 1916	31st: Death of Francis William Clyne (40), North Sea	31st: Battle of Jutland
July 1916		1st: Start of the Battle of the Somme
Dec. 1916		6th: David Lloyd George (49) becomes UK PM (Coalition War Cabinet)
Mar. 1917		15th: Abdication of Tsar Nicholas II (48)
Apr. 1917		4th: USA declares war on Germany
Nov. 1917	23rd: Death of Alice Clyne (43), Bexley Cottage Hospital	8th: Vladimir Lenin (47) becomes Leader of Soviet Russia
Jan. 1918	15th: Herbert George Clyne to Quetta with 1/4th RWK	
Feb. 1918	2nd: Death of William Clyne (48), 24 Green Walk, Crayford	
Mar. 1918	18th-19th: Journey of Clyne children from London to Bowermadden, on a *Jellicoe Express*	3rd: Signing of Brest-Litovsk treaty (Russian withdrawal from war) 21st: Start of the German Spring Offensive, Western Front
July 1918		17th: Murder of Tsar Nicholas II (and family), Yekaterinburg, Russia
Aug. 1918		8th: Start of the Allied Hundred Days Offensive, Western Front
Sept. 1918	30th: Marriage of Ernest Ralph Fullbrook (28) & Bertha Burt (26), Pokesdown (Bournemouth)	
Nov. 1918		9th: German surrender by the Chancellor, Prince Max von Baden 11th: Signing of Armistice, Compeigne
Jan. 1919		18th: Start of Paris Peace Conference
Feb. 1919		6th: Creation of Weimar Republic in Germany
Apr. 1919		13th: Massacre of Amritsar, Jallianwala Bagh, Punjab
May 1919		6th: Start of 3rd Anglo-Afghan War, NW Frontier 27th: Storming of Spin Baldak fortress, NW Frontier
June 1919		21st: Scuttling of the German Fleet, Scapa Flow 28th: Signing of Paris Peace Conference Treaty, Versailles
Aug. 1919	31st: Marriage of Francis Cecil Clyne (20) & Gladys Victoria Balchin (20), Crayford	8th: Signing of Armistice to end 3rd Anglo-Afghan War, NW Frontier 25th: Start of first commercial airline service (London to Paris)
Nov. 1919	24th: Herbert George Clyne arrives back in Tonbridge, for demobilization	
Jan. 1920		10th: Formation of the *League of Nations*
Feb. 1920	20th: Birth of Charles Ralph Fullbrook (JUM), to Ralph & Bertha, Millbank Barracks (RAMC), Westminster	
Mar. 1921		4th: Warren Harding (56) becomes US President
Nov. 1921	17th: Birth of Pamela Gwen Fullbrook (PAM), to Ralph & Bertha, Millbank Barracks (RAMC), Westminster	
Dec. 1921		6th: Signing of Anglo-Irish Treaty, London
Oct. 1922		23rd: Andrew Bonar Law (64) becomes UK PM 31st: Benito Mussolini (39) becomes Prime Minister of Italy
Nov. 1922		14th: First BBC radio broadcast
May 1923		22nd: Stanley Baldwin (56) becomes UK PM
Aug. 1923		2nd: Calvin Coolidge (51) becomes US President
Nov. 1923		8th: Munich Putsch (failed attempt by Nazi Party to overthrow Weimar Republic)
Oct. 1923		29th: Founding of Turkish Republic (by Kemal Atatürk)
Jan. 1924		21st: Death of Lenin (53): Stalin (45) now Head of Russia 22nd: Ramsey MacDonald (57) becomes UK PM (minority Labour government)
Feb. 1924		3rd: Death of Woodrow Wilson (67), Washington DC
Nov. 1924		4th: Baldwin (57) becomes UK PM
May 1925	30th: Death of Walter Douglas Clyne (13), Cliffs at Mid-Clyth	
Sept. 1925	24th: Alice Lena Clyne (18) leaves Liverpool on *SS Doric*, bound for Quebec City	
May 1926		4th: Start of General Strike in UK

July 1926	3rd: Marriage of Stanley Clyne (24) & Annie Caroline McCarthy (26), Wandsworth	
May 1927		20th: Charles Lindbergh (25) flies solo from New York to Paris
Oct. 1927		6th:"*The Jazz Singer*" released, with Al Jolson (ending silent films)
Mar. 1929		4th: Herbert Hoover (53) becomes US President
June 1929		5th: MacDonald (63) becomes UK PM
Oct. 1929		24th: Wall Street Crash (Black Thursday)
Aug. 1931		24th: First UK National Government, led by MacDonald (65)
Oct. 1931		27th: Second UK National Government formed, led by MacDonald (65) - who is then expelled from the Labour Party
Sept. 1932	Len Clyne (18) travels from Bowermadden to London	
Jan. 1933	11th: Birth of Betty Victoria Clyne (BETTY), to Frank & Gladys, 16 Hart Grove, Southall	30th: Adolf Hitler (43) becomes Chancellor of Germany
Mar. 1933		4th: Franklin D Roosevelt (51) becomes US President, initiating "*New Deal*" to alleviate unemployment & the situation of the poor
June 1934		30th: "*Night of the Long Knives*" - purge (many assasinations) of members of the Nazi Party out of favour with Hitler
Feb. 1935		26th: First demo of radar, by Robert Watson-Watt (at Daventry)
June 1935		17th: Baldwin (68) becomes UK PM
Oct. 1935		3rd: Invasion of Abyssinia (Ethiopia) by Italian forces
Nov. 1935		20th: Death of John Jellicoe (75), Kensington
Jan. 1936		20th: Death of King George V (70), at Sandringham: Accession of King Edward VIII (42)
Mar. 1936		7th: German militarization of the Rhineland 12th: Death of David Beattie (65), London
July 1936		17th: Start of Spanish Civil War
Aug. 1936		1st: Start of Berlin Olympics
Oct. 1936		4th: Battle of Cable Street (pro- and anti-fascist groups in London)
Nov. 1936		2nd: Launch of first regular television service (by the BBC)
Dec. 1936		10th: Abdication of King Edward VIII (43), at Fort Belvedere: Accession of King George VI (40)
Apr. 1937		26th: Bombing of Guernica, in Basque country, mostly by Luftwaffe
May 1937		28th: Neville Chamberlain (68) becomes UK PM
June 1937	22nd: Marriage of Harry Clyne (31) & Grace Marian Sibley (25), Hampton Hill	
July 1937		7th: Start of Second Sino-Japanese War
Jan. 1938		30th: Francisco Franco becomes Prime Minister of Spain
Mar. 1938		12th: "Anschluss" of Austria by Germany
Sept. 1938		30th: Signing of the Munich Agreement (regarding German annexation of the Sudetenland) by Britain, France and Germany
Oct. 1938		1st: Annexation of the Sudetenland by Germany
Nov. 1938		9th: "*Kristallnacht*" (violence against Jews in Germany)
Feb. 1939		25th: First Anderson shelters constructed
Apr. 1939		1st: End of the Spanish Civil War
Aug. 1939		23rd: Signing of Molotov-Ribbentrop (Stalin-Hitler) pact, in Moscow
Sept. 1939	30th: Marriage of Frank Lunn (48) & Williamina Maud Clyne (35), Aldershot	1st: Germany invades Poland 3rd: Britain and France declare war on Germany
Oct. 1939	20th: Len Clyne (25) joins CMP	
Nov. 1939		30th: Start of the "Winter War" (Russian invasion of Finland)
Dec. 1939		17th: Scuttling of the Graf Spee, Montevideo
Mar. 1940		13th: End of the "Winter War"
Apr. 1940		9th: Start of German invasion of Norway

May 1940		10th: Churchill (66) becomes UK PM (coalition government) 10th: Start of German invasion of France and the Low Countries 23rd: Oswald Mosley imprisoned 27th: Start of Dunkirk evacuation
June 1940		10th: Completion of German invasion of Norway 10th: Italy declares war on Britain and France 25th: Completion of German invasion of France & Low Countries
Sept. 1940		7th: Start of the Blitz (first German bombing raid on London) 9th: Start of attempted Italian invasion of Egypt, from Libya
Dec. 1940		8th: Start of British invasion of Libya 29th: Second Great Fire of London (bombing raid)
May 1941		11th: End of the Blitz
June 1941		22nd: Start of "*Operation Barbarossa*" (German attack on Russia)
Dec. 1941		7th: Attack by Japanese air force on Pearl Harbor, Hawaii 22nd: Start of (Anglo-American) Arcadia Conf., Washington, DC 28th: Formation of Burma Independence Army, Bangkok
Jan. 1942		7th: End of the Battle of Moscow - repulse of German forces
Feb. 1942		15th: Fall of Singapore (surrender of British forces) to Japanese
Mar. 1942		8th: Fall of Rangoon (abandoned by British/Indian forces) to Japan
Apr. 1942		18th: Doolittle raid (by USAF bombers) on Tokyo
May 1942		12th: Completion of the Japanese invasion of Burma
June 1942		4th-7th: Battle of Midway Atoll
Aug. 1942		7th: Start of Battle of Guadalcanal (Solomon Islands) 19th: Dieppe Raid
Nov. 1942		8th: Start of "*Operation Torch*" landings in Morocco and Algeria
Dec. 1942		2nd: Beveridge Report (founding of the "*Welfare State*" in Britain)
Jan. 1943		14th: Start of Casablanca conference, Morocco
Feb. 1943		2nd: End of the Battle of Stalingrad (Volgograd) 9th: End of Battle of Guadalcanal
May 1943		16th: End of Battle of North Africa
July 1943		5th: Start of the Battle of Kursk 9th: Start of Allied invasion of Sicily 25th: Coup in Italy, removing Mussolini from power
Aug. 1943		23rd: End of the Battle of Kursk
Sept. 1943		3rd: Start of Allied invasion of Italy 8th: Surrender of Italy
Nov. 1943		15th: Louis Mountbatten (43) becomes Supreme Commander of South East Asia Command (SEAC) 15th: Joseph Stilwell Deputy Supreme Commander of SEAC 22nd: Start of Cairo conference, Egypt 28th: Start of Tehran conference, Persia
May 1944	5th: Len Clyne (29) leaves UK for Burma	
June 1944		6th: Initiation of Allied invasion of mainland Europe (D-Day) 13th: First V1 Flying Bomb hits London
July 1944		20th: Assasination attempt (failed) on Hitler, Rastenburg
Aug 1944		23rd: Coup d'etat in Rumenia
Feb. 1945		13th: Firebombing of Dresden
Mar. 1945		27th: Last V2 Rocket Bomb hits London
Apr. 1945		12th: Death of Franklin D Roosevelt (63) 12th: Harry S Truman (61) becomes US President 28th: Death of Benito Mussolini (61), Como, Italy (firing squad) 30th: Death of Adolf Hitler (56), Berlin (suicide)

May 1945		8th: Victory in Europe (VE) day
July 1945		5th: General election in UK 26th: Clement Attlee (62) becomes UK PM
Aug. 1945		6th: Atomic bomb dropped on Hioshima 9th: Atomic bomb dropped on Nagasaki 15th: Victory over Japan (VJ) day
Oct. 1945		24th: Formation of the *United Nations*
Jan. 1946	25th: Len Clyne (31) arrives back in UK	
May 1946	11th: Marriage of Charles Ralph Fullbrook (26) & Annie Doreen Clark (24), St. Luke's Church, Chelsea	
Sept. 1946	14th: Marriage of Leonard James Clyne (32) & Pamela Gwen Fullbrook (24), St. Luke's Church, Chelsea	
Feb. 1947		21st: Mountbatten (47) appointed Viceroy of India
Aug. 1947		15th: End of British rule in India / formation of India & Pakistan as separate states
Nov. 1947	12th: Birth of Lindsay Leonard Clyne (LINDSAY), to Len & Pam, St. George's Hospital, London	20th: Marriage of Princess Elizabeth (21) & Philip Mountbatten (26), Westminster Abbey
Jan. 1948		1st: Nationalisation of UK industries (coal, electricity, railways etc) 30th: Assassination of Mahatma Gandhi (78), New Delhi
May 1948	24th: Marriage of Andrew Melville (34) & Alice Lena Clyne (41), Deptford	
July 1948		5th: Founding of British National Health Service (by Aneurin Bevan)
Nov. 1948		12th: Birth of Prince Charles, to Philip & Elizabeth, Buckingham Palace
Oct. 1951		25th: General election in UK 26th: Churchill (77) becomes UK PM
Feb. 1952		6th: Death of King George VI (56), at Sandringham: Accession of Queen Elizabeth II (25)
Mar. 1952	27th: Birth of Trevor William Clyne (BILL), to Len & Pam, St. George's Hospital, London	

Bibliography

This is not a scholarly or archival document, so it's not really appropriate to provide a set of citations in the text or a detailed list of the sources that have been consulted concerning particular points. However, I feel that I should at least acknowledge the books that have proved most useful in obtaining background information of various types, and also to make some comments about the many relevant on-line resources that are now available. Of course, these books constitute just a minute fraction of the many that are relevant. They're all still in print, in some cases reprinted by a new publisher, or at least are still obtainable on-line in some way – even if only as second-hand versions.

A suitable starting point, at least in terms of how I approached the daunting task of researching the history of my forebears in the Great War, is: "*The Queen's Own Royal West Kent Regiment - 1914-1919*", by Captain CT Atkinson, originally published by Simpkin, Marshall, Hamilton, Kent & Co Ltd (1924, ISBN 9781843426905). This is a highly detailed compendium of vast amounts of information, presented in a very readable and accessible way. Of course, it does relate only to the activities of the RWKR during the Great War, but even so it runs to over 600 pages. The amount of work that must have been involved is staggering. Doubtless there are similar works relating to various other regiments. Unsurprisingly, its tone is in tune with the ethos of the time, with war clearly being regarded as a terrible thing, but also an opportunity for glory. This is only slightly reined back in what might be regarded as its companion volume - "*The Queen's Own Royal West Kent Regiment - 1920-1950*", by Lieutenant-Colonel HD Chaplin, published by Naval and Military Press (2004, ISBN 9781845741501). This runs to over 500 pages and again clearly represents the culmination of a monumental amount of research and effort. Of course, it also is largely focused on activities during the war years, spread now over much of the globe. Pride in the regiment, which is entirely justified, permeates every page. Both books contain a wealth of detailed information about individual battles, skirmishes, troop movements etc, plus at least some of the relevant socio-political background.

In the context of scholarly, but relatively obscure and specialized, magnum opus publications, I should perhaps mention "*The Succession of Ministers in the Church of Scotland from the Reformation*", by Hew Scott, published by Oliver and Boyd (1928, ISBN 9789354033414). This runs to 800 pages. To say that it's readable is perhaps stretching things a bit, since it's basically just a list of Ministers, with brief CVs for all of them. However, it's still a stunningly impressive feat of scholarship, covering as it does, not only Scottish Presbyterian Parishes, but also the Missions established in all corners of the world, over a period extending to almost 400 years, and with extensive indexing and cross-referencing. Almost 4,000 Ministers are listed. The effort needed to compile and organize this amount of information, which of course all had to be done manually, is almost beyond imagining. As with the Army, the Church (and even just one branch of the Christian Church) used to be an organization of breathtaking scope. Of course, the Scots have always been impressively systematic and scholarly. It almost seems a shame that it figures in the current book only as a single, rather obscure, point of reference.

Another book that was helpful regarding Scottish history in the late 19th and early 20th Century is "*The History of Clydebank*", by John Hood, published by Parthenon (1988, ISBN 1-85070-147-4). A lot of this is naturally focused on shipbuilding, but the Singer factory comprises an almost equally important part of the history of the area and the book also conjures up a vivid picture of local social conditions and developments.

For the Burma Campaign in particular, there are excellent books that cover "The Forgotten War" – hopefully it actually has a rather higher profile now than in the immediate post-war period. Certainly its strategic significance, and the truly terrible conditions of the warfare on the ground, are better understood now. Of course, the most definitive in many ways is "*Defeat into Victory – Battling Japan in Burma and India 1942-1945*", by Viscount

W Slim, published by Cooper Square Press, originally in 1956 (2000, ISBN 9780815410225). Bill Slim was undoubtedly a great commander and his book is both comprehensive and readable. He tends to be rather generous to all involved, with the notable exception of the Japanese. Describing similar exploits as heroism on one side and mad fanaticism on the other is perhaps excusable and, to be fair, he does recognize that the enemy was truly formidable in many ways. In any event, it's certainly an authoritative and detailed account. The perspective offered by "*The Burma Campaign*", by Frank McLynn, published by Bodley Head (2010, ISBN 9780099551782) is just slightly different. It was, of course, written much later, after extensive research of various types. There is considerable focus on the main characters (Slim, Mountbatten, Wingate and Stilwell, plus Chiang Kai-shek). The complex interactions between the British, Americans and Chinese, and the various political machinations involved, are also very well described.

There are not very many books focused on the CMP and in fact the only one I've found giving good information across its complete history is "*The History of the Corps of the Royal Military Police*", by Major SF Crozier, published by The Naval and Military Press originally 1951 (2014, ISBN 9781783310951). It provides a very good compilation of information, as well as plenty of maps and illustrations. It's also very readable.

There are also certain other types of book that I've found useful in providing background and insights. Of course, the battle at sea was important in both of the major wars. A book I would recommend to anyone is "*Castles of Steel*", by Robert Massie, published by Pimlico (2005, ISBN 9780224040921), which covers all of the maritime activities during the Great War. I had actually read this before I started any serious preparation. It is based on outstanding historical scholarship, but is also highly readable. Of course, the story is an epic one, although a feature that emerges strongly is the unsustainable nature of the huge investment of resources that was involved (particularly in Britain and in Germany). Also clear in many of these pages is the injustice of the treatment of Jellicoe after Jutland. In fact, not only was Jellicoe a great commander, and a modest man who cared about the people under him, but he was also an accomplished scholar in his own right – this is clear on glancing through his book "*The Grand Fleet 1914-1916*", originally published in 1919 by Harvard University Library (2020, ISBN 9781974872295). I still maintain that there are no heroes in real life – or, perhaps more accurately, there are countless numbers of them, mostly completely unsung – but, from what is known about Jellicoe's life, he probably merits the accolade as much as anyone. Another scholarly, but highly readable, book, which provides valuable insights into what happened during the aftermath of the Great War, is "*Paris 1919*", by Margaret MacMillan, published by Random House (2001, ISBN 9780719559396). The main players in the Peace Conference may have had (reasonably) good intentions, but the unfortunate consequences of the outcomes of their deliberations have cascaded down through the decades ever since. This book is a masterly description of exactly what happened there and afterwards.

The history of the Ottoman Empire and its descendants is almost infinitely complex. Its relevance to the current work is not so strong, although the various battles in Gallipoli and Mesopotamia, certain developments during the inter-war period and the effect of activities in the Middle East on the course of the Second World War cannot be fully understood without this historical background. One of the most concise and readable books in this area, although also authoritative and comprehensive, is "*Turkey – A Short History*", by Norman Stone, published by Thomas and Hudson in 2010 (2019, ISBN 9780500292990). The role played by Mustafa Kemal Atatürk is, of course, pivotal, but much of the earlier history is important and this also is very well covered in the book.

There are several other, slightly more parochial, areas of background that I needed to understand, at least at some level. These include certain aspects of Scottish history, particularly the Clearances and the Crofting Communities in the Highlands and Islands. "*The Making of the Crofting Community*", by James Hunter, published originally by Berlinn in 1976 (2010, ISBN 9781841588537) provides a wealth of information. Hunter is a professional historian and has published a number of books about Scottish history. His Scottish links are extensive and he clearly feels strongly about the historical injustices and the need to allow these Celtic fringe communities to thrive, while retaining their character and independence. The book covers both historical background and many detailed personal stories and developments. Interesting snippets are also provided by "*Coal Mining at Brora 1529-1974*", by John Owen, published by Inverness Highland Libraries (1995, ISBN 1874253005) – a short, well-researched book by an evident enthusiast for obscure mining histories. It's difficult to feel entirely negative about the Earls and Dukes of Sutherland, despite their Clearance activities, when one appreciates quite how much effort and cash they pumped into the stimulation of industrial activities (particularly in the Clyne family heartland).

There are, of course, many books that relate to London during the Second World War. Its central role, and the experiences to which ordinary Londoners were subjected, were certainly exceptional, and perhaps unique in history. A book I found to be helpful and interesting is "*The Battle of London 1939-45*", by Jerry White, published by Bodley Head (2021, ISBN 9781847923011). This contains information about the experiences of a wide range of people living in the city during the war, with a lot of original material. It's the latest of a string of books he has published that are based on life in London over the past century and a half; he clearly has a wealth of background knowledge about the city.

Mention should also be made of the usage I have made of the internet. It's easy to forget that it has been operational on a wide-ranging scale for only a couple of decades, such has been the transformation it has effected in the retrieval of information (and in communications more generally). Furthermore, enhancements over the past decade or so in bandwidth and data storage capacities have ensured that there is effectively no limit now on the size and number of files that can be downloaded and saved. This certainly facilitates certain types of research, although the plethora of accessible information does raise the question of whether it is all accurate and reliable. My first port of call in almost any area is *Wikipedia*. Not only does their admirable sourcing and cross checking system normally ensure reliability, but the freedom from commercial links means that the sites are not encumbered with advertisements or attempts to extract cash. Most of the images on Wiki sites are free from copyright constraints and this also can be helpful for users. It is an invaluable resource. I regularly contribute (miniscule) sums and I do feel that its value is such that all frequent users should consider doing this.

Of course, there are other sites offering access to information relevant to various types of (non-scientific) research. These can be broadly divided into those that are commercial and those offered by government agencies or charities. The National Archives (www.nationalarchives.gov.uk), which was founded in 2003, is the official archive and publisher for the UK government, and for England and Wales. It provides access to records of various types – particularly relating to military history, but also to many other topics. These cover areas as diverse as passenger lists on ships, the Metropolitan Police, old maps, national census information and taxation records. Copies of certain types of documents can be obtained for a (small) fee, but others are available without charge. Inevitably, given the complexity and range of available resources, it can take a while to work out how to access particular types of document or information. The site is distinct from that of gov.uk (www.gov.uk), which was launched in 2012. This is a public sector information website, providing a single point of access for UK government services. It mainly relates to current activities, rather than historical archives, but it is possible to obtain information and documents concerning military service records, births, marriages and deaths etc. The latter can be accessed via the General Register Office (www.gro.gov.uk), which is part of HM Passport Office and maintains the national archive of all births, marriages and deaths (dating back to 1837). Many Scottish records are held separately. Scotland's people (www.scotlandspeople.gov.uk) is a site operated by National Records of

Scotland (NRS). It's mainly oriented towards historical records and ancestry. As with the UK sites, there is a (small) charge for downloading of certain documents.

There is also a lot of (declassified) information available on US Government sites. For example, https://history.state.gov/historicaldocuments/frus1943CairoTehran/index#in36 contains comprehensively indexed information about various aspects and outcomes of the Cairo and Tehran summit meetings. There appears to be no charging system for accessing information. Following various links in such sites can often lead to interesting documents and snippets. As with several such sites, navigation can be a little complicated, but it may nevertheless be worthwhile to spend some time on them. These are the types of site that professional historians would tend to use.

As anyone who has even tentatively explored their family history via the internet will be aware, there are also many commercial sites that offer access to information and documents. They can usually be distinguished from government-run sites, or those offered by certain charities, by the nature of the charging system employed. Once a user has been registered, commercial sites tend to offer time-limited access, often with several levels available, such that regular subscriptions must be paid in order to obtain continued access, whereas government agency sites charge only per file downloaded (and also offer a lot of free access). Of course, the commercial sites are motivated by a need to promote ongoing income, and they can't be castigated for that. Nevertheless, the model doesn't always work so well from the customer's point of view, particularly since the site search engines may not be very efficient and it's not always clear exactly what types of file can and can't be accessed. My own experience of such sites has certainly been rather mixed. Of course, it should also be noted that initial attempts to explore a topic or start an individual quest, by using a search engine such as that of Google, will often bring up a list of sites in which commercial ones figure prominently.

A final point concerns obtaining information about the (military) activities of individuals during World War 2. As many people will know, this tends to be more difficult than for earlier periods, at least back to the late 19th Century. More restrictions cover on-line access. In fact, to obtain archived information about, for example, my father's activities during World War 2, the only recourse was a paper request to the Army Personnel Centre in Glasgow, where extensive paper records are stored. This is a useful service, mainly restricted to relatives of the (deceased) person and with just a small fee – waived in my case because it formed part of a digitizing exercise. Unsurprisingly, it has been strongly affected by the Covid-19 pandemic, and the measures taken to combat it, with a huge backlog being created. Nevertheless, the people there did kindly exchange e-mails with me and I did eventually get sent photocopies of at least part of his army records. The digitizing exercise will doubtless be very helpful, although that is certainly a large and time-consuming job.

Index

Printed in Poland
by Amazon Fulfillment
Poland Sp. z o.o., Wrocław
03 March 2023

379f8ed7-b464-4f77-a970-6ad177ab7371R01